OUTLAW

ABBI GLINES

NEW YORK TIMES BESTSELLING AUTHOR

Outlaw

The Mississippi Smoke Series

Visit my website at https://abbiglinesbooks.com

Cover Designer: Sarah Sentz, Enchanting Romance Designs
www.enchantingromancedesigns.com
Editor: Jovana Shirley, Unforeseen Editing
www.unforeseenediting.com
Formatting: Melissa Stevens, The Illustrated Author
www.theillustratedauthor.com

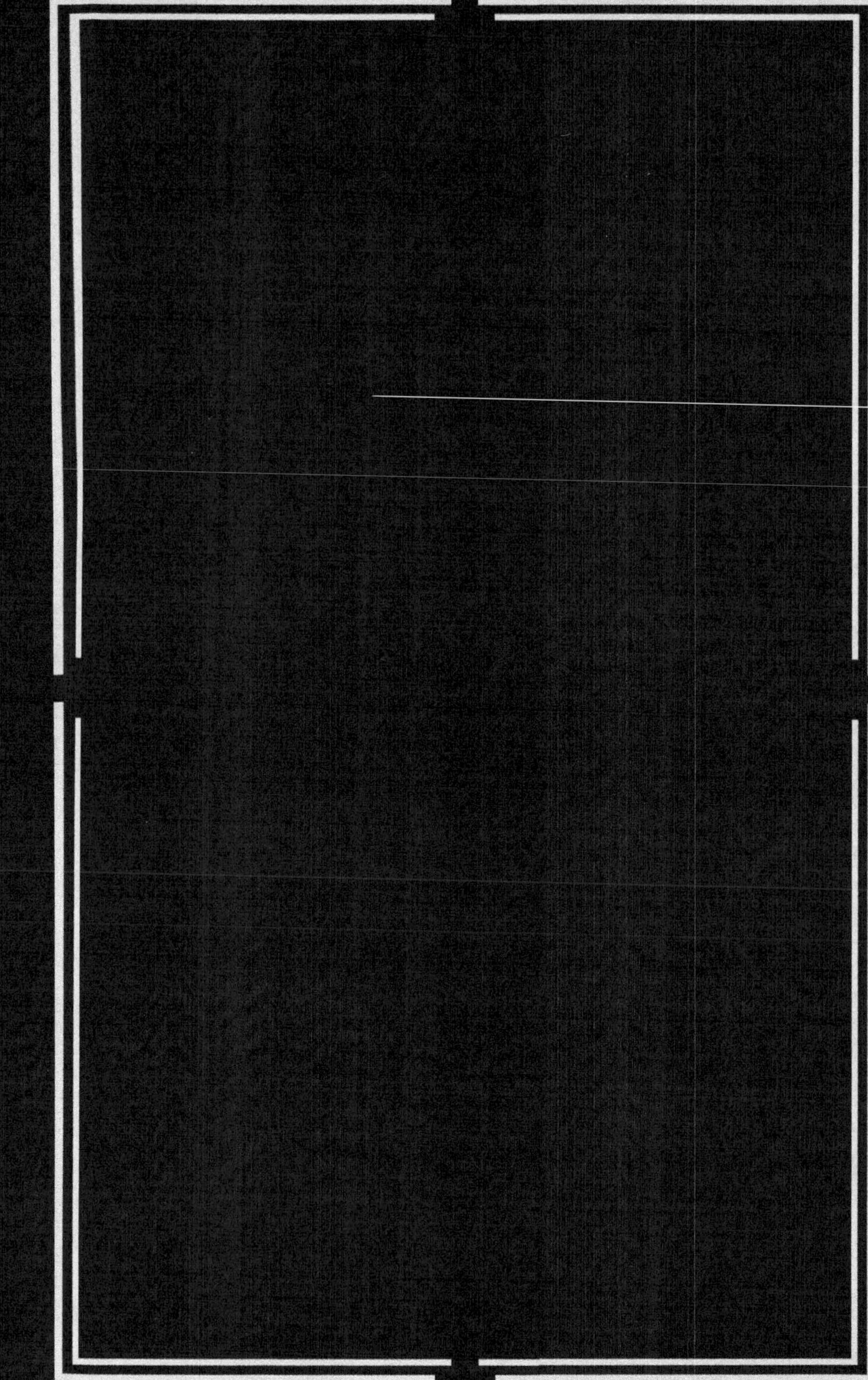

• THE FAMILY •

started by Jediah Hughes. It began with horse racing, moonshine, and illegal arms in the early 1900s

Jediah Hughes

Eustis

Elmer
(died from Typhoid at ten years old)

Feldman

Tipper

Garrett

Gregory
(died at three years old in a house fire)

• THE HUGHES •

Hughes Farm

Garrett Hughes (BOSS in books 1-9)
Wife: **Fawn Parker Hughes → *SCORCH***

Blaise Hughes (Current BOSS/oldest son)
Wife: **Madeline Walsh Hughes**
(parents Etta Marks/dead and Liam

Cree Elias Hughes →
SMOKESHOW and
FIREBALL

Trev Hughes
Fiancée: **Gypsi Parker** (also stepsister) →
FIRECRACKER

• THE SHEPHARDS •

Oldest family inside the southern mafia other than the Hughes

Charles Livingston Shephard
Best friend of Jediah Hughes

Gerald

Joseph
(became a priest)

Jeffrey
(died from Spanish influenza at fifteen years old)

Charles II

Darwin
(died from gunshot at twenty-four)

Charles III
(drowned in childhood)

Joshua
(became a missionary)

Lincoln

Lincoln II (Linc)

Stellan

Mississippi Branch

Linc Shephard
(left Florida to run Mississippi Branch when **Levi** was twenty-two)

Florida Branch

Levi Shephard
Wife: **Aspen Chance Shephard**→ ***WHISKEY SMOKE***

Georgia Branch

Shephard Ranch

Stellan Shephard
Wife: **Mandilyn Shephard**

Thatcher
→ ***DEMONS***

Sebastian
→ ***SMOLDER***

• THE KINGSTONS •

Mars Kingston joined the family in 1921

Mars Kingston
Childhood friend of Jediah Hughes

Hollis

Son
(died in childhood)

Atticus

Son
(died in childhood)

Rollin

Raul

Creed

Barrett

Florida Branch

Creed Kingston (dead)
Wife: **Abigail Kingston** (dead)

Huck
Wife: **Trinity Bennett Kingston**
→ ***SMOKE BOMB***

Hayes (dead)
engaged to **Trinity**
at his death

Georgia Branch

Barrett Kingston
Wife: **Annette Kingston**

Storm
→ ***SIZZLING***
and ***STORM***

Lela
Book coming in 2025

Nailyah
Book coming in 2025

• THE HOUSTONS •

Joined the family through horse racing in 1938

Kenneth Houston Wife: **Melanie Houston**

|

Saxon Houston
Wife: **Haisley Slate Houston** → *SMOKIN' HOT*

|

Winter Noel Houston

• THE LEVINES •

Joined the family in 1977

Alister Levine

|

Mississippi Branch

Luther Levine
Ex-Wife: **Chloe Wall**
(Moved from Florida when **Kye** was nineteen)

|

Florida Branch

Kye Levine
Wife: **Genesis Stoll Levine** → *BURN*

|

Jagger Henley Levine

• THE PRESLEYS •

Joined the family after graduation

Gage Presley

Best friend of Blaise Hughes in high school

Wife: **Shiloh Carmichael Presley** → *STRAIGHT FIRE*

• THE SALAZARS •

Joined the family through horse racing in 1958

Georgia Branch only

Efrain Salazar

Gabriel Salazar (dead)
Wife: **Maeme Salazar**

Ronan Salazar
Wife: **Jupiter Salazar**

Birdie
w/Ex Wife: **Estela Salazar**

King Salazar
→ ***SLAY*** and ***SLAY KING***

• THE JONES •

Joined the family through joined real-estate in 1966

Georgia Branch only

Hoyt Jones

Monte
Fiancée: **Bay Mintley**

Roland
Wife: **Luella Jones**

Wilder Jones
Wife: **Oakley Watson Jones →*ASHES***

Wells Jones
Book date coming soon

Teller Jones
Book coming in 2025

Sarah Jones

• THE RICES •

Oldest family in Mississippi Branch. Hiram Rice left Ocala in 1912 to move to Madison, Mississippi and run a speakeasies in Jackson and one on Madison both Jediah Hughes had purchased. Illegal gambling as well as moonshine was sold inside the bars.

Mississippi Branch

Hiram Rice

Whitmill

Frances

Junior

Hart

Gannon (former head of Mississippi Branch. His Parkinson's progressed until he had to step down 12 years ago. Linc Shepherd was moved there to become head over Mississippi Branch)
Wife: **Edy Rice**

Fia Rice Castron (married to a member of Louisiana Branch)

Saylor

• THE CARVERS •

Awbrey Carver joined the family in 1928 through bootlegging and running illegal gambling rings.

Mississippi Branch only

Awbrey Carver

|

Robert

|

Hale
Wife: **Lethia Carver** (dead)

Ransom | **Opal** | **Than**

• THE CASHES •

The Cash Ranch

Mississippi Branch only

Hawkins Cash
Joined the family in 1922 through horse racing

Samuel
(shot and killed at 20 years old)

William

Fender
Wife: **Grissele Cash**

Bane
→ *TORE UP*

Crosby

• THE SAVELLES •

Savelle Stables

Mississippi Branch

Oz Savelle

joined the Family in 1967 through horse

Jonas

Wife: **Ellender Savelle**

Oz | **Forge** | **Kash**

Alabama Branch

Kash Savelle

moved to Alabama Branch when he turned 21

• THE BOWENS •

Lewis Bowen joined the family in 1975

Mississippi Branch

Lewis Bowen

Oz Savelle's best friend since childhood

Malbrough 'Mal"

Ex-Wife: **Celeste**

Locke | **Gathe**

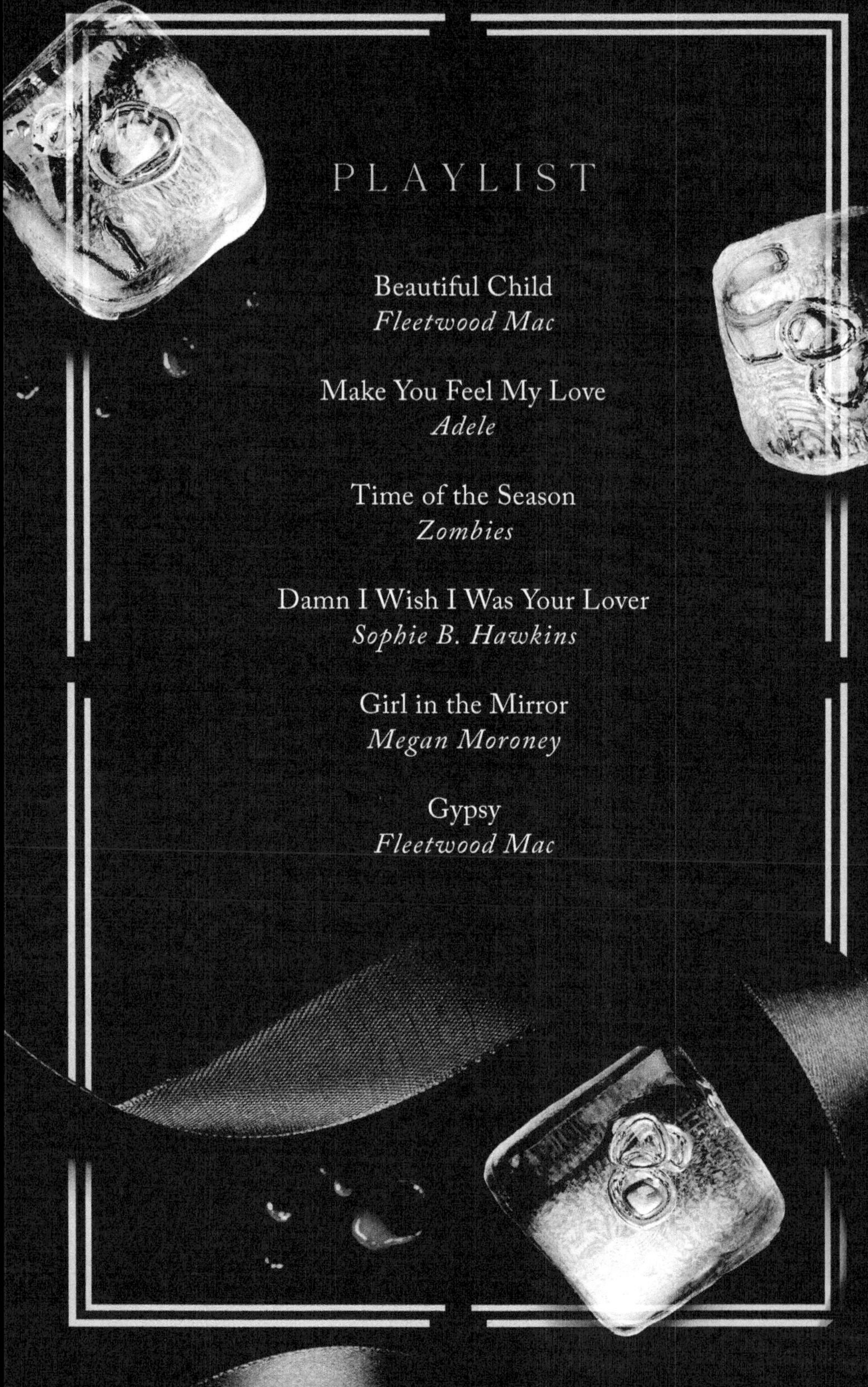

PLAYLIST

Beautiful Child
Fleetwood Mac

Make You Feel My Love
Adele

Time of the Season
Zombies

Damn I Wish I Was Your Lover
Sophie B. Hawkins

Girl in the Mirror
Megan Moroney

Gypsy
Fleetwood Mac

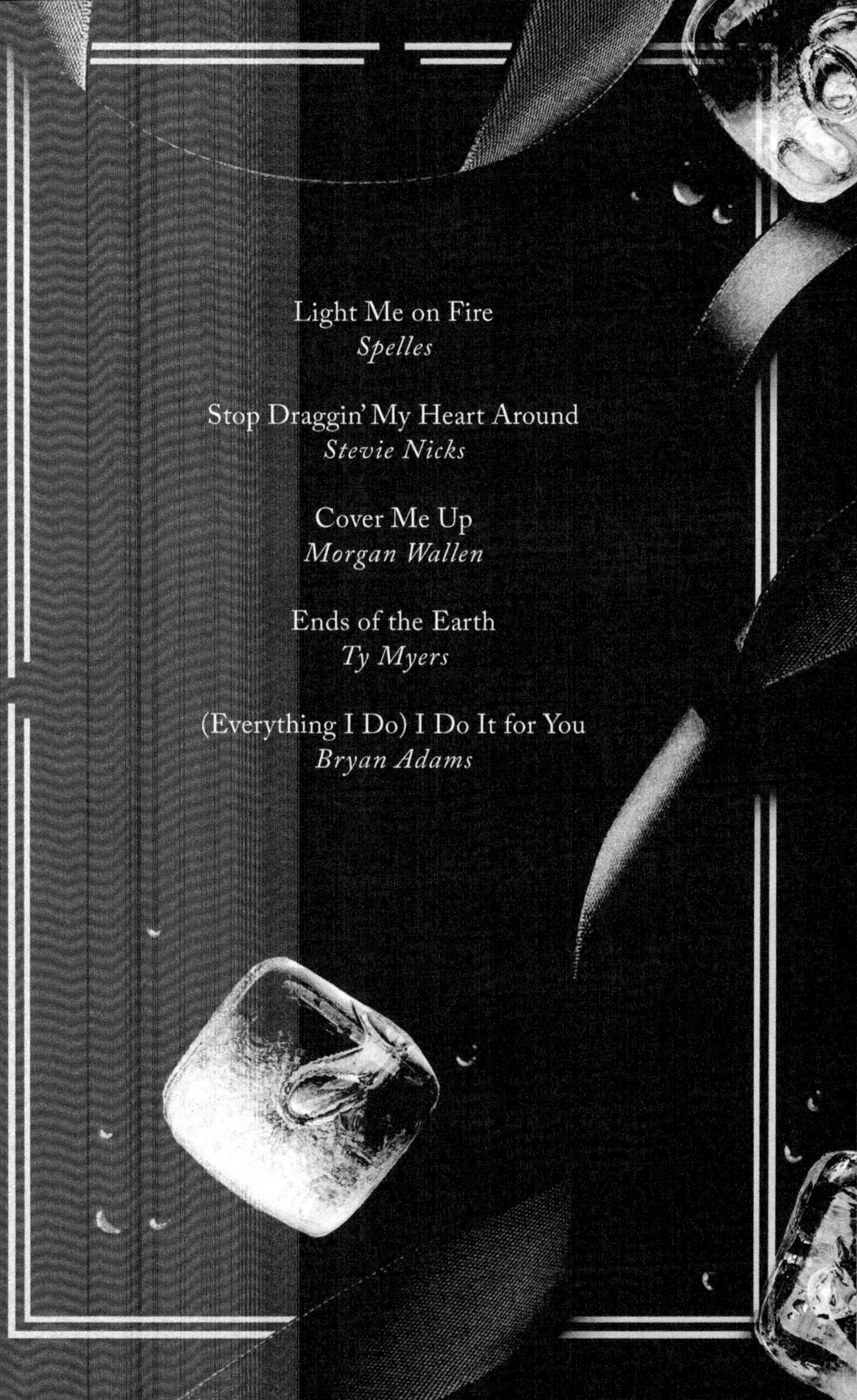

Light Me on Fire
Spelles

Stop Draggin' My Heart Around
Stevie Nicks

Cover Me Up
Morgan Wallen

Ends of the Earth
Ty Myers

(Everything I Do) I Do It for You
Bryan Adams

ACKNOWLEDGMENTS

When I started this book, I did NOT expect it to be over 100,000 words. My books normally run 70,000 to 85,000 words. Heck, when I hit 85,000 I think I've written a monster. Then Linc happened. My family got annoyed. I was always writing. I had to send it in parts to my editor as I finished because I was cutting it so close to having it ready for release day. As I write this, I have just finished it and sent the last part to my editor. I need sleep but I enjoyed every minute of this story. I hope you did to.

To the people who suffered, stood in the gap, and worked magic to make this story happen:

Britt is always the first I mention because without him, our house might literally fall apart.

Emerson for surviving without me. I would say she didn't complain but that would be a lie. There is always a lot of standing at my office door and scowling at me.

My older children, who live in other states, they called and texted and were also ignored. I felt bad but I replied "Writing, deadline, will call when finished." And they didn't mind but they also didn't stop calling and texting so… anyway.

My editor, Jovana Shirley at Unforeseen Editing. She worked with my tight schedule, and I would be screwed without her. She's a God send. (this seems to be happening monthly so I might as well copy and paste this with each

Acknowledgments section) THIS MONTH she was a major rock star.

My formatter, Melissa Stevens at The Illustrated Author. Who has never let me down. She always does a speedy turn around for me (monthly I might add). She makes my books beautiful inside. Her work is the best formatting I've ever had in my books. I am always excited to see what she does with each one. Each book seems to be better than the last!

Autumn Gantz, at Wordsmith Publicity, for saving me from losing my mind and taking over all the things that I can't keep up with anymore. Her help allows me to write this quickly. She reminds me of the things I need to do. I don't think I would have been able to keep up with this one book a month schedule without her.

Beta readers, who come through every time: Jerilyn Martinez, and Vicci Kaighan. I love y'all!

Sarah Sentz, Enchanting Romance Designs, for my book cover. Again, she nailed it. I have no visual creativity to give her any help in the matter. But she manages to create something I adore every time.

Abbi's Army, for being my support and cheering me on. I love y'all!

My readers, for allowing me to write books. Without you, this wouldn't be possible.

To that little girl whose first crush was already grown, but she found him again almost thirty years later, and the man who made her childhood dreams come true. They were the inspiration behind this story.

Happy anniversary to us.

PROLOGUE

BRANWEN

The smell of hay, cigars, and sunshine still haunted my dreams all these years later. My dad's deep belly laugh, his big smile, and thick Southern drawl were also weaved within them. Reminding me of a time when everything had seemed simple. Perfect. Easy. If only it were just my father's memory that came back to me when I slept, then I would wake up with a warmth in my chest instead of an ache that had become my constant.

Eyes the color of the sky as a storm churned; dark brown hair, left long enough to pull it back at his nape with string from a feed sack; a black cowboy hat on his head; dirty, worn snakeskin boots; and a crooked grin that was mine alone. He'd never smiled at anyone else like he did me, and it'd made me feel special.

Linc Shephard had stolen my six-year-old heart from the instant he walked into the stables at my daddy's new job and looked down at me.

He had smiled and reached for one of my wild curls that were never tamed. Wrapping it around his finger, he chuckled. "Well, hello, Ringlets. I didn't know Demeter had such a pretty little helper."

It hadn't taken me long to realize he was important. Him and the others who were always around. They were kings, and for a brief part of my life, I was allowed to live inside their kingdom. The way others respected them wasn't lost on me. When they arrived, the workers at the stables all quieted with a reverence as they went about their jobs more diligently. Even my daddy, who was the head horse trainer and told the others what to do, treated them with a respect he didn't show anyone else.

When I got a glimpse of them, no matter how far away they might be, my eyes would search him out. Looking for the face that outshone the rest.

That was what I'd lived for. Seeing Linc smile at me.

He would always wink, and I'd go running to him. His amused laugh as he waited for me would make my heart flutter like a swarm of butterflies in my chest.

A memory flooded my mind, and I let it play out, knowing I shouldn't…

"Miss me that much, Ringlets?" he asked me, dropping down to his haunches so he could look me in the eye instead of towering over me.

"You've been gone for days," I accused him, not realizing why he would go missing for gaps at a time.

He reached behind him and pulled out a yellow daisy. "But I came to check on my favorite girl as soon as I had the chance," he told me, then tucked the flower behind my ear. "Remember what I told you about boys and flowers?"

I nodded. "That even an outlaw can give a girl flowers. But not to trust one because he brings them to me," I replied. "But I trust you, and you always bring me one," I added. Because I did trust him. Maybe even more than my daddy.

He shook his head. "See now, that's where you're wrong. I'm the worst kinda outlaw, Ringlets."

I rolled my eyes. "I don't think you're an outlaw. I think you're a king."

He smirked, and I heard laughter behind me, but I ignored it.

"You can fool them at any age with that fucking charm of yours." The voice that I knew belonged to Creed Kingston sounded gruff and sarcastic.

I didn't turn around and glare at the giant man. I kept my focus on Linc.

Linc's eyes flicked up to him. "Not this one. She's too smart."

"Let's hope so and that her taste changes with age," he drawled, then nodded his head toward the big house. "Garrett is waiting on us. We need to go."

Garrett was the boss. I'd heard Daddy say that many times. They were all scared of him, even if they didn't say it. Everyone at the stables would speak about him as if he was to be feared. He looked the same age as Linc, but he owned all this. The stables, the big house, the land that Daddy said went on for miles.

Linc's eyes met mine again. "I'll be back later, and you can show me the new colt."

I nodded my head vigorously. Wanting nothing more than a reason to have Linc all to myself. When I had his full attention, my world was complete.

"Boss called. Everyone, up to the house now!" Kenneth Houston shouted from the entrance on the other side of the stables.

Linc tapped a finger to the tip of my nose, then stood up. "You take care of that colt for me, Ringlets," he said.

Then, I watched as he walked away with Creed, wishing more than anything that he could have stayed a little longer.

I touched my bright yellow daisy and smiled. I'd add it to my others tonight when I got home. I kept every single one that my outlaw had given to me.

ONE
BRANWEN

Present Day

I could do this. I had no choice but to do this. Taking a deep breath, I slowly took in the tall iron gate in front of me.

It had taken me three weeks of staying in Madison, Mississippi, five years ago to find the location of Linc Shephard's home, only to be refused entry through the gate. I'd been told by some man over the intercom that Linc was currently involved in a threesome and he'd give me a call when he was ready for a new cunt. That was all I needed to hear to send me running back to Tennessee. I'd sworn that I would never seek him out again.

Going to find him was something I'd battled with for a month before finally convincing myself that it was the right thing to do. Finding out that he was the kind of man he had always warned me about as a child was a cold, hard slap in the face. That day five years ago, at thirty-three years old, I had finally accepted that the man I had built up in my head and kept on a pedestal all these years was a child's innocent memory. Not reality.

Having to come back here and demand to see him this time was the very last thing I wanted to do. But I had no choice. I had to see him. Fate had decided to once again toss me a twist, and to say it was cruel would be an understatement. I'd pissed off the gods that be at some point in my life because they kept circling me back to this man.

There was a small chance he might not live inside this fortress that I hadn't been admitted to five years ago when I came to find him. If he had left here, then I knew where in Ocala to go looking for him. Getting onto the Hugheses' property would be easier than this. Unless it had changed since my childhood and Garrett added an iron gate around it. I really hoped I didn't have to find out. As a child, that might have been a magical place, but as an adult, I now understood who and what they were. And Ocala was the location of the leader. The man they called boss. I shivered, thinking about how important it was to keep my secrets.

The rumble of an engine snapped me out of my thoughts, and I lifted my eyes to the rearview mirror to see a large, expensive-looking black truck pull up behind me. My heart began to race at the sight of it. I glanced down at the backseat and the sleeping form of my daughter before quickly reaching for the door handle and exiting the vehicle. Mentally preparing myself to see Linc again, I held my shoulders back and steeled myself as the driver's door to the truck opened.

Memories began creeping back in, even though they were unwanted. Not just from the last time I'd seen him that night in Vegas five years ago, but from my childhood as well. Nope. Not going to allow that. Memory lane was off-limits.

The blond man who stepped out of the truck, stopped all other thoughts. I relaxed some at the realization that it wasn't Linc, followed by the small dose of panic that maybe he had moved and I'd be forced to go to Ocala. The man closed his truck door and took another step in my direction. He tilted his head slightly as he studied me. His dark blonde hair was pulled back into a messy bun, and his short beard did little to hide his attractive face. The darkness in his gaze had me on high alert. It was dangerous, almost that of a predator.

"Can I help you?" he asked me as his eyes made their way back to mine after doing a quick take of my body.

I cleared my throat. This was one of them. I knew it without being told. He had that presence about him. The power, threat, and intimidation were all there, surrounding him like an invisible force that set you on edge. It stirred the urge to flee when met with it.

"I, uh, I'm looking for Linc Shephard," I said, thankful my voice didn't waver.

The corner of his mouth quirked slightly, but he didn't smile. "Is that so?" he drawled. "And what is it you need with Linc, sugar?"

The way he said *sugar* sounded like a caress that I was sure made most females throw themselves at him. He wouldn't be getting that reaction from me. I knew what he was.

"I have some business to settle with him. An issue that I really need to see him about."

The man rubbed his bearded chin with his thumb and forefinger. His arm was covered in tattoos, and it reminded me of Linc. He'd had so many tattoos five years ago. I'd inspected each one up close.

"As stunning as that face is of yours, I'm still gonna need a little more information."

Right. Fine. I was here to get this handled, and what did I care if some man I didn't know wanted the reason why? It wasn't going to affect me or the outcome. It would get Linc's attention at least.

I lifted my chin and looked him directly in the eyes. Probably a bad idea because the threat in this man's gaze was unsettling.

"If you must know, I need him to sign divorce papers."

That still sounded bizarre, and I'd had this revelation dropped on me over a week ago now. But I hadn't said it to anyone. I couldn't. No one in my life could know about this. I had to get it fixed and pretend it'd never happened.

The man stared at me as if I had lost my mind.

Apparently, five years ago, I had indeed lost my mind. I had the proof of it in the passenger seat of my car. A state of Nevada marriage certificate, saying I was married to Lincoln Shephard II. I just hadn't realized how drunk I had been until the marriage certificate was presented to me by the county clerk's office. A marriage I hadn't known existed and was standing in the way of my future happiness.

He let out a low chuckle. "I think you might have the wrong man. Linc ain't married. He's been divorced from his ex-wife for fifteen-plus years now."

Yes, I knew all about Maggie. She'd been the cause of my first heartbreak at the age of seven. Linc had married the mother of his child, and I had been devastated since I had planned on marrying him one day.

"I'm aware of all that. But it seems, five years ago, a marriage happened in Vegas after we both had too much to drink, but we assumed it wasn't real."

The man stood there, silent, his eyes narrowed.

I waited, wishing he'd say something. I hated being his sole focus.

"You're fucking serious?"

I nodded. Why would I lie about this? I didn't ask that out loud though.

The man let out a bark of laughter, and his eyes crinkled at the corners. "Fucking hell," he said. "This might be the best shit I've heard all year."

I stared at him, not sharing his amusement in the situation.

He nodded his head toward the gate. "I'll open it up."

Relief and anxiety battled for first place inside me. I was going to find Linc, and this would be fixed. Yet, seeing him again…well, I'd never been very good at ignoring the effect he had on me. Not as a child or as the thirty-three-year-old woman I had been five years ago. But this time, things were different.

I was engaged, and I had a child to think about.

I turned and headed back to the car. Thankfully, Stevie was still sleeping peacefully. She'd been nonstop chatter for hours on our drive here from Nashville. The lie I had told Hudson, my fiancé, about why I had to come to Madison wouldn't have worked if I had left Stevie with a sitter. Attending the funeral of a former friend of my father's was the best excuse I could come up with. Hudson hated funerals, and I'd known he wouldn't offer to come along.

Besides, Linc had been a friend of my father's. My dad worked for him and the rest of the Southern Mafia until he had a heart attack and left me alone at twelve years old with no one but my mom's sister—Aunt Catherine. Not only had I barely known the woman, but she had also taken me away from the life I loved- the den of vipers I thought were kings.

I pulled my new ocean-gem-colored Toyota Camry—which Hudson had bought me as an early wedding gift after my fifteen-year-old Mazda finally gave up on life—through the open gate and immediately into a tunnel created by a canopy of trees. Branches from the live oak trees that lined the road on either side had grown out and connected, creating a stunning, shaded drive. I sucked in a breath at the sheer beauty and almost wished Stevie were awake to see this. She would be fascinated.

When the trees ended and the sunshine beamed down brightly, I squinted to see the extravagant house up ahead. A circular drive sat in front of it with a water fountain in the center. Again, Stevie would love this. But her being awake was not a good idea. My gaze went back to the house. It was as spectacular as the trees. A matte-black Georgian-style mansion shouldn't surprise me. Sure, it wasn't as massive and sprawling as the Hugheses' mansion in Ocala, but this was pretty freaking incredible. So much wealth.

I shook my head and blew out a breath.

"Not what I pictured you living in, Linc," I whispered as I parked my car.

I left the car running and the air-conditioning going for Stevie. I'd have Linc come outside so I didn't get far from the car, explain our drunken mistake, get his signature, get back in, then drive away. Never to see him again. Solid plan.

Hudson would never know about this. I'd get married in three months to a man who was good to me. Had a successful dental practice, a home with a backyard—perfect for a swing set. Stevie had never had a yard to play in before. My income had been a struggle all her life. We lived in a small apartment in a safe part of town.

But that was all about to change. She would have the things I wanted for her so badly. I just needed to get this signature and leave.

Before opening my door, I grabbed the marriage certificate and divorce papers, then I stepped out into the warm summer heat and waited on the man in the truck. He could go get Linc, and we'd get this all cleared up.

I stared up at the house and the staircase that led up to the front double doors. Above the entrance was a small veranda that looked over the front yard. Round topiary bushes sat on either side of the stairs and along the front of the house.

This place was something out of a magazine. I'd hated the black paint on one house in Hudson's neighborhood, thinking it was a ridiculous color for a house. Wrong. On the right structure, it was perfect. Even the columns on the front entrance and on the veranda were black. The only things breaking up the color were the windows.

Did a woman live here with him? I knew he wasn't married to her. But that didn't mean he couldn't have a live-in girlfriend. The thought bothered me, and in return, that pissed me off. I did not care who or what Linc Shephard did.

One of the doors to the house swung open, and I stiffened.

Linc stepped out, and for a moment, I forgot about the papers in my hand that needed signing, the empty Vegas hotel suite with the short note he'd left for me, and the morning-after pill sitting on top of it. The fear, desperation, and pain that I had been dealt by this man's actions seemed to slip away. Right now, I felt six years old again. My heart fluttered wildly in my chest.

The cowboy hat on his head was tilted back as he stared down at me, then continued in my direction. A plaid pearl-snap shirt with the sleeves rolled up, showing off the artwork on his forearms, jeans that fit his lower half in a way that made mouths water, and black combat boots made up his attire. He was rugged-looking. Less polished, like he had been in Vegas. More like the Linc from my childhood. The one I had wanted above everything else.

His gaze did a swift take of my body and locked back on my face, as if there had been nothing of interest to see there. That stung, and I wished it hadn't. I didn't care what this man thought of my appearance. He'd sure liked it well enough five years ago, but I guessed I'd changed since then. I was a mom, I'd struggled more than I ever had in my life, and I was stronger because of it.

"How can I help you?" he asked as he closed the distance, taking the steps with his long strides.

He didn't appear angry, just slightly inconvenienced. As if I had interrupted something important. I glanced back as my nerves began to snowball down a hill, going full speed. The other man appeared amused, biting back a smile or possibly laughter as he leaned against his truck door, his arms crossed over his chest. When he nodded his head at me to answer Linc, I realized he was looking forward to this. He might have let me inside the gate, and he might have that dark, sexy thing going for him, but I didn't like that man.

Turning back to Linc, I knew standing here silently was only going to prolong things. Tell him, get it over with, and remember that he wasn't the man I had once believed. He was what he had always warned me he was. An outlaw. The very worst kind.

I cleared my throat and straightened my shoulders. There was no flicker of recognition in his eyes, and that was a slap in the face I hadn't been prepared for. I would have thought he would remember me from our night five years ago. I mean, sure, we had drunk a lot, but we hadn't been completely messed up when it started. Yet not even a tiny trace of recognition was there in those dark blue eyes of his.

Stupid, stupid girl. Why did I keep thinking that Linc had any redeeming qualities? Childhood fantasies should all be gone by now.

"I see you don't remember me." My words sounded as bitter as they tasted. "I'll give you a small recap. We met in Vegas five years ago. You were there on business. I was at a bachelorette party that I didn't want to be at. We danced. We drank. We drank so much that the pretend wedding package with Elvis sounded hilarious. Then, you bailed before I woke up the next morning, leaving a note that said, *Take the pill. I don't want any surprise kid showing up. Checkout is at eleven. Order whatever you want for breakfast.*" I had memorized the note. I'd read it hundreds of times, wanting to find something in it hinting that our time together meant more to him than it appeared.

His brows drew together, and he studied me harder. I felt like a spotlight had been put on me, and every flaw on my face and body were beaming brightly at him. I didn't let my insecurity show on my face though. He would never know the truth. Who I really was. How I had thought I loved him that night. How I had believed destiny had played a part in putting us there at the same time.

He gave nothing away. His expression never changing. "Okay, yeah, I remember you now."

I tensed from the invisible blow. He remembered me… now. Whatever. This wasn't why I had come here. I didn't need anything more from this man than his signature.

"Lucky me," I replied with sarcasm dripping from my words.

He raised his eyebrows, as if I had no reason to be annoyed. To think, I'd been infatuated with this man for the majority of my life. Jesus, I needed my head examined.

I stepped forward and held out the papers with the marriage certificate as proof for him to take. "Seems we made a mistake. The marriage was legal. The county clerk had a copy of our marriage certificate. Here are divorce papers. They are simple and to the point. Just need your signature."

The incredulous look on his face was followed by a bark of laughter behind me.

"Now, that is why I let her inside the gate," the blond man said. "Priceless."

Linc ignored him as he reached out to snatch the papers from me and looked down at the certificate, then back at me. "This can't be right."

"Trust me, I thought the same thing. But we can fix it easily enough."

The hard gleam in his eyes startled me. He was angry. This wasn't my fault. He was the one who'd paid for the supposedly bogus marriage. I was the one who should be pissed.

"Are you after money? I have lawyers—you realize that? A fucking team of them. They will know this is complete horseshit the second they see it. I'm not giving some hot fuck I had in a casino five years ago a dime." He shoved the papers at me, causing me to stumble back as I tried to take them and keep from falling at the same time.

His furious expression shifted to the blond man. "Fucking hilarious, Luther. Grow the hell up," he snarled.

I was speechless as I clutched the papers to my chest. Was he serious?

"You can leave," he barked at me.

My shoulders jerked, and I winced at the volume and tone of his voice. He wasn't going to sign them. This was not something I had planned for. Crap! I had to get these signed.

"I'm not lying to you, and I don't want your money. I just want to be divorced!" I said, raising my own voice and taking a step back from him. I didn't know if he would do more than shove me next time. I'd never been hit by a man, and I didn't want to experience it today.

"I was married, and I sure as fuck wouldn't make that mistake twice. Especially to someone like you," he said with disgust.

He was successfully shattering my self-esteem. Not that I wanted him to have married me on purpose, but still, he could have chosen his words more carefully. That was a rather nasty way of saying it. No one deserved to be spoken to like this. I was here to fix an issue neither of us wanted.

"These papers say that you did make the mistake of marrying someone like me. Unfortunately for me, I had to drive almost six hours to find you and get your signature to fix this. Not only do I not want anything from you. I want nothing more than to get the hell away from you and never lay eyes on you again. So, if you'd sign the papers, that would be fantastic!" My voice had risen with my anger until I was shouting. Unable to stop myself, I continued, "Furthermore, if I wanted something from you, why would I wait five years?! You might find me unattractive and beneath you, but not everyone feels that way. I need this divorce because I'm engaged." I held up my hand to show him the diamond ring Hudson had placed on it. "But I can't get married until I am divorced from YOU!"

I was panting when I stopped and lowered my hand back to my side. I wasn't a verbally aggressive person. This was so out of character for me that I was slightly stunned that I had just spoken to him like that. He seemed to bring out the worst in me.

"Might want to get the papers to the lawyers to check over," the blond man said.

Linc's eyes dropped back to my hand, and his jaw clenched.

Yep. Proof, you asshole, that I want out of this farce we're stuck in.

Did women actually do this kind of thing to him to get his money? Were they stupid? Or maybe they didn't know who he was. That was probably it. No sane woman would try to screw over a member of the Mafia.

"Mommy! Why awah you yellin' like that?" the sweet voice that my world revolved around called, and my heart sank.

Dammit.

I spun around as Stevie hurried toward me. How she had managed to get the car door open I didn't know. Time to start using the child lock. The concern on her little face hurt my heart. I had woken her up because I'd let Linc get to me.

I bent down to look at her. "Listen, Vivi Lu," I said, brushing her curls back from her face. The headband I had placed in it this morning had been tossed onto the floorboard hours ago. "Go back to the car and look at the books Mommy brought, okay? I will be done in just a few minutes, and then we can go get some ice cream."

She loved ice cream. I'd have to go to the grocery store to get it since finding oat milk ice cream anywhere else was almost impossible. The excitement at the word lit up her eyes briefly, but vanished as she turned to stare up at Linc. Her little mind was so curious and he was someone I didn't want her curious about. They were never supposed to meet.

"Who awah you?" she demanded, her chin up and not one ounce of intimidation on her face.

I stood and moved her back, feeling the need to shield her from any of the cruelty he could spew from his mouth. The very mouth I had once thought was perfect. Not anymore. He was the enemy.

"Go back to the car," I told her, my focus on Linc's face.

He'd better not say one word to upset her.

He didn't respond to her innocent question, but his eyes were studying her too closely. There was little about her that I felt gave away who her father was. She was my mini me, all except for her eyes. Panic began to seep in, and the thought of him figuring it out had me grasping at something I could say to veer his thoughts in another direction.

"Awah you the outlaw?" she asked him, narrowing her eyes and glaring at him as intently as he had been doing to her.

I froze. I should have never called him that in front of her. She repeated everything. I just hadn't imagined she would see him. Speak to him. This was supposed to be quick. An *oops, the marriage was real, now sign, and goodbye, have a nice life* kind of thing. Instead, Linc was being difficult.

His eyes shot back to me, and I said nothing. It was just a description. Maybe he wouldn't remember the little girl who had worshipped him. At least, I prayed he wouldn't. Because Stevie was a replica of that girl.

We stood there for what was probably less than a minute but felt like an eternity. I struggled to breathe normally. I was planning out my escape in my head. *Pick up Stevie and run. Never look back. Figure out a way to get a divorce without Linc's signature. Maybe I could forge it.*

"You marrying her father?" he asked me.

The way he was scowling at me made me feel as if he could read my thoughts. The sun seemed to have gotten hotter as it beamed down. I started to sweat.

"Yep!" Stevie blurted out when I said nothing. "I get to be a flowah gawha and wayah a pwetty dwess like Mommy," she informed him proudly. "Then, Hudson will be my dad 'cause I don't have one wight now."

Linc held out his hand to me. "Give me the papers," he said.

The rush of relief crashed over me, and I wanted to weep with joy. He was going to sign them. Everything was fine.

"Thank you. Just sign, and we can go," I told him.

He raised an eyebrow at me. "I'm still having my lawyers look at them."

A slight inconvenience, but how long could that take? A couple of hours?

I nodded. "Okay. We can go get something to eat. Look around town."

"You'll need to get a hotel room," he interrupted me. "Might take a day or two." His eyes dropped back to Stevie. "How old are you?" he asked.

I opened my mouth to tell him a lie and haul her off to the car when she replied, "Fowah yeahs old!" She held up four tiny fingers.

When his eyes came back to me, he said nothing, but I could see it. The words he wasn't saying. Would he ask? Would I tell him the truth? If I did, it would change Stevie's world. Her safe bubble I kept her in. The life that was just within our grasp would crumble.

Please, God, don't let him ask me if she is his.

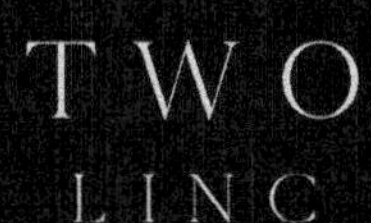

TWO
LINC

With my chosen figurado clamped between my teeth, I glared out over the front lawn of the house from my office window. That fucking blue car had long since driven away, yet the tension that had come with it hadn't. Instead, it coiled tighter inside me, like a rattlesnake just before it struck. I should have kept her here. Demanded more information. If she wasn't after money, did it mean that the marriage was real? Sure, I'd been messed up that night. But had I been that out of it?

The opium I'd had in the hookah pipe just before walking into one of the many clubs inside the casino that the family owned had been a poor decision, but I'd needed to release some stress. It had sent me to a place where I didn't give a fuck about anything. The peace I had been searching for came so easily. Then, I saw her, and she took my breath away—literally—just like when I woke up in my suite with her beside me, naked in bed. The woman was possibly the most beautiful female I'd ever laid eyes on, and I'd fucked a lot of gorgeous women.

I let the cigar smoke linger in my mouth as I swirled it, enjoying the flavors. This specific cigar had become my comfort crutch. When I needed to take off the edge, this was what I reached for. Probably more often than I should.

Letting the smoke go with an exhale, I replayed all that I could remember from that night. Most of it was clear. So damn crystal clear in my mind that I'd used that face to get myself off more than a few dozen times over the years. She was still the most stunning creature I'd ever seen when she orgasmed. Thinking about the way she'd looked when she got off had my cock hardening in my jeans. Long blonde curls, the color of the finest champagne, sliding over her shoulders like warm caramel had been a sight that took the top spot on the mental highlight reel for best fucks of my life.

The fascination she'd held for me was the main reason I ran like hell the next morning. Because for the first time in my life, I had wanted to stay. I had wanted to fuck her more. Put her on my face and drown myself in that sweet, tight cunt.

Taking the cigar from my teeth, I glared at it for failing me. The stress wasn't ebbing away. Only the storm of emotions that ranged from frustration to disbelief, to doubt, to full-blown fury.

Not because the number one memory from my spank bank had walked back into my life. And not because of the way her eyes had seemed to knock me on my ass. Hell, even the marriage certificate—if it was real—could be handled easily enough. It was the little girl I was struggling with. I hadn't pressed because I was afraid of the truth. The what-if. She looked nothing like Levi had as a child, but then she was her mother's mini me. There was just something…a gut feeling. A draw to her. As if my instincts were screaming at me that I should know her.

I had left her the morning-after pill. She would have fucking taken it. Right? I'd even put a bottle of water beside it. She wouldn't have wanted to be knocked up with some one-night-stand's kid. She hadn't been on a manhunt that night. I'd hit on her. In fact, if I remembered correctly, she had been rejecting men or sending them running—until me.

But what if I had walked right into a trap? What if she'd been wanting a kid and the right sperm donor hadn't come along yet? She hadn't smoked opium, and I honestly didn't know if she had been that drunk. The whole thing could have been premeditated.

Fuck.

If the little girl was mine, would she have brought her here? It'd been five years, and she was engaged. She wasn't after me for anything. So, why would she have shoved the kid in my face if she had something to hide? That didn't make sense. The timing added up though. Women had done worse things. This one wasn't after my money, but she might have wanted my sperm.

The door opened behind me, but I didn't turn back to see who it was. I already knew. Only Luther would open my office door without knocking—that, and he was the only other person here. We shared the six-thousand-square-foot home. He kept to the west wing, and I stayed to the east. Neither of us planned on having another family. We'd both failed at the first attempt. He hadn't even married the mother of his child. She'd refused, and he hadn't loved her enough to demand it.

"You think the kid is yours?" Luther asked, the humor gone from his voice.

He had enjoyed the marriage shit, but the instant the little girl had stepped out of the car, things had taken a turn. The threat that she could be mine wasn't funny.

Hell, I had fucked up, being a father to my son. Staying with his mother for his benefit all those years had done him more harm than good. All he saw was the toxic relationship Maggie and I had. Whatever love I'd thought I had for her was long gone by the time he was old enough to truly remember things. She'd held him over my head, and because he loved her, I'd allowed it. I shouldn't have.

"Fucking hope not," I replied.

Once I had the background information on her, along with the marriage certificate, then I'd know if a paternity test was needed.

"You sure know how to pick 'em," he drawled.

Scowling, I turned around to look at him. "What's that supposed to mean?"

He lifted the shoulder not leaning against the doorframe. "No need to get pissy. I was just pointing out, when you decide to fuck one raw, you pick stunners. Hell, you took Maggie right from under Garrett's nose back in the day. He'd had his eye on her, and you managed to charm her within minutes. But this one?" He let out a whistle. "Damn, man. If she fucks as good as she looks, then this might not be a bad thing. When she stepped out of her car outside the gate, I was struck speechless."

I shot him a disgusted look. I didn't need the fact that she was so goddamn beautiful shoved down my throat. I was aware. It was the reason I had run like hell five years ago. Beautiful women made me stupid at times, and she was a level above beautiful.

"Garrett was already engaged to wife number one. Maggie was never going to be his sidepiece," I replied.

"What's her name?" Luther asked me.

I shrugged as if I didn't care, although until I had read the marriage certificate, I hadn't known it. All I had called her that night was Dollface. I hadn't wanted her to know my name, so I never asked for hers.

"Which one?" I asked because I hadn't gotten the kid's name. I was hoping it wasn't Vivi Lu, or whatever she'd called her. The poor kid would be bullied over a name like that.

He chuckled. "God, you're an ass. You have the fucking marriage certificate. Did you not read her name on there?"

"Branwen, I think it said. I don't know how she pronounces it. I never asked her name. We fucked. It was one drunken night in Vegas. Knowing her name wasn't important."

He shook his head, still grinning at me. "Not so sure about that. I've seen you drink a fifth of Jack many times in our past, and never did you think that taking some cunt to a wedding chapel was a good idea."

"It wasn't a fucking chapel! It was some pretend Elvis shit. And I wasn't just drunk. I'd smoked some opium before I saw her."

He threw back his head and laughed. I was done with this conversation. He could go now.

"That makes much more sense," he said when he stopped his annoying cackling.

My phone started to ring, and my eyes dropped to where it lay on the desk. I stared at the number. I hadn't wanted to get Levi involved in this, just in case there was no need for him to ever know about it. So, I'd called Wilder Jones. He was the family's computer genius and could find more information than Levi could anyway.

Wilder's name on my screen had me lowering my cigar to the tray. I could hear the phantom rattler waiting there, taunting me with its bite. My gut was something I trusted. Right now, I wished it were a liar.

THREE
BRANWEN

Five Years Ago

The bottle of Tito's sitting on the mirrored shelving behind the bar might be enough to make this bearable. I would rather be literally anywhere but here. A dentist chair, getting three cavities filled; listening to my aunt preach at me about virtue; or, hell, even at my yearly gynecologist checkup. But I wasn't so lucky.

I had to be here. In Vegas, celebrating my best friend's last days as a bachelorette. Next weekend, she would be walking down the aisle to marry not only the man she claimed was the love of her life, but also my ex-boyfriend. Oh, and not just any ex-boyfriend. The one who had told me he loved me, convinced me to spread my legs for the first time, and had our future planned out for us. That was the problem—his planning.

Bastian Draughn hadn't broken my heart. I wasn't looking at the bottle of Tito's, contemplating getting blackout drunk over his marrying Idris. It was more of the painful fact that

I was having to stand back and watch her make a huge mistake. But she didn't see it that way.

Bastian had targeted her a year ago after I turned down his marriage proposal and broke up with him. But she refused to believe he'd ever proposed to me. As if I would lie about that. Being the nonconfrontational person I was, I let it go. Gave her my blessing, although I didn't think she really would have cared either way, but at least she'd asked me. Granted, they had been talking on the phone and meeting for coffee for over two weeks by the time she got around to asking me if I was okay with her going on a date with him. I hadn't wanted her to because I knew she was the rebound. He was trying to get to me. When his calls, flowers, love notes—sent to the office I worked in at his father's dairy farm—hadn't worked, he had gone after my best friend.

The love notes hadn't stopped right away. He had been dating Idris and was still swearing I was the only woman he would ever love. Bastian was a spoiled rich kid who had been given everything he wanted. He was attractive and never had a female tell him no. My doing so was something he hadn't expected or handled well.

Now, here we were, one week away from his wedding to my best friend—although I couldn't really call her that anymore. The girl I had met in high school and who I'd survived our twenties with, living in a shitty apartment together that we loved, was gone. She didn't text or call me much these days. I was her fiancé's ex, and even though I wasn't in the wrong, she seemed to feel as if she had to keep me close but still at arm's length.

That was what hurt the most. Losing Idris. In the end, Bastian had gotten the last laugh, it seemed. He'd stolen her. The person I trusted most. She had been the closest thing I had to family. After my father's death, I'd been left with an aunt who put up with me until I was old enough to move out. Idris had filled that void. Until she chose Bastian over me. I hadn't even asked her to choose.

There had been other guys before Bastian, but none I had gotten as serious with. It wasn't until I moved out of my aunt's that I went on my first date. She never allowed me to date. Most guys I went out with a few times, then ended things. I always saw their flaws. I started dating Bastian when I was twenty-six and my being a virgin at that age gave him some weird sense of ownership over me. He hadn't believed me when I told him I had never had sex, up until the blood on the sheets and his penis had proven I wasn't lying.

Shaking my head, I rolled my eyes at my stupidity and drank down the rest of my cosmopolitan. I was thirty-three years old. I had wasted six years of my life with that man, never really loving him. He was just someone who wanted me. I had finally let go of my fantasy man. The one who would check all my boxes. The ones that had been set in place since I had been a kid. The reason I had held on to my virginity for so long. No one was ever the right one. No one was ever the outlaw my memory wouldn't let me forget.

I turned on the stool to see Idris already drunk, dancing with her hands in the air, along with two of her other bridesmaids. They were her new friends. Danielle was Bastian's best friend's new girlfriend—well, new, as in he hadn't started dating her until after I broke up with Bastian. They had been together eight months now. Evie was her current roommate. Seemed Idris had felt awkward, having Bastian over to our place after they got serious, and in a fit of tears, she'd told me she had to move out and hoped I understood.

What I had understood was, she was leaving me with a rent payment I couldn't manage on my own. We'd long since moved out of the shitty first apartment. Once we got real jobs that paid well, we moved on up in the world. She had decided college wasn't for her after only one year and gotten her real estate license, then began working for her mom and stepfather's agency. I hadn't been given the opportunity to attend college. My aunt wouldn't cosign with me for a loan, but then I'd never expected her to. I had gone right into the work field, having been a bank teller, bartender, and lastly a secretary at Draughn Dairy, which was where I met Bastian. It had good insurance, a 401(k), and paid me well. However, the apartment we had been living in was still too steep for my paycheck alone, so I'd also had to downgrade to a studio, but I had found being alone wasn't so bad.

"Hello, gorgeous," a man's voice said as a body sat down beside me.

Great. Another annoyance. I had sent three of them off already.

I cut my eyes to the guy who had decided to sit on the stool next to mine. He was young. Possibly still in college. He had the frat-boy look about him. The cocky glint in his eyes told me he knew he was attractive. I was sure his greeting worked on most females. But he'd picked the wrong one. Nothing about him was my type.

"Get her another of whatever she's having," he told the bartender.

Nick—who, I'd found out from talking with him, was twenty-five, had married his high school sweetheart, and had a five-month-old baby—glanced at me.

I nodded my head. The kid wouldn't be paying for it though. He'd be gone in less than five minutes. Three if I spun my story faster. Nick had been on duty since I'd sat down, and he'd gotten used to my pattern. They showed up and offered to buy me a drink, and then I sent them away with one horrible lie after another. When I'd asked the last guy how he felt about genital warts, Nick had choked on his water, and I'd struggled to keep a straight face.

I licked my lips, my mind already spinning my next tall tale to send this one running. I'd done the STD thing and the *five kids under six years old at home* thing. The age role play one, where I asked a man how he felt about being diapered and put in a crib, had been fun too. Nick had bent over in a fit of laughter when that man made his excuse and escaped.

"Tell me how a woman as beautiful and sexy as you is sitting here alone," the guy drawled. Then flashed me a crooked grin that was so practiced that he probably did it in the mirror every morning.

Nick placed the cosmo in front of me, and the twinkle in his eye as he fought off a smile made me want to laugh this time. He was ready for it, and I needed to make this one good. I had my audience now, and I might as well keep him entertained. He'd said he couldn't wait to tell his wife, Cindy, about this when he got home. She was going to love it.

"Oh," I replied, "I don't know." I picked up my drink and took a sip, then winked at Nick before turning my attention to Frat Boy. *Time to deal the hand.* "Perhaps there hasn't been a man brave enough to take me on."

The challenge in his eyes was just too easy. He didn't even think about the hand I had dealt before tossing in his bet. Silly boy.

"Seems we both just got lucky then. Because I can promise you, I'm more than willing to take you on."

I pulled my bottom lip between my teeth and let it slowly slide back out as he watched, transfixed. My turn to deal the flop.

"Is that so?" I asked in a sultry voice. "You seem very sure of yourself…I didn't get your name."

"Devin," he replied, leaning on the bar and closer to me.

Someone should tell him to lay off the CK One. I recognized that scent from a guy I'd dated before Bastian. It seemed Devin had bathed in it.

"I can keep calling you beautiful all night, but I'd like a name to go with that showstopping face."

Showstopping face? What was he, ninety? Not rolling my eyes was difficult, but I held my smile.

"I don't like my real name. I prefer to go by Candy. It was my stage name." I batted my lashes at him as I dealt out the turn. "But I'm not allowed to go by that name anymore."

I was pretty sure there was drool forming in the corner of his mouth. He probably had watched many Candys dance on a pole, void of clothing.

"Stage name, huh?" he asked, moving in closer.

I was going to have to get this over with before he damaged my lungs with the cologne fumes wafting off him.

I ran my tongue over my bottom lip, letting him watch me. Before I could deal the last hand in my story time, the stool on my other side scratched against the floor, and thinking it might be one of the girls I was here with, I did a quick glance.

It wasn't.

It was another man.

And for a solid second in time, the world stopped. Froze like a drop of water in an Alaskan winter. I didn't even blink. I did a quick tally of the drinks I'd had. Maybe I'd had one too many.

The dark blue eyes that still appeared in my dreams met mine, but only briefly before lifting to look over my head at Devin. "You can go." The deep, raspy voice was more mature.

Even with a short beard covering his chiseled jaw and laugh lines in his tanned skin, I knew him. That face was still the same. He was a man now, not just a young guy trying to live in a man's world. He'd aged all right, but like a fine wine. One I would give my last breath to taste.

Devin said something, but the roaring in my ears as I stared at Linc Shephard drowned out everything else. His eyes dropped back to mine. The interest in that steady gaze caused my heart to race. I'd never seen this look in his eyes before, and wow. It was like a blazing fire that you knew was dangerous, but you couldn't stop moving closer to it. Mesmerized by the beauty of its devastation.

He shifted slightly, and his arm moved.

"Holy fuck, dude!" Devin exclaimed.

That snapped me from my trance. I blinked. The sound of a glass being dropped onto the ground brought back the rest of the noise that had gone silent at the sight of Linc. Glancing around, I realized life hadn't stopped because my world had. I stared up at Linc to see his expression had gone from panty-soaking to lethal as his eyes were fixed on something behind me.

"Sir, I'll have to call security," Nick said nervously.

I shifted my gaze toward him as he stared in Devin's direction, wide-eyed. What had Devin done?

"You can call, but they won't come," Linc replied. His calm tone was so out of place with the horror on Nick's face.

"How did you get through security with that?" Nick asked.

With what? I started to turn and look at Devin to figure out what the heck had happened while I was in la-la land, thanks to Linc's sudden appearance.

"I don't go through security," Linc replied.

It wasn't Devin's terrified expression or the way his entire body was trembling that I noticed first. It was the gun pointed at his head. I sucked in a breath as my hand flew to my mouth.

What the heck was Linc doing? We were in a casino! He couldn't go pulling out a gun on people in here. Or…maybe he could.

Two tall men in black suits appeared behind the three of us. Wide shoulders, shaved heads, and intimidating scowls on their faces. Great. Linc had gotten the casino's security involved. How was he going to get out of this one?

"Is there a problem, Mr. Shephard?" the largest one asked. His eyes went from Linc to Devin.

"Escort this one out," Linc told them as he lowered his gun, then slid it back into the hidden holster under his brown leather jacket.

"Yes, sir," the man replied.

They moved toward Devin, who was still pale. The fact that he was being kicked out started to sink in, and his anger flared up, giving his skin more color.

"Wait! I didn't do anything! He pulled a gun on me—"

The guard who had said nothing grabbed Devin's arm and jerked him up. "Shut up," he snarled, cutting him off.

They hauled him off, even though he continued to rant and fight against their hold. The word *lawyer* was thrown out, but then they were too far away for me to hear the rest. I turned back around and realized Nick had moved down to help another customer, but there was a new cosmo in front of me and a glass of amber liquid in front of Linc, which I assumed was whiskey.

I looked at our glasses, then back up at him as he lifted his and took a drink. His entire body was completely relaxed as if all that hadn't just happened.

"What was that?" I asked.

He slowly turned his head until his eyes were once again on me. "Which part?"

I waved a hand over where Devin had been sitting. "All of it."

He lowered the glass and placed it on the bar. "Did you want him bothering you?"

"No, but I had it under control. I was about to deal the river, and he'd have jumped up and run with very little explanation. They always do. A gun was not required."

The corner of his mouth quirked. "The river," he said.

I nodded.

"Hate that I missed the flop and the turn," he replied, almost smiling. "You use Texas Hold'em deals to label the lines you give men to get rid of them?"

I'd never told anyone that before. "Yes."

"Why?" he asked.

Because once, this man, who I'd thought was meant only for me, taught me to play Texas Hold'em on a haystack underneath the late summer sun, and now, I was pretty much unbeatable at the game. I didn't tell him that though. I wasn't sure if he realized who I was. Unlike him, I looked nothing like the little girl I had once been. I was a woman, and I doubted he could see past the me of today to the girl he had known in her youth.

"I like the game. Makes sense in all parts of life really."

He took another drink. "So, that's what you've been doing tonight. All those men who walked over here and sat down, then took off shortly after. I'm curious"—he twirled the liquid in his glass around as he studied me—"what was it you told them? Because I can't think of one fucking thing you could tell me that would make me get up and walk away." He reached over and cupped my chin in his large, callous hand. His eyes scanned my face through his dark lashes. "Up close, you're even more incredible than you were from a distance."

All my little-girl dreams collided with the desires and dreams of the woman I'd become. Seemed that nothing had changed. Linc Shephard still made me feel like nothing or no one else ever had. Fate had brought him back to me. This was my chance to finally live my very own fairy tale.

FOUR
BRANWEN

Present Day

Waiting on my phone to ring had my anxiety so ramped up that the knock on the door to our motel room caused me to jump up. Who was that? Housekeeping again? I'd sent them away two hours ago.

"What's wrong, Mommy?" Stevie asked, her angelic face turned up to look at me from where she sat cross-legged in the middle of the double bed we had slept on last night while watching cartoons on the television.

She had thought staying the night in a motel was an adventure. Yesterday, we had gotten the supplies to make sandwiches and eaten them down at a park I'd found. Stevie took a slice of bread and tore off small pieces to feed the ducks, giggling with delight as they waddled over to eat them. It had helped keep my mind off things and get through the rest of the day.

This morning we had only gone out once to get her some breakfast. One scrambled egg, a slice of buttered toast, and two strawberries—it was her favorite thing to eat in the mornings. Finding that hadn't been too hard. The first diner we went into had all three items available. That made her happy. I'd only drunk coffee. My stomach was in knots, and eating was not appealing.

"Nothing. I was just startled," I told her, patting her leg as I walked over to the door.

I unlocked it and didn't even glance in the peephole, although I should have. I would have been prepared for the sight of Linc when I swung open the door. He was just as ridiculously sexy, powerful, and rugged as he had been yesterday.

"I thought you would just call," I blurted out, not sure if his coming here was bad or not.

I was veering toward it being negative. There were no signed papers in his hands. That was definitely not good.

"There are a few things we need to discuss," he replied. Then, his eyes flicked over me and into the room, where Stevie sat, probably watching us. "Might be best if she doesn't hear this."

Oh God, oh God, oh God. Did he know?

I mean, other than guessing, how could he know? He'd left me a morning-after pill. He wouldn't ask if she was his. He didn't want a kid. That had been very clearly stated in his short note. I was overreacting. That was all.

Maybe the divorce was going to cost money, and he wanted to tell me how much I had to pay. That could easily be it. Although I didn't know where I was going to get the money without Hudson finding out about this. It would be tricky. I didn't have any jewelry left to sell. I'd sold all of what Bastian had given me after finding out I was pregnant with Stevie and losing my job because of it. Not that they'd told me that was why I was let go.

They said that my position was no longer something they had a use for and gave me three months' pay, then sent me on my way. That was a lie. I'd worked my ass off for that company, taking up slack in many other areas. They had needed me, but Bastian had hated that I was pregnant.

I turned back and looked at Stevie, who was watching us. She waved at Linc and smiled. Guilt crawled up my back, and I fought against it. I couldn't feel guilty for protecting her. Giving her the life she deserved. Keeping her from one that would likely break both our hearts.

"Stevie, I need to have a chat with Mr. Shephard. I'll just be right out here, okay?" I told her.

She nodded her head, then turned her attention back to the television. Seemed she wasn't going to argue or pepper me with a million questions. Small miracles.

I closed the door and looked back at Linc. He wasn't wearing the cowboy hat today, and his hair was still like it had been five years ago. Thick, wavy brown locks, brushed back in a messy yet perfectly styled look that I doubted he ever spent much time on. Just one more unfair advantage in his appearance. Even the tiny touches of silver in his beard were sexy. Damn him.

"Her name is Stevie?" he asked me. His hard edge had softened some.

I was afraid to look at him.

I nodded. "Yeah," was all I said wanting him to stop asking about her.

"Odd name for a girl."

His words said one thing, but his tone said another. He liked it, but then I had known he would. The drugs or the high of holding her in my arms the first time had made me sentimental.

"Not if you grew up listening to Fleetwood Mac," I replied, then bit my tongue before saying any more. Too much, and he might connect the dots.

He didn't need to remember. In Vegas, I had wanted him to, but not any longer.

"That was before your time."

I lifted a shoulder and stared out at the parking lot instead of him. "I didn't have a normal childhood."

And that was all he was getting from me about that. The days of him singing "Gypsy" to me while ruffling my out-of-control curls, which my father had no idea how to manage, were long gone.

"Is she mine?" The three words came out hard, laced with accusation.

Lying to him, I found, was going to be more than difficult with his dark blue eyes lasered in on me. I swallowed, straightening my shoulders. I had Stevie's future to think about. Her life and everything that was almost hers. The two-story house that Hudson lived in that would soon have a swing set in the backyard. The private school he was going to pay for and the security that when it came time for college, she would get the chance I never had. Hudson wanted her. Linc had not. I couldn't hurt her by telling her that she did have a father, but he didn't want her. He had given up any right to her when he left me that pill.

"She's mine," I finally said.

His eyes narrowed. "She's not Jesus. There was no immaculate conception. Who is her father?" he snapped at me.

I took a deep breath. He would not intimidate me.

"I've never had a paternity test done," I replied, leaving out there was no reason for a paternity test.

I had slept with three men in my life—Bastian, him, and Hudson. There was only one man it could have been; at that time, it had been a year since I'd slept with Bastian, and I hadn't met Hudson yet.

His nostrils flared, and his eyes darkened with distaste. What? Did the idea that I might have slept with other men around the same time make me a bad person in his eyes? Hypocrite. His body count was in the hundreds or possibly thousands. Like he had the right to judge anyone.

"Then, I will require one before I sign anything."

My flash of anger spun into dread. What would happen when he found out? How could I explain this to Hudson? I'd told him Stevie's father was dead. Because to me, he was. I'd rationalized my lie to make it something I could sleep with at night.

He pulled his phone from his pocket and pressed a number before holding it to his ear while his gaze bored into me like he wished he could grab me and toss me over the railing. When he knew the truth, he just might do that. Or worse. I shouldn't have come here. This was a mistake. I could have found a way around this if I'd tried. Maybe an annulment. But he'd have had to be contacted for that too, right?

GOD! Why had I brought Stevie with me? If he had never seen her…

Sweat trickled down my back as I scrambled for a way to save this situation. Stop him from doing this. He didn't want a child. Why was he so set on knowing if she was his?

"Burl." His gravelly voice heightened my fear. "I need a paternity test done. I'm at the Madison Inn. Room 210."

Who was Burl? Was he asking him to send a doctor or lab person here? To our room?

I wrung my hands in front of me. What would I tell Stevie? She thought her dad was dead too. I'd told her the same lie to protect her. I hadn't wanted her to go looking for him one day and find…well, this. The man in front of me. The one who hadn't wanted her.

Linc shoved his phone into the back pocket of his jeans. The fury in his gaze narrowed on me. "You'd better fucking pray she's not mine." The threat was the last thing he said before turning and walking away. Back toward the stairs.

I watched him go, wanting to ask, *What if she is? What then?*

He wouldn't kill me, would he? My death wouldn't change anything. Maybe I should run. He was leaving. We could go. Drive north and not look back. No. Hudson would send out a search party, and we'd be on the news. I couldn't do that to Stevie. I wanted to give her a perfect life. The one I hadn't gotten.

When he was gone from sight, I closed my eyes and tried to calm my breathing before going back inside. I had to explain this to Stevie or prepare her that someone was coming to do…well, I wasn't sure. I needed to google how a paternity test was done. If they were going to take her blood, then this was about to get dramatic. There were few things that Stevie hated more than needles.

Taking my phone, I quickly did a search on what to expect with a paternity test. Finding the answer, I sighed with some relief. He would just need to swab inside her cheek for a sample of her tissue. There would be no wailing from her. I could solely worry about my potential upcoming death.

I read the last text from Hudson. He was checking on us. Making sure we were doing okay and asking if I needed him. He was the first real security I'd had since…well, since my dad.

Once, I would have balked at marrying a man who didn't give me butterflies at the sight of him. But that had all been before Vegas. That night had changed me. I'd woken up the following two months. Realized that love wasn't tingles and flutters in your stomach. That was silliness that the little girl in me had had to grow up and move on from.

Love was being safe. Knowing you were wanted. Love was being comfortable. It wasn't about hot sex and multiple orgasms. It was having someone to raise your child with, build a life with, and grow old with. Not worrying that you'd lose them or that they would leave you.

When Hudson looked at me, it was as if he saw no one else. I was it for him. He wanted to be my safe place and Stevie's father.

I could lose it all. Linc Shephard was about to blow up my carefully laid plans.

Since my first day of working as a dental hygienist for Hudson, I'd seen a future for me and Stevie. He couldn't take his eyes off me. Finding reasons to have me in the room with him. Seeking me out to talk about the simplest things. Then, he asked me to dinner. It escalated from there. Within a month, we had started dating exclusively. Before him, I hadn't dated since Bastian. Being a single mom made it hard, and having to work and go to school for my dental hygiene degree was enough time away from Stevie. I hadn't wanted to add to it by bringing a man into our lives.

Hudson had been the perfect fit. He took me and Stevie on dates. We became a family—or the closest thing to one that we could be.

But my lies were all coming back to haunt me now, and I was pressed into a corner.

Tears stung my eyes, and I fought off the need to cry. I was going to let Stevie down in more ways than one today, and it was all my fault.

FIVE
LINC

I was smoking a fucking cigarette. Leaning against the hood of my F-150, I inhaled deeply in hopes that something would help take away the tension radiating through my body. My eyes stayed locked on the second floor of the motel, not taking them off the door that read 210. I didn't trust the woman. She looked like a deer caught in the headlights and ready to take off running. Which didn't make me feel better. It only heightened the dread slowly working its way through my veins.

She might not know who the father was, but it was clear in those eyes of hers. What the fuck color were they? Jade? Was that even an eye color? You sure as hell couldn't call them green. That was too basic of a description. Something about them tugged at a memory that seemed to be dangling just out of my reach.

Scowling, I pulled more of the poison into my lungs. It wasn't like I hadn't pulled up that face hundreds of times since the night we'd fucked. My memory just hadn't been doing her justice. Which I thought had been impossible. Until yesterday, I'd assumed the opium high had created that perfect face in my memory. But fucking nope. She was even better than the fantasy.

None of that mattered. If the kid was mine, that meant she'd not taken the pill I'd left for her, knowing she had no way of ever contacting me if she was pregnant. I'd been used.

I took the cigarette from my mouth before I bit off the tip. Fuck! What was I going to do if that little girl *was* mine? Letting her walk away with my daughter and allowing some other man to raise her would be best for her. That had been her plan after all. The marriage certificate had led her to me, and she hadn't come to tell me I had a kid. She'd just come for the divorce. So, she was guilty of not only having my kid, but also keeping her from me.

The silver Mercedes sedan pulled up beside my truck, and I dropped the cigarette to the concrete before covering it with the toe of my boot. Burl was here. The urge to send him away and let this go was there. But I'd not be able to get it out of my head. I'd think about the kid. Guilt would creep in, and it would eat me alive. I had to fucking know.

Dr. Burl stepped out of his luxury vehicle, and his gaze swung to mine. I hadn't given him any information other than I needed a paternity test. In the past, I'd had to call him to do this for one of the guys, but not me. This was going to be a first.

"Morning," Burl said, tipping his cowboy hat back on his head.

He looked like he had been down at his stables. His worn jeans were dusty, as were his boots. Unlike the family, Burl didn't have a stable full of thoroughbreds that he bred and raced. He had quarter horses and a couple of Tennessee

Walkers. His wife had once been a champion barrel racer and now taught riding lessons.

"Are we testing a baby or a kid?" he asked me.

I glanced up at the door. "Four-year-old girl."

"And, uh..." He cleared his throat. "Which one of the guys do I need to swab?" The hesitancy in his voice gave away his unease at having to ask me that.

I cut my eyes back to him. "Me."

The flicker of surprise was gone as quickly as it had come. He was a master at shutting down his expression and masking his thoughts around us. "Okay. Then, we can go ahead and swab your cheek before we go to the room."

He set his small case down on the hood of the truck then reached into it. When he turned back to me with the sterile cotton swab, I opened my mouth so that he could rub the tip inside my cheek several times. I'd never had to do this since fucking without wrapping my dick up was something I didn't do. My one exception with the blonde goddess, who I'd fucked like a damn dog in heat, had brought me to this.

There had been two condoms on the floor that morning—the only ones that had been in my pocket—which I tossed in the trash. I walked away, knowing that the memory of her tight, hot, wet pussy as I had taken her raw wasn't a hallucination since we had fucked many times. Not just twice. Yet I told myself that she was most likely on birth control. If she hadn't been, she'd have said something.

I'd gone to the nearest pharmacy and gotten the morning-after pill, just to be safe. Covered all the bases.

When Burl had the swab in its container, he put it in the case, then closed it. "The child's mother is with her?" he asked.

Legally, the mother had to be with her, but Burl knew I didn't care about legalities. He was paid well to overlook the times he was asked to break a law.

I nodded. "Yeah. She's expecting us."

I started toward the stairs, and he fell into step beside me.

"You think this is another female looking for money?" he asked.

I fucking wished. I shook my head. "No. I'm the one demanding it."

"Oh."

The startled sound in that one word wasn't lost on me.

We climbed the stairs in silence, and the closer I got to the door, the more the foreboding squeezed my chest. I didn't have to do this. I could sign the fucking divorce papers and let them walk. My lawyers had verified that they were in fact legal. They suggested that I file a petition for an annulment since we never lived together and the marriage wasn't valid. If not, then they needed to prepare paperwork for her to sign, stating she gave up all rights to my assets and money.

Before a decision was made on that, I needed to know if the kid was mine. Because if she was, it would change things. I might not have wanted another kid, but if I had one, I would support her. Even if her mother didn't want my money, she'd goddamn take it. Another man wasn't going to financially support what belonged to me.

Burl didn't ask any more questions, but then he never did. He didn't pry; he only knew what we shared with him. He wanted it that way too. The less he knew about the workings inside the family, the better. He handled all our medical needs that we didn't want taken to the hospital, as well as being available for things such as this. Making house calls for our convenience.

I rapped my knuckles against the door. There seemed to be a struggle on the other side with unlocking it, and I glowered as I waited. When the door eased open, Branwen wasn't standing there. My eyes dropped to see blue eyes staring up at me, along with a big grin, causing dimples in her cheeks. There was a sprinkling of freckles over her nose that I hadn't noticed yesterday.

"Hello." She paused and scrunched her nose. "Mommy is in the bathwoom."

Burl cleared his throat behind me, masking a chuckle.

The kid was fucking cute. She was going to be a beauty, like her momma. The unease that she might be mine and the males in her future rattled me. I hadn't thought about that. What if I had a daughter? Especially one who was going to grow up to look like her mother. Fuck. I'd end up murdering teenage boys with my bare hands.

"I'm watching *SpongeBob*," she informed me. "And I don't nawmally get to watch that show. Mommy says it's wude and 'noxious." Her eyes were big and round as she shared that information with me. "But theah isn't anything else for me to watch."

She couldn't say her *r*'s.

She turned her gaze to Burl. "Who awah you?"

"He's a friend of mine. A doctor, and he just needs to swab the inside of your cheek," I told her.

She tilted her tiny body as she peered around me, trying to get a better look at Burl. Her smile had dropped immediately when I said the word *doctor*. Her brows puckered. "You don't look like a doctow," she told him. "You look like a cowboy."

This time, Burl did laugh.

The door to the bathroom opened, and my eyes swung up from the kid to the woman walking out. Long legs, the perfect flare to her hips, narrow waist, and tits. Jesus Christ, the set of tits on her. Then, all those pale blonde locks draped over her bare shoulders, curling just over her cleavage. My hands were clenched so tightly that I could feel my short nails biting into my palms. It seemed my cock didn't care that she might have lied and intended to keep a child she'd had without my knowledge from me. It just wanted to fuck her again.

"Vivi Lu!" she called out. "You know better than to open a door without me."

The little girl spun around so fast that her blonde curls floated around her head. "But we awn't at home. We awe at a motel," she explained as if that made all the difference.

Branwen placed a hand on her hip, and I fought the urge to look at the small sliver of flat, tanned stomach that the shirt she was wearing flashed. The hem didn't quite meet the waist of her blue linen shorts. "That rule goes for wherever we are. It's dangerous. Someone bad could be on the other side and snatch you."

I liked that she wasn't sugarcoating it. The kid was too fucking adorable for her own good. She needed to be aware that she couldn't trust people.

"I'm sowwy, Mommy." She sounded remorseful. "But it wasn't a bad guy. It was just Mista Outlaw, and he bwought a doctow that looks like a cowboy."

Branwen's light-green eyes lifted to me. I wondered if they would be so damn striking without that dark rim around the pale jade color. Why was I thinking about this? It didn't fucking matter.

I tore my eyes off her and stepped inside so that Burl could follow me.

"This is Dr. Burl," I told her, closing the door behind him.

When I didn't say more, Burl moved farther into the room.

"It's nice to meet you," I heard him say.

"Uh, yes, I'm, uh, Branwen Hester, and this is my daughter, Stevie," she replied. Her voice reminded me of a smooth, expensive whiskey.

Her last name was bothering me. It was familiar, but I couldn't place it. When I had read it on the marriage certificate yesterday, I'd paused and tried to think of where I had heard it before. Not that it mattered. Highly unlikely the two were connected. It was just a surname.

"What is a swab?" Stevie demanded.

I smirked at the way her expression suddenly looked fierce.

"It won't hurt," her mother quickly informed her, bending her knees and lowering herself until her eyes were level with her daughter's. She took the girl's hands in hers. "I promise. This is quick and easy. When it's over, we can go back to the park we found yesterday. Have another picnic and feed the ducks."

The little girl looked from her mother back to Burl. "But I'm not sick. Why is a doctow hewah?"

The pink tip of Branwen's tongue came out and licked her lips quickly, and she took a deep breath. I assumed she was trying to think up a lie to tell the kid.

"You're right. You aren't sick. But..." She paused, and the fear in her eyes gave away shit that only made me question this.

I could stop it. Let them go and forget about all of it. Sign the fucking papers. Never know.

There was only one reason she would be scared. And that reason would change my life. Immediately. It would change theirs too. If I let it. That was up to me. Branwen had already made it clear that she had no problem not knowing who the father of her child was. That, or she knew and wanted to keep it a secret.

It was going to shock the hell out of me if the kid was mine, and she knew it. Coming here and not demanding money from me once she had my name and could track me down wouldn't make sense. Unless this was about the fiancé.

He might be rich. I hadn't taken the time to read the full background check that Wilder had pulled on Branwen. I got as far as the girl's birth date and did some math. That was the main reason I'd wanted this test. The date of conception was spot-on with the time we'd fucked.

"It's a test to see if you have more family. If there is someone else who might want to be a part of your life. Or just know about you." Branwen's eyes flickered to me briefly, then back to her daughter.

"I got mowah family than you and Hudson?" she asked, her voice going up an octave.

Hudson wasn't her family. Not yet. Annoyance hit me—that her mother had let her think that he was her family—and I had to unclench my teeth and force myself to calm down. This kid might not be mine. That man was going to be her future stepfather. I had no reason to get pissed off because she thought that he was family.

Branwen bit her bottom lip. "Yes, baby, you do. Family that I couldn't find before now."

I held my breath as I narrowed my gaze. My eyes locked on her, as if I could draw out the fucking truth myself. That response sounded an awful lot like she knew who the kid's father was and had looked for him. For me.

"Let's get this over with," I barked.

The little girl jumped, startled by my sharp demand, and her eyes swung up to my face. She studied me through her thick lashes. I rubbed my jaw, wishing I hadn't been so damn harsh. But, fuck, I wanted to get this done. I was tired of all the what-ifs.

"You got tattoos on youwah fingaws," she stated, studying my hand.

I dropped it back to my side. "Yeah, I do."

She pulled her hands free of her mother's and walked over to me, her attention captured by what she'd seen. "Mommy has a tattoo, but Hudson don't like it. He said tattoos awah twashy and she's gonna get hewahs taken off."

My gaze lifted from the girl to see Branwen looking slightly pale as she stood back up. The tight smile she gave me didn't meet her eyes.

"Let's not talk about tattoos, Vivi Lu, okay? Let's just get this swab done so we can go to the park."

A faint memory of a tattoo on her body came back to me. It had been on her hip bone. I was pretty sure I'd licked it on my way to eat her pussy. What was it?

"But, Mommy, he's got thwee fingaws tattooed. I just want to see them."

Her tone sounded so damn pleading that I found myself fisting my hands so she could see the three tattoos on my fingers. She didn't ask her mother as she quickly made her way closer to me to look at my ink.

"You like the lettah A?" she asked me, lifting her eyes up to my face.

My lips quirked. "I like those *a*'s," I replied. "That's the ace of spades, ace of diamonds, and ace of clubs," I told her. Then, I opened my hand and turned it over. The back of my ring finger was the last one. "And that's the ace of hearts."

Her eyes widened as she peered at it. "You got fowah on your hand," she said in awe. Then, her eyes went to my arms. "Awah those chains around youwah awms?"

I nodded. "That they are. Reckon Hudson would think I'm the king of trashy."

Her eyes darted back up to me, and I winked at her. A small giggle escaped her, and she covered her mouth, then nodded her head in agreement. I almost told her I had more, but then I figured the little curious beauty would want to see those, too, and I didn't think taking off my shirt would be the appropriate thing to do.

Burl coughed, and I glanced over at him. The *we need to do this* look in his eyes reminded me why we were here.

I nodded at him to proceed.

He walked over to Stevie and dropped down to his haunches. "All right. I just need to stick this swab in your mouth and rub the inside of your cheek with it. That's all. You open wide, and it won't hurt a bit."

She nodded, then gave him a serious frown. "You pwomise you won't wub my thwaot with that thing? 'Cause that makes me thwow up and cwy. Don't it, Mommy?" she said, looking back at her mother for confirmation.

Branwen smiled at her daughter. "Yes, but you aren't getting tested for strep throat. This will not make you cry."

"Or thwow up?" she pressed.

The kid was sharp. She was making sure she wasn't being tricked. I smirked.

"Or throw up," her mother assured her.

The girl seemed appeased with that and turned to Burl, then opened her mouth wide. I watched as a million fucking things went through my mind, like a herd of cattle stampeding out of control. She could be my kid. I'd know soon. What would I do with that? Just give her mom money? Did I want to know her? Have her in my life? Did I want to be a dad to her, or was this Hudson guy better? No. If she was mine, I didn't think I could let some other man take my place. Even if he was a better choice. I blinked, then jerked my eyes off the kid as weird shit I wasn't familiar with hit me in the chest.

"I'll get this to the lab, and you should know within the next two hours," Burl informed us both.

He looked at me for further instruction or permission to leave. My singular nod was all he needed. He smiled once more at Branwen and Stevie before heading for the door. I waited until it closed behind him to look at Branwen.

"I'll let you know, and we can proceed from there," I told her.

She didn't ask anything more. "Okay." Her voice was barely above a whisper.

Turning, I exited the small space, needing something more than a cigarette. I needed an entire fifth of whiskey.

SIX
BRANWEN

Trying to stay in the moment with Stevie while tossing small pieces of bread out to the ducks was a struggle. My mind was on the results of the test. What would I do if Linc fought me for custody? He wouldn't do that. He hadn't wanted a kid. It was my biggest fear, yet I knew that it was very unlikely. I was a good mom. There was no reason for the courts to take my daughter from me. But this was Linc Shephard. He had pull and power in places that unsettled me. That wouldn't be an issue though because he did not want a child.

Stevie's laughter made my heart clench tightly. He might not have wanted a kid, but he'd been taken by her. I'd seen it, and part of me wanted to wail because what if I had kept her father from her and he'd have been a good one? The other part of me had wanted to grab her and dash out the door. She was mine. I was terrified at the thought of sharing her. It was incredibly selfish, and I knew that, but it was still there. I couldn't help it. Trusting him to not break her heart would be hard. How would I be able to do that?

Hudson had called, and I'd sent it to voice mail. I just couldn't talk to him right now. Not until I knew what Linc intended to do about the fact that he had a daughter. There was no longer a chance that I could keep this from Hudson. Stevie would tell him all about it. If I asked her to not tell him, then that would be asking her to lie for me. There were many things I could rationalize away, but that wasn't one of them. This wasn't her fault.

I was going to have to tell Hudson something, even if Linc sent us back to Tennessee with my signed papers. I would have to admit to my lies and hope he could forgive me. Not only could he call off the wedding, but he could also fire me. I'd be without a job. My hand went to my chest, and I rubbed. Panic was growing by the second, and it hurt to breathe deeply. I could not black out in a full-blown attack. I'd not had one in years. I was stronger than I had once been.

"Hey! He's back!" Stevie's voice called out, and my head snapped up to look at her as she waved her hand excitedly.

Linc was here. He'd come looking for us. He knew.

Slowly, I stood up from the patch of grass I had been sitting on and dusted off my bottom before turning to face him. All I could hear was the pounding of my heart and the rush of blood as it pumped in my veins. This was it. I sucked in a breath, but it was a sharp pang instead of relief.

I couldn't see his eyes behind the sunglasses he was wearing. But the firm line of his mouth wasn't happy. That almost spurred my anger enough to overcome the terror rising in me. I hadn't come here, asking for anything other than a divorce. What was he angry about? Not knowing he had a daughter? Well, he hadn't exactly left me with a way to get in touch with him. Just a note and a freaking pill.

"There's no need to tell you the results. You knew."

The accusation in his tone only fueled my temper.

I lifted my chin and glared at the dark lenses covering his eyes. "You didn't leave me a way to contact you. Not even a name. Just a pill." I tossed out that reminder before he could start in with the *you kept er from me* thing.

"Which you didn't take."

My eyes flared, and I was so close to slapping his face. How dare he! She was standing feet away from us, feeding the ducks.

"I did take the pill," I hissed at him, hating to even admit it. That pill could have robbed me of the little girl who owned my heart. "It isn't one hundred percent effective." Thank God.

His jaw worked back and forth. He knew I was right. Arguing with me about it and throwing out blame were pointless. The marriage we hadn't known was legal was the only reason I had come to find him—again. The first time he never needed to know about. That was my secret to keep.

"I'll follow you back to the motel to get your things. Then, you're coming to my house. We have things to discuss. My lawyer will meet us there at my office."

His house? Lawyer? I didn't like that idea. It sounded threatening. He hadn't wanted a child. He didn't get to want her now.

"Why?" The franticness in my tone made me wince.

I was trying to act calm, but I was afraid that I was failing.

He cocked an eyebrow. "What did you think would happen? I'd find out I have a four-year-old daughter and sign the papers, then let you leave with her?"

"OH! I'm fowah too!" Stevie said, rushing up to us. "Can I meet huwah? She can come feed the ducks with us."

My sweet baby girl. The path I had set up for her had just taken a turn I'd never expected. One I had never wanted.

I stared at him for a brief second, then bent down to look at her perfect little face. "Honey, we need to go to Mr.

Shephard's house so Mommy can go to a meeting there. Let's get our things together, and we will go to the car. You can ask me questions on our way."

Her eyes sparked with excitement for going back to the house she'd thought was a villain's castle. I was afraid her description might be accurate after all.

"Yay!" she squealed and bounced on the balls of her feet.

Standing back up, I held my hand out for her to take. More so for my reassurance than hers. She was perfectly happy, and that was as it should be. The weight on my shoulders wasn't hers to bear. My gaze went back to Linc.

"Our things are already in the car," I told him.

We didn't have much, seeing as I hadn't been planning on the overnight trip. I always kept a change of clothing for both of us in the trunk. It was a habit I'd started when she was a baby and always messing up both our outfits.

"I'll follow you," he repeated in a clipped tone.

What did he think, that if he didn't follow me, I would take off back to Nashville and have the Southern Mafia showing up at my front door? Um, no thanks. But then he didn't know that I was aware of his ranking inside the Mafia. I'd honestly thought when he read my first and last name on that marriage certificate, it would have dawned on him. The realization of who I was and how he would respond was something I'd played out many ways in my head. None of those things had happened though, seeing as he didn't remember me at all.

With my hand wrapped protectively around Stevie's, I walked to the car and unlocked it. She climbed inside and sat in her car seat. The anticipation of going back to the black mansion and getting to see the inside making her bouncy. Taking my time, I buckled her in, then kissed the top of her head.

This would be okay. It had to be. Linc wasn't a monster. He had questionable morals, and I didn't trust him, but he wouldn't want to do anything that would hurt Stevie. I had to believe that much.

Even when he had been a young man, I remembered his struggle at being a father. I'd overheard him talking to Garrett and Creed more than once about how he was failing his son. How he wasn't cut out to be a dad. He would agree that the best thing for Stevie was Hudson. He wanted to be her father. He wanted children of his own too. His house even had a white picket fence.

TWENTY-EIGHT YEARS AGO

I huffed with frustration at my dad's refusal to let me ride the new two-year-old colt that had arrived yesterday from the family in Georgia. Dad thought I didn't know about the family or who the Hughes were, but I did. It was hard not to hear things, always being here. Adults would talk around me, thinking I was just a kid and didn't understand. I probably knew more than Daddy did.

Picking up the saddle and placing it on the bench, I scowled at the other tack around me. I wanted a saddle like these. Mine was used and beat up. Garrett's wife had a saddle with turquoise-blue leather and crystal beads outlining it. I loved that saddle. I'd asked for one this past Christmas, but Daddy had said that was out of his budget. That pretty saddle was never used. It just sat there, making me envious.

"Hey, Ringlets," the voice I loved above all others said, wiping away my foul mood.

I snapped my head around to see Linc walking into the room. His head tilted, and his eyes narrowed slightly as he studied me. "That was some serious scowling you were doing. Which one of these saddles offended you?"

My heart fluttered, and the giddiness that came from seeing him bubbled up inside me. He had been gone all week. Normally, he stopped by once or twice. I'd missed seeing him. The hand that was behind his back came around to the front, holding a bright yellow daisy.

He stopped in front of me and tucked it behind my right ear. "All right, my wild gypsy girl, tell me what has you in a mood."

"My dad," I grumbled.

He looked surprised. "Your dad? You got a great dad. One of the best."

I knew that. But sometimes, he wasn't fair. Like today, when I'd wanted to ride the colt.

I shrugged. "He's being unfair."

Linc threw his leg over the bench and sat down, straddling it so that he was closer to my eye level. "That's a parent's job. To be unfair. But he has a reason. I'm sure of it. Hell, I wish I could be the kind of dad yours is. I happen to suck at it, Ringlets. Parenting is hard."

I hated the reminder that he had a family. A wife and son. People that he belonged to when my heart believed that he belonged to me. I was his Ringlets.

I bit my bottom lip and dropped my eyes to the ground. "I bet you don't boss Levi around all the time. Tell him no when he really wants to do something."

I didn't see him with Levi that much, but I did see Garrett with his son, Blaise, who was the same age. Garrett never corrected the kid, and he was a hellion.

Linc chuckled. The deep rumble always gave me goose bumps.

"Levi is a six-year-old boy. All I do is tell him no. You've seen him. Last time I brought him here, what did he do?"

The corner of my mouth drew up, even when I didn't want to smile. The memory of it was funny. I'd wanted to hate Levi because Linc loved him so much. I was jealous. I didn't like seeing him with another kid. One he seemed to care about more than me. But Levi had been cute and hard not to like.

"He let out Wolfgang after breaking the railing on the south pen, walking on it like he was on a tightrope in the circus," I replied.

Wolfgang was one of Garrett's champion horses. He'd won more races than any other horse at the stables.

Linc reached out and tugged on one of my curls. "That last part he did was to impress you," he told me. "Couldn't really blame the kid. He might be young, but he isn't blind. But what did I do to him after all that?"

I thought back. "Um, you tossed him over your shoulder like a sack of potatoes and hauled him to your truck while he screamed and pounded his fists on your back."

Linc nodded. "Yep. He wanted to stay and ride, like I'd promised him, but he didn't listen, and I took him home without getting to ride. Reckon he thought I was unfair then too. Like I said, being a dad is hard work, but whatever your dad did, it was for your own good."

I crossed my arms over my chest, not liking the fact that he was taking my dad's side. Linc was supposed to always side with me.

"I just want to ride the new colt. Garrett let Blaise ride him, and he's only six. I'm ten, and I've been riding longer than that."

Blaise Hughes was a terror. Levi might have broken a railing, but Blaise did much worse than that on a regular basis. His mom might never come to the stables, but Blaise was here too often. Daddy never corrected him either. He just let Blaise do what he wanted.

Linc studied me as I fought off the tears welling in my eyes. I didn't want to cry in front of him and look like a baby. I liked it when he called me fearless. He let out a sigh, then stood up. Disappointment that he was leaving had me scrambling to think of anything to keep him with me for a little longer.

"Why don't you get your saddle ready?" he said. "I'll go see if I can talk to Demeter."

I blinked, my heart soaring as I stared up at him. When he glanced down at me, his blue eyes twinkled, and he winked before heading toward the door. I watched him go, sure that I would love Linc Shephard with all my heart forever.

SEVEN
LINC

Present Day

I opened the front door to the house and stood back so that Branwen and Stevie could enter. My eyes followed the little curly-headed blonde, unable to stop watching her. Now that I knew she was mine, it was all I wanted to do.

I'd never wanted another kid. Life with Maggie had been rough, and we managed to raise Levi, but the day he turned eighteen, she packed up and left us both. Took off to fucking Europe. I hadn't expected it. As toxic as we had been together, she had been my wife. We'd made it through some bad times. She always forgave me for my mistakes and weak moments.

When she was gone, it was then that I realized I loved her. Not the way a woman wanted to be loved by her husband, but I did love her. I cared about her. I had to face all the shit I'd done to her over the years because I hadn't been in love with her. Or obsessed with her. Or whatever the fuck a man needed to be to not want other pussy. The regret had been difficult. It caused me to withdraw and deal internally.

She'd given me my son. For that, I owed her my life, and she had deserved my fidelity. Forgiving myself for the way I had treated her had been a long road. I wasn't sure I ever had, if I was honest. Knowing Maggie was now happily married to a man who adored her helped though. I liked that she had what she'd deserved all along.

Blue eyes looked up at me. Levi had his mother's hazel eyes. But my…daughter, she had mine. My chest felt tight as she smiled. I had another kid. A girl.

Jesus Christ, what had fate been thinking, giving me a daughter?

"I like yuwah castle."

My lips tugged at the corners. "Thank you."

Her brows puckered as she frowned. "Do you have a dwagon hewah?"

Had she said dragon, or was I misunderstanding her?

"No, Vivi Lu," Branwen told her as she shook her head. "I told you in the car that this was just a house."

She gave her mom a sheepish glance, then lifted her small shoulders in a shrug. "I was just makin' suwah you was wight."

"It's *were right*, not *was right*," Branwen corrected her gently.

Luther cleared his throat, and I shifted my gaze from the two of them to see him standing in the arched entryway that led down the hall to my office.

He held a bottle of Corona in one hand as he studied Stevie before looking at me. "Stanz and Hoyt are here and waiting."

Stanz and Hoyt were two of the lawyers who worked for the family. They handled all family issues within the firm. It was rare that I myself needed them, but being in charge of the Mississippi branch, I was always involved in the others' legal issues, so I knew them both well.

"Where is Jayda?" I asked.

I wasn't about to leave Luther to watch over and entertain my daughter. He wasn't great with kids.

Jayda was our housecleaner and cook, who lived here six days a week. Sunday was her off day. We'd hired her two years ago when Maxine, who had been with us since I had taken over the Mississippi branch, retired. Maxine had brought Jayda in to meet us, and I was against it the second I got a look at her. Having an attractive young woman under our roof would only lead to her in one or both of our beds. Drama neither of us wanted at this age.

That was, until we found out that Jayda wouldn't be angling to get fucked by us or any other man. Her girlfriend, Beth, stayed the night here often. They had been together for five years.

Luther smirked. "What, you don't want to leave her with me?"

I rolled my eyes and let out a sigh, pulling out my phone and tapping Jayda's number.

"Yes, sir," she replied after only one ring.

"I need you in the central great room," I informed her.

"On my way."

Sliding the phone back into my pocket, I met Branwen's tense expression. She didn't like the idea of leaving Stevie. It pissed me off that she didn't trust me to protect my daughter. The one she hadn't planned on telling me about. She'd lied to me. She had known that Stevie was mine, and if I hadn't done the test, she would have never told me.

Biting back a scathing remark for Stevie's sake, I went over to the entertainment system and picked up the remote. We had plenty of channel options, and although I'd never watched one meant for children, I'd seen something like that on here. I turned on the screen, and it lit up.

I glanced back at Stevie. "I've got any channel you want, or is there a specific show I can search for you?"

Her eyes were wide as she stared at the screen. "It's like a movie theataw," she said in awe. "Look, Mommy! It's just like when we go to see a movie with popcown." Her eyes swung back to me. "Do you have popcown?"

Damn, she was adorable. The popcorn machine in the theater at my brother's home in Georgia wasn't looking so pretentious right about now. I'd need to buy one of those and hope he didn't come for a visit, only to see it after I gave him hell for his in his home theater.

"I do." I looked at Luther. "Go pop her some popcorn," I told him.

"With buttah, please!" she piped up.

Luther did not look amused, and for a second, I thought he was about to refuse, but his gaze went to Branwen. Whatever he saw made him change his mind. It had better be him having some out-of-place sympathy for her and nothing more. Luther was a whore, but he wasn't going to fuck the mother of my child. We'd need to get that cleared up and fast before he started trying to charm his way into her panties.

Apparently, it's not hard to do, I thought bitterly.

"Mr. Shephard, you needed me," Jayda said, entering from the other side of the room.

"Stevie, this is Jayda. She will get you anything you need. Change the channel for you. Just ask," I told her. "Jayda, this is Stevie, a very special guest. Take care of her for me. Her mother and I will be in my office if you need me."

Jayda turned to smile at Stevie.

"You look like Awiel," she told Jayda. "She's my favowite pwincess. I like youah hayah."

"Oh, I much prefer yours. All those beautiful blonde curls." She glanced back at Branwen. "You got those from your mother, I see."

Stevie nodded her head, causing the curls to bounce around her head.

"We will be just fine," she said, looking at me, then giving Branwen a reassuring smile.

"Luther went to get her popcorn. Make sure he did it right before you give it to her," I instructed.

Jayda laughed. "I'm not sure he's ever done that before. Stevie and I might need to make a trip to the kitchen."

"This way," I told Branwen, barely glancing at her before starting toward the office.

"I'm, uh, Branwen," I heard her say. "Thank you for watching her. You need to know that Stevie is allergic to tree nuts. Popcorn will be fine as long as it is being popped here and hasn't been cross-contaminated. She will ask for a soda, but it makes her bounce off the walls, as does anything sugary. She likes water and oat milk, if you have it. Dairy gives her a stomachache, and she doesn't like soy milk. If you have any questions, she knows what she can and can't have, but please come ask me. Being in a new place, she's excited, and she might not pay close enough attention."

I stopped and looked back at her. What happened when she had tree nuts? Was it serious? Finding that there were instructions that came with Stevie wasn't something I'd even considered. I wasn't used to food allergies, and knowing Stevie had some concerned me. No, it fucking scared the shit out of me.

"Oh, and she loves grapes. If she asks for them, she is allowed to have them, but I slice them in half. She's probably old enough to not choke on them now, but it still worries me. If one were to slip down her throat..." she winced. "Please slice them before giving them to her. It's a fear of mine. The popcorn makes me a little nervous, too, but I let her have it. I just never leave her alone with popcorn, and I watch her while she eats it. If she were to choke, there wouldn't be a sound, and you wouldn't know she wasn't breathing." She paused, biting her lip and looking at Stevie nervously. "Vivi Lu, chew the popcorn very good. Don't put more than one piece in your mouth at a time. Keep something to drink beside you, okay?"

Stevie nodded. "I pwomise to eat it slowly."

Branwen's smile softened. "Be good. I won't be too long, but if you want me or need me for anything, tell Jayda, and she will bring you to me."

Fuck. Maybe I shouldn't leave her with Jayda. What if she looked away and missed Stevie choking? I no longer wanted her eating popcorn. Why didn't we have ice cream? We needed to get ice cream. Wait! Shit. She couldn't have dairy. My head started to pound behind my eyes as I worked through what was safe for her and what wasn't.

"I'm trained in pediatric CPR and AED. I used to work as a counselor at a summer camp. And my sister has a peanut allergy. I will be extremely careful and consult you before she has anything. I promise. She is in good hands," Jayda told her reassuringly.

"That's wonderful. Thank you," Branwen replied.

I made a mental note to have Jayda buy oat milk and go through the entire kitchen and get rid of anything with tree nuts. There was a weird, anxious feeling in my chest that I wasn't familiar with. We needed to get to the office and handle things, but even with Jayda's assurance that she had this, I wasn't sure I wanted Stevie out of her mother's sight.

Did she leave her at a preschool? What if someone else didn't watch her as carefully as Branwen obviously did? Who watched her when she was at work?

She turned to me. "Okay, we can go now."

She seemed more relaxed about leaving, but for the first time, I was questioning Jayda's ability to do as she had been told.

"Nothing happens to her," I said sternly, making sure Jayda understood.

"I will guard her with my life," she replied.

"I have an EpiPen in my purse if, by some chance, she does get ahold of tree nuts or something cross-contaminated. She will begin projectile vomiting and wheezing immediately. I'll need to inject her leg while an ambulance is called. Don't hesitate to bring her to me."

What the fuck? My entire body stilled as I stared at the little girl I'd just found out was mine hours ago. The horrific image that Branwen had just put in my head wasn't helping. Had that ever happened to her? Branwen had explained it as if they had experienced it before. My throat was tight as I stared at Stevie. Was this a good idea? Could we do this meeting in front of her? No. That wasn't acceptable. She was a kid.

Jayda didn't look as if she was doubting her ability to handle things. I needed her to be more concerned. She didn't look alarmed.

"Jayda, I need a word with you." There was a hard edge to my tone that she didn't miss.

Quickly, she hurried over to me. "Yes, sir."

I grabbed her arm and pulled her farther away from my daughter's earshot. Staring from Stevie, who was now hugging Branwen, back to Jayda, I had to unclench my teeth.

"That girl is mine," I told her. Jayda's eyes widened, and I continued, "Nothing happens to her. Do not take your eyes off her. Not for a fucking second. Am I clear?"

She nodded. "I swear I won't let anything happen to her."

"I want oat milk in this house. And find some ice cream made with oat milk. When we are done, the kitchen is to be rid of anything with tree nuts and get rid of fucking peanuts too. All nuts out. Clean the kitchen thoroughly so that no traces of any nut are left behind. I'll let Luther know his peanut butter cookies have to stay in his room on his side of the house. No more baking them in the kitchen either."

"Yes, sir, but tree nuts and peanuts aren't the same—"

"I don't give a fuck. Do it. Don't question me."

"Yes, sir."

I looked over to see Stevie watching us with a curious expression as she stood slightly behind her mother's legs. I let out a breath and tried to relax my tense body. She was an observant little thing, and I didn't want her scared of me.

"Let's go," I told Branwen.

The meeting was going to take a turn that my lawyers weren't prepared for. I had planned on coming to an agreement on joint custody with Branwen. Stevie staying with me every other week and taking turns with holidays. That was what my lawyers had suggested, but that was before I'd just been enlightened on how fragile a little girl could be. Levi had been different—or that was how I remembered it. At that age, he'd been with Maggie most of the time. I hadn't been around as much as I should have been. Not until he was old enough to understand the legacy he had been born into.

Changing the plans in the short walk to my office was rash. I was doing it without consulting my lawyers. But I had missed four years of Stevie's life already. I wasn't going to miss any more, and I sure as fuck wasn't about to have her leave her mother. Branwen was required to keep her safe. I didn't want them separated. She needed her mom.

My chest got tight and uncomfortable again as I thought about all the things that Branwen had listed that could happen to her. I rubbed my fist over it, trying to ease some of the tension, as I stalked down the wide hallway.

Fuck. Was this what having a daughter was going to be like? Would I always have this panicky feeling clawing up my back, trying to suffocate me?

Stevie wouldn't be safe from my enemies when they realized I had this weakness. She wasn't going to go to some fucking school. She had to be guarded. Protected.

The only other option was letting them go and not claiming her.

I wasn't going to be able to do that. There was no going back now. Whatever I had to do to keep her safe, I'd do it. Now that I knew she existed, and I'd met her, I wasn't letting her be raised by some other man. She was mine. Her mother was just going to have to get on board. I wanted my daughter, and my daughter needed her mom.

Being the leader of a branch of the Southern Mafia had never made my knees feel weak or my stomach clench, but with a tiny little blonde beauty with a head full of curls in my life now, I was ready to fall the fuck apart.

EIGHT
BRANWEN

I followed Linc inside the room, and the two men who stood both looked to be in their fifties. Unlike Linc, they looked their age. One was even balding. The other had thick silver hair and glasses. If I hadn't known Linc's age, I would have thought he was early to mid-forties.

"Branwen, this is Garth Stanz and Matthew Hoyt," Linc informed me as he walked past the men and straight to a bar, which appeared to be stocked with five different whiskeys.

Like the rest of the office, the bar was a dark wood, almost black. A rack with lowball glasses and a few short, odd-shaped, almost pear-like, glasses hung to the right of it while the left was a built-in humidor case. My eyes drifted over the room, and I stopped at the portrait of a black thoroughbred. I wondered if that horse had been his—or maybe still was. Obviously, it was important.

Behind his desk were tall windows with drapes that hung from the crown molding to the hardwood floor. A cylindrical chandelier, with the same bronze as the rest of the hardware, hung in the center of the room. Bookshelves lined the walls, filled with just books. Nothing more. I had no idea if Linc was a reader or not. There was a lot I didn't know about the man I had thought I loved for most of my life.

When Linc took his glass of whiskey to stand behind his desk, he motioned for me to take a seat as the two men sat back in the caramel-colored leather chairs. I glanced around and decided to sit in one of the same-styled chairs to the left of the black leather chesterfield, whereas they were seated to the right.

The room smelled of Linc. His distinctive scent that had stayed with me long after I left that hotel room in Vegas. Recently, I hadn't been close enough to him again to get a whiff, and I would be lying if I said I wasn't inhaling more than necessary. It was addictive. I could dislike the man and appreciate the way he smelled.

I looked from Linc to his lawyers.

Linc was looking through some papers on his desk then stopped to read one. His jaw was rigid and whatever he was reading didn't help matters.

"As you already know, the marriage certificate is legal." Linc's tone didn't hide his annoyance about that fact.

Well, I didn't want to be married to him either. It was why I had come here in the first place.

"I understand you want a divorce because you're engaged to be married."

His eyes, flickering to the three-carat ring on my hand, held a trace of disgust. I fought the urge to cover it. That was a silly reaction, but old habits died hard, I supposed. My desire to please this man was well past its expiration date.

"However…" he continued.

My already-straight posture grew rigid at that one word. I didn't like it. Dread pooled in my stomach.

"We both have something we want here. You want to marry the dentist, and I want my daughter."

If he were anyone else, I'd have balked at him knowing that Hudson was a dentist, but this was Linc. He had the world at his fingertips. I hadn't prepared myself for it though. I should have. It was an invasion of privacy. He hadn't gone back all the way in my past, or he would realize who I was.

The determined expression on his face was causing my throat to close and my heart to pound so loudly that I was sure they could all hear it. What did he mean about wanting Stevie? I had convinced myself he wouldn't want her. Just like he hadn't wanted her five years ago. I fought to inhale, and my hands trembled in my lap so hard that I had to clasp them together to stop it.

"What do you mean by that exactly?" My words sounded raspy, but without proper oxygen, it was difficult to speak.

He raised an eyebrow at me as he took a drink from his glass. Neither of the men to my right said a word. They'd been mute since I'd walked into the room, as if waiting until they were given permission to speak. He set his glass down slowly, not breaking eye contact with me. The room felt as if it were closing in on me, and I wondered if I was going to black out.

He couldn't take my daughter from me. She was my world. My reason for living.

"It means that I missed four years of her life," he stated. "I won't miss any more. I realize she needs you. You're her mother, and taking her from you would be devastating for her, even if it was every other week. Little girls need their mothers."

I sucked in a deep breath as his words helped ebb the panic that had been overtaking me. Tears stung my eyes. I wanted to weep with relief.

His jaw clenched tightly, and his eyes darkened, as if my reaction angered him. "For me to sign the divorce papers, you will have to agree to move in here with Stevie for one year. I want the chance to build a relationship with her. *I* will be her father. She will know me as her father. Not some," he snarled, "fucking dentist who golfs and plays tennis. She's a Shephard."

I shook my head. This wasn't possible. How could he think that would work?

"Our lives are in Nashville. I have a job and an apartment there. Stevie just got accepted to the best preschool in the city—"

"I was robbed of four years of her life," he interrupted me to repeat himself. "I won't miss another goddamn day. My kid doesn't belong in some fucking apartment, going to a preschool. She belongs here. With me, where I can give her a world that the dentist could never afford her." Linc leaned back in his chair and nodded his head at the men beside me. "Now, you can agree to my generous offer, or I can win joint custody. Then, she will live here with me every other week, and we will alternate holidays. She will not be attending a preschool, and security will have to be placed with her at all times when she is not with me. Those are nonnegotiable, and if you fight me on it, you will lose."

I'd never felt so helpless. He was taking all my plans for her away. Snatching them out from under me. Giving me no choice. Not really. If I stayed here, then Hudson would have to know all my lies. He would most likely call off the wedding. Take back his ring. Move on and find another woman to give that safe, perfect life to. But if I didn't agree to this… then I'd be without Stevie half of the time. That was…that was impossible. I couldn't do it.

"You s-said you d-didn't want a kid. You said—"

"That was before. She exists, and that changes everything," he interrupted me.

The fact that he had told me to take the morning-after pill no longer held any significance since he'd met her. Again, all my fault for bringing her here.

"You realize that this will change her entire life. Hudson won't marry me. She won't get the house with the white picket fence, the dog, the swing set in the backyard. All of that will be taken from her. You can get to know her and still allow us to continue the path we were on. Hudson is a good—"

"*Not* her father. He's weak. He can't protect her. As for the house, she gets a mansion. Forget the fence. We have an iron gate. If she wants a dog, then I will buy her whatever breed she chooses. As for a swing set, there is a resort-worthy pool with a waterfall and slide out back. Hell, I'll have a goddamn playhouse fit for royalty if that makes her happy." He looked as if he was disgusted by the sight of me. "She is mine. *I* will give her the life she deserves."

He wasn't going to budge. Not even a little. I felt the world I'd worked so hard for being snatched away while I sat there, unable to salvage any of it. Doing what he demanded would destroy everything I had in Nashville. Friendships that had been built around my relationship with Hudson. My career. There would be nothing to go back to when the year was over. But he probably already knew that. Just like he never intended to allow me to take her back there. I'd be required to live in this town. He just wasn't saying it.

"I won't have a life to go back to when the year is over."

He took a drink, and his eyes were that of a stormy sea. Both in color and the threatening glint in them. "That's not my problem. This is your decision to make. I suggest you choose wisely."

I gripped my hands together so tightly in my lap that the tips of my nails were going to break the skin. This was a scenario I hadn't thought up. One I hadn't worked through. I'd come in here, thinking he would request to see her on occasion. Possibly once a month. Even that much time away from her seemed horrible.

"I don't have a choice," I said, my voice barely above a whisper. "But you know that. You made sure of it."

Placing his elbows on the desk, he leaned forward, his eyes narrowing as he stared at me. "Tell me, Branwen, why is it you aren't threatening to fight me in court?"

I blinked, confused at first. Was this a test and I'd failed? Did he think I had set this up and wanted the outcome he had given me? That I wanted to live in this house with him? I'd not once given him a reason to think that. I'd give anything to be allowed to leave here with my daughter and return to our lives in Nashville. It was safe. His life, albeit one with extravagant wealth, was not. I shook my head, not sure if I was understanding him correctly.

"You heard the question. You are accepting my threats without a real fight. I want to know why."

I blinked and watched as he tilted his head to the side, studying me closely. There was a challenge there.

He was powerful and had too many people in his pocket at his disposal—that was it. I shouldn't know that. He'd never told me what he did. Where his wealth had come from. If I hadn't known, if I were any other female, one he'd only met that one night in Vegas, I would believe I could fight him in court and win. Money didn't buy a judge's decision. Power did.

I could lie, but why? He'd done a background check, yet he still wasn't aware that our families were connected. That I was from his past. I had never been a stranger to him.

Lifting my chin, I met his glare. "I know who and what you are, Linc. I'm not stupid enough to fight a battle we both know I can't win."

His eyes widened slightly. He'd thought I'd set this entire thing into play to get the outcome he was handing me. Did he think I'd truly gone to all that trouble when I had a ring on my finger from another man? Was the fact that a woman would choose a man like Hudson over him that hard for him to believe? What a fucking ego.

No, Linc Shephard, I'm not trying to weasel my way into your life. All I wanted was to get you out of mine, and I've failed miserably.

"Who and what am I?" he drawled.

It wasn't a secret that there was a Mafia that ruled the South. One where wealthy men controlled the hands and actions of those supposedly in charge. They were whispered about and feared. While the majority did not know who they were exactly, they had their guesses. Towns were owned by them. Senators, governors, mayors, judges were put into office by them.

Part of me wanted to blurt out who I was. See the realization hit him. Watch as he recalled the little girl who had worshipped him. The one he'd brought daisies to and placed in her hair, who he'd taught to play Texas Hold'em, the one he'd called Ringlets. But I wouldn't. That was the past, and we weren't those people anymore.

I licked my dry lips before replying, "You're a member of the Southern Mafia." Also known as *the family* among their ranks, but I didn't say that. He'd have more questions if I said too much.

He leaned back in his chair, the expression on his face unreadable. "And you know this how?"

I would have to lie or tell the truth.

I chose to lie.

"You told me."

His eyes darkened, and he blew out a breath. "Fucking opium," he sighed, then shook his head, as if disgusted with himself. He reached for his whiskey. "I guess that saves me the trouble of telling you why our daughter will always require protection. With that knowledge, will you be living here with Stevie or choosing to fight me in court?"

As if that were ever an option.

NINE
LINC

What all had I told her that night? Jesus, I'd been more fucked up than I'd realized. Granted, opium mixed with alcohol wasn't the best combination. There were definitely moments and time that were blacked out for me that night. I remembered seeing her. I'd watched her for over an hour before approaching her. I recalled how I'd been pleasantly surprised that not only was she fucking gorgeous, but she was also funny. She had personality. I'd enjoyed just listening to her talk.

I didn't have a memory of leaving the club or where we had gone to next. There were images of the chapel and Elvis, but that was mostly a blank spot in my memory. I could see us outside and her walking barefoot along the edge of a fountain while I held her hand and her high heels. Her laughter and the way the lights of the city seemed to illuminate just her. That had been the opium, but still, I'd thought she was a goddess.

The parts I could recall in the best detail was fucking her. We'd ripped off each other's clothes the instant the door to my suite closed. I picked her up and impaled her with my cock for the first time up against the wall, unable to go any further. Although I could still see her face when she had gotten off and hear her sexy moans, I could not remember taking out a condom at any time. That could have been the moment I'd knocked her up. I wasn't sure because there was also a memory of taking her in the shower, on the bed, bent over the counter in the kitchen, and on the balcony as she gripped the railing and I took her from behind. I'd had only two condoms.

At some point, I'd apparently told her about the family that night. I was pissed at myself for getting that messed up, but also glad she'd been aware and it wasn't one more thing I'd had to explain today. She hadn't seemed to have any questions about it though, which surprised me. It wasn't like she could google it and find the answers. There was an odd sense of surrender to her expression, in the way she spoke to me, that was causing an odd reaction from me. It wasn't the way women normally responded with the want and need controlling their every move. She didn't want me. She'd made that clear with more than just words.

I turned from the window as one of the men still in my office cleared his throat.

Stanz held out the new paperwork to me. "She needs to sign these. It's the NDA and prenup. Although you're already legally married, we need these signed so that when the year is over, she isn't going to fight you for half of your assets or demand alimony. There's also the custody agreement for the child. We added another clause that covers the things you went over with her about security detail for her and the child, as well as the bank account you will set up in her name and keep funded for her needs while she is living here without a job."

I took the paperwork and placed it on my desk. I had let Branwen go to be with Stevie already. The longer she was away from her, the more stressed I got about her safety. I trusted Jayda, but the food allergies and choking shit had me on edge. I hadn't asked if Stevie could swim. We needed to get special locks on the doors and an alarm at the pool in case she ever got away and went out there alone. My mind started reeling at all the things I needed done to make the house safe.

"Are you sure you don't want to end the marriage now? Waiting a year will cause more issues. It would be best if you didn't live together while married. That will make the marriage seem real. Legally, that can get dicey if she chooses to fight you for anything when this is over."

Stanz was only repeating himself. I'd heard this when he said it the first time.

"If you do your job correctly, it won't. She will sign whatever I give her. Make sure it is clearly stated that the marriage is for convenience only and will terminate one year from tomorrow," I told him, not liking the way he felt he needed to question me.

"Yes, sir. The changes have all been made, and we will redo the filing when we are back at our office," Hoyt replied, not allowing his partner to say more.

"I'm not questioning your decision, Mr. Shephard," Stanz said, his voice cracking, betraying his anxiety. His fear was palpable.

"If we are done here, then I have things that need handled," I told them.

Both men nodded, taking their bags and heading for the door without another word. I waited until they were gone to pick up my phone and decide on who to call first. The security concerning the pool, making sure Stevie couldn't get near it while alone outside, seemed the most pressing. But first, I needed to send Jayda to buy things that they needed now. I didn't want them leaving this house again without me setting up their security detail and assigning a driver for Branwen to use when they needed to go somewhere.

Then, there was Luther. I should probably let him know my kid was moving in, along with her mother, who was off-limits to him. I needed to make that clear first, then reiterate it daily—because the man often let his dick rule his actions. More so than most.

TEN
BRANWEN

How to explain all this to a four-year-old was as complicated as how I was going to tell Hudson. I wasn't sure who to start with.

When I had gone back to find Stevie, she'd been in the kitchen with Jayda, elbow deep in cake batter. Her big eyes had twinkled with excitement as she explained that they were making a strawberry cake with real strawberries.

When Jayda had first walked into the great room earlier, I'd misjudged her. The fact that she was beautiful and young had made me assume the worst. Not that I was jealous of her, but because I wasn't sure I wanted to leave my daughter with her father's entirely too young plaything or girlfriend. His saying she worked for him had made me want to laugh. I still believed she did more than clean and cook for Linc and Luther. But that wasn't my business. As long as they kept that away from Stevie, then whatever.

The woman had won over Stevie, and if we were being forced to live here for a year, I needed to learn to overlook a lot. They would have to clean up their lifestyle in Stevie's presence. Whatever orgy or sex parties they used to have here ended today. They now had a four-year-old under their roof. This was something I should have brought up to Linc in his office, but his demand that we live here had thrown me for a loop. I couldn't think clearly. Being away from his dark gaze made it easier to consider all that this really meant for us.

I still had no idea what Linc was going to demand we do about the apartment and our things. I needed to tell this all to Hudson face-to-face. I wanted to pack up our things and speak to the apartment leasing agency about getting out of the lease early or subletting. A steady throb behind my temples set in as the many different things that had to be handled rattled off in my brain.

Jesus, how had this all snowballed so quickly? I had gone over so many scenarios before coming here to get him to sign the papers, and this was not even close to any of the outcomes I had planned for. The man who had demanded I take the pill and told me he didn't want a kid, then left without any way for me to contact him shouldn't have wanted us to move in so he could make up for lost time. He wasn't supposed to want her in his life. Yet I would be lying if there wasn't a part of me that warmed toward him for it. Stevie was my greatest joy, and having the man who'd helped in giving her life see what a gift she was and want her did lessen the ache in my chest I hadn't even realized was there. I'd carried it for so long that it had become a part of who I was.

Jayda opened the door to the oven while Stevie stood on a stool, leaning over the sink and washing her hands. I would have to think about all this later. My curious little munchkin was no longer distracted, and I was going to have to explain this to her somehow. She hopped down and hurried over to me, smiling. Today had been another adventure for her. She was happy. I just hoped that she handled it well when I told her that this adventure was going to be rather prolonged.

"Jayda is going to show me the pool!" she exclaimed.

"That is, if it's okay with your mom," Jayda said. "She might have other plans."

I shrugged. "No other plans. Let's go see that pool."

With Stevie's hand in mine, we followed Jayda out of the kitchen. I knew she probably had a list of things to do and entertaining us had to be annoying. But I didn't know my way around or where Linc expected us to go next. Keeping the smile on Stevie's face was important today. I wanted her to like it here since she had no other choice.

We were almost to two large glass doors leading out onto a patio when Linc appeared.

"Thank you, Jayda."

She nodded, then quickly exited the room without a word.

My hand tightened on Stevie's as he approached us. I didn't want him bringing up anything to her yet. I needed to explain it to her and let her ask me questions first. Dropping it on her would upset her and confuse her. I was sure Linc had very little knowledge of four-year-olds. He hadn't had one in a very long time.

"Can she swim?" he asked me.

"Yes. She's taken swimming lessons the past two summers," I replied.

The flash of relief in his eyes was followed by his shoulders relaxing. "Good. I have a security system being put in that will ring if any door that leads to the pool is open. There will also be an alarm that goes off if there is movement by the pool and no one is out there supervising. Just for precaution. I wasn't sure about her swimming abilities, but even so, she never needs to go out there alone."

I agreed that it wasn't safe, and I'd never allow that, but the fact that he was doing all that to ensure her safety was impressive. "Thank you."

He cut his eyes from me to the doors. "Her safety is my priority. Would you both like to go have a look outside? Perhaps tell me what kind of swing set you want." He dropped his gaze down to Stevie, who was watching him with keen interest.

She glanced at me with a look of apprehension, then scrunched her nose as she turned back to him. "Mommy took me to pick one out, but the one I weally love is too big for Hudson's yawd," she told him matter-of-factly. "But she said she would find me one that fits."

The swing set she'd wanted was one meant for a playground and multiple children. Hudson had a small vegetable garden in his backyard, along with his storage shed that took up a good amount of space. There was a small area where he'd said we could put a swing set for her. She hadn't been happy about not getting the one she wanted and pitched a tantrum when I told her that we were shopping for a swing set only. Maybe with one slide attached, but that was it. Not an entire playset with all the extras.

"What kind did you want?" he asked, his attention solely on her.

"It had a cuwy slide and a stwaight one, a clubhouse, a lemonade stand, a wope ladduh, and thwee swings!" she exclaimed, using her hands to describe it.

He nodded and reached to open the door. "Sounds like a winner."

"It is! But Mommy is getting me one that I will like too," she added the last part and smiled at me, as if she needed to reassure me that she would be happy with the swing set I chose for her.

I had warned her she wouldn't get one at all if she acted ugly about it. That had changed her tune quickly.

Linc opened the door leading outside.

"Oh wow!" she squealed.

She let go of my hand to run out onto the stone patio with a fireplace, flat screen television, a swinging bed that hung from the ceiling, and a kitchen area with a grill and a well-stocked bar. I had to agree with Stevie. Wow.

"Who lives out hewah? I want to live outside too!"

I smiled, watching her. She couldn't seem to take it all in fast enough. Rushing from one thing to the other.

"No one lives out here. This is just a place to relax," Linc informed her.

She pointed at the television. "You can watch *Bluey* outside," she told him as if he were the luckiest human on earth.

He had no idea who *Bluey* was, but he would soon enough.

He glanced at me, taking out his phone and tapping the screen. "What station would, uh, I find *Bluey*?" He said the last word as if he wasn't sure he had it right.

"Any chance you have Disney Plus?" I asked.

His brows drew together. "I've seen that on the app options, but never clicked it."

The screen lit up as the television came on, and he began to use his phone as a remote. When he found the Disney Plus app, he clicked it.

I held out my hand to him. "I'll log in to my account," I told him.

He handed it to me, and I quickly logged in. When *Bluey*, season two, started playing, I gave him back his phone. The opening song began, and she scrambled to the sofa and climbed up onto it with her eyes fixed on the screen. I was surprised she hadn't gone to the swinging bed, but it was only a matter of time. Right now, *Bluey* had her complete attention.

"She really likes this, huh?" he said, watching her.

"Oh, yeah," I agreed. "She's her favorite."

He tore his gaze off her as if it was hard to do, then turned to me. "Let's walk over here, where we can still see her and discuss things."

I had a list of things to ask him since I'd had time to think and let it sink in that he was making us live here. Hopefully, he was about to give me some answers. Following him out onto the uncovered portion of the patio, I began to list my questions in order in my head. I didn't want to forget anything.

"I will have two of my men take you back to your apartment to get your things. For now, you can keep it, and there is no need to bring everything back here. Both your bedrooms are already furnished, and you can go shopping to decorate them however you would like. If Stevie would like different furniture, then I will send in an interior decorator to work with you both to turn it into whatever makes her happy."

I took his brief pause as my chance to speak. "I can't pay for rent without an income," I pointed out before he could dictate more of my life.

"I'll cover your rent for the next year. You can decide what you intend to do when the year is over. I will still want to see Stevie regularly, so living in Nashville will be an issue. I'm sure you've thought of that."

I took a deep breath, trying not to get overwhelmed with having everything taken out of my hands. "What about speaking to Hudson? I can't tell him all this on the phone." The bitterness in my voice was thick in every word. "Not that he will understand or forgive me, but he still deserves an explanation."

Linc's gaze gave me a once-over before the hint of a smirk turned his lips, but his eyes remained cold. "You don't seem very torn up over that," he drawled.

Was he serious? Of course I was upset. But he hadn't given me any other choice.

"I am keeping it together for her," I hissed at him, my eyes cutting back to Stevie. "If she sees how upset I am, it will affect her."

His expression didn't change. "Come now, Branwen. You can't be that heartbroken over it. The dentist looks exactly like all those other preppy losers you cast off while sitting at that bar in Vegas before I rescued you."

I hated how he'd called him *the dentist*, as if that were an insult. "Hudson is a successful dentist. He is one of the top in the city. He is kind and thoughtful. I'm lucky that he even gave me a second glance. Every female patient that comes in flirts with him. His last girlfriend was a pediatrician," I finished, snapping my mouth shut.

He hadn't needed to know all that. My need to defend Hudson to him was pointless. What good did it do? He could think whatever he wanted.

Linc rubbed his bearded chin and let out an unamused chuckle. "You were lucky he gave you a second glance? He's a man. We are visual. We don't give a fuck about a medical degree. We think with our dicks, and degrees don't get them hard. Tits, asses, curves, legs, and plump lips with stunning eyes do. I think about fucking eighty percent of my day. When men put a ring on female it because it's one they want to sink their cock into over and over. I made that mistake once, so I know better. But since his pasty, boring ass hasn't married yet, he doesn't know better, and he got a look at you and wanted to claim you. Don't kid yourself. He probably walks around with a boner all fucking day when you're working."

I opened my mouth, then closed it. I wasn't sure what to say. I thought, in a roundabout way, that was a compliment. Maybe.

"Tell me, does he take you to the bathroom and bend you over the sink during working hours or find a closet to spread your legs and eat your pussy?"

My eyes shot to Stevie again, who was happily watching the screen. I felt flushed all over. Hearing Linc talk about me being bent over a sink and fucked the way he'd done to me in Vegas, or my pussy in general, set a tingle off between my legs that did not need to be there. I was going to have to live under the same roof as this man. Getting messed up in the head over him was not going to happen. I refused to give in to my attraction to him or think of him as anything more than the dictator he was.

"He doesn't, does he?" Linc asked. "Because he is boring. Polite. Thoughtful. *Kind.*" He clipped out the words as if they were insults rather than the way I had meant them. "Not one of those traits equals a man who knows how to fuck."

I licked my lips and took a steadying breath, not wanting him to see that he affected me at all.

"My sex life isn't something I will discuss with you," I told him, sounding too breathless. Dammit. I cleared my throat and tried to scowl. "This is inappropriate and off topic."

Linc's eyes trailed down to my chest. "I've fucked your pussy raw. I know exactly how your cunt tastes, and you've pulled my hair while calling me God. I'd say we are past the uptight bullshit. I'm not your dentist."

Now, the tingle was an ache. Dammit! I hadn't had sex in over a month. Hudson had been so tired in the evenings that he often fell asleep on the sofa before Stevie went to bed. Then, he'd wake up to leave. That was all this was. I was clearly in need of an orgasm.

"You're blushing. That's cute, seeing as I've had your legs wrapped around my head while you came all over my face."

Jesus! Would he shut up about it already?

"Linc, stop," I said, holding up a hand, and a deep, sinister laugh sent a shiver over me. "We have a child together. She is my only concern here. You have given me no choice but to uproot our lives and come here to live with you. I don't need a recap of five years ago. I need to know when we are going to get our things and when I can talk to Hudson. I also need to explain all this to Stevie, and she's going to have many things to ask you. She's inquisitive, and seeing as how I have lied to her about her real father, this is going to be an even bigger shock."

That got his attention.

His eyes narrowed. "What did you tell her about me?" The husky tone was gone.

At least I'd stopped his trip down memory lane.

Time to face up to this lie for the first of three times I would have to do it.

Sucking in a deep breath, I steeled myself before replying, "I told her you were dead."

He said nothing as he stared at me.

Wanting to defend my lie, I continued, "You walked out of the hotel room with no way for me to contact you. I was left with a pregnancy that cost me my job—although do not get me wrong; I wouldn't change it. I was given Stevie, and that was worth all of it. I struggled to eat and keep a roof over our heads, and at times, I hated you for it. Because she deserved more. Eventually, I was able to give that to her. But it was you I blamed for the times she went without. To me...you *were* dead."

I watched as his eyes showed the range of emotions that his expression did not. It remained the same. He studied me, then shifted his focus to Stevie. "And I paid for it. By missing four years of her life."

Fine, whatever. He had missed a lot, but I'd done what was best for her. Not that any of it mattered now. He was getting his revenge. He'd snatched everything I had wanted and worked for away from me with the snap of his fingers.

"That lie gets cleared up today. She needs to know I'm her father. That everything I'm going to hand to her is from the man who will take care of her. Protect her. I don't want to hear her refer to the dentist as her new dad ever again." Controlled rage flared in his eyes as they swung back to me. "Change in plans. Tomorrow, I'll go with you to get your things. Once you know what you'd like to bring back here, we can leave my men to pack it up, and I'll take you to speak with the dentist. Stevie can stay in the car with me. There's a television in there, and I'll be sure, uh, *Bluey* is available for her to watch."

He was going to sit in the car while I went in and talked to Hudson? That would make it worse. There was a sliver of hope that Hudson might possibly forgive me. How could he even consider it with Linc waiting outside for me? It would just be rubbing salt into the wound.

Hudson told me he loved me regularly, but I'd never said the actual words back to him. He never mentioned it, but I knew he'd noticed. Every time he said them, I saw the pleading in his eyes. The hope that I'd say them back. Doing it now would not only be yet another lie, but it would appear calculating. I did love him, but I wasn't in love with him. I was going to make it up to him by being an excellent wife. And when he was ready, maybe have a child with him. It was all slipping away. Melting in my grasp like a piece of ice until it was all gone. Splattered on the floor, unable to return to what it once had been.

"I don't suppose I can talk you into staying here. Stevie could stay with you," I finally said after a brief second of panicked silence.

He shook his head. "No. She needs to stay with you until I am secure with how to handle any allergic reactions or choking. We'll go together."

This time, his words hadn't been spoken as a demand. They weren't harsh. Instead, there had been a flickering of unease. Was he scared to keep her? I watched him carefully. Taking in the moment of weakness I'd never thought I would see on this man. All over Stevie. He didn't want anything to happen to her. Already, he cared about her safety. An odd feeling settled in my chest. One I couldn't yet define.

ELEVEN
BRANWEN

Linc had gotten a phone call and excused himself to go take it after telling me to make myself at home. I wanted to laugh at that, but he was stalking toward the glass doors before I could respond at all. I'd gone to sit on the sofa and pulled Stevie into my lap, where we watched two more episodes of *Bluey*. Burying my nose in her hair, I forced myself to relax. Her hair smelled like wildflowers from the shampoo we'd used at the motel last night. Focusing on her and only her, I was able to bring my anxiety down enough that the pounding behind my temples slackened.

We remained like that for well over an hour, and then Stevie wanted to go find the pool. She was over the moon and begged to go swimming. I promised her she would get a chance to. She didn't know yet that the pool would soon be a part of her daily life. I had almost told her several times but stopped myself. I wanted to wait until Linc was here. She'd want to ask him things, and I felt like his presence would make it more real for her.

Jayda came to collect us and show us the bedrooms that would be ours. The rooms were across the hallway from each other and identical in size and layout. Both had en suites and walk-in closets that were as big as the bedrooms in our apartment. The only difference was that mine had a balcony overlooking the backyard. Stevie's room had a window nook with fluffy pillows and a small ledge, where several books were currently tucked.

There was a selection of swimsuits for Stevie to choose from hanging inside her closet, along with clothing, underclothes, and pajamas. I'd not expected that, and Jayda informed me that if anything wasn't to my or Stevie's liking, I should let her know, and she'd take it back. Apparently, she'd been sent out on a shopping spree.

Not just for Stevie either. I had several bikinis, cover-ups, a couple of sundresses, some shorts and tops, and a drawer full of panties, bras, and nightgowns. The sizes were accurate, and the lingerie looked more expensive than anything I'd ever owned. Most of my underthings had come from Target. When I did splurge, it was at Victoria's Secret. The ones that had been bought for me here were from neither. The delicate lace and silk ranged from white to a dark rose.

The bathrooms were also stocked with every toiletry we could possibly need. High-end lotions sat on the counter, along with face creams and salon-quality hair products—from shampoo to heat-protecting oil. I didn't own half of this stuff and wasn't sure what to do with some of it. How she had managed to buy all this in such a short amount of time I didn't know, but I was impressed.

The large, oval tub that looked big enough for three people had bath salts, body wash, soaps, bubble bath, and something called bath potpourri in a basket on one side and a cluster of white pillar candles on the other. The thought of soaking in there, under the warm, scented water with the candlelight, sounded heavenly. It still didn't make me want to live here for a year, but it wasn't a bad perk to the situation. My tubs had always been small shower combos.

Stevie was high on life. The entire day had seemed to bring her one new exciting thing after another. After spinning in circles and running around to explore her room, which she had labeled the princess room, she was determined to go swimming. Knowing that, this evening, she was going to be told about the change in our lives, I gave in.

She chose a shiny pink two-piece with a tutu attached. She was well aware of how adorable she looked and admired herself in the mirror while I coated her with the sunblock that had been among all the other items in our bathroom.

I'd had a harder time choosing a swimsuit from the three that Jayda had chosen for me. When I had gone with the sky-blue one simply because it covered my bottom more than the other two, I'd been thankful for the cover-up even if it was slightly see-through. I wouldn't have chosen any of the bikinis for myself or even tried them on. They were too revealing. Jayda had much different taste in swimwear. I was flattered she thought I could pull these off.

When I stepped into the hallway, Stevie came twirling out of her room to meet me with a huge grin on her face. "I feel like a weal-life pwincess, Mommy," she said in a singsong voice, then slipped her hand into mine.

This was fun and new, but I feared that when she found out it was about to be a more permanent thing rather than a short visit, it might not be so exciting. She had been planning for her new room in Hudson's house and the school she was going to attend, and then there was the wedding. Being a flower girl was a big deal to her. All of that was going to be taken from her. I was still struggling to process it all. How would a four-year-old?

"You definitely look like one," I agreed.

She bounced, barely able to control her anticipation.

Following the same route that Jayda had used to bring us to our rooms, we went back down a long hallway, turned right, then went to the winding staircase that led down to the foyer. It was a straight shot back through the house, passing the great room, a library, a toilet room, another hallway that led to the kitchen, and then a large sunroom before coming to the doors leading out onto the patio. Disney Plus still lit up the screen, and Jayda turned around from placing items in what I hadn't realized was a refrigerator by the bar. It blended in with the cabinets. Her eyes scanned us with a pleased smile.

"Everything fits okay then?" she said, closing the door.

"Yes, thank you," I told her.

She waved a hand. "I enjoyed it. If only I got paid to spend someone else's money every day," she said. "This refrigerator has bottles of water and oat milk in cute little boxes that have straws, and in the freezer up here are Popsicles." She glanced from Stevie to me. "They're all-natural fruit with no artificial colors, flavors, or added sugar."

I appreciated that she'd thought of that.

"Thank you," I said as Stevie tugged on my arm.

"Let's go swim!"

"I'll walk over with y'all and show you where the towels are," Jayda offered.

We followed her down the smooth black stone tiled path to the pool that really should be at some fancy resort. Stevie released my hand and took off at a run for the slide. I waited until she got to the top and came down with her little fists in the air, beaming, before I turned to look over at Jayda, who was watching her too. When Stevie emerged from the water, Jayda shifted her gaze to me with amusement tugging at her lips.

"This is where you will find towels. The doors are kept closed because this is a warmer and keeps them toasty for you."

A warmer for pool towels. I almost rolled my eyes but refrained.

"That's fancy," I said instead.

Jayda pressed her lips together, grinning. "Yep," she replied with a pop at the end, sounding as if she thought it was ridiculous too.

"Mommy, watch!" Stevie called out.

I turned back to her. She was clambering out of the pool. The slide wasn't going to get old anytime soon.

Jayda excused herself after telling Stevie to have fun.

Slipping off the cover-up, I left it on one of the teak bed-sized loungers, which were covered, like a cabana. Sheer white curtains hung from all four corners of the slated ceiling that I assumed could be drawn together to close yourself inside. There were three of the loungers on both sides of the freeform-style pool. One end had two different rock waterfalls that cascaded down in gentle waves. The slide curving around the right of them. The other end had a gradual slope to enter the pool with two umbrellas coming out of the shallow water and lounge chairs underneath for those who wanted to sit and enjoy the cool water, but not submerge themselves in it. I decided that was more my speed and went to sit under the shade while watching Stevie exhaust herself.

Another cheer went up just before she hit the water with a splash. Smiling, I sat down and spread my legs out in front of me. I tried to take her to the neighborhood pool where Hudson lived every weekend, but it didn't compare to this.

She didn't seem to miss having the other kids to play with, and I sure didn't miss the noise.

With all this...fantasy-style living, I was beginning to think that Stevie might not mind this so much. But Hudson...my stomach sank as I thought about him. He was going to be hurt. He had become my friend. We talked every day. Worked together. Spent our free time together. I was going to miss that. I was going to miss having a life. One where I went to work, had friends, lived.

What would I do here other than sit by a pool? I had no friends. I had nowhere to be. It was going to get lonely. I didn't see me and Linc becoming friends or spending time together. Even with Stevie's laughter ringing out and her sheer joy, my heart sank. No amount of nice things, fancy tubs, or elaborate pools could replace having someone. The feeling of belonging. Being wanted.

Two hours in the pool had worn her out. We showered, and then I dried her hair and put her in one of her more comfortable outfits that Jayda had bought her before lying down with her on her new canopy bed for a short nap. She needed to be rested before I told her about Linc. When she was tired, things were more dramatic. She fell asleep quickly, but I lay there and stared out the window while running my fingers through her soft locks.

It felt as if I had accidentally jumped on an out-of-control, speeding train and couldn't get off. My decisions and choices had been snatched away. I wanted what was best for Stevie, and although Linc seemed very taken with her, I couldn't see him being what was best for her.

Getting up, I tucked the covers around her before leaving her room to go over to the one given to me. I needed to call

Hudson. I'd barely responded to his text, and before facing him tomorrow, I wanted to talk to him. Ease his mounting concern. Tomorrow would be bad. At least for tonight, I could let him rest easy.

Taking my phone, I stepped onto the balcony and pressed his number. I knew he'd had left the office by now and should be home. Unless his mother had called for him to come eat with her this evening. That happened a couple of times a week. She wasn't very fond of me or Stevie, no matter how much Hudson claimed otherwise. I was a single mom, saddling her son with a kid that wasn't his. She made comments that, somehow, Hudson misinterpreted differently. His mother could do no wrong in his eyes. It was something I had come to accept and live with.

"Hey," Hudson said, sounding relieved. "I was just about to call you again. What happened with the car? I could come get you."

I'd told him that the car's engine light came on and I had to leave it at a repair shop overnight while they ordered a part. That was the last form of communication we had before I finally fell asleep last night. Now, I had to admit to that being a lie as well, but I would do so to his face. Even if that made it all the more difficult.

"I'm sorry. Things have been, uh, busier than expected. We will be home tomorrow." *To tell you that I am a liar and am moving in with Stevie's very alive father for a year.* Guilt weighed heavy in my chest.

"Good. I miss you," he said, sounding as if he truly meant it.

"I miss you too," I replied.

"I should have gone with you. I've felt bad about it since you left."

That, too, was my fault. I'd told him I was going to the one thing I knew he wouldn't want to attend. My secret had been carefully covered up.

"You can't close down the office for something like this," I replied.

"Branwen, I would do anything for you. If you'd have asked me to, I would have gone. Even though I hate funerals, I would have been there for you."

I closed my eyes, wanting to weep at the sincerity in his tone. A man like this didn't come along every day. I'd found one who not only loved me, but also loved my kid. The idea of losing him and what we had was painful. I doubted anyone would ever love me like this. Give me the safety and security that he provided.

"I know." My voice was barely above a whisper. "It's why I didn't ask you." Every word out of my mouth tasted sour because, tomorrow, this moment would never come again. I would have to look him in the eyes and tell him everything.

I heard his mother's voice in the background, asking him if he wanted tomato gravy on his biscuits. She'd be happy when she found out. I wasn't good enough for her son, and she'd known it all along.

"Yes, ma'am," he called back. "Dinner is ready. Mom is fixing my plate. I'll see you tomorrow."

"Yeah. See you then."

"I love you." The three words he used so easily that I struggled to say.

"You too," was the best I could do.

"Bye."

"Bye."

The call ended, and I stood there, holding the phone to my ear, wishing there were another way. That I didn't have to tell him about Linc or leave him. But wasn't this the way that it always was? Those who loved me were taken away from me.

TWELVE
LINC

Stevie's face when she saw the macaroni and cheese placed in front of her for dinner secured Jayda's future employment for as long as she wanted the job. Jayda winked at Branwen and gave her a small nod. She must have asked what Stevie's favorite meal was. I didn't much care for mac and cheese, but after the way my daughter reacted, I'd fucking learn to love it.

"Do you go to school yet, Stevie?" I asked her as I watched her take a drink of her oat milk. I knew this answer, but I wanted to hear her talk. Reading about her and Branwen from a report wasn't the same as hearing Stevie's version of her life.

Her eyes widened. "I'm going to go to school in… Septembah, wight, Mommy?" she asked, looking uncertain, as if she wasn't positive she had told me the correct information.

Branwen started to nod and stopped. Her brows drawing together, as if she wasn't sure how to respond. "Uh, yes—well, you were going to go in September, but things, um, well, they might change."

There was no *might*. They would change.

Stevie frowned, not liking that response. "You said I was going to Bwight Minds."

Branwen's eyes flickered over to me as she set her glass of cabernet back on the table after taking a drink. "I know, but there are some changes that you and I will be making. I was going to tell you about them tonight."

Stevie stared at her, as if she was waiting for her mother to continue. Branwen picked up her glass again and took a much larger gulp. Her chest rose and fell as she took a deep breath. My eyes immediately went to her tits. The image of her large, round pink nipples flashed in my head, and I jerked my eyes off them and took my whiskey and drank what was left in my glass. That had to stop. I couldn't keep thinking about the night I'd fucked her.

"Come here," Branwen told her as she pushed her chair back and held out a hand.

Stevie scrambled down from her chair and hurried over to climb into her mother's lap. I studied them. My DNA had done little to create her. All I could see of me was the eyes. Otherwise, she was her mother. Branwen's hair wasn't as curly, but it was longer and thicker. The weight causing the curls to loosen as they hung down her back and over her shoulders. Women spent hours trying to achieve that look, yet she woke up with it.

Branwen cupped her daughter's—*our* daughter's—small face and pressed a kiss to the tip of her nose. "You like it here, right? The pool and the slide. Your new room," she said.

Stevie nodded her head, not taking her eyes off her mother's face.

"Well, you see…" She paused and glanced at me before continuing.

I saw the concern in her eyes, but there was nothing I could do to make this easier. I wanted my daughter to know who I was. Branwen had lied to her, and perhaps the circumstances had kept her from letting me know about her pregnancy and our child, but she had found me and still not planned on telling me. That was what I couldn't get over. It fucking infuriated me.

"Remember that day when you asked me why some kids had a mommy and a dad, but you just had a mommy, and I told you that your dad wasn't alive anymore?" Branwen said slowly. Her tone was gentle, almost as if she was asking for forgiveness for what was to come.

She nodded her head. "Yes, but Hudson is gonna be my dad now."

The way those words twisted me up was more than uncomfortable. I wanted to take my plate and throw it against the motherfucking wall. Branwen had almost allowed it too. After finding out my name and hunting me down, she had intended on robbing me of knowing my child. Letting another man raise Stevie as his own.

Branwen tucked a lock of blonde curls behind her ear. "You see, honey, that can't happen anymore. Because your dad is alive and"—she glanced at me, then back at Stevie—"he wants to spend time with you. He didn't know about you until very recently, and he is anxious to get to know you. To be…your dad."

I didn't like the hesitation in her voice, as if this was something bad.

"My weal dad?" she asked, her eyes as round as saucers. "I have a weal dad? But why didn't he live with us in owah apawtment? Wheah is he?" Her little voice was a mix of curiosity and confusion.

Branwen cleared her throat and took another deep breath. "He didn't live with us because he didn't know he had a little girl."

"Why didn't you tell him?"

I was holding my breath and hadn't realized it. Fuck, I was nervous. Why was I so nervous? Because there was a chance my daughter might not want me to be her dad. That she might want the pasty-ass dentist instead.

I'd kill him.

"I didn't know where to find him. But I finally found him, and now he knows about you, he wants to be a part of your life."

Her shoulders straightened. "Is he gonna move into Hudson's house with us?" she asked, sounding hopeful at the thought.

Branwen shook her head. "No, no, sweetie. It doesn't work that way. I mean, no. He has his own house. One you like very much. He wants us to live there for a while so he can get to be around you. So you can do things together."

"Wheah is his house?" she asked, those big eyes searching her mother's face.

"Well"—Branwen looked around and held out her hands—"this is his house. Mr. Shephard—uh, Linc is your dad."

Stevie's head swung around, and her gaze locked on mine. I couldn't imagine what all was going through that little head of hers, but I could see so many different things swirling in her eyes.

"Yowah my weal dad?" she asked.

Emotion I hadn't expected clogged my throat, so I simply nodded.

"I'm gonna live in this house?"

All I could do was nod. I swallowed, trying to clear the shit that had come over me. Damn, I hadn't been ready for that. I'd thought I was, but I wasn't.

She looked back at her mother, and I took the moment to compose myself.

"I get to swim in his pool again?" she asked.

Branwen smiled at her. "Every day," she replied.

"That's bettah than going to pweschool!" she said, then turned back to me. "I got this many new swimsuits upstay-was," she told me, holding up six fingers.

"We can buy you as many as you want," I told her, thankful my voice didn't fucking crack. "Your mom tells me you want a puppy. I'll buy you whatever puppy you want. We can even go together to look at them when you decide what breed."

Her little palms slapped down on the table. "Weally?!" she exclaimed.

"And that swing set you want? I'll have one even bigger and better put in the backyard."

Stevie wiggled out of her mother's lap and ran down the length of the table toward me. I didn't know what to do or expect. When she reached me, she climbed up into my lap with my help, then threw her arms around my neck.

"I'm weally glad yowah my weal dad. Yowah not an outlaw," she said, then loosened her hold to look back at her mother.

Branwen was watching us, her eyes shimmering with tears. I wasn't sure what kind of tears they were, and I didn't think I wanted to know. She wasn't going to ruin this for me.

"He's not an outlaw, is he, Mommy? You was wong."

Her lips hesitantly turned up at the sides. "I was wrong," she responded simply.

For a moment, I studied her. Once, there had been another little girl who called me that name. I told her I was one, and because I had nicknamed her, she had done the same to me. I dropped my gaze back to the little girl in my lap. Her curls were well kept and not a messy riot, like the one from all those years ago, but they reminded me of hers.

I hadn't thought of her in years. Thinking about her now brought a smile to my face. Back then, I'd always thought I might have been a better girl dad. She loved me more than my own kid. Levi never lit up like she did at the sight of me. When I'd felt like a failure or shit with Maggie had me in a funk, she'd come running for me out of the stables, smiling at me like I'd hung the fucking moon. Those pale blonde ringlets flying around her. That kid had saved me from losing my soul more times than I could count.

Blinking, I came out of my memories and focused on my daughter. Maybe I wouldn't be bad at this. I'd been loved before by a little girl, and I hadn't had to do more than bring her a daisy to put in her hair when I saw her. I could hand Stevie the world.

THIRTEEN
BRANWEN

The turmoil that had taken root inside me last night had kept me awake, staring at the chandelier above my bed. Stevie had asked thousands of questions, it seemed, when I lay down with her. She even fell asleep in the middle of one. The day had exhausted her, and I was glad she hadn't struggled to sleep in her new room. I had needed some time alone.

The way she had just accepted the massive turn of events without issue was a relief. She had kept Linc busy by telling him everything he could ever want to know and asking him questions. As I sat there, witnessing them together, the blame grew heavier and sank slowly onto my shoulders. It came with regret that I'd been keeping this from her because it was something she obviously needed, and I hadn't even realized it. She'd barely taken her eyes off Linc.

Twice, while we were in bed, she had beamed at me and said, "I have a weal daddy." As if she was amazed.

The pang of remorse was sharp, and I had to live with it. This was my penance. Facing what had to be done today had only been more of what I deserved.

Dad used to tell me, "You made your bed, darlin'. Now, you got to lie in it."

Although the sound of his deep, husky tone had long since faded from my memory, as his scent and laugh had, his words were still there. He'd have been ashamed of me. I'd stolen time that could never be taken back from not only Linc, but my daughter too.

While he might have deserved it, she hadn't. She was innocent. My fear had ruled everything else. I thought I was giving her the best. The family that I thought would be complete with Hudson. Yet not once had she brought him up again. She hadn't acted sad that he wouldn't be her dad anymore. I couldn't remember a time in her life that she'd been this giddy.

Standing in front of the mirror, I studied myself. The cotton-candy-pink sundress I had decided to wear made the sun I'd gotten yesterday by the pool stand out. The desire to look my best when I talked to Hudson no longer held any importance for me. My life would never be the same. The one I had been living when I kissed him last and got in my car to drive here was gone. It was time I accepted it.

Needless to say, extra time spent on under-eye concealer was a must this morning. I'd taken a shower, dried my hair, and finished my makeup, and Stevie was still sleeping. The king-size bed with a mattress from heaven, combined with her full day, had her sleeping late. It gave me time to get ready, and I knew she needed the rest for another full day. This one with several hours spent in a car.

Stevie's happiness was number one priority, and having watched her with Linc, I knew I'd never be able to take her away from him. When the year was over, we would rent something in Madison. I'd find a job here or in Jackson. The fifteen hundred dollars in savings wasn't going to be much help though. I couldn't keep the car that Hudson had bought me. I'd need to leave that with him. That was another cost I would have to prepare for.

I could talk to Linc about my getting a job once he felt more secure about me not being with Stevie all the time. In Nashville, she'd had a sitter who came to our apartment and stayed with her two days a week, and the other three days, Hudson had childcare at the office. Three of the ten women who worked there used it for their younger children. He'd put it in place after he asked me to work full-time and I explained I didn't have full-time childcare and couldn't afford it.

Taking a deep breath, I tried not to think about all that he'd done for me. It would only add to the other heaviness I was carrying. I picked up my phone to check the time. It was almost eight, and Linc wanted to leave at eight thirty.

Slipping my phone into my purse, I made my way over to Stevie's room. She needed to get dressed and have some breakfast before we left.

Her bedroom door was slightly cracked. I'd closed her door after checking on her over an hour ago. I hurried across the hallway and pushed it open to look inside. The bed was empty.

"Stevie!" I called her name, taking longer strides than normal to her en suite, but the lights were off in there too.

My heart started picking up pace as I swung my gaze around to see any signs as to where she might be. The slippers that I had left beside her bed were gone.

Where had she gone? Why hadn't she come to my room?

Rushing out the door, I moved as fast as I could in my heels. This house was too big. She could have gotten lost. She could have gone outside, alone. When I reached the stairs, I slipped off my heels and broke into a run as I headed down them. I hadn't told her not to go exploring here by herself, and I should have. Panic tightened my throat and stung my eyes as I scanned every area I passed.

Then, I heard her trill of laughter. I slowed and placed a hand over my heart as I sucked in a deep breath. She was okay. Closing my eyes, I took a second to calm down, then put my shoes back on before heading toward the sound of voices. I smelled the bacon before I got there.

By the time I reached the door that led into the kitchen, my heart rate had slowed, and I wasn't about to burst into tears.

"Can I have thwee mowa, please?" Stevie asked as I stepped into the kitchen.

The windows went from the floor to the ceiling, facing the back of the house. The sunlight poured in and made the white and black kitchen appear even more spacious than it already was. The island sat between two sets of double ovens, and the gas range stovetop looked like something out of a commercial kitchen with at least ten different eyes. The circular bar, which had twelve barstools, was covered in food.

Stevie was on one of the barstools, sitting on her knees, with a glass of oat milk that had a curvy pink straw in it. Her gaze swung to mine, and her smile stretched across her face, causing the dimples I loved so much to pop out. "Good mownin', Mommy! Jayda made bweakfast, and she gots lots and lots of bacon," she called out to me.

"I see that," I replied, making my way over to her. "I didn't know you had woken up. I was scared when I couldn't find you."

Her face fell. "I'm sowwy. I thought you was asleep, and I was weally hungwy."

Brushing her curls back from her face, I placed a kiss on her forehead. "I understand that. Just don't go running off without telling me, okay? This house is big, and you could get lost."

She shook her head. "But I didn't get lost. I came wight hewah. And Jayda was making bweakfast. She got me some milk."

I glanced over at Jayda. "Thank you. This looks amazing."

She shrugged. "I like to cook. When I have people to cook for, I go a little overboard. When the guys have women over, they aren't invited to stay for breakfast, so unless Linc's son is visiting with his wife, I don't get to do big breakfasts. Luther rarely eats until noon, and Linc is a *four eggs, two pieces of toast, and a coffee* guy. No room for creativity."

I wasn't a big breakfast eater either, but Stevie was.

"You might become her favorite person," I told her. "Although we don't require all this every morning. I would gain a hundred pounds. But Vivi Lu here loves her some breakfast food. She'd eat it for all three meals. We've done pancakes, cheese grits, and bacon for dinner many nights."

Jayda smiled at Stevie. "I will remember that," she told her and winked. "We might just have us some breakfast for dinner soon. Sounds like a fun way to mix it up." She finished putting three pieces of bacon on a plate and placed it in front of Stevie.

"Thank you," she said before snatching up a piece and taking a bite as if she hadn't already had a plate of food.

"I can make you a plate, or you're welcome to do it. I don't know what all you like just yet, but I am a fast learner," Jayda informed me.

I liked this girl. And if I wasn't at least ten years older than her, we might just become good friends. She didn't seem to have any claim on Linc or Luther. She wasn't being territorial, which, honestly, was what I had expected to happen. The comment about the women they had over not being invited for breakfast was so blasé, as if it was no big deal to her. She didn't sound catty or anything. Maybe I was wrong, and she didn't screw around with the guys. It was just so hard to believe. She was gorgeous.

"No need to worry about me. I will feed myself," I told her, not about to let someone wait on me. I might have to live here for a year, but I wasn't going to turn into some diva who let other people wait on her.

I walked over to the island, and Jayda handed me a plate.

"Here you go. Are you a coffee drinker? Or maybe espresso? I make a killer caramel vanilla latte."

I looked from the food back to her. "Really?" I asked, my voice giving away my excitement at the word *latte*.

Jayda grinned. "Before this job, I was a barista," she replied. "Which one do you prefer?"

"That caramel vanilla latte sounds wonderful."

"Cold or hot?"

I laughed. "I feel like I'm at Starbucks. Hot, please."

"Tall, grande, or venti?"

My eyebrows shot up, and she smirked.

"That's a joke."

Another chuckle bubbled out of me as I turned back to the food and chose some berries, a pancake, and a slice of bacon.

"The bacon is weally good," Stevie told me.

"Vivi Lu, I don't think bacon can be anything but good."

She giggled and stuck the end of the fancy straw into her mouth while she watched me.

I was almost to the stool beside her when Linc walked into the kitchen. If I had been eating, I would have choked on my food.

Good Lord. That man.

His eyes met mine, and I had some difficulty swallowing. I'd thought Hudson was handsome. But he seemed ordinary when compared to Linc. Self-preservation had perhaps dulled my memory of his perfection. Right now, it was here, slapping me in the face.

Broad shoulders with muscular arms stretched the blue pearl-snap shirt he was wearing. The faded jeans it was tucked into looked as if they had been tailor-made for him. Complete with dark brown cowboy hat and boots, the man was breathtaking. Literally. I wasn't getting enough oxygen.

Linc's gaze didn't have any trouble looking right past me to Jayda, who was busy at a complicated-looking coffee machine, then to Stevie.

"Good morning," he said, causing her little head to snap around to look at him.

"Hey! It's my weal dad!" she exclaimed happily, pointing as if I hadn't seen him the instant he stepped into the room.

The corner of his mouth tugged up, and the way it made his eyes crinkle reminded me of the Linc I used to know. My outlaw. I tore my gaze off him and pulled the stool out to sit down. He wasn't smiling at me. He was smiling at our daughter, who was impossible not to smile at.

"Morning, Mr. Shephard," Jayda called out. "I'll have your plate to you in just a minute. I finally have someone to make a latte for."

Linc walked into my line of vision again, and like moths to a flame, my eyes were right back on him.

He studied the array of food, then cut his eyes over to Stevie. "Was there something here to your liking?" he asked her.

Blonde curls bounced as she nodded her head vigorously. "The pancakes was weally good. You need to twy them.

Jayda puts whipped cweam and bewwies on them. And the bacon was my favowite," she said, holding up the half-eaten piece in her hand to show him what bacon looked like, I guessed.

"I normally just have eggs and toast, but if you say I need to try the pancakes, then pancakes it is," he replied, his expression serious, as if her words had changed his mind.

Again, she nodded and bounced on her knees. "You can sit by me. Thewah is a seat wight hewah." She patted the spot on her other side.

"That's the best offer I've had all week," he told her, then glanced back at Jayda. "I'll take the pancakes the way Stevie had them with the bacon, please."

Jayda looked up at him, her expression a mixture of surprise and amusement. "Got it," she replied, then placed the latte in front of me.

"Thank you," I told her again before she turned to start making his plate.

"We awah going to pack up my things and bwing them hewah to youah house," Stevie told Linc.

He leaned in closer to her. "I'm looking forward to you showing me your favorite toys."

"That's my Bluey house!" she exclaimed. "We can bwing that, can't we, Mommy?" she asked, turning to look at me.

"Yes, of course."

"Hudson gave it to me."

And there it was. What I had hoped my oversharing daughter would not mention. I didn't look at Linc, but I could literally feel the air around us get thick.

"Is there by chance a larger Bluey house that you might want?" Linc asked her.

This time, my eyes swung to him. Was he serious? He couldn't do this with everything in her life. She'd be spoiled.

"Yes!" she said, bouncing again. "And thewah is a beach house and a campah and a school! Mommy said I can get them fowah my buffday."

I watched as the smug expression came over his face. Like he had just been given the information he needed to win the game. Although this wasn't a game. It was a little girl who did not need to be bought with toys. He was going to win. He'd already won. He would be the most important man in her life until the day came that she fell in love.

"I believe we can make a stop on our trip today and go ahead and get those items. I would hate for you to have to wait months for them."

I held in a groan as Stevie let out a squeal.

Jayda handed Linc a cup of coffee, then slid his plate in front of him.

He didn't even glance her way. The sight of Stevie celebrating her upcoming trip to buy all the items on her wish list had his complete attention.

His eyes finally shifted toward me, and I gave him a pointed look that said I wasn't happy about this. The confused frown that drew his brows together made it clear he had no idea what was wrong with his decision. We would talk about this, but not while Stevie could hear it. I finished my breakfast in silence while listening to Stevie tell Linc about the dog she wanted. He seemed to be determined to make all her wishes come true in the span of twenty-four hours.

FOURTEEN
LINC

The only reason Branwen hadn't lit into me yet, the way her eyes said she wanted to, was because of Stevie's excitement. Even buckled into her car seat, she seemed to be bouncing as she kept pointing at things inside the Bentley limo that I never used. However, today, it'd seemed like the more comfortable option for Stevie. I'd made sure it was stocked with drinks and snacks for both of them, not that Branwen seemed to care. She was too busy shooting me scathing looks.

It had started at breakfast when I told Stevie I'd get her the toys she wanted. I didn't see the problem with it. My daughter's favorite toy was not going to be something another man had given her. Branwen could get the fuck over it. And when we stepped outside and the limo was waiting, her comment about my truck being able to hold more stuff was said with annoyance. Then, she said she would be driving her car because she needed to return it to Hudson since he had bought it for her.

The flare of temper in those eyes of hers had made me almost laugh when I told her that I'd already sent her car that way. I'd read in her background check where the car was in the fucker's name, and I didn't want it here. She wasn't driving my kid around in a car bought by another man. She wouldn't be driving at all. She would be driven and have security detail when she and Stevie left the house. My sending the cheap, ugly-ass car back without her consent had ruffled her feathers.

She sure as hell was enjoying her cold bottle of bubbly and leg room right now though. At that thought, my eyes drifted down to her legs, and I wished like fuck they hadn't. It wasn't the first time I had checked them out because, well, they were right there…crossed and bare. Her toenails were painted the same red color as her fingernails. The dainty gold anklet looked like it had tiny diamonds in it.

Had the dentist given that to her? She didn't wear much jewelry. Other than the ring on her finger, that was the only other piece I'd seen on her.

I realized my teeth were clenched, and I tore my eyes off the damn thing and her legs to stare out the window. The show that Stevie loved so much was playing on the television screens so she could see the blue dog in all directions. Otherwise, the vehicle was silent.

I tried to think of something to distract me, but the need to know who had given her the fucking anklet was gnawing at me. What did it matter? Our marriage wasn't a real one. Legally, yes, but that was it. She didn't belong to me. Unlike our daughter, she wasn't mine. My damn possessive streak, which had woken up the instant I knew I had a daughter, seemed to be spilling over onto the mother as well. I had to get a rein on that. This was day one of three hundred sixty-five that she would be sleeping in my house. Down the hall from me.

If I was completely honest with myself, I loathed the fact that she was going to see the dentist today. I wanted to snatch her away from him, just like I was going to do with my daughter. But if the man had any pride, he'd break things off when he found out she was married and would be living with me for the next year. There could be no wedding in a few months. With that thought, I relaxed my jaw, then turned my attention to the television that Stevie was watching.

The blue dog and a tan-colored one were climbing all over the larger blue dog. After a few moments of trying to follow what the fuck was going on, I glanced over at Branwen, who was looking down at her phone.

"Do the parents have a job on this show?" I asked her.

She glanced up at me, and for the first time since breakfast, the corner of her full mouth curled up slightly. "Yes. The dad is an archaeologist, and the mom, I believe, is airport security," she replied with a touch of amusement in her voice.

"They seem to have an awful lot of free time."

A small laugh trickled from those lips, and my eyes gave in and dropped to look at them. They were covered in a shiny pink gloss that made their natural pouty form a temptation. A memory of seeing them wrapped around my cock appeared, and I had to hold in a hiss as I swung my gaze back to the television in hopes that the talking dogs could distract me enough to stop the thickening inside my jeans. Getting a fucking boner with my kid in the car wasn't acceptable.

I cleared my throat before asking, "Are they Australian?"

"Yep. I think the accent is part of the draw for kids. It's very popular right now. When they came out with the playhouse, it was almost impossible to find..." She trailed off, her voice lowering, and then she dropped her eyes to her phone again.

What? Did she think talking about the toy was going to set me off because of the damn dentist?

"Mommy, can I have some of those Goldfish?" Stevie asked as the credits on the current episode came on.

Branwen glanced back up, then reached over to the tray filled with snacks that Jayda had stocked the car with. The neckline of her sundress dipped down as her tits pushed up from the move. Cleavage that I'd only allowed myself to look at once this morning now became impossible to ignore. She wasn't wearing a bra because of the way the bodice of the dress was made, I assumed, and the tease of one of her large, round nipples was right there. The areola almost pressing up enough to see.

Dammit! I needed to stop. It was because I hadn't fucked in days. I'd need to fix that tonight. Go sink my dick into a mouth and a cunt until I was sated enough not to get hard over this woman.

"Here you go," Branwen said as she held the opened bag out to Stevie, who grabbed it.

"Thank you."

"You're welcome."

The kid was so damn polite. That was Branwen's doing. I couldn't fault her for that at least. The fact that she had intended to keep my kid from me though? I doubted I could ever forgive her for that. But for our daughter's sake, I had to find a way to be nice to her and not end up fucking her.

FIFTEEN

BRANWEN

At some point during the drive, I'd let go of my anger at Linc not consulting me about anything that concerned me or Stevie, and I began to grow more anxious about my seeing Hudson. I stayed focused at the apartment and pointed out things to the two men who had apparently driven my car to Nashville and would be packing up what we wanted to bring with us. I wished I could do this alone and have time to think, but Linc stood outside the door with a cigar, leaning against the rail, talking on the phone, waiting, while I was inside with Stevie and the men who I assumed were Mafia members.

"This box going?" the one who had introduced himself as Gathe asked as he pushed his surfer-boy blond hair out of his face.

"Yes, please," I replied.

With my thoughts on what I was going to say to Hudson, there was a good chance that I would forget several things. He often talked over me to get his point across. I couldn't let him do that this time.

Stevie came walking out of her bedroom, rattling away about something that had to do with her baby dolls to the tall, muscular, tanned one with messy, dark brown hair and light-blue eyes. His name was weird. Something like Than, I thought. My mind wasn't computing things that well today. Too much to think about.

"You mean to tell me she can eat food and poop in a diaper?" he asked with a well-played look of surprise.

Stevie nodded her head. "Yep! She can! It's gwoss too."

"I sure hope she doesn't do her business on the trip back to Linc's," he said, shaking his head and looking truly worried.

If I wasn't so worked up with dread, I would have smiled.

"Than," Gathe called out, and the guy carrying a box of Stevie's toys looked up at him.

"Yeah?"

"How many boxes left in her room?"

"Five."

"I've cleared out the other bedroom. Linc wanted to know how much longer." He turned his gaze to mine. "You got anything else we need to box up?"

I studied the room, then looked back toward the bathroom. There really wasn't much we needed from there. Our bathrooms at Linc's were better stocked than ours had ever been.

I shook my head. "No. I think that's gonna be it."

He gave me a nod. "All right, we will get the rest in the moving truck and head out."

When we had arrived, the two guys had already been parked outside with a U-Haul. Everything had been so efficient.

I glanced around for my purse and went to pull out some twenties I had tucked inside. "Here. Let me tip y'all. You've been so helpful."

The blond one raised his brows and shook his head. "Thank you. That's real nice, but we don't want any money. This was nothing at all. Happy to help."

His momma had raised him right, but I was still giving him something for doing this.

I held the money out. "Please take it. It would make me feel better."

He shifted his eyes to Than, as if asking for backup.

"What he isn't saying is that if we take your money, Linc will lose his shit. Besides, you're family now, and we take care of family," he said, shifting the box in his hands.

Family. They were Mafia. Born into this life, just like Linc had been. They looked close to Linc's age when I had been a little girl. The brief moment of nostalgia helped ease the ball of tension in my chest.

"Okay," I replied. "If you're sure."

"Positive."

The door opened, and Linc stepped inside. The cigar was gone, but the breeze that blew in brought the scent of it inside. I wished it hadn't. Not because I disliked it, but because that was his smell. I guessed I wouldn't be coming back here for a year, so I shouldn't care. It wasn't as if I would ever get to live here again. That decision had already been made for me. My time in Nashville was over.

"You done?" he asked me.

I nodded. Walking out that door meant going to see Hudson, and the vicious dread was back. I had to get this over with.

Linc looked at the other two guys. "Finish up. Get this back." His gruff voice made his words sound like an order.

He didn't have to be rude. They had been a huge help.

"I have to leave with my weal dad. Be cayuhful with my toys," Stevie told Than.

"I'll guard them with my life. They're in good hands."

She smiled, seemingly pleased with that, and started toward Linc. He watched her with a smirk that held a touch of pride. That kind of thing was going to do me in. It wasn't getting easier to witness. My heart only seemed to ache more every time I was reminded of what I had kept from her. But I hadn't known that he'd be like this. That he would want her. If I had, it would have all been different.

Stevie reached up and grabbed his pointer finger, wrapping her small hand around it, and grinned up at him. "Let's go watch *Bluey*."

He nodded his head, and she started out the door, leading him. I watched them exit, then glanced over at the other two. Than looked ready to burst into laughter. Gathe's eyebrows had risen, and he stilled.

"Fuck, that's funny." Than chuckled when they were gone, and then he swung his blue eyes over to me and winced. "Sorry."

I held up a hand. "No need to apologize. It is amusing."

"Seeing a female ordering him around is priceless. Especially one who is pint-sized." Gathe smirked. "And what the hell is *Bluey*?"

"It's a cartoon with talking Australian dogs. Main character's name is Bluey, and she's blue," Than told him.

Gathe frowned at him. "You know this how?"

I was kind of wondering the same thing.

"It's one of Hawk's favorite shows. We watch it during breakfast every morning."

Understanding lit Gathe's face. "Oh, okay. Yeah, that makes sense."

Who was Hawk? Did Than have a kid?

I glanced at his hand, and there was no wedding band, but then that didn't really mean anything. Linc had never worn one when he was younger. I wasn't going to pry though.

"Thanks again," I told them, making my way to the door.

"Y'all will get there before we do, but your things will be there by tonight," Than said.

I glanced back at him as I reached the door. "We aren't leaving yet. I have another matter to handle first," I explained.

"Still, it's a short flight. You barely get up before you start back down."

Flight? I scrunched my nose. "We drove."

He nodded. "Yeah. But Linc has the plane ready at the private strip to take you back."

I stared at him, letting that process. We were taking a private plane back to Madison? He hadn't said anything. What was this life he lived? I'd known it wasn't like mine, watching the Hugheses as a child, but experiencing it was something much different.

I managed a smile, then headed for the limo. Stevie had never flown before, and she was going to be thrilled. Seeing her face when we drove up to the plane would be priceless. I would look forward to that and not think about my upcoming talk with Hudson.

When I reached the car, the driver was standing outside the door and opened it for me. I thanked him, then climbed inside to find Stevie already buckled into her car seat, her attention on the television screen while she ate a banana and held a box of oat milk in her other hand. Linc learned fast, it seemed. He was only on day two of this *having a little girl* thing, and he was figuring it out.

"I assumed bananas weren't a choking hazard," he said as the door closed.

They could be, but I decided against telling him that. He might never let her eat without me present again. She wasn't a baby anymore, and it was mostly my own fears that had me still slicing grapes. The one time I'd tried to be brave and let her eat an apple without me peeling it and cutting it up, she choked. I had been traumatized.

"She looks content," I told him.

The limo began to move, and I stared out the window at the other cars as we left the parking lot. Seeing them reminded me that I didn't have my car. I had wanted to take it to Hudson.

"Where did they leave my car?" I asked.

"It's parked in his driveway," he told me, then reached into his jeans pocket and pulled out the key fob. "Here."

I reached forward and took it.

He had known where my apartment was without having to ask me. He knew where Hudson lived. He'd known Hudson had bought me the car. I wanted to know what all he did know because I knew his information didn't go all the way back to my childhood. It seemed to be that he had researched only current things about me. If he realized who I was, then it would uncover yet another thing I had hidden from him. Not that it mattered really. It wasn't something that would change anything.

The drive to the dentist office was the shortest trip from my apartment I'd ever had—or my increasing dismay at having to tell Hudson all of this made it feel too quick. Prolonging the inevitable didn't sound so bad about now. When the limo stopped, I took a deep breath, trying to calm my nerves.

Stevie looked around and then smiled brightly. "We awah at the office!" she said and clapped her hands together. "Let me out. I want to go show Hudson my weal dad!"

Oh good Lord. My eyes swung to Linc, who was sitting back with his long legs slightly spread and an arm resting on one of his muscular thighs and the other behind Stevie. He was smirking. I was torn between wanting to lean over there and slap him or rub up against him. I wasn't sure which one of those was winning. He was the picture of raw, masculine power. Ugh. Damn him for being so incredibly sexy.

Straightening my shoulders, I turned back to Stevie. "Not today. I need to go inside alone. I've got to tell Hudson that you and I are moving to Georgia to live with your dad for a while. It is better if you and him stay in the car."

She frowned, and I could see her trying to work this out in her head. She hadn't been concerned about Hudson after finding out about Linc. But now that she was faced with it, the questions were starting to pop up.

"Will Hudson let us live with my weal dad?"

I didn't look at Linc. I already knew he wasn't going to like that question.

"Hudson doesn't decide where we live. But he needs to know about it."

"Will he live with us, too, aftah the wedding?"

Linc made a noise that was somewhere between a growl and a cough. Whatever. He deserved it. He had demanded we do this and given me no other choice. She had just met him two days ago, but she'd known Hudson much longer.

"The wedding isn't going to happen this year," I told her, preparing for tears. She had really been looking forward to that flower-girl dress.

Her brow puckered. "Why not?"

I should let Linc answer all these questions.

"Well, you see, since we've found your real dad and he wants to spend time with you and have you live with him, then that changes things. Madison is a long drive away from Nashville, and this is where Hudson lives and where his dentist office is. He can't move with us."

How was I supposed to explain this to a child?

She was silent for a minute, and thankfully, there were no tears yet.

"It's okay," she told me, patting my hand that rested on her leg. "We don't need him now. I got a dad. My weal one. Hudson can be someone else's dad."

Unable to help myself, I cut my eyes over to Linc.

The bastard had a smug grin on his face as he lifted his shoulders slightly. "She's got a point. Maybe you could just go tell him that."

Glaring at him, I narrowed my eyes, unable to say what I wanted to in front of Stevie.

"I won't be long," I said and went to get out of the already-open door.

For a moment, I stood there and looked at the building in front of me. I'd been here four days ago, yet it no longer felt the same. The comfort and security that being here had provided was gone. Now, I would rather be anywhere else.

SIXTEEN
LINC

Stevie went right back to watching her show once Branwen stepped out of the limo. My eyes followed the sway of her hips as she walked up to the entrance. Fuck, I wanted to grab her ass. I blew out a sharp breath and forced my gaze in another direction. The decision to fly home rather than drive had been made for Stevie's benefit, but, damn, it was for mine too. Another six hours with her sitting across from me, and my dick would have had a permanent zipper imprint on it.

My cell started ringing, and I leaned forward so I could slide it out of my pocket. Garrett's name lit up the screen, and I frowned. I didn't hear from him too much since he'd handed over the running of things to Blaise.

I hit Answer, then put the phone to my ear, leaning back in my seat again.

"What's going on?" I asked, preparing for some shit I was going to have to deal with.

"I'm the one who should be asking you that," he replied.

I glanced over at Stevie. "I'm assuming you are talking about the background check I had run."

"That, and I was curious how she was doing. It's been years since I checked in on her."

I frowned, trying to figure out what the fuck he was talking about. Checked in on who?

"Uh, I'm not following you. I only had one background check pulled in the last week—on a Branwen Hester. Who are you talking about?"

"Branwen. How is she? And why didn't you mention you'd fucked her five years ago?" He let out a deep, amused chuckle.

I shifted in my seat, trying to figure out how Garrett knew Branwen and why he thought I knew her too. Before Vegas. "I met her in Vegas. At a club. Am I understanding that you know her?"

I'd not read through her entire background check. I didn't care about her childhood or even her twenties really. That wasn't my concern.

Had she been connected to someone within the family? Or a business associate? She was too young to have been a friend of his. Unless he'd dated her once. Before he met and married Fawn, he had fucked around with some young ones.

I sat up, my hand tightening on the phone. If she'd fucked Garrett, then had she known who he was? About my connection to him?

"Linc"—his tone sounded incredulous—"you're kidding, right?"

No, I wasn't fucking kidding, and if he hadn't been the boss for most of my life, then I would be demanding he tell me what the hell he was talking about.

"No," I replied as calmly as I could. "I'm not. How do you know Branwen?"

There was silence for a moment, and I was starting to feel caged. A pounding behind my eyes took root as I waited for him to tell me who she was.

"She's definitely grown up now, and not recognizing her is understandable, but you have the same background check that came through Blaise's office. I can't believe you don't remember her, of all people. She was your fucking shadow. You called her something…some nickname."

My eyes swung over to look at Stevie as she giggled at whatever the dogs were doing. The pale blonde head, full of curls, and her perfect little features. Then, she turned to look at me and smiled.

"Jesus Christ," I whispered.

Garrett was saying something, but all I heard was her laughing, and another laugh from years ago began to replay in my head. That was why she'd looked familiar. Even the freckles that peppered her nose.

"Linc." Garrett said my name into the phone, and I blinked, then swallowed hard.

"Yeah?" I croaked out.

"Everything okay?"

I shook my head, although he couldn't see me. No, I was not okay.

"Yeah," I replied. "I, uh…yeah."

He chuckled again. "I can't believe you didn't remember her when you saw her name. And she didn't say anything to you? She might have been a kid, but she was twelve when Demeter died. She'd spent six years of her life at my stables with him. And she worshipped the ground you walked on."

Holy fuck. This was not real. How could Branwen be her?

My gaze went to the office building she'd walked into.

She had known who and what I was. So, she did know me. She recognized me in Vegas. She could have found me before. She lied about it. She'd kept Stevie away from me on purpose. That marriage license was the only reason she had shown up at my door.

"I don't think I ever called her by her name before. The first time I met her, I nicknamed her. The name just didn't register. The last name rang a bell though. But it was a lifetime ago when Demeter worked for the family."

The surge of anger was being met with sheer fucking shock as I tried to replay every interaction with Branwen in Vegas that I could remember. Had she mentioned it, and I missed it? Or had it been during one of the spells where I blacked out from the opium and booze? Why hadn't she said something when she came to get me to sign the divorce papers?

She'd probably expected me to see her name and realize who she was…but I hadn't.

"She's good now?" he asked. "I kept a check on her until she was grown. Made sure her aunt had what she needed financially to provide for her. I only checked in on her one more time when she was around twenty-six, I believe. She had a secure job at a dairy farm and was dating the owner's son. Seemed serious from the report I got back. I was surprised to hear she hadn't married the guy. From the pictures I've seen, she turned into a real beauty."

Garrett hadn't forgotten her. He'd checked in on her. Made sure she was okay. Out of loyalty to her father, who had been one hell of a trainer and bookie. One of the best the family had ever had.

The day he'd dropped dead from a heart attack was brutal. I held her while the paramedics came, and she sobbed hysterically. The funeral was the last time I had seen her. She'd rushed to me with tears streaming down her face and told me she had to go live with her aunt.

I knew nothing about her life after that.

I wasn't the same person I had been then. Life had changed me. Made me darker, colder, and detached. I didn't get involved. I didn't show affection.

It seemed it had changed her too. She had grown into a liar. A cruel one. She had planned to keep my child from me and let another man raise her.

"She's good," I finally said.

Looking over at my daughter, I knew I wouldn't put my hands around Branwen's neck because of her. But she was going to pay for this. The betrayal stung, but my grief over the four years I'd lost from Stevie's life was greater than anything else. No excuse or apology could give that back to me. Or to my daughter. She had wanted a dad. She had wanted one, and I couldn't be one because of Branwen.

It wasn't just me she had stolen from, but our daughter too.

SEVENTEEN

BRANWEN

From the first day that I'd laid eyes on Hudson Wolfe, he'd reminded me of a Ken doll. His blond hair, cut short and neat; smooth jawline, always shaved; golden skin; green eyes; and a runner's fit body. When he had smiled at me the first time, I held my breath, waiting for the butterflies that I had yet to experience with any male except Linc. They didn't come.

The disappointment was swift, but I kept waiting. Hoping that the closer we got, the more my feelings would grow into something passionate and exciting. They didn't.

I hadn't let my inability to feel these things stand in my way. Hudson was exactly what we needed. He was stability, comfort, and security. After having been a single mom to a baby and toddler, where I had struggled to supply for us, that had sounded wonderful. Much more powerful than silly tingles and butterflies.

Stepping into Hudson's office as he walked in behind me and closed the door, I knew I had been selfish. He was such a good man, and I had taken advantage of his feelings for me. I was never going to love him the way he deserved. He was successful and attractive. There were so many women who could love this man properly. There was probably one out there that he would give those damn elusive flutters to, and I'd almost robbed her of that. My butterflies had been claimed at the age of six, and I was starting to accept that they would always be Linc's.

"God, I've missed you," Hudson said as he walked up behind me, wrapping his arms around my waist and pressing a kiss to the side of my head.

He was only four inches taller than me at five foot ten. His height wasn't something I'd noticed before. But after I'd been around Linc and his six-foot-three stature, muscular build, and even his beard, Hudson seemed weak. Almost feminine. That wasn't a fair comparison, and I knew I should stop comparing them.

I had only been gone for three days. Would anyone ever miss me again like Hudson had? Thoughts like that didn't help. This wasn't about me. It honestly never had been. Since the moment my precious baby girl had been laid in my arms, my life had revolved around her. I wanted her to be happy. I wanted her life to be full.

When she went to take her driver's test, I wanted to be there with her. When she got ready for her first date, I wanted to do her hair and help her choose what to wear. When she went to prom, I wanted to take pictures and tell her how beautiful she was. When she said yes to the man she loved, I wanted to go shopping with her for the perfect dress. And when she held her baby in her arms for the first time, I wanted to be there with tears of joy in my eyes. All the things I'd never had. It was what I dreamed of, what I was determined to give her. I had thought that Hudson would be the way to have that ideal life.

But Hudson had never looked at Stevie the way Linc did. As if he would take a bullet for her. The pride, love, and awe in his eyes was what I wanted her to have and I hadn't considered that Hudson wasn't going to give her that. I had thought I could give her that all on my own. I'd built her future on her needing me, and I had been wrong.

I should have known better. Because at each of those moments when I hadn't had a mom, I also hadn't had my dad, and it had been a hollow ache in my chest. I had needed and wanted him too. Not just a mother, but my father as well. Linc might not be the best man, but he was her dad, and I knew he would protect her and love her.

Taking a deep breath, I laid my hand over Hudson's and prepared myself for what I had to do.

"I lied to you." I said the words while he still held me and my back was to him.

He was silent for a moment, then released me to turn me around to face him. There was a concerned expression on his face, but his eyes clearly told me he was prepared to forgive me. That would make this much worse. My guilt would continue to mount if he did. At some point, I was going to suffocate in it.

"About?" he asked me.

Nervously, I licked my bottom lip. *Just say it, Branwen. Get it out.*

"Stevie's father isn't dead," I blurted out. "I said he was because, to me, he was. I never intended for her to know him. It was selfish, but I had my reasons, and they were wrong. I won't justify myself or my actions."

Hudson's face looked surprised, but there was no anger or accusation in his gaze. He reached out and took my left hand in his. "Okay. You lied. It's good that you're clearing that up. Stevie's father being alive doesn't affect us or how I feel about you."

Oh, but I wasn't done yet. I took another deep breath.

"But it does," I said. The regret in my tone was thick.

I tucked a lock of hair behind my ear and then crossed my arms over my chest, as if they could protect me from this. "I couldn't find my birth certificate. I looked for it for over a week. I wasn't sure if I needed to drive to Florida to get a copy of it or if I could get one online, and if so, I didn't know how long it would take. I decided to call and find out from the clerk's office." I paused realizing I was talking fast.

No longer able to look at him, I tilted my head back slightly and looked at a water stain on the ceiling. "The lady told me I did need a birth certificate to get a marriage license. She asked me questions about the date of the wedding and was checking to see the quickest way for me to get a copy… and then she asked me when my divorce would be final. I was so confused. She went on to say that my records showed that I was married and had been for five years. To him. Stevie's dad."

I didn't tell Hudson his name. He never needed to know that. Linc was dangerous. I'd already lied to Hudson. I was hurting him. I would not let him get near the world that Linc lived in. He needed to remain oblivious to it.

"What?" he gasped as horror filled his eyes. The same horror I'd felt when I found out.

"That night—when I met him at the club in Vegas, when I got pregnant with Stevie—we drank a lot. I know I told you that already, but it's important because that was how it happened. We were talking about favorite movies. I said something about *The Hangover* being one of mine. He told me there was a chapel that did a fake wedding, complete with Elvis, for people to do *The Hangover* thing. We thought it sounded hilarious at the time. Or I did at least. He took me there, and we did it. But it seems we didn't get the correct package." I stopped and closed my eyes as I took a deep breath.

"I didn't want you to know. I was embarrassed and afraid you'd call off the wedding." I looked at him again. "There was no funeral. I went to find him. With his name on the marriage certificate, I had tracked him down. I had divorce papers drawn and took them with me, along with the marriage certificate. If I could get him to sign them, then after they were filed and finalized, it would be a thirty-day wait period before I could remarry."

Hudson ran his fingers through his short blond strands of hair. "Jesus, Branwen," he breathed as he began to pace, looking pale and slightly panicked. "You could have told me the truth. It sucks, and, yeah, I would have been upset, but you don't need to lie to me. We are getting married, and I need to know I can trust you." He was talking as he rubbed the back of his neck.

He still thought we were getting married. I wanted to hug him and tell him how sorry I was, but I wouldn't. I wasn't done yet. He was about to change his mind.

"He saw Stevie. He was suspicious and refused to sign the papers until he had a paternity test done. When he got the results, he used the divorce as leverage. He would sign them, but only after Stevie and I lived with him for a year."

"WHAT?!" Hudson shouted, his face turning red now.

I'd never heard him raise his voice, and I stiffened but continued, "He doesn't want to be married to me, but he wants to get to know his daughter. He feels robbed of the four years of her life he missed."

"Like fuck! He can't blackmail you, Branwen. He's manipulating you. I'll call my lawyer, and we will go see him today."

"Hudson, no," I said, shaking my head. "You can't."

He stared at me, his brows drawn together, his face was flushed. "Why? Do you want this?" he asked, looking anguished.

"Of course not. But you don't know him. He can demand it, and if you try and stop him, you won't only fail, but you'll also be putting yourself in danger."

"Danger?" He spat the word like it was ludicrous. "I have the best lawyers in Nashville. I sure as hell can stop him. This isn't legal, Branwen."

"Trust me when I tell you that even your lawyers can't fight him. He has power. A lot of it. That power goes to very high places."

He shook his head. "No one is above the law."

"He is."

Hudson let out a hard laugh. "He has you brainwashed. You don't know this man. You met him and fucked him one time. He can't—"

"That's not the truth either. I do know him. He just didn't know me."

Hudson's eyes narrowed. "What does that mean? Is he famous? Are you married to a celebrity?"

I let out a hard laugh. "No. He's not famous. It's just that he hadn't seen me as an adult. He didn't recognize me."

"You're going to need to give me more than that. If he isn't a celebrity or the fucking president, then he doesn't have any power that is greater than a court."

Yes, he did. Should I tell him? Admit it so that he would back down? Letting him try and fight Linc on this would likely get him killed. I'd have to live with that, and I wasn't sure I could.

I knew you didn't share details about the family if you were in the know. You kept that secret close. Only those they chose to tell knew about who and what they were. But this was Hudson's life I was considering here.

"Hudson," I said, and he stopped the pacing he had started up again, "he is a dangerous man. And when I say that, I mean *Godfather*-level dangerous. You can't fight him. Those who try..." I stopped. Saying the word *die* seemed dramatic, although it was true.

"*Godfather*?" he asked, scowling like he didn't believe it. "He's not the Mafia, Branwen. Is he a felon? If he is a criminal, then we'll have even more leverage in court."

"Stop. There will be no court. I will not allow it. I won't do it."

His face was a mix of disbelief and pain. He looked betrayed. I'd expected this though, hadn't I? It was why I'd dreaded coming here. Facing him. Telling him all this.

"Why are you so scared of him? You expect me to just let you go live in a house with a man you are that terrified of? I can't do that."

He didn't mention Stevie. Just me. Had he always done that, and I hadn't noticed? I tried to think back to other decisions and plans we had made. Did he always just talk about me and him? Or had he mentioned Stevie? Would I have missed that when my world revolved around her? His concern was for me, and he hadn't even brought her up or asked where she was right now. He wasn't worried about her.

Linc was.

I was doing what was best for her.

"Stevie wants to know him. She wants us to live there for a year. She deserves to know her father."

"The one you are so scared of that you are afraid of us taking this to court? That father? Because he sounds like a psycho. Not all parents are worthy of knowing their kids."

My face felt hot, and I clenched my fists until I felt my nails biting into my palms. "He isn't a psycho. He would kill for her. He is already completely taken with her, and she is with him too."

"You said *kill* like it's a good thing, Branwen. What has gotten into you? You were gone for three days, and I feel like I am talking to a completely different person."

Linc. He was in my head. In my life. He always seemed to throw it off-balance. Change its course.

"I didn't come here to ask you to understand. I came to tell you the truth and to apologize." I unclenched my hands and slid the diamond off my finger. "I'm sorry."

"What are you doing?" he asked me, his tone no longer angry but softer.

"I can't keep this," I told him. "And I left the car at your house. I have the fob for you."

He shook his head and grabbed my wrist, then put the ring back on my finger. "You aren't taking this off. He wants to know his daughter. I'll live with it. But he doesn't get to have you too. I love you, and we are getting married. We'll wait a year. That's fine."

"He lives more than six hours from here, Hudson."

"I don't care. I'll drive to you. We can meet halfway. But I will not lose you, Branwen. I won't."

I stared up at him, baffled by this. I hadn't expected this outcome.

"He is going to want us to live close to him when the year is over. He wants to see Stevie regularly."

"Divorced parents do this all the time. There are ways to make it work. We have a year to figure it out. But this ring stays on your finger. That car is yours. You will still need a car. Take it with you." He let go of my hand and cupped my face with both of his. "You lied. I forgive you. I will always forgive you."

This wasn't good. My gut told me it would prolong the inevitable, but right now, I was too emotionally drained to keep fighting. I simply nodded, knowing I would regret this.

EIGHTEEN

BRANWEN

There was no way to stop him unless I made a scene. I had to let him walk me out to the limo. But it should be fine. Linc wasn't jealous of Hudson because of me. He just didn't want Stevie calling him Dad.

This was not how I had seen today going. The way he'd reacted? Yes, that was pretty spot-on. But not breaking things off with me? That had been a surprise.

I had already convinced myself that he was going to call off the wedding and I'd realized that he deserved someone who loved him. However, he was not listening to me, and if I stayed in here any longer, I feared Linc would come looking for me. Stevie was going to get hungry, and Linc also had a plane waiting on us. What harm would it do to leave here with things like they were? Hudson knew the truth for the most part—at least what I could tell him—and when this situation became too hard, he could break it off. A long-distance relationship with me living in Linc's house was a long shot.

I waved at my fellow coworkers and told them hello as they called out to me. Hudson held my hand in his as we went outside the building. My heart was racing, but there was no need. Hudson was my fiancé after all. Linc knew that. Just like he knew I wanted to marry Hudson. He didn't care.

"There." I nodded toward the Bentley.

Hudson squinted against the bright sun. "The limo?" he asked.

"Yes."

He shifted his eyes to me. "Does he always travel by limo?" There was a mocking tone and expression that came with that question.

"No. He normally drives a truck. He just didn't want Stevie to be uncomfortable on the long drive," I explained.

"It's six hours. Not fifteen."

I shrugged. "I know, but..." What was I supposed to say to that?

He was right, of course, but Linc was going to spoil his daughter, and I couldn't seem to stop it.

Hudson slid a finger under my chin and tilted my head back, as if he were taller than he was and it was necessary. "It doesn't matter. He can do what he wants for Stevie. I'm just worried about me and you. That's all I care about."

He leaned down and pressed his lips to mine. Typically, I could enjoy his kisses, but the way he had once again blown off Stevie, as if she and I weren't a package deal, bothered me. When he straightened, a smug smile touched his lips, as if he'd won something. Had that been for Linc to see?

"Come on," he said and began walking toward the Bentley.

The driver-slash-bodyguard stepped out of the car and went to stand in front of the back door with his arms crossed over his chest.

"What's with the Secret Service?" Hudson asked sarcastically.

He had noticed the driver wasn't your typical chauffeur, but then it was hard not to with his towering frame and build.

"Like I told you, he is powerful," I whispered.

"Looks pretentious to me. Besides, how dangerous can he be if he needs his own bodyguard? I'd think he could defend himself."

I sighed. "The security is for Stevie. Not him. He'd likely take down anyone before the giant could. That's just backup."

Hudson snorted and looked amused. "Whatever. Call me tonight when you can. We will talk more about things."

I hadn't been calling him because lying to him about where I was and what I was doing felt wrong. Hearing his voice would have only made it worse. But he knew now, and talking to him might be what got me through this. At least until I adjusted to this change.

"Okay. I'm going to give it a week, then start looking for a job. So, if you get a call from a dental practice about me, make that referral a good one." I added the last part teasingly.

I'd worried about that before, but it seemed Hudson loved me more than I'd realized.

"That won't be hard to do. But could you stick with an old man or a female dentist? I'm already having to accept your living under another man's roof. If you are working for a male dentist, all I will be able to think about is the hard-on he's going to have while working for you."

I jerked my eyes off the car and looked up at him, then let out a startled laugh. Hudson never said things like that to me. "What?"

His eyes met mine. "You heard me, Branwen. Don't act like you didn't know I had been salivating over you since day one."

I mean…I had known he was attracted to me, but he'd never said it like that before.

Just before we reached the door, the driver opened it, then stood in front of Hudson, blocking him from getting closer, while he held out a hand for me to proceed. This was awkward. I should have thought of this. Of course Linc wouldn't want him near the vehicle. Hudson backed up looking startled.

"I, uh…well, this is as far as you go," I explained, wincing.

He raised his eyebrows. "Seriously? Stevie is going to be my stepdaughter. She doesn't need protecting from me."

"I know," I replied quietly, not wanting Linc to hear us. That might cause a problem. "It's just…" I said gently, placing a hand on his chest. "This is new. All of it. For all of us. Give it some time."

Hudson glared at the vehicle, and the driver took a step toward him and tilted his head down to look at him. I wasn't sure if that was meant to be a warning or a challenge, but I was going with both.

"Please just go back inside," I pleaded.

Although he was trying to appear like he wasn't scared of the man, his skin had paled, and his eyes were wary. This was never going to work. He'd see soon enough that it was best to end it.

Hudson barely nodded his head. "Okay. Go get your car and drive it back. You need it, and it's yours. I want to know you have something safe to drive in."

I was ninety-five percent sure Linc wasn't going to let me go get that car. I needed to give him the fob back, but he did have the second one at his house. It had come with two of them. I could always mail this one to him. Arguing with him about it with the current audience we had wasn't smart.

I opened my mouth to tell him okay when the door on the other side of the limo opened. My head snapped around, and my stomach sank as Linc stepped out. I shouldn't have let Hudson come out here. Shit!

Linc placed his cowboy hat on his head, then pulled something from his back pocket. I moved quickly to stand between him and Hudson. But when he turned around, I realized he hadn't reached for his gun. He stuck a cigarette between his lips and was holding a lighter up to the tip. His eyes brushed past Hudson as the flame went out, and he tucked it back into his pocket. When his eyes met mine, I let out the breath I had been holding. He didn't look ready to kill anyone. He just appeared bored.

"She's asleep," he drawled. "If y'all are gonna keep talking, then I need a smoke."

When he leaned against the limo casually, like some badass cowboy from a movie, the tension radiating off Hudson just got worse. I could feel it, and I wanted to slap my hand over his mouth to keep him from saying anything that might make Linc pull the gun he kept on him at all times. If Stevie were awake, then there was a chance he wouldn't, but with her asleep, Hudson wasn't safe.

"The doors are open," Hudson said tightly. "The smoke can drift inside, and that's not good for Stevie's lungs."

Oh God. Why couldn't he keep his mouth shut?

Linc's gaze shifted to him slowly. As if it were a chore he didn't enjoy. "Then, I reckon you oughta shut the fuck up and let Branwen inside the limo."

I turned to look at Hudson, placing both hands on his chest to try and get his attention. He could not react to Linc.

"It's fine," I almost hissed. "We need to go. I'll call you tonight."

"Gotta admit, I didn't think you'd keep that tiny diamond on her finger after you found out she'd be living with another man for a year."

I closed my eyes for a moment and sucked in a breath. He was purposely trying to get a rise out of Hudson. This wasn't a game, and if it were, he had already won. So, he had no reason to do this.

"I trust her." Hudson's anger was heavy in his tone.

Linc let out a deep chuckle. "Do you now?" There was a pause, but I didn't turn to look at him. "Aren't you a little old to let a pretty face get in your head?"

Hudson's body was rigid. He was going to walk right into whatever Linc was doing. Defusing the situation was the only way to end this. I had no control over Linc, but it seemed I did over Hudson.

"Ignore him. He is trying to piss you off," I whispered, pushing at his chest, but he wasn't budging.

"Not that it's your business, but I love Branwen. What we have is real, and this ridiculous setup you are forcing on her isn't going to change that. She might be scared of you, but I'm not. I've got the best lawyers in this city at my disposal."

Another chuckle, but this one held a threat that I wasn't sure Hudson would pick up on. It was dark and sinister. There were no rules for Linc. Hudson hadn't believed me when I explained that inside.

"You go right on ahead with that," Linc replied. "Branwen." My name came out as a demand in a sharp snap.

Having no choice, I turned to face him, letting my hands fall from Hudson's chest.

He inhaled deeply, then took the cigarette from his lips. "Get in the limo."

The glint in his eyes made it clear that if I didn't do exactly as he said, then this would get ugly. But leaving Hudson alone out here with him wasn't smart either.

Lifting my chin, I glared back at him. "Only if you do."

A slow smile spread across his mouth, and he took another pull from the cigarette, then dropped it, covering it with his boot. "What's wrong, Dollface? You afraid the dentist won't be safe without you to stand in front of him?"

Dollface. That was what he'd called me in Vegas. My face heated at the reminder of the things he'd done to me while calling me that. Damn him.

"Linc, please get in," I tried pleading. Demanding anything of him would never work.

"All right, but only because you asked so sweet," he replied, then winked at me, reaching up to take his cowboy hat off so he could get inside.

The driver moved aside for me, and his cold expression stayed on Hudson. I moved to get in, watching Linc to make sure he did the same.

With a smirk, he lowered himself, then slid back into the vehicle. I didn't dare glance back at Hudson as I hurried to get inside too. He would be upset that I had gotten in without saying anything more, but this was for him. I didn't want to see how much further Linc could be pushed before he reacted.

`The door closed once I was in and seated. My eyes went to the dark tinted window, and I looked out at Hudson. He was hurt. He was also angry, but the pain in his expression was more visible. I knew he couldn't see me, but he still stayed there as the limo began to move away. I should have ended things. He was just going to continue to get hurt by this. By us.

"He's got small hands," Linc said, snapping my gaze from the fading view of Hudson to him.

"They're perfectly sized for him. He's not as tall as you are," I bit out, annoyed with him.

He smirked. "Small hands, small dick."

I rolled my eyes. I wasn't going to defend the size of Hudson's penis. It was average in length and girth. About the same size as Bastian's. Not everyone had monster-sized ones like Linc did. In fact, if I hadn't been intoxicated, it would have probably been painful. No woman wanted to be stretched that much.

I dropped my eyes to my phone as it vibrated with a text. I sighed and swiped my finger over the screen.

Hudson: You went the wrong way. Are you not going to get your car? What will you drive?

I couldn't ask, and not because Linc would just say no, but because it was one last connection to Hudson. I didn't need to be driving something around that he had bought for me. It would make my not letting him go free worse. But he had been so adamant that we would work. That he wanted to wait. Because he loved me.

Branwen: I can't. We are headed to an airstrip and flying back.

I wanted to add that I was sorry, but there was so much to be sorry for that I didn't know where to begin.

"He's a stage one clinger. No woman's cunt is that damn magical." Linc's deep drawl snapped me out of my thoughts and away from watching the dots on the screen as Hudson typed.

Ignoring his remark was the smart thing to do, but I chose to be stupid.

"Not every man is led by his penis." I whispered the last word, just in case Stevie wasn't completely asleep.

The corner of Linc's mouth quirked as his hooded gaze watched me, making my entire body rebel against me as it tingled.

"You're right. I'm not. But the dentist is. You're probably the hottest piece of ass he's ever had."

I opened my mouth to tell him that Hudson's ex was gorgeous when my phone vibrated, and I looked back down at it.

Hudson: I've got a root canal to do. Call me tonight.

After all that typing, that was it? He must have erased whatever he was going to say.

Branwen: I will.

I turned to look out the window instead of continuing the conversation with Linc. When the limo turned onto a road I'd never been down, Stevie yawned, drawing my attention to her. Both small fists were rubbing her eyes as she stretched out her legs. The first smile I'd had since dealing with Hudson spread across my face as I watched her.

She opened her eyes slowly, and they met mine. The soft, happy grin that appeared on her face made my heart warm. She was my cure for everything.

"Hello, sunshine," I said.

She giggled, then turned her head to look over at Linc. Watching her expression brighten at the sight of him reminded me why I could do this. I owed it to her.

My eyes shifted to Linc. He wasn't just in awe of her; he already loved her. It made the other things he said and did less important.

"Awah we going to the stowah now?" she asked him.

He shifted in his seat, leaning forward slightly to look around her and out the window. "No need to go to the store," he told her. "I believe everything you want might be inside there."

He pointed to the window, and she turned her head to see the jet that sat parked out on the runway.

"A plane!" she squealed, her eyes as wide as saucers as the tip of her little finger pressed against the glass. "Mommy! It's a plane, and my Bluey toys awah in it!"

I had known this was going to thrill her. The Bluey toys would have been forgotten when she saw it, but it wasn't enough that Linc had a plane flying us back; he had to have the toys waiting inside it for her.

"I see that," I replied. "You're going to get to fly. That's exciting."

She nodded her head, and her curls bounced.

"Yeah! Let's go." She began to tug at the buckle and work to unlatch it.

The limo door opened about that time, and she kicked with glee. Linc reached over and helped her with the release button.

She looked up at the driver. "I'm gonna wide on that plane!" she told him.

His mouth almost smiled, and he nodded his head once. The man never spoke. I didn't even know his name. He held out a hand to her as she scrambled out of her seat and started to exit the car. Without hesitation, she placed her tiny one in his and let him help her.

Linc had already exited the limo and was walking around to get her before she was completely out. I stepped onto the asphalt and thanked the driver before following Stevie, who now had her hand clasped with her father's. She was skipping as she went beside him toward the plane. They made a sight that would melt the coldest of hearts. Rough and rugged cowboy, holding hands with a small pixie.

I held up my phone and took a picture. It was one of those things I wanted to keep. When this got too hard, it'd remind me of why I was doing it. Not just because Linc had left me with little choice, but because of Stevie too.

NINETEEN

LINC

Along with the Bluey items that Stevie had wanted, I had asked for every available Bluey item. There was a plane—which was her favorite, it seemed—an ice cream stand, a kitchen set, cell phone, dolls of all the characters, a beach towel, a chair for her to sit in, and a cash register. While Stevie was ecstatic and I enjoyed the fuck out of watching her, Branwen had a different reaction. She wasn't pleased. But Stevie was, and that was all I gave a shit about. Maybe giving a kid everything was a bad idea, but fuck it. I'd missed four goddamn years of buying her things.

With the knowledge of who Branwen was, I wanted to study her more. See if there was anything of the girl I remembered there. I'd immediately seen it in Stevie the moment I got off the phone with Garrett. It was like blinders had been ripped off my eyes, and I wondered how the fuck I had missed it. I couldn't *not* see the little girl at the stables when I looked at Stevie.

Stevie was making a plate of pretend food and taking it to her mother. I watched them as I took a drink from my glass of whiskey the attendant had brought me.

I hadn't expected the dentist to handle it as well as he had. I wanted him out of Stevie's life. No other man was going to act like her father. She had me.

Seeing him put his hands on Branwen and kiss her had pissed me off. It shouldn't have, and I didn't like that it had. Stevie was mine, not Branwen. She'd lied to me. Kept my kid from me. I should despise the sight of her. I'd kill a man for less.

If she wasn't so fucking gorgeous, then it would be easier to hate her. The flashbacks of her tight cunt weren't helping me either. I wasn't sure how much of it was real and how much of it was just from the dreams I'd had about her since that night. My subconscious had conjured her up—and still did often. Many times, my head was between her legs, like a crazed man who couldn't get enough of her taste. She'd either tasted like a candy with a hint of lemon or I'd made that shit up in my head. I had eaten a lot of pussies, and they were either slightly salty, metallic, or perfumy, like they'd sprayed it, which always turned me off, and then some had no taste. None had tasted sweet or lemony. I'd even kept bags of hard lemon candy so I had it to suck on when I woke up from dreaming about licking her cunt for well over a year after fucking her.

Maybe my dreams had been memories. Looking at her could get a dick hard. If she truly fucked and tasted like my dreams said she did, then getting rid of the dentist might be harder than I'd thought it would be. Problem was, when I got rid of him, another one would come along. When I moved her into somewhere else in a year, she'd get a job and meet people, like a man who wanted her.

I tossed back the rest of the amber liquid in my glass. I wanted to punish her for what she'd done to me and to Stevie. Make her pay for it. Have her feel half of what I did when I thought of the years I'd lost with my daughter.

I also wanted to fuck her. Get my mouth on her pussy. See those big pink nipples. Suck on them. Hear her scream while I stretched her and slammed into her tight hole over and over. I might not get owned by a cunt, but I could make one addicted to my dick. I could control her with it. Keep her from bringing another man into my daughter's life. I didn't have to like her. I sure as hell would never love her. But that didn't mean fucking her was off the table. It would fix this dentist shit. Get him to move on without violence being required.

Just thinking about it had my cock throbbing painfully.

"Can I get you another drink, Mr. Shephard?" the attractive brunette asked, bending down in front of me to take my glass, taking her time. She knew her tits were pushed up and right in my direct view.

I didn't know her name, but she'd been an attendant for us more than once. Luther had bent her over one of the sofas and fucked her on a flight while I watched. Her tits weren't that big from what I could remember of them bouncing as he pounded into her, but they were nice.

When I lifted my gaze from her cleavage to her eyes, the invitation was clear. She stood up, smiling at me, then walked back to the front of the plane, closing the door behind her. I could sit here with my raging hard dick, thinking about the dirty shit I wanted to do to Branwen, or go let the pretty attendant's mouth suck me off.

I chose the latter. When I stood up, Stevie was too busy with one of her toys to notice, but Branwen's eyes met mine. Thinking about how they looked, hooded and needy, only made my erection worse. I headed in the direction the attendant had gone, making sure to lock the door behind me. I knew it was soundproof for the purpose of needing privacy in the main cabin.

The girl turned around, and her eyes flared with want when she saw me. She couldn't be older than twenty-five, but I didn't give a shit. She had a mouth, and she was hungry for it.

"Get on your knees," I told her as I unzipped my jeans, needing to free my cock. I shoved them down, along with my boxers, and all ten inches of my dick stood erect against my hard lower stomach.

"Oh God," she breathed, kneeling in front of me.

The angry, swollen head was leaking pre-cum, and she ran her fingertip over it, then stuck it in her mouth and moaned like she enjoyed the taste. As nice as her little show was, I wanted to come. I didn't have time for her to do sexy shit. I was already fucking hard.

I grabbed her dark hair and fisted it in my hand. "Suck it," I ordered and gave her no other option as I took my dick in my other hand and guided it into her mouth.

Most women I had suck me off were professionals at taking it down their throat. I liked to be balls deep, but it was a lot of cock to take.

"Open your throat and let it all in, or I'll slam it down," I warned as the head was encased by a warm, wet hole.

Fuck, that was it. Just what I needed. It continued to go further, and I smirked and glanced down at her. Maybe she was a professional. She wasn't even gagging yet. I eased up on her hair and groaned.

"Ah, yeah, that's good."

She made a sound, and I closed my eyes and laid my head back on the wall behind me. No need to instruct this one.

She was clearly used to having a cock in her mouth. I'd have to remember this. Request her more often. A gag came when it was three-fourths of the way in, and I let the image in my mind take over.

It wasn't the brunette, but a blonde head down there. I could see my cock bulging in her slim throat. Tears running down the sides of her face as I sank fully into her. The nails that clawed down my thighs were red, and jade eyes stared up at me with wet, spiky lashes. God, she was even more gorgeous like this, and I hadn't thought it was possible for her to get any better.

"Take my dick like a good girl," I rasped as the pleasure pulsed through me.

Her head began to bob as she ran her tongue along it, gagging every time I went balls deep.

"Ah, baby. That's it. Suck my cock like a little slut. Such a pretty little thing. You want it, don't you?" I was lost in my own fantasy. And the scene taking place in my head was going to make me come fast. "You want my cum?" I panted. "I'm gonna give it to you. Shoot my load down your tight throat, just like I did your cunt."

My balls tightened, and the tingles started. I gripped her hair tighter, keeping my eyes closed. The image in my head was what I wanted to see when I shot off. The mouth I wanted my seed to fill was one I also wanted to punish.

"Yeah, fuck. Fuck, that's it. Fucking keep gagging. That's what you deserve," I ground out through gritted teeth. "I'm gonna make you pay for it."

More tears fell from her eyes, and she whimpered.

"That's—GAH. Dammit, yesss." My body jerked as my dick exploded. "Ah, God, Ringlets, baby, fuck." I fell back against the wall, letting go of the hair I'd been holding, hating that I had to open my eyes.

When she let my dick pop free of her mouth, I straightened and reached for my boxers and jeans, then pulled them up. The attendant stood, and I knew she'd told us her name when we boarded, but I couldn't remember it. Not that it mattered. She'd served a purpose, and I'd tip her well for it. Not only had she given me an excellent blow job, but I'd realized exactly what I was going to do about Branwen.

"Do you need me for anything else, sir?" she asked.

I looked down at her as she batted her eyes up at me. "No, that'll be all."

TWENTY
BRANWEN

Stevie ate a Popsicle while wrapped in a towel, sitting on the lounger beside me. She had been swimming for two hours, and my guess was, she was going to need a nap soon. Today had been a more pleasant experience as compared to yesterday. By the time we had gotten off the plane, I'd been so angry and emotionally spent, trying to act like I was fine for Stevie's sake, that I had gone to bed, dreading the next three hundred sixty-four days.

After successfully ignoring Linc during breakfast, he had said he had to go handle some work and would be gone until late. I wanted to cheer with relief. Stevie pouted. Having been on the receiving end of that pout many times, I knew its power. Linc promised her a movie night with ice cream sundaes and said he would bring her back a surprise. That sent her flinging her arms around his legs and thanking him and calling him Dad. The scene was almost enough to soften me up.

But then I remembered he had gone and had sex with that young flight attendant, Leslie, with Stevie on the plane. We didn't hear or see anything, and rationally, I knew that Stevie had no idea what he was doing, but I did. It had been disrespectful, and if he thought he was going to parade women in and out of this house in front of her, he had another thing coming. I didn't know how I was going to stop him, but I was working on that.

My not speaking to him had no effect. He hadn't even noticed.

I wasn't who he wanted to spend time with anyway. I was just the baggage that came along with having Stevie here. God, I wanted to think of something else besides him.

It was a beautiful, sunny day, and Stevie was having a blast. I wanted to soak it in, but right now, I had too many things wearing on me, and I was unable to shut my brain off.

The call with Hudson had been hard, but he had assumed my bad mood was because of us not being together. That seemed to pacify him. I had ended it after ten minutes, telling him I had a headache and needed sleep. He wanted to talk again tonight, which gave me one more thing to dread. Although I might not be invited to this movie night that Linc had promised Stevie. He hadn't looked at me. It was almost as if he was ignoring me, like I was doing to him.

I sighed heavily and glanced back over at Stevie, realizing she had gotten quiet. Her Popsicle stick was thankfully all that was left of the pink treat as it lay in her open hand because she was sound asleep. I leaned forward and took another dry towel and laid it over her. It wasn't cool out, but the wet towel and suit might give her a chill. Sinking back on the plush lounger, I stared up at the slated ceiling that let very little sunlight through. I'd put sunblock on her twice now, so she should be fine to sleep where she was.

The sound of the waterfall as it gushed over the rocks and hit the water might lull me to sleep, too, if I closed my eyes.

At least then, I wouldn't be thinking. I could get rest from the things plaguing me. Just as I decided to give it a try, I heard heavy, booted footsteps, and my eyes snapped open. I turned my head toward the sound to see Linc walking in this direction. He had on a snug-fitting black T-shirt with his jeans today. The sight of his corded, tattooed biceps was eye candy that I did not have any business partaking in.

Without Stevie to talk to him, I was going to be forced to, and vice versa.

He stopped when he reached our cabana lounger.

Not fair, God. So not fair. No man should look like that. It was cruel.

I couldn't blame Leslie for flashing him her cleavage and spreading her legs for him when he went after her. I was sure most women did. Heck, I had done it myself. I wondered if he carried those morning-after pills around in his pocket for all the available vaginas wanting to be filled.

I rolled my eyes behind my sunglasses at the thought.

"I thought you were going to be gone all day," I snapped, aggravated at myself for speaking first.

"You talking to me now?" His drawl sounded amused.

Damn him.

I lifted a shoulder, but said nothing.

He chuckled. "How long is this jealous fit supposed to last?"

I stiffened and glared at him. "I am not jealous. This is not a fit!" I hissed, trying not to yell and wake up Stevie.

He smirked at me. "Like hell it ain't. You haven't said a word to me since I came back from letting the flight attendant suck my cock like she had been begging to. I was unaware your mouth was available. Can't go getting pissed at me for not knowing." He paused, and his eyes went to my mouth, then slowly down my body. "If you want to suck it,

I'm open to negotiations. Starting with you doing it while wearing that bikini."

I sat up straight, feeling several things, but clasping tight to the anger. The others were not to be acknowledged. "I do not want to…suck your…thing, and I don't care who you screw around with," I whispered. "But I don't want you bringing women around in front of Stevie. Keep your…your sex stuff personal and hidden."

His heated gaze didn't meet mine, but instead was on my chest. "Please continue with your hissy fit. Those big tits keep bouncing and jiggling around enough, and a nipple might pop free."

The instant tingle between my legs made them harden as he continued to stare at them. What was he doing? Why was he doing it? My body felt warm, and it had nothing to do with the sun.

"Stop looking at them," I said, reaching over Stevie for my cover-up.

"You put them on display like that, and they're impossible not to look at."

I prayed he did not see the shiver that ran through me. My body was a fool.

Snatching the cover-up and clutching it to my chest, I stared back at him. "What do you want?"

He ran the pad of his thumb over his bottom lip. "That's a loaded question." His gaze flickered to Stevie, then back to me. "Tell me, Branwen, does your pussy taste like lemon candy? Because I have this memory of it."

My breathing was getting heavy, and I had to rub my thighs together because of the ache that had started between them.

"If you don't know, I can check."

I gasped, my eyes going wide. Had he just offered to go down on me?

He leaned down, and I was frozen, unable to move or speak. His hand reached up and took my sunglasses from my eyes, then put them on top of my head. I blinked, staring at him. He was so close that I could smell him. The smoke-and-spice scent only caused my heart rate to speed up.

"It'll just take a second." His deep voice was husky.

I managed to shake my head, and he shushed me. Then, his warm, large hand touched the skin just below my belly button. The breath I sucked in was loud enough for him to hear, and he shushed me again with a small shake of his head. His fingers slid underneath the fabric of my bikini bottoms, and instead of grabbing his wrist and jerking it out, I dropped my eyes to watch him.

Why wasn't I moving? Telling him to stop?

It was if everything had gone into slow motion until he ran his middle finger over my pulsing clit, and I let out a yelp, my eyes flying back up to his face.

"Easy," he said hoarsely with a glint of smug satisfaction in his eyes. "That pussy is soaking wet."

He dipped his finger inside me, then pushed it up into my very deprived entrance, and I had to cover my mouth to muffle my moan.

"Still tight," he said, his low voice sounding almost like a groan. "With a face like yours and a body like this, I'd think someone would be fucking this hole properly, but, damn, it's sucking my finger like it's hungry."

He let out a sadistic laugh and pumped it three times as my mouth fell open and my eyes rolled back in my head. That was so good. His finger was rough and thick. Instead of jerking his hand away, I wanted to hold it there now so I could ride it until I orgasmed. I was so close already. Just a little more.

And then it was gone. I let out a cry, and he stood back up. I wanted to weep, slap him, get up, and rub myself off on his leg. Damn him!

He stuck his middle finger inside his mouth, and I watched as my body trembled from the pleasure that had been snatched away from it. The way he continued to clean off my wetness from his finger was as if he was savoring it.

Hudson and Bastian had told me I tasted sweet before. Bastian hadn't been one for giving pleasure though. He liked to get it. Hudson went down on me often—or at least he used to—but I didn't ever get off on it. Sure, it felt good, but neither of them seemed to know how to use their tongue on me.

Five years ago, when Linc had been between my legs, I had gotten off twice as my body bucked and I pulled his hair like a woman possessed. It had been incredible. That image was all I could think about right now.

He finally pulled his finger from between his lips. "Not a dream," he murmured, then turned and walked away.

I lay there, panting, my clit screaming for attention, and I equally hated and wanted Linc Shephard more than anyone else on earth. It was a twisted truth that I had to accept.

TWENTY-ONE
LINC

Standing under the warm shower, I wrapped my hand around my cock and placed my other palm against the stone wall. I'd leaked so much pre-cum that my fucking boxers had been sticking to me. I was a fifty-five-year-old man who had fucked hundreds of women, but one lemon-candy-tasting pussy milking my finger, and I was ready to erupt.

Jesus Christ, what kind of voodoo did she have? No fucking wonder the dentist had looked ready to run after the limo and hold on with both hands.

I'd just cut him off from her cunt.

He wouldn't be touching it again.

I snarled as I began to pump my cock. That cunt was gonna be mine exclusively.

If Stevie hadn't been next to her at the pool, I'd have ripped Branwen's damn bottoms off and spread her legs open, then feasted. Fuck, it'd tasted incredible, and why was she so damn tight still?

I let the vision of her lying on the lounger like a goddess, opening her long and tanned legs up for me, take over my thoughts. Her cunt glistening with that sweet juice coating it as she squirmed and begged for me.

"Such a pretty pussy," I said, stroking the hard length in my hand.

I imagined listening to her beg for me to fuck her hard. Licking my lips that still tasted like her, I grabbed her ankles and flipped her onto her stomach.

"Put that ass in the air for me. That's it. Show me both your tight holes."

Pulling her butt cheeks apart, I leaned down to spit on the small, puckered pink one. She begged and whimpered. I pressed my fingertip just inside, and a low, sexy moan came from her. Taking my dick, I aligned it with her cunt and pushed it in, just the head, and stilled. Her cries got louder.

"Such a dirty girl, letting me fuck you and play with your ass at the same time. Oh fuck, baby. That's it. Bounce back on my cock. Slap those perfect, plump cheeks against me. Fuck, that pussy is tight." I squeezed my dick harder, my groans and pants the only other sounds in the shower. "You like my finger in your ass? Beg for more. You're gonna let me fuck that hole too. Shoot my load deep inside, then watch it ooze out."

The image sent me flying over the edge.

"FUCK!" I shouted.

My cum shot out in thick, creamy ropes, hitting the shower wall. More curses ripped from my chest as I trembled while the last of my seed pumped out of me.

Leaning forward, I rested my forehead on the stone wall. If just thinking about fucking her got me off like that, then what the hell was the actual act going to do? Even when I'd been high, I couldn't stop fucking her. What would I be like sober?

It would be a win-win. I was going to fuck her and punish her. There would be no worshipping at her cunt's altar. I would continue to fuck whoever I wanted and her too. I'd make sure she knew about it. If getting my dick sucked by the flight attendant had made her that angry, then how much would it bother her once I had her obsessed with me? Knowing she couldn't have my cock exclusively. It would never be hers. I would never be hers.

Smirking, I straightened and tilted my head back as the water hit my face. I was going to have to eat her pussy. That was something I wouldn't deprive myself of. Having her obsessed with my tongue, too, would only make it all the better. She'd be rid of the dentist in a week's time, and there would be no other man in my daughter's life. And just like when she had been a kid, Branwen would only want me.

TWENTY-TWO

BRANWEN

I didn't look or speak to Linc during dinner, but Stevie was busy telling him about her day. His eyes felt like lasers locked on me at times, and I almost met them, but didn't. I was strong. The bastard had gone too far, and I refused to be some form of amusement for him.

My plan was to excuse myself after we finished eating and go to my room instead of joining them for movie night. Let them bond over *Moana*, and I would call Hudson.

When Linc stood, chuckling at Stevie's excitement over dessert being in the great room while she watched the movie, I did the same, taking my plate, then going over to pick up Stevie's.

"Jayda will clean the table," Linc told me as I collected the flatware that Stevie hadn't used.

"I'm not leaving my plate at the table. That's rude. She cooked the meal." My words were clipped.

I could see Stevie pulling on his hand in my peripheral vision.

"Come on. Let's go," she urged.

Normally, I would correct that behavior, but he had promised her an ice cream sundae, and she loved ice cream.

"We need to wait on your mom," Linc told her.

With my hands full, I made my way to the sink. "You two go ahead. I'm going to make a phone call after this," I said with my back to him now.

"That doesn't sound like fun, does it?" he asked.

"Nope," Stevie replied. "You gotta come too, Mommy. You love *Moana*."

But I did not love her father. I actually wanted to stay the hell away from him and his arrogant smirk. I began cleaning what was left on the plates into the disposal while trying to think of a way out of this.

"I'll join you after I call Hudson," I told her, glancing over my shoulder and giving her an apologetic smile. *Please just go along with this*, I silently begged her with my eyes.

"Come on, Ringlets. I have a bowl full of cherries waiting for you. I know how much you like to do that little trick where you tie the stem with your tongue."

The plate I was holding clattered loudly as it slipped from my hand, and I stared down at it. I was suddenly lightheaded, and I had to grip the edge of the sink to steady myself. Sucking in a breath as the thud of my heartbeat filled my ears. Stevie was saying something, but I couldn't hear it.

"You—" I choked out the word, my throat tight. I swallowed and tried again. "You know." My words sounded like a raspy whisper, but that was the best I could manage.

He knew who I was. Which meant that he knew that I had known who he was and said nothing. What did this mean?

I tried to calm my racing heart and trembling body so I could think.

A small hand touched mine. "Mommy, awah you okay? You just dwopped the plate. Wemembah that accidents happen," she said, as if to soothe me.

I stared down at her sweet hand on top of mine and inhaled deeply. I could not do this in front of her. He'd chosen this moment to confront me when he had several other options.

"I'm fine," I assured her, doing my best to smile.

"I've got plenty of plates." Linc's voice made my back stiffen. "Now, ladies, let's go have our movie night."

Stevie grabbed my wrist, pulling my hand away from the edge of the sink, and beamed. "YAY!" she said while tugging me to come with her.

Giving in, I turned around, and my eyes met Linc's. The amusement in his gaze didn't seem angry. He was enjoying the reaction he had gotten out of me.

How long had he been holding on to this? Had he known all along? When he had read my name on the marriage certificate, had he realized who I was then and just said nothing?

"Let's go!" Stevie let go of my hand once I was moving in the direction she wanted and ran ahead of us.

Once she was out the door, I wanted to chase after her to save myself from being alone with him. Even if it was for a second.

Keeping my head down so as to not have to look at his face, I followed behind her. The sound of his boots on the hardwood seemed to be all I could hear. My steps quickened, and a deep chuckle rumbled in his chest. I didn't react to it, but continued the *ignoring him* bit and almost caught up with Stevie.

Her loud squeal startled me, and my head snapped up to see her dart into the great room. What had he done now? Hopefully, he hadn't bought every Moana toy ever made.

When I stepped into the room, I stopped and took in the table, where Stevie was currently scanning the items that filled it. He'd had Jayda set up an ice cream sundae bar. There were at least thirty toppings, arranged in clear containers of every shape and size. The centerpiece was a chocolate fountain. It was Instagram-worthy.

A hand slid around my waist and flattened on my stomach. The warmth of his body closed in behind me. I was frozen, except for my gaze as it dropped to stare at his touch. His large hand almost covered the entire area.

"You didn't think I wouldn't figure it out, did you, Ringlets?" his voice, close to my ear, said in a husky whisper. "You oughta know better than that. Keeping things from me isn't possible."

I shivered as he took a lock of my hair and twirled it around his finger.

"That sweet little girl...she'd have told me." His voice was heavy with disappointment. As if he had the right to that.

He had been the one to disappoint me. If he wanted to play that card, he needed to get in line. I was there first.

"She'd have done anything for my attention," he told me as his lips brushed the edge of my ear, causing me to shiver. "Why not now? Hmm?"

"Mommy! Look at all the chocolate!" Stevie cried out with glee, spinning around to look back at us.

He was gone so quickly that I had to grab the doorframe to steady myself. My smile was wobbly as I nodded my head. His scent was still wrapped around me with each breath I took. The spot on my stomach where his hand had been felt as if he had branded it with a hot iron.

"I reckon all you need is a bowl," Linc said, stepping around me and heading in her direction.

Her eyes stared up at him with complete adoration. It hadn't taken him long to win over his daughter—not that he would have had to work at it as hard as he had with extravagant gifts, a private plane, and now this. He might as well be Daddy Warbucks, and she'd be his Annie.

My phone vibrated in the pocket of my leggings, and I ignored it. I knew who it was, and right now, I wasn't going to be able to talk to Hudson or respond to his text. I had a movie to get through with a man I didn't know if I trusted or not.

"Which ice cweam is oat milk?" Stevie asked him as he handed her a bowl.

There were three different ice cream flavors—chocolate, strawberry, and vanilla—displayed in a serving piece that seemed to also be a freezing unit so that it didn't melt. Stevie was on her tiptoes, peering up at them with interest.

"All of them are. Take your pick," Linc informed her.

"Weally?" she asked in amazement. "I want all thwee!"

Linc grinned down at her and went to scoop her some from each vat. I would normally say something about the portion size, but right now, that was the least of my worries. The less I had to talk, the better.

As soon as she had three scoops in her bowl, she went to the chocolate fountain. He went behind her and showed her how to hold her bowl. I watched them for a moment. Memories I had repressed, not allowing myself to dwell on them, hit me, one right after another.

It was only when he did things like this that I saw a glimpse of the guy I had once known. Because the man he had become was someone altogether different.

TWENTY-SIX YEARS AGO

The chaos around me felt a thousand miles away. My chest ached with every sob that racked my body. I heard a siren in the distance. The smell of hay, horses, and cigarettes was the only constant around me. The rest…the rest was my world tilted on its axis.

No one was telling me what had happened or why my daddy had collapsed on the ground.

I'd run to him, but never made it, Kenneth—had stopped me. His hands clamping over my shoulders and holding me back as others began to call out and rush to Daddy.

One of the stablehands, Patrick, was doing CPR on him. I screamed for him, but Kenneth held on to me, telling me it was okay. That I needed to let them work on my daddy. It wasn't okay though. My wails tore from me as he continued to lie there, not moving.

This wasn't real. It couldn't be. My daddy was larger than life.

Just this morning, he had come into my room at five, like he always did, singing "Wake Up Little Susie" by The Everly Brothers. I groaned and threw my pillow at him. The full belly laugh from him had been followed by him telling me the bacon was going to get cold.

He wasn't sick. Why was he not sitting up?

The siren was louder, and the roar in my head, along with more voices yelling, began to pull me under.

Then, I heard him. Not my dad, but Linc's voice. When I turned around, Kenneth let go of me, and I saw Linc taking long, quick strides toward me. I let out a loud sob, then broke into a run. He would make this better. I just had to get to him.

When I reached him, he opened his arms, and I threw myself into them. He held me against his chest, and my tears soaked the front of his T-shirt. "I got you. Shhh," his tone was meant to soothe, although not even Linc could do that. Not when my daddy wouldn't get up off the ground.

"He's gone," I heard someone say, and I fisted Linc's shirt in my hands.

"Fuck." Linc's voice was laced with pain.

I knew. He didn't have to tell me; I knew it.

My daddy was never going to get up. Linc's arms tightened around me as he rocked me back and forth. He didn't lie to me and say it was going to be okay, like Kenneth had. He said nothing, just let me cry. While the grief engulfed me, Linc kept me from going under with it.

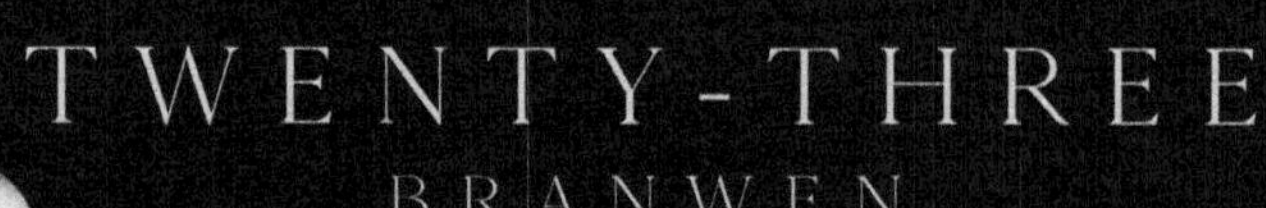

TWENTY-THREE

BRANWEN

Present Day

Leave it to Stevie to fall asleep after eating all that sugar. I had been sure she'd stay awake until the movie ended. One hour in, and her eyes had closed.

I knew Linc was watching me and not the movie. If he was trying to rattle me, he had already succeeded at that.

"Unless you want to be sure that Moana returns the heart of Te Fiti, I think we can call it a night," I said, glancing from Stevie up to him.

"I'll carry her," he said, standing.

I didn't argue. I was used to carrying her to bed after she fell asleep on the sofa, but not that far and not upstairs. I just hoped he laid her in bed, then left. There was so much of this house I hadn't seen or been to, and I wasn't sure where Linc's bedroom was located. I imagined it was on the opposite end though. I didn't think he would want his privacy invaded completely.

He scooped her up in his arms effortlessly, and I stood up to follow them. The ice cream bar was still sitting out, and I wondered if it would be out all night or if Jayda was coming to put it away. I started to ask, but stopped myself. I didn't know where anything went, and being down here alone, where he could come back and try to discuss my not telling him who I was, was a risk I didn't want to take.

There were also going to be a few missed calls and texts from Hudson. My phone had vibrated several times. Dealing with him felt exhausting. I wanted a bubble bath and to crawl into bed. Tomorrow would be another day to face.

Linc's shirt was stretched tight across his back, making it easy to see every flex of his muscles as he walked up the stairs with Stevie. My eyes drifted down to his butt, and I wished I could stop looking at this man. It would make my life so much easier. Ignoring him was impossible.

Tonight, the distance from the great room to our bedrooms seemed to have become extended. Never-ending. Or it was because I was being taunted by Linc's body after what he'd done to me outside today.

Finally, we were outside Stevie's bedroom, and I wanted to sigh in relief. Now, he could go, and I could get alone time. Much-needed alone time. Some I had needed since he'd left me aching. I didn't need his fingers when I had my trusty, faithful vibrator. It had never failed to get me there.

Standing back, I waited until he was done before I went to tuck her in properly, but he began doing it after laying her down. She curled into the covers and buried her nose in the pillow. Linc stood over her, watching, and the stupid emotions that came from the sight of that were unwanted. I pushed them back.

He glanced back at me, and the corners of his mouth quirked. "She looks exactly like you did."

I knew that. I'd shown her pictures of me as a child, and she'd been convinced it was her. I had proven it wasn't by pointing out her eye color.

I just nodded, saying nothing. Glancing at Stevie one more time to make sure she was good for the night, I then headed for the door. If Linc wanted to watch her sleep, then he could do so. I'd done it plenty of times in her life, so I understood it.

Turning the knob on my door, I heard the one behind me close. I pushed mine open, ready to escape. I hurried inside then started to shut it when Linc's hand reached out, and his palm hit the door with a solid thud, stopping my effort to get away from him. My eyes went from his hand to meet his gaze, and he smirked at me.

"Not even a good night, Ringlets?" he drawled.

"Don't call me that," I snapped.

He pushed the door open further and stepped closer to me. "Why not? I thought you liked that nickname."

I moved back two steps, not liking that I could smell him. "Because I am not that little girl anymore," I said angrily.

His eyes drifted down my body, and I hated the warmth that started stirring in my belly.

"No, you definitely are not." His voice deepened. "I knew you were gonna be a beauty, but, damn, I had no idea you'd turn into this."

I didn't need him to tell me that "this" was a compliment. His eyes said it for him as he eyed me hungrily.

Slowly, his gaze traveled back up to my face.

"If you're done, I want to go to bed," I said, crossing my arms over my chest to hide my hardening nipples.

"You're so angry." He took a step toward me. "Why is that? Did I not have everything you liked at the sundae bar? And you didn't eat one of the cherries."

He was playing games with me, and this had to stop. Mentally, I could not handle this. But telling him that he affected me would show him my weakness, and a man like Linc did not need that power. He had enough already.

I took another step back, and he continued closing the distance until my back hit the wall. An almost chuckle came out in a breath, and he reached up to cup the side of my face.

His thumb brushed over my lips. "In Vegas, you showed me how you could use your tongue and tied at least five cherry stems into a knot. Why not tonight?"

I didn't respond, but focused on breathing normally. Acting unaffected. Although the area between my legs was anything but.

"I have an idea to loosen you up." The gravelly tone in his voice made it very difficult for me not to press against him and bury my nose in his chest. Inhale and soak him in. "Why don't you take off these tight-ass pants that you've been teasing me with all night and your wet panties, then lie on the bed and spread your legs? I'll lick and tongue-fuck your pussy. You can pull my hair while you come in my mouth."

My knees buckled slightly, and I sucked in a breath.

His hand went to my waist and held on to me. "Easy, Ringlets," he said gently.

Blinking, I stood there, considering it. Yes, I was that stupid. But I knew what his tongue could do, and I wanted it. The regret that would come was the only thing keeping me from doing exactly as he'd said. His fingers began to slide into the waist of my pants, and I shook my head.

"No," I breathed.

"Shh," he whispered, bending his head and brushing his lips against my temple.

"Stop," I said with a little more force as the tips of his fingers made it inside my panties.

"It's okay," he whispered against my skin. His breath smelled of mint and whiskey. "I left it wet and swollen today. Let me take care of you."

With my body screaming *yes* and my head shouting back *no*, I shook my head again as I trembled and panted for breath. I was going to come the second he touched me, and I didn't want him to have the satisfaction, but the urgency to feel it was taking over. My body was winning the battle.

His middle finger slid between my folds as his hand cupped me. "You keep telling me no, but your pussy is so wet that it soaked through your pants." His tone was scolding. "When are you gonna stop lying to me, Ringlets? Where did my good girl go?"

Using his fingertip, he circled my entrance slowly, then ran it up to my clit and did the same to it. The pulsing was almost painful, as its need for attention turned fierce. My head dropped forward against his chest, and I grabbed his arms to keep from falling to the floor.

"You don't want me to stop, do you?"

His words taunted me. I didn't care. I just wanted that release.

"You're dripping with need. Let me lick it up for you."

"Oh God." The words tore out of me, and I shook from the thought of it.

"That's right. I'm your god. I take care of all your needs. You just have to be my good girl." His teeth nipped my earlobe. "Go lie on the bed."

My brain did its best to stop me. To remind me why this was a bad idea. But the desire had become my demon, and I was weak.

He continued to tease around my clit without touching it. "I can feel your clit throb. Let me lick it." His tongue swiped at my neck. "Suck on it. I want your pussy juices in my beard so I can smell you."

That was it. I nodded, and he stepped back enough to let me move to the bed. My body was so worked up that I struggled to get my bottoms off. With Linc's eyes on me, it was even harder. Once I had them to my ankles and kicked them off, I turned and climbed onto the bed.

"Wait." Linc's hand grabbed my left thigh and held me still. "Stick your ass in the air, then spread your legs and show me that pussy."

As if I needed anything more to make me crazed. I laid my cheek against the bed and did as he'd said, widening my legs.

"Better than my imagination," he said gruffly.

The mattress sank in as he moved in behind me. His warm breath had me gripping handfuls of the cover beneath me. The first swipe of his tongue made me jolt as a whimper came from me.

"Fuck, that's incredible. That's a good girl's pussy," he praised, then ran his tongue from my folds to my other hole.

I tensed as his tongue circled the forbidden, untouched spot. It felt taboo and dirty, yet I felt a small gush, and my excitement began to trickle down my thighs.

I rocked my hips. "Please," I begged.

Linc's mouth moved back toward where I needed him most, and this time, he didn't stop. His tongue flicked my clit, and I cried out, then buried my face in the mattress to muffle it. He began to lick, then gently sucked as he thrust a finger inside me.

The world became a colorful explosion as I shuddered in bliss. With the release of my pleasure, Linc's tongue became more frantic, and my muffled scream filled the room. My legs were going to collapse.

"No!" Linc barked the order as the cool air hit where he had been.

His hand squeezed my butt, and then I heard the sound of his zipper. My head snapped up. I shouldn't have done this, but sex was definitely out of the question.

I opened my mouth to tell him that I wasn't having sex with him and tried to move, but he slapped his hand against my ass. The sight of his thick, hard, veiny cock caused my words to get stuck in my throat. I'd forgotten how incredible it was.

He slid a hand back between my legs, and I moaned as he coated his fingers with me. With his other hand, he gripped his erection and slowly began to pump it. His eyes locked on what he was doing to me. He trailed the tip of his finger up until it was back at my tight, clenched hole.

"No," I gasped as panic began to stir in place of the pleasure.

"Shh," he said as he caressed the spot. "I'm just going to play with it. Relax."

Play with it? I stared up at him, wide-eyed.

His hooded eyes flared with lust. I started to feel more comfortable with this, getting distracted by his face. Then, he pushed in with his finger, and I yelped, tightening up.

"Easy," he groaned. "Just let me play." His eyes met mine, and the blue was almost black. "Your ass is as fucking perfect as the rest of you."

I decided that if touching me there was putting that look on his face, then I could let him.

I nodded and tried not to tense up as he continued to stroke himself while he poked gently at the puckered entrance. When I completely unclenched, his fingertip went in farther, and I let out a strangled moan.

"That's it," he panted, his hand moving faster over his erection.

It slid farther in, and I held my breath, waiting for pain but only feeling…well, it felt good.

His mouth went slack as he watched what he was doing.

"Touch your pussy," he growled.

I reached back and began to work my fingers over my nub as he sank farther in.

"Ah, yeah. Jesus, that's tight. It's a virgin ass. Fuuuck." As he grew closer to his release, his beautiful face was that of a god.

He worked his finger in and out. Rubbing my clit vigorously, I climbed higher, pushing back on his finger.

"Oh fuck, that's it," he snarled. "Bounce that ass on my finger. Fuck, fuck—GAH!" His mouth fell open as thick white shots of his cum hit my thighs, my butt, and my hand between my legs.

"OH GOD!" I cried out, jerking against my hand as I reached another peak.

"Jesus," he breathed out as his palm covered one of my cheeks.

I was spent. Unable to stay like this any longer, I sank onto the bed as my breathing slowed. What had I just done?

TWENTY-FOUR
LINC

"If you need to talk about it, then Bane will probably listen. He's more sensitive since his cock is owned and he's got a kid," Luther said, leaning back against the wall with a cigar clamped between his teeth.

"There is nothing to talk about," I snapped, wiping the blood on my knife off on the shirt of the asshole who smelled like he had shit himself as he held a hand over his ear and moaned from the pain of losing half of it.

"No, of course not. You just found out you have a wife and a daughter, and they're now both living in the house with us. Not one damn thing to talk about. I'm sure you're handling it fine. I mean, I would be, but then I'd also be back at the house, waiting for the smokeshow you accidentally married to head out to the pool in one of those little bikinis of hers. They're my favorite part about this."

I shot him a warning look. "Don't," I snarled.

He cackled with laughter. "Yep. Nothing to talk about. You're fucking peachy."

Using the knife in my hand, I pointed toward the bedroom of the apartment we were in. "Could you possibly go make yourself useful and help Locke?"

The disgust on his face as he looked around at the filth this man lived in told me that, no, he would not go help Locke. "Do you smell this place? I don't want to touch anything." He pushed off the wall, straightening, and took the cigar from his mouth. "Why do you think I lit this up? I'm trying to kill the stench."

"That's not going to work. He shit his pants," I told him and headed over to the bedroom door to see if Locke had found the key yet.

He had taken out three dresser drawers and dumped them on the floor, flipped the mattress and sliced it open. Boxes had been tossed everywhere, and he was currently standing on a chair.

"Any luck?" I asked.

He glanced over at me. "No, but I should have looked here first. He had it hidden behind a poster. Took me a minute to think about the fact that the poster was in an odd location. Ripped it down, and here we are."

I waited while he stuck the flat head screwdriver under the edge and popped the vent cover off. Reaching up, he pulled out a bag of white powder, then stuck it back. We weren't here for cocaine. He felt around some more, and then the corner of his mouth curled as he pulled out a single key.

"Think we got it," he said, then tossed it to me.

"I'll call Bane. He can take Luther with him to check the warehouse and see if this is it while we stay here with Moe."

Locke jumped down and dusted off his hands on his jeans. "I'm gonna need to take a shower with fucking bleach after this. The fucker is nasty."

"He shit again!" Luther called from the other room. "Can't we just kill him and leave?"

Locke smirked as I shook my head, then pressed Bane's number.

"Locke found a key in the bedroom vent. Come get it and go test it. If it works, we will end this here and meet you there. Oh, and I'm sending Luther with you. I'm tired of him bitching about the smell."

"Five minutes away," he replied. "Send him out with the key."

"Yeah." I ended the call, sliding my phone back into my pocket.

Locke glanced past me and into the other room. "If he shit, can I just stay in here?"

Jesus, they could kill a man and then go have a drink and watch tits and ass dance on a pole, but they couldn't handle filth and the scent of shit.

"Go on outside and keep an eye on things. If the fuckers he's working with think we might be onto them, we could have company."

Locke looked relieved. "On it."

Luther was glowering at Moe, the idiot who had been hired by Marsha Conway's people to get photos of Governor Baskin fucking a stripper, along with video for another grand.

Jericho Baskin was in office because we had put him there. Marsha Conway was some uptight bitch who was intent on running against him. She was already playing dirty. Once this was cleared up, we would have to pay her a visit and make sure this was the last time she pulled this shit.

If Baskin could keep his dick in his pants, that would be helpful, too, but the man liked to fuck college coeds, and we'd been covering up his tracks for years. In return, when we needed someone to look the other way, he made sure it happened. This was by far the most inconvenient instance because this place was disgusting. We'd all need bleach after.

"Here's a key. Take it out to Bane, who is almost here. Y'all are going to test it."

"Thank fuck," Luther said in relief as he moved to take it.

I turned back to Moe, slid the knife into my back pocket, and crossed my arms over my chest. The other two men could not get out of here fast enough.

I waited until the door closed behind them before speaking. "I got shit to do, Moe. You're wasting my time. If that key isn't the right one, it'll be your balls that come off next."

His eyes were red-rimmed as his bottom lip trembled. "They'll kill me," he whispered like there was someone other than me who could hear him.

"Moe, I'm gonna kill you. That's a given. But what we are wagering on here is how I'm gonna kill you. It can be fast and painless. Or I can drag it out for days. Endless torture," I told him. "You ever been around pigs, Moe?"

He shook his head as he began to let out a low whimper.

"Funny thing, those pigs," I went on, taking the one cigarette I'd brought with me out of my pocket and sticking it between my lips. Pulling the lighter out next, I lit it up and inhaled deeply, letting the nicotine seep in. "Pigs are indiscriminate eaters. They will eat anything you put in front of them. In fact, they won't just eat a human body; they will eat all of it. Bones, teeth, and soft tissue. Until there is nothing left."

He began to sob as I took another drag, watching him.

No one would miss him. He was a junkie who was gonna eventually die in this filth with a needle up his arm. The cocaine was the least of the drugs Locke had found here. It also seemed he'd put hidden cameras in public restrooms to watch women go to the toilet. Shitting was apparently the twisted fuck's thing because he had more videos of that than the other.

"I got a whole pen full of pigs, Moe."

"It's the key," he wailed loudly.

Good.

"And are all the copies in there?" I asked.

Although the stripper who had fucked the governor had already sworn those were the only copies, I wanted to double-check. She knew her life was on the line. Baskin had been too damn easy to set up. I was going to start sending him vetted girls who I knew weren't working for someone else.

He nodded. "All except the one in there."

I tensed. "In where?"

"My-my video collection. They don't know I took a copy. I liked to watch it though."

I pointed at the restroom videos. "With those?"

He nodded. "Yeah. It's labeled *Gov*."

I walked over to the stacks of DVDs and found the one labeled *Gov* and held it up.

"Yeah."

"You know, there is a better way to store and watch videos. It's 2025."

My phone rang, and I pulled it out, then hit Answer.

"We are inside," Bane said into the phone.

"Is it all there?" I asked.

"Yep, and then some. Seems the governor wasn't the only one they were getting shit on. We are loading it all up now."

"All right. Take everything," I told him, then glanced over at Moe.

The sound of Locke's shout snapped my attention toward the window.

"Who's here, Moe?" I asked him, snatching the Glock from my waist and stalking to the door.

"I-i-it's Kedar and Rebel," he stuttered out. "They wired the place," he added frantically. "I couldn't tell you, or they'd hear me."

"Fuck!" I snarled, pointing the gun at Moe and giving him the easy death because the dude was pathetic. His life had been torture enough.

His body went limp, and I headed for the back door. I should have had two men out there, not just one. Moving fast and silently, I exited the house and listened as I made my way around to the side. Other than Locke's shout and one gunshot from a silencer, I heard nothing else.

Footsteps, crunching in the grass, were coming in this direction. Pressing my back against the wall, I inched closer to the edge.

"It's me." Locke's voice sounded off.

Lowering the gun, I turned the corner. Locke was wrapping the bottom part of his shirt that he'd ripped off around his arm. Blood was all down his side. He'd been shot.

"Where are they?" I asked.

"Dead," he replied. "Here, tie this for me. I can't get it."

Shoving my Glock back into its holster, I tied the fabric around the gunshot wound. "How bad is it?"

"Grazed me. Just bleeding like a bitch," he grunted, sounding more pissed than anything.

The black Escalade pulled into the drive.

"Did we get it?" he asked, squinting against the sun.

"Yeah. They got it, and I have the copy Moe stole in my back pocket."

Bane, Luther, and Oz climbed out of the vehicle.

"You good?" Bane asked Locke, his gaze dropping to his arm.

"Yeah."

"I take it, they're all dead?" Luther said, still smoking that damn cigar.

Locke looked at me. "You kill the shitter?"

"Yeah. They're all dead."

"I'll call Forge and Than, tell them to meet us here with the farm truck," Bane said.

I was done with this fucking day. I wanted a hot shower and something to eat. We'd been tracking these fuckers for two days. I was exhausted.

"You got a preference on what we do with the bodies?" Bane asked me.

"I didn't buy the pigs because I like bacon," I replied and headed toward my truck.

"Call Gathe," Locke said. "If he doesn't get to watch this time, he's gonna be pissed, and I'm not in the mood for his bitching,"

I shook my head and smirked. The boys were some twisted fucks. Watching the pigs dispose of bodies for us entertained them. Last time we'd done it, they took a keg of beer out there and built a bonfire, then got smashed. When I went out to check on things that evening, they'd added females, and it had become a goddamn fuckfest.

On that note, my strides got longer as I thought about going home. Sure, I was looking forward to seeing my daughter after having been gone, but I was also looking forward to some plans I had for her momma.

Opening the truck door, I climbed inside, finally free to think about Branwen's ass up in the air, letting me finger-fuck it. That woman's body had been made to be licked and fucked. She'd been flushed the next morning when she looked at me. Even acted shy. That had only made my dick hard.

Thinking about sinking myself balls deep into her cunt made my cock throb. I'd have to be careful though. This was to make her addicted to my cock, not for me to get obsessed with her pussy. Condoms would be a must since I intended to still fuck other women. In fact, that was probably what I should do tonight, but I hadn't fucked her yet, and I had to have that. Feed that need. Then, I'd be over it. I could go have another hot, wet snatch.

I might not be able to eat another one though. Not when I was getting to taste her. But the fucking, I'd be fine.

TWENTY-FIVE
BRANWEN

Two days to sit and scold myself for taking off my pants for Linc was nothing compared to seeing him walk out to the pool, wearing nothing but a black pair of swim trunks. The colorful ink that covered his body was one thing, but the canvas that held it was another. It was as if a sculptor had chiseled every inch to perfection, then breathed life into him.

When was he going to start looking his age? Make it an even playing field for other men.

"Hey! My dad is hewah!" Stevie called out from the top of the slide. She pointed at him and then clapped her hands. "And he's got on a swimming suit to swim with me."

Yes, Vivi Lu, Mommy noticed. You're alive because Momma always notices the man. It's her biggest weakness.

She waved her hand excitedly at Linc. "You was gone!" she said. "But you came back!"

Linc's grin was more than I could deal with. I decided to stop looking at him.

"I have to leave for work sometimes, but I will always come back," he told her.

I wondered how many people he'd killed or what illegal activity he'd participated in.

"That's what Mommy said!"

Not exactly. I hadn't said *always*.

His body cast a shadow over me. A warm towel hit the side of my leg as he dropped it onto the seat.

"You want to go swimming with us, Ringlets?" he asked.

Ugh. That freaking name.

"I'm fine," I replied, not looking up at him. I didn't correct him about the name because the bigger deal I made out of it, the more he would do it.

"Did you not look in the mirror?" He drawled the question with his southern accent coming out thick. "You are a hell of a higher level than fine."

Okay. He was using pickup lines on me? Seriously?

I finally glared up at him through my sunglasses. "Don't do that," I snapped.

His gaze was on my legs before moving up to my face. "What don't you want me to do, Ringlets?"

I waved a hand at him. "This. Flirt, or whatever you're doing," I paused and saw that Stevie was playing under the waterfall, not paying attention to us. "What we did was a brief lapse in judgment. We aren't doing it again. I'm engaged."

And oddly, the guilt I should feel about that was not one of the things I had been dealing with. I had to end things with Hudson. Break it off. It hadn't even been a week, and I had spread my legs for Linc.

He reached down and took a strand of my hair and twirled the loose curl around his finger. "I saw you first."

I blew out a breath of frustration, more at myself than at him because this was getting to me.

"What are we, ten?" I asked sarcastically.

He let out a deep chuckle as my hair fell free from his hand. "You keep acting like you haven't had your hand between your legs, thinking about the other night," he replied.

He walked over to the edge of the pool near Stevie, and I watched him do it. Because it was hard not to. His narrow waist and golden skin. Even the scars that hadn't been covered by the tattoos were sexy. They were proof of how dangerous he was, and God help me, I wanted to lick them.

Groaning, I laid my head back and closed my eyes. I was a bad person.

"Watch this!" Stevie called out when she saw Linc approaching.

I listened but was afraid to look. Seeing him playing with her in the pool was another demon I wouldn't be able to fight. It would gnaw at me and get under my skin. Then, I'd end up having sex with Linc again.

Tonight, I was breaking things off with Hudson. I could not let him think that we had a future.

For starters, I was lusting over another man—one I would never have, but who would always be in my life because of our daughter. Another thing was, seeing Linc with Stevie, I'd realized that Hudson wasn't going to be a good stepdad. Sure, he'd invited her on dates, but comparing him to Linc made me see that Hudson had ignored her for the most part. Her constant talking would get on his nerves. Linc hung on every word she said.

Why hadn't I noticed the ways Hudson was not a good fit? I'd had an excellent father. I knew what a good one was.

I'd wanted him to be a good fit. He loved me, and that'd made me feel secure.

Again, I had been selfish. When had I become that person? I didn't used to be selfish.

"Don't get hewah wet. She will be mad," I heard Stevie whisper.

Keeping my eyes closed, I continued to listen. I was pretty sure I had dozed off to the sounds of them in the water. But they were close to me now.

"I think she's asleep." Linc's deep voice was definitely right next to my ear. Goose bumps covered my skin, even with the warmth from the sun. "Ringlets, I think you might be playing possum," he whispered so close to me that his cigar-and-mint breath heated my skin.

When what felt like his knuckles ran down my arm, causing goosebumps, I gave up and opened my eyes. "I'm awake now," I said, trying not to sound angry for Stevie's sake.

Linc chuckled, and then he stood back up.

"Mommy!" Stevie said with excitement dripping in her tone. "Tomawah, we awah going to get me a puppy!"

My gaze went from her to Linc. "We are?" I asked, not sure that was a good thing.

She'd get attached, and when we moved out in a year, would the dog stay here? Why hadn't we discussed it first? I had told Linc about her getting one when I married Hudson, but that had been a different situation.

"I've got a friend who just bought a goldendoodle puppy from a couple who breeds them in Jackson. I was going to take her to pick one out," he explained, wrapping a towel around his shoulders.

I loved goldendoodles, and because I was going to push Stevie in that direction, I knew that they were all sold before they were even born. Especially if it was a trusted breeder.

"Linc, those dogs sell fast. As in as soon as the mother is pregnant with them. They aren't going to have any left."

I wished he hadn't told her this before assuming because of who he was that he'd get to just go pick one out.

He ran the end of the towel over his damp face, smirking. "They kept two of them because they were their favorites. I convinced them to sell me one." He glanced at Stevie. "That is, if she makes a connection with one of them."

I should have guessed he'd covered all his bases.

Stevie was bouncing and smiling so big that her dimples were at their deepest. "Let's think of a name, Mommy!"

If there was a word more descriptive than smug, then it would fit Linc's expression perfectly.

"You can make a list of names, but until you see the puppy and see its personality, I don't think it's fair to label it with a name yet."

Stevie's eyes widened. "Like me. 'Cause you didn't name me until you held me. Wight?"

Talking about this—holding her for the first time and naming her—around Linc made me uncomfortable.

It was the most wonderful day of my life, and yet I had never felt more alone. No parents were anxious to rush in and see me and the baby. I had no one in the room with me who loved me, holding my hand and telling me I was doing great. When tears fell as I gazed down at my baby girl for the first time, I had no one there waiting to hold and adore her next.

Maybe that was the moment I changed. I got selfish. Because I never felt the same again. The woman who had walked into the hospital after driving herself there at midnight with contractions four minutes apart and seven centimeters dilated was not the same one who left with a baby wrapped in a pink blanket.

But I had chosen that.

I had thought it was the best for Stevie.

So, no. I'd been selfish before. Because Linc would have been there. He might not have loved me the way I wanted, but he'd have loved her. I had stolen it from him. The most precious moments in my life—he could have shared them with me. Held her close and whispered that he'd always protect her. The things I had wanted for her so badly.

Blaming him because he was a womanizer wasn't fair. He was still her dad.

I nodded. "Right," I replied as a lump formed in my throat. I couldn't say more.

TWENTY-SIX

LINC

The call that had come last night from the governor, wanting to see the videos and photos, was annoying. I'd had plans after Stevie was tucked in tight, and I'd been working that angle, reeling in Branwen all evening. Having to leave before Stevie was even in bed pissed me off. Bane went with me and said nothing about my foul mood. It was why I'd taken him and not Luther. He'd not have shut up about it.

I wanted that fucking excuse for a diamond ring off her hand. To get what I wanted, I needed less distractions and more time with both Branwen and Stevie.

Today's outing had been just that, and my mood had improved immensely.

Taking a drink from my glass, I watched as Branwen and Stevie sat on the floor in the corner of the great room with all the things that Stevie had wanted for Maui. The blue merle goldendoodle she had chosen had clear blue eyes the color of the ocean.

He had also not been for sale. The couple hadn't even mentioned the third puppy because, according to them, he was a rare pattern, and they hadn't known the gene was in his line. But the owner was holding him, and Stevie fell in love.

The amount of money I had to pay them to get them to let me have the damn dog should have lessened their heartache. If they didn't get a divorce. The wife had left the room, slamming the door behind her.

But Stevie was happy. She had her puppy, and from the looks of it, Branwen was pretty damn happy too. I hadn't seen her smile that big or laugh like that before. At least not since Vegas, but I hadn't truly been in the state of mind to appreciate it the way I was doing now.

This was all playing right into my plans. She'd drop the fiancé and be addicted to my cock soon enough. Then, I could rest easy, knowing no other man would be in Stevie's life.

My gaze traveled over Branwen's face as she held her head back, laughing as the dog licked her chin. It wasn't like having a woman who looked like her wanting your cock was a bad thing. This wouldn't be a chore. The drama that would probably come from it would be annoying, but we wouldn't be living like a married couple.

What I had gone through with Maggie was different.

With Branwen, I would make no promises. There would be no understanding that I wouldn't fuck other women. This wasn't about love. It was ultimately about Stevie. I also wanted Branwen to pay for having lied to me. This was the best way to do that and get to have my daughter in my life.

"We got a dog?" Luther asked as he walked into the room, wearing nothing but a pair of athletic shorts and tennis shoes. He had a sheen of sweat covering his body, which meant he'd been in the gym, working out.

"Stevie got a dog," I corrected him.

The corner of his mouth curled up as he looked at the scene they made.

Stevie took the dog from her mom and stood up with him, then proudly held him to show Luther. "This is Maui!" she exclaimed as if she were holding an award.

"Maui?" he repeated, his eyes cutting to me.

"It was almost Bluey," I said.

"Mommy said he don't look like Bluey. He has eyes like the ocean. So, we named him Maui," she explained to a man who had never watched a kid's show in his life.

His grandson was three years old, and you'd think he'd know something about Bluey and Maui by this point.

"I see," he replied, although he didn't see shit.

His eyes shifted from my kid to her mother, and I watched him check her out. What was it with those damn tops of hers that didn't reach her waist and her stretchy, tight-ass pants? She needed to wear something else.

I cleared my throat to get his attention, and he took his time tearing his eyes off her tits to look over at me with an amused glint in them. Bastard.

"You leaving?" I asked hopefully.

I had been enjoying watching them with the dog I'd paid three times more for than the other two they had for sale.

He shrugged and sauntered over to sink down onto the leather sectional, closer to them than I was. "Wasn't planning on it. You?" he shot back at me.

I glared at him, which only seemed to amuse him more. He could be a dick. I turned my gaze back to the girls and their puppy to catch Branwen looking at Luther. What the fuck? Hadn't she just been telling me she was engaged?

"Look at him, Mommy!" Stevie exclaimed, drawing her mother's attention off Luther's bare chest.

She laughed as she watched whatever the dog was doing, and, damn, that sound was nice. Not only did she look like an angel, with the body of a fallen one, but she had a laugh like one too. The woman needed some physical flaw. She had plenty of personality flaws, which would be what saved me from feeling anything for her. I had enough beautiful, selfish, and shallow women in my life. Other than fucking them, I wanted nothing else to do with them. I was too old for their bullshit.

The puppy sank its teeth into a blanket and started to pull it from the basket where Jayda kept them neatly folded. Branwen moved onto her hands and knees to crawl over and get him. My hand tightened around the glass while her ass was in full view, leaving little to the imagination with those damn pants.

Cutting my eyes back to Luther, I caught his complete attention on her ass. This had been enjoyable until he came in and ruined it. His eyes needed to go elsewhere, as did his naked chest. I stood up and he turned to look at me.

"I have some business we need to handle in my office," I said tightly.

He raised an eyebrow, then shook his head with a small chuckle. "All right."

I waited on him to get up and followed him out of the room to block any view of him that Branwen might have. I wasn't intimidated by how he looked shirtless. Hell, we'd shared women before. But I didn't like her looking at him. I had no reason for it. I just didn't like it.

We were almost to my office when he asked, "She's got you fucked up already, huh? Didn't take her long, but then with an ass like hers and those tits—"

"Shut up, Luther," I snarled.

He walked into my office and went straight to the bar. "I thought she was engaged," he said, taking a glass.

"Not for long," I clipped.

"Really? You wanna stay married to her?"

If I did, then she couldn't marry anyone else. I wasn't planning on marrying someone again. Love wasn't for me. We'd been married for five years, and it hadn't affected my life. Why let it now?

"I was kidding," Luther drawled. "But the look on your face tells me you are seriously considering it."

"I thought you told me to talk to Bane if I needed to talk about it," I reminded him, wishing he would just stop talking altogether.

He shrugged. "I did, but here you are, glaring at me for looking at her and making up shit about needing to talk business in your office because of it." He took a drink. "Someone needs to remind you how bad you are at marriage. Hell, Maggie moved continents to get the fuck away from you."

As if he could say shit.

"At least she married me. You couldn't even get Chloe to the altar. She refused your ass."

He smirked. "And I am ever so grateful. Not that Chloe isn't a beautiful woman, but she wouldn't have been enough. I'd have wanted a variety. Not just one cunt." He pointed his glass at me. "Which is why your marriage was a fucking disaster. You couldn't keep your dick out of other cunts."

My marriage to Maggie had had way more issues than my infidelity, but I didn't want to talk about that or her. It was the past. A mistake made in my youth. Those days were well behind me.

"The fact that we have sons who are so fucking pussy-whipped confounds me," he added, then took a drink. "Well, more so Levi than Kye. I saw the Kye and Genesis thing back when they were kids. He just lived in denial; plus, the boy has a lot of his momma in him. The faithful shit. But Levi?" Luther let out a chuckle. "He couldn't be more like you if he tried. Then, he went and got obsessed with a magic pussy. Must be the virgin thing that did it for him."

I shook my head. The shit that came out of his mouth sometimes. I did not want to think about my daughter-in-law's pussy. Jesus.

TWENTY-SEVEN
BRANWEN

Convincing Stevie that Maui had to sleep in the crate tonight for potty-training purposes was not an easy task. She'd been sure that Maui would be sleeping in her room, preferably in her bed. I assured her when he was a little older, he could sleep with her, but not yet. The breeders had already started his training, and we were following the steps they'd given us to continue. Although the crate really bothered me, he seemed content in there.

Linc was keeping him in his room to get up with him and take him to use the bathroom during the night.

As negative as I had been about this, today had been fun. When Stevie had wanted the puppy that wasn't for sale, I was worried, but Linc had magically made it happen. I didn't think I wanted to know how much money his magic had cost.

Laying my head back, I closed my eyes as I soaked in the hot bubble bath. I was really going to be spoiled by this tub. The only things that would make it better were a glass of wine and perhaps some music. I should try and remember to bring a glass up tomorrow night.

A faint click had my eyes flying open, and I turned my head toward the door that led into the bedroom. What was that, and why did it sound like a door closing? I hadn't locked the door because I wanted Stevie to be able to get to me if she needed me. Thinking it might be her, unable to sleep because of her worry over Maui being in the crate, I started to call out her name when Linc appeared in the doorway.

Gasping, I sat up, crossing my arms over my chest. "What are you doing in here?" I sounded breathless and a little frantic, but I was taking a bath!

He leaned a shoulder against the open door and cocked his head to the side as he studied me. His eyes trailed down as if he could see through the covering of bubbles, and heat washed over me from his gaze.

"I came to see you. And lucky me, I found you naked."

The husky timbre in his voice was one of those things that made me stupid when it came to him. He didn't need to know about it though.

I held my chin up and glared at him. "You could have knocked. What do you want?"

He smirked then, and the seductive gleam in his eyes caused things to start up in my core that needed to stop. "Would you like me to list the things I want? Or can I just show you?"

I stared at him as my breathing picked up.

"You weren't wearing the dentist's ring today," he said, shoving off from the door and walking over to me.

I'd broken off the engagement with Hudson last night. It hadn't gone well, and there had been some yelling on his part, which I hadn't been prepared for, but it was done. All I had to do was ship this ring to him somehow. I didn't think

USPS was a safe option. But I could stop feeling guilty. He could move on with his life.

But I hadn't ended things with him because I wanted to do things with Linc. I never intended to do sexual things with Linc again. The past few nights, staring at the ceiling, I'd mentally coached myself on how to resist him. Why I had to. That it would keep things from getting complicated.

So, why was it that I couldn't remember any of those reasons with him standing there, looking at me like that?

The man was a predator. The sexy, dangerous, tempting kind that made you forget that the pleasure was fleeting and you would be left cold.

I swallowed. "We broke things off."

He didn't even try and hide the fact that he liked that.

"That doesn't mean you can come in here and…do what we did the other night. I didn't break the engagement off because of you."

The cocky grin on his face said that he didn't believe me. He was so full of himself.

"Is that so?" he asked, taking a seat on the edge of the tub.

I moved back a little, but I couldn't get very far. Not far enough.

"Then, tell me, Ringlets, why did you call it off? A week ago, you were determined to marry him."

I blew out a breath. I was covering my boobs, but the way he was looking at them made me feel like he could still see them.

"It wasn't fair to him," I bit out.

Linc didn't look like be believed me. He reached out and brushed some bubbles from my shoulder. "You sure that's why? Or was it because you had forgotten what it felt like to have a man who knew how to make you come, give you pleasure, and bring out your naughty side and I reminded you?

That pussy has either gone without a cock for a while or the dentist has a micro penis."

A shocked laugh burst out of me. Had he really just said that?

"Hudson's cock is not micro," I argued. I didn't know why I was defending it, but I was.

Linc's finger trailed down my arm, and I shivered, unable to stop it.

"My one finger sure got squeezed in your hot little hole."

Talking about my hole had that entire area alive and alert. The ache that bordered on pleasure pulsed between my legs. My thoughts went to how thick and long Linc's cock was. The veins and angry purple head as it jutted out. No, Hudson's penis had never looked like that. And I'd never had the urge to lick it. But, God, thinking about Linc's made my mouth water.

"What are you doing?" I asked him as his fingertips moved over my collarbone, then down to the cleavage my arms couldn't cover.

His eyes lifted to meet mine. "Trying to get you to lower your arms so I can see your pretty titties."

My chest rose and fell as my nipples let me know how much they'd like that.

I licked my lips. "Linc, this is a bad idea."

"Your body is trembling, and you're panting," he told me.

My body was a slut. My brain was not. I was trying to get them to work together. So far, it had been a massive fail.

"How my body reacts and what is smart are two different things."

Linc leaned toward me, his eyes never leaving mine, and then he lowered his lips to press them against my shoulder. They trailed a path to the curve of my neck. "My cock is leaking—it's so hard—and your body is humming with need, to the point that I can feel it. Taste it. Let me give us what we both want. Your cunt needs stretched and filled. It needs to be taken care of."

The gravelly tone in his voice was about to snatch away all my reserve. Or maybe it was the words. Possibly both. No, it was his lips and hot breath on my neck as I arched to give him better access. One of his hands grabbed my arm and tugged it down. I gave up, letting them fall away. My breasts felt full as they ached for attention.

A deep, low hum came from me when his hands covered them and squeezed. Yes. That was it. God, that felt good. I pressed against them, making another pleading sound.

"That's a good girl. Let me take care of you," he murmured in my ear. "This feels good, doesn't it?"

I nodded and moaned again, pushing them into his touch. I wanted his hands other places too. He needed more arms.

"You're gonna open those legs for me, aren't you? Let me thrust my cock inside you," he said, then bit my earlobe.

Yes. I knew I shouldn't, but I would die if he didn't do that now.

"Stand up," his harsh tone commanded, which only turned me on more.

I stood slowly as the bubbles and water rolled down my bare flesh.

Linc's eyes watching the action felt like a bright flame being brought too close.

"Fuck, you're stunning." His words took away any nerves or uncertainty.

I wanted him to look. To see me. Want me.

He stood up as his hand trailed from my outer thigh, over my hip, and around to cup my butt. "I want you like this in front of the mirror first."

I felt hypnotized. "First?"

"First. One time with this body tonight won't be enough," he replied. He took my hand and walked me over to the marble counter and turned me to face the mirror. "I brought plenty of condoms this time." He grinned wickedly.

"I have an IUD," I blurted. I shouldn't have. But the idea of his cum inside me made me stupid.

His eyes flared as he studied my face in the mirror. "Condoms aren't just for that."

I inhaled. I was aware. Which was why I was stupid for wanting him bare.

His eyes dropped to my butt. "Lean forward and hold on to the counter."

When I did, he began to unzip his jeans. The building ache between my legs began to grow so much that my arousal was coating my inner thighs. He had his cock in his hand, but I couldn't see it from this position, and I wanted to.

"I'm just going to feel this slick, dripping pussy on my head a little before I roll one on," he rasped.

With my palms flat on the cool marble, I watched his face as the swollen tip sank just inside my folds. A deep, low mewl came from me, and the veins in his neck stood out as he continued back and forth. I wanted it shoved inside me now. Just like it had been. I squirmed, ready to start pleading.

"Just the tip," he said, then clenched his teeth as the large head slid into me, reminding me just how big it was.

"OH!" I cried out, my fingers curling in.

"Fuck, that's a pretty sight. Those plump, glistening lips, trying to suck me in," he said, sounding as if he was struggling as much as I was. "I'm gonna move it just a tad. Be still."

I nodded and held my breath, waiting. He let it pop out, and I wanted to cry, but he eased it back in, just barely. Then again.

"Fuck," he panted. "That greedy cunt is like a goddamn suction cup."

I was clawing at the marble, not sure how much longer I could take this before turning around and pushing him to the floor and riding him.

He slid in farther this time, and I let out a cry.

"Ah fuuuck," he groaned.

I wiggled my bottom, trying to get him inside me farther. His hand grabbed a butt cheek and squeezed it painfully.

"STOP!" he snarled loudly, which made me gush between my legs. "Jesus," he whispered, and his eyes closed for a moment while he clenched his teeth.

He had felt it, and I didn't care.

I'd wanted him to. I wanted him inside me. Now.

"You want it," he taunted, sounding as if he was as far gone as I was.

His eyes opened, looking at me in the mirror. He sank in some more, and my mouth fell open as the fullness increased.

"YES!" My one word was almost a shout.

His eyes dropped back to where he was maybe a fourth of the way inside me. "It feels so good," he said through his teeth, and another inch sank inside me. "You keep soaking my dick with your little squirts."

He slid in some more. His mouth fell open a little, and he moved even deeper. I wasn't breathing. It was stinging, and although I wasn't sure he wouldn't rip me open with his girth, I was willing to chance it because there was nothing on earth that compared to this.

"I need to pull out," he said in a pained whisper.

If he did, I might burst into tears.

"No," I begged. "Please don't stop."

His eyes narrowed.

"Linc, please. I want your cock inside me. I want to feel your cum as it unloads."

His fingers dug into my skin, and I saw the moment his last thread of resistance snapped. With a guttural growl, he plunged into me so deep and hard that I felt his balls hit my clit. Throwing my head back, I cried out his name.

All that had happened before. All that would happen after did not matter while we let our primal need take over. Our bodies claiming what they craved.

"Such a good pussy," he praised.

His name, God's name, pleading—it all fell from my lips as I held on while Linc's thrusts took me higher. The rest of the world was left far behind. I was lost in a nirvana I never wanted to leave.

Linc leaned forward and slid his hands around to grab my boobs as they swung and bounced violently. "Goddamn, these big, full titties."

His eyes were on them in the mirror, and the animalistic expression on his face as he chased his orgasm sent me spiraling.

Linc grabbed a handful of my hair and pulled my head back. His mouth was against my ear. "Come on my cock. That's it. Such a pretty girl to fuck like such a slut."

My body convulsed as he talked ugly in my ear.

"You like it. Taking my dick. You want to be my cockslut. I can feel it. That naughty pussy creaming all over me."

The free fall, the moment of bliss, held me in the air. I gasped. When Linc let my hair go, his hands went back to my tits, and he jerked me up against him. I felt him shudder.

"Fuuuck." He squeezed my breasts painfully, and the warm, thick rush of his release began to fill me as his cock pulsated against my tight walls. "That perfect body, taking my seed," he groaned, staring at me in the mirror as he jerked and let out another groan.

When he stopped, I finally began to slowly sink back to earth. My walls clenched again, and he hissed in my ear. His brutal grasp on my boobs relaxed. We stood there, staring at each other, saying nothing. That was insane. It was a realm of pleasure that was dangerous. When you got there, you wanted to stay. Do anything to get back to it.

Linc moved a hand up to wrap a curl around his finger. "I have a clearer picture as to why I kept fucking you that night in Vegas."

The corner of my lips tugged up.

"Sweet-tasting cunt that feels like a virgin, yet takes my ten inches like a pro."

He smirked, then let the strand he had been playing with go. He then ran his palm down my stomach as we both watched our reflection until his hand slid between my legs. With his other one, he grabbed a fistful of my hair and jerked my head back and to the side. His mouth leaning down close to my ear. "There it comes. Open those legs wide. We are gonna watch my seed leak out of your cunt."

Oh God. I had barely recovered from what we'd just done, and he already had me starting to tingle again. I opened my legs, and he grabbed my upper thigh.

"Put your foot up on the counter so I can see better."

When I did, he let out a pleased sound, then sunk his finger inside my sensitive entrance. "Used, cum-filled little pussy on such a good girl," he said in a sadistic voice that shouldn't have turned me on but did. "Look at that perfect pink cunt. Slick with my seed." He hummed his pleasure and began pumping his finger in and out of me. "What happened to my sweet girl, Ringlets? Standing here with your legs open, showing me how messy you let me make you. That's not what good girls do."

He shoved two fingers in, and I cried out, leaning harder against him.

"But you always did want to make me happy, didn't you? Ah, and I do like the sight of your pussy dripping with my load."

I shuddered. His words were edging on taboo, and I knew he was doing it on purpose. I was trying not to let it get to me, but he made it impossible. I was going to come again with him doing this. It made me feel depraved, and even that was turning me on.

"Look how naughty you've been," he murmured against my ear. "Even now, watching my fingers pump in and out of you. Letting me have what I want. Sweet girl wants to be my slut." He growled the last word, and his fingers sank inside me hard.

I crested and shouted his name. My body convulsed, and I lifted my hips to rock against his fingers as he held me up, still pressed against his chest. He was hard again; I could feel it against my bottom. Then, he pulled me up his body to rub his erection against me.

"You got me throbbing already," he said accusingly. "And I was going to clean you and take care of you. But now, I'm gonna fuck this filthy cunt again."

TWENTY-EIGHT
BRANWEN

I kept my eyes closed, pretending to be asleep while Linc got out of bed and began to dress. We'd ended up having sex a third time after our shower, and I'd been so exhausted that maybe I dozed off. I wasn't sure, but the moment the bed had moved from him getting up, I had been aware of it.

Without him distracting me, I could think about what we had done. What I'd let him do—and so easily.

Had it been mind-blowing? Yes. Had I been lost in the dark pleasure? Yes. Did I now feel good about it? I wasn't sure.

The guilt of being engaged to Hudson wasn't hanging over me, but I'd gotten used to being treated differently. Sure, Hudson hadn't given me orgasms, but he had kissed me. Not one time had Linc kissed me—on the mouth at least. He kissed me other places, if it could be considered that. It was more licking and sucking things that he had done with his magical tongue.

The click of the door as he left the room left a cold presence drifting over me. Had I just been a booty call? He had needed sex and used me for it. Wouldn't he have kissed me if it had been more? And, God, why did I want more?

Groaning, I rolled onto my back and stared at the ceiling. That stupid fantasy of Linc being mine was still there, manipulating me. Thirty-two years of this man being in my head, haunting my dreams, and after all he'd done, here I was. He snapped his fingers, and I came running. I had to stop this. Get control of myself, but how? I knew good and well that if he walked back into this room tomorrow night, it would take him a few words, some intimate touches, that freaking face of his, and I'd be opening my legs once again.

It would never be enough! I'd always want more. I'd want him. His heart. I would want him to kiss me, not make me feel like Julia Roberts in *Pretty Woman*. Now, that outcome I would take, but the other…I wasn't his paid live-in whore. Although tonight, that was exactly what I'd acted like. He'd called me his cockslut, and I'd gotten off on it. Ugh! He made me twisted.

Either the man was always virile and hard to sate or there was something more to it. Because tonight and in Vegas, he couldn't stop fucking me. It was as if he couldn't get his fill, and I wasn't so sure that if I hadn't been so spent and closed my eyes, he wouldn't have taken me again tonight.

Hudson was ten years younger than him, and after he got off, that was it for the night. He wasn't getting it back up again. The past few months, he'd made jokes about getting old and it being harder on men to do that every day. Their testosterone or something wasn't what it used to be. Linc had disproven that theory.

Hudson had made me feel secure and comfortable. Linc made me feel wild and alive, but only when he was stripping me down and taking me to levels of pleasure I hadn't known existed. Otherwise, he was…infuriating, controlling, demanding. Except with Stevie. He treated her in a way he never treated anyone else—that I had witnessed at least. He loved her. That was the difference.

Me...well, he had to make a space for me in his life because he loved her. I had to suffer through the turmoil he was going to put me through emotionally because I loved her. I could and would do anything for my daughter, I just didn't know if my soul would survive this. Not that I had a choice. Linc had given me no choice. Not really. Hating him for it was impossible when I watched Stevie with him. I was only reminded that my decision five years ago had been the wrong one. Simply because my heart had been hurt.

I'd lied to myself, saying that I didn't want the life the Linc lived near her. But if he had wanted me, if he hadn't left that letter, if he'd been there the next morning, or even if he hadn't been having an orgy when I came to tell him the first time, I would have let him be in her life. That was the first lie I'd told myself. The second lie was that I had been protecting her from it. Yet...my dad had allowed me to live in it, and those were the happiest memories I had of my childhood.

The truth was mine to accept. I'd made decisions that affected both of them based on my emotions and the hurt that Linc had inflicted on me.

This time, I had the chance to do the right thing. Not think about me.

The kitchen was full this morning, and as I stood there, unnoticed, and took it all in, the only things that made my heart warm was the sight of Stevie's big smile and the sound of her laughter as Linc constructed a face on her pancakes with a bowl of berries. My reminder of why I could survive Linc Shephard. God knew I'd needed one this morning.

The rest of the scene unfolding only made me want to turn and go back to my bedroom.

Jayda's hand was on Linc's waist in a very familiar way as she leaned over him with a can of whipped cream, laughing at his attempt to make the face look like his. Jayda told him, while standing entirely too close to his body, that he had to add a beard. They would make a perfect commercial. The beautiful family, all smiles and loving.

If Linc did decide to marry again and love someone, then would this be what it looked like? She'd be beautiful and young, like Jayda. For Linc to fall in love, she'd have to be. He was getting older, and he'd eventually want someone to spend the rest of his life with. I had to face it. And while Stevie was at his house, would she have another family? Another mom who she loved? My chest ached at the thought. She'd been all mine, but this could happen, and I would have to be tortured with this image in my head every time I left her with her father.

No longer able to look at them, even if Stevie was being entertained by it all, I shifted my gaze to the large, round kitchen table. Luther sat with Maui in his arm as he took a drink from the coffee cup in his other hand while watching me. I felt the instant flush in my cheeks. I had no idea what my facial expression had been or if he had any idea that the three of them had bothered me. I did my best to smile at him as I walked into the room, no longer able to stay back and observe now that I had been caught.

Jayda spotted me first, and her stunning face appeared happy to see me. God, she was impossible to hate. Even my jealousy of her close relationship with Linc couldn't stop me from liking her. She was too nice.

"Good morning," she beamed. "We have pancakes again for breakfast. Stevie woke up early and came down to make her request."

I shifted my eyes to my daughter, who was pointing at the pancake that Linc had decorated. "Look, Mommy! It has my dad's face!" She giggled, covering her mouth.

She always referred to Linc as "my dad," I was realizing. As if she wanted everyone to be sure he belonged to her. I understood that need completely. He had never been mine though. Even if I had spent countless hours imagining it. At least Stevie could claim him as hers.

"There is a clear resemblance," I replied, trying to appear as if I were completely fine. That Linc hadn't fucked me three times last night, then walked out of my room without a goodbye or a…kiss.

"It's the whipped-cream beard that makes it. I can totally see Linc's beard being that white in the next, what…two to three years? I mean, you're getting close to sixty," Jayda teased as she picked up a plate and began to put pancakes on it.

"Careful," Linc warned. "You'll find yourself unemployed."

"No, the hell she won't," Luther called out from the table, where he was now rubbing Maui's head. "She can stop cleaning your side of the house and cooking for you, but she's right. You're old, and I'm not losing her because she tells the truth."

As she turned to me, holding out a plate, I assumed Jayda's trill of laughter would make Linc scowl, but he was fighting back a grin. Then, he winked at her. My stomach felt as if a brick had been rammed inside. I took the plate, murmuring a thank-you, and walked over to sit down beside Stevie.

He hadn't even glanced at me. I was trying not to read into it, but with him winking at Jayda and touching her, how was I supposed to eat? I hadn't been hungry to begin with, but now, I was bordering on nauseous. With myself.

Stevie put a strawberry, which had been used as a nose for the pancake face, and popped it into her mouth, then gave me a toothy grin as she chewed it. Needing some source of comfort, I kissed her cheek. She leaned into me, as if savoring it, and that was a balm to my soul. I had love. My daughter's.

"Here are some berries and maple syrup. There is also the raspberry syrup I found at this cute little farmers market in town," Jayda told me as she slid the items over to me.

"Thank you," I said, feeling awkward.

I'd never had to interact with someone else who had slept with Linc. I mean, I wasn't positive they had, but it appeared as if they had some connection. Unlike him and me.

My mood wasn't going to improve if I continued thinking about this.

A phone rang, and Linc's deep voice said, "Yeah," as he took long strides out of the kitchen.

Not even a hello to me. Nothing. I looked back down at my plate and felt like if I tried to eat it, the first bite would get stuck in my throat.

TWENTY-NINE
BRANWEN

Glancing down at my phone, I frowned at Linc's name lighting up the screen as it rang. When had his number been put into my cell phone? I was tempted to ignore it.

Yesterday morning, he had shown up in the great room while Stevie played with her new toys to tell her he had to leave to do some work. She'd thrown her arms around his neck, and he'd hugged her before giving me a nod, then walking away. Again, not one word.

It was almost thirty hours later, and we hadn't seen him since. Yet his number had been programmed into my phone, which I had not put in there, and he was calling me. The third ring, I gave in and picked it up.

"Yes," I said in a clipped tone.

"I need you both ready by four. Jayda knows what you need to pack and will help you. Than will pick you up and drive you to the airstrip."

I waited for a moment for more information, but he said nothing.

"Okay, but where are you taking us?"

"Florida. Stevie needs to meet her brother."

Oh. OH. I had known she had a brother. I remembered the wild little boy Levi had been. But I hadn't really considered the fact that Stevie had a sibling.

I'd not been back to Ocala since I'd left at twelve years old. I wasn't sure how I felt about it. This might be good for us. Going somewhere. Stevie and I needed out of the house. The pool was great, and the house was huge, but we had been here for days. Although it wasn't like I had a choice.

"Okay," I agreed, but said nothing more.

"Is she good?" he asked me. His tone was still businesslike and detached.

"Yes, but she needs to get out of the house. I mean, after this trip. We can't stay here all the time." I tried to keep my voice equally cold.

He cleared his throat. "Yeah, I will make sure that happens more often."

"Good."

"See you then," he said, and then the call ended.

I pulled the phone from my ear and stared at it. He'd really just hung up. If I didn't have a bite mark on my shoulder, where he had locked into me when he unloaded inside me the last time, and my butt didn't have small bruises from his fingertips digging into it, then I'd have thought I'd dreamed up the other night. The man he'd been that day was someone else. He'd dropped his charm on me, and I'd done whatever he said.

Seemed he had gotten his fill of me all in one night.

Jayda came walking outside to the pool with concern etched on her normally smiling face. Maui went running to her with his tail wagging as a wet and giggly Stevie chased him. I sat up from my reclined position on the lounger.

When she reached me, she glanced back at Stevie, who had picked up Maui and was playing with him, then swung her gaze back to me. "Hey, uh, there is a man at the gate for you. Hudson? I'm not allowed to open the gate for anyone unless given instruction to by Linc or Luther." She winced as she said it.

I swung my feet off the seat and onto the ground. Shit. What was he doing here? How had he found me? I hadn't given him an address. More than that, it was dangerous for him to be here. Thank God Linc wasn't home.

Snatching up my cover-up, I pulled it on and looked over at Stevie. "Can you watch her for me? I need to call him and get him to leave."

She nodded. "Of course. I'm sorry. I'd let him in, but…"

I shook my head. "Don't apologize. I wouldn't want you to. God knows what Linc would do."

Slipping my feet into the flip-flops I'd worn out here, I hurried for the patio, then decided to go inside in case Stevie could hear me. She hadn't asked about Hudson in days, and I didn't want to confuse her. This was all still very new, and she was happy with it.

I dialed Hudson's number while I stepped inside the house.

"Why is there a security gate to get up to this house?" Hudson demanded when he answered.

If you knew, you would not be sitting there.

"Hudson, why are you here? You need to leave."

"No. Not until I see you. I came to talk to you. Beg you to reconsider. And you're locked behind a gate, and I can't get in. This is concerning, Branwen. I don't feel good about this. You breaking things off seemed so…so not like you. I'm now seeing some major red flags here. Are you okay? Is he…is he holding you in there? Fuck, I don't know. The man seemed dark and twisted. He might be Stevie's father, but he isn't someone you need to be around."

I rubbed my temples with my forefinger and thumb. He had to stop thinking and go.

"I told you he was wealthy and powerful. This comes with it. I am safe. We are safe. But you can't be here because you won't be."

"I won't be?" he asked. "Do you hear yourself? You are saying that I won't be safe. That means you believe he will do something to me. That he isn't stable. You need to let me help you. You don't love him. I know that."

Oh God, Hudson. Shut up and go.

I had brought him into this. Another thing to add to my list of fails.

"This isn't about love. It's about Stevie. He wants to get to know his daughter. Form a bond with her. You being here makes him feel threatened. Just go. Find someone new. Someone worthy of you. Be happy."

Please, for the love of all that is holy, get out of here.

"I can't find someone new and be happy, Branwen! I love you. I want you. You make me happy."

How was it that I struggled to get rid of men who wanted me, yet the one I wanted thought of me as a hookup that wasn't even worthy of polite conversation? This was Bastian all over again. Except I didn't have a best friend for him to start dating. Although she had tried hard to reach out to me and rekindle our friendship after their divorce two years later.

"Hudson, please. I can't do this with you. My life right now…it's a lot, and emotionally, I can't handle this."

"Might want to try harder."

Luther's voice caused my head to snap up, and I stared at him as he sat down on the sectional.

"I love you. I will be there for you. Just let me, please, baby," I heard him pleading as I stood silently, my gaze fixed on Luther.

Did he mean that Linc was on his way home? Shit. Shit. Shit.

"If you love me, then you will respect my decision and let me go," I pressed, not taking my eyes off Luther.

If he was in here, then no one was outside, killing Hudson.

He stretched out both his arms and rested them on the back of the sofa, then propped his right foot up onto his left knee as he watched me. "He won't kill him here. Too messy. But the dentist will go missing. No one will ever find him. It will be a tragedy that makes the Nashville news for weeks, until another big event happens."

My eyes widened in horror as he spoke. He was serious. I swallowed the bile in my throat.

Hudson was swearing his undying devotion, and all I could do was picture him with a bullet in his head. All my fault.

No. No! I wasn't going to let Hudson do this.

"Hudson," I said firmly, shutting him up. "For the next year, I am focusing on Stevie and her needs. Letting her get to know her father. I have no time for this. If you still feel this way in a year, then we can reconnect, but right now, you need to go home. Nothing you say will change my mind."

He was silent, and for a moment, I feared Luther was wrong. Maybe Linc had arrived and killed him. He could be sitting in his Mercedes, bleeding out or with a broken neck.

"Okay." His tone sounded defeated. "But I wish you'd let me see you. Kiss you goodbye."

I rolled my eyes to the ceiling, and my shoulders sagged. "I can't do that. It wouldn't help this."

"I'll wait," he said fiercely. "When this year is up, I will be waiting."

I wished he wouldn't. I had to believe he would get tired of this and change his mind.

"Goodbye, Hudson," I replied, not going to feed into that at all.

"I love you, Branwen."

I ended the call, praying he drove away.

"What naughty tricks do you have, sweetness?" Luther asked with a smirk.

I frowned at him, not sure what he meant. He picked up his phone and tapped something. The large theater-sized television screen came to life on their wall, and the front gate appeared. Hudson was still there. His car parked and him pacing back and forth, glaring toward the gate.

Dammit!

"That man is obsessed," he said. "And as gorgeous as you might be, to have a man that fucked up in the head, you must have some euphoric witchery going on between your legs."

I could assure him I didn't. He could ask Linc all about it. This had nothing to do with sex. My sex life with Hudson hadn't been that great. The other night had reminded me how much it had lacked.

Hudson finally jerked open his car door and climbed inside.

"Thank God," I sighed, then held my breath, waiting for his car to back up.

"If he tries to crash through that gate, I'll give you whatever you want to let me have a taste of that pussy," Luther said, cutting his eyes to me and letting them ease their way up my body.

My face flushed. He couldn't be serious.

"Fuck, the way you blush is even sexy." His tone turned into a raspy purr. "I'd make it feel real good, I promise."

I opened and closed my mouth, unable to think of words to say. There was no way in hell I'd be sleeping with Luther. The fact that I'd done so with Linc was bad enough. I didn't intend to become the house whore. Was that what Linc had led him to believe? Humiliation sank in, and I clenched my cover-up together in the front tightly.

"You ever had a pierced cock in your cunt?"

Holy shit. He had a pierced penis!

"Had the metal bar slide over your slick, wet clit?" he said, his voice getting deeper and smoother. "Fuck." He took one hand and grabbed his crotch. "Now, I'm hard, thinking about it."

I needed to turn and leave. However, I was in shock at the moment and struggling to get my feet to move.

"You like that, don't you? Those cheeks are such a pretty pink. Are your nipples hard? Thinking about having your pussy teased with the head of my dick. Wondering how the metal feels. Fuck, you've got great tits. I bet your nipples are like ripe raspberries."

Raspberries? My nipples?

The desire in his eyes had his pupils dilated. He tugged the zipper of his jeans, and I jumped back, startled.

"You got my dick fully erect, sweetness. There isn't enough room for it in my jeans when it's like this."

He was getting out his penis? Oh my God! I didn't want to see this.

Thankfully, my legs began working again, and I turned, then ran out of the door, not stopping until I reached the pool. Jayda glanced up from where she sat on the edge of the pool, dangling her legs in, while Stevie swam around, showing her tricks.

"What's wrong?" she asked, frowning as she stared up at me.

I shook my head. I couldn't tell her what had just happened.

"Nothing," I said, then cleared my throat. "I got him to leave."

She pulled her legs out and stood up. "You sure? You look rattled."

I was beyond rattled. Why would someone pierce their penis? And had he really intended to just pull it out right there?

"Good. Just drama with…him," I said, trying to wave it all off.

She didn't look convinced. "All right. But if you need anything, just tell me."

I forced a smile. "Thank you."

She waited for a moment, and I thought she was going to say more, but she didn't. She turned to wave at Stevie and told her she was going back inside to clean the bathrooms. I stood there, attempting to act normal, while she walked away.

THIRTY
LINC

The entire flight and drive from the airstrip to Hughes Farm, and not one fucking word about the dentist stopping by. I'd waited it out. Given her time. But even while Stevie played with the toys she had chosen to bring with her, Branwen said nothing. I'd wanted to watch her and try to read her expressions, but keeping my eyes off her was the only way I could manage to not think about the other night. When I thought about it, I began craving her cunt again. I was like an addict that had his first hit after years of being clean.

I'd thought I had it all under control until I saw the damn security video of the dentist and heard the shit he was saying to her. He wasn't going to let her go easy. I would need to step in and make sure he didn't show up again. This wasn't just about Stevie anymore. It was also Branwen's cunt. He wasn't getting near it. No one was. But me. The thought of someone else having it made me want to go on a murderous spree. I might not like her, but, goddamn, that body belonged to me. I'd have it when I wanted it. She would put up a fight, but if I talked to her just right, she became real agreeable.

When we drove under the archway that read *Hughes Farm*, I couldn't stop myself from glancing over at Branwen. My thoughts had been centered on Levi meeting Stevie when I chose to bring them here instead of him and his wife, Aspen coming to us. I hadn't considered Branwen's reaction to being back after all these years.

A small smile played across her lips as we passed the stables.

"I see hawses! Look, Mommy!" Stevie exclaimed, pointing toward the window.

Branwen nodded and took a deep breath. "Yeah, baby, I see them," she replied softly and turned her head away.

I heard the sniffle she was trying to hide. Fuck.

"You can wyde hawses, can't you, Mommy?" Stevie's voice was full of pride.

"Yes," she said in a shaky voice.

I was real close to unbuckling her and pulling her into my arms. The fact that she'd basically lied to me by not telling me about the dentist's visit seemed almost trivial at the moment. I knew she was remembering. The last time she'd been here. My hands fisted. Dammit. I should have thought about that.

"See the big house, Mommy?" Stevie asked.

Branwen smiled, her eyes shimmering, as she nodded, but didn't speak.

"It's pwetty."

"It is," she agreed.

"Are you okay?" I asked, and she tensed.

Her eyes shifted to mine, and she stared at me as if my asking her that was confusing.

"Yes," she said, but her voice gave away her emotion.

When the car stopped, she reached up and wiped at her eyes, sniffed, and then straightened her stance. Seeing her transform so quickly and hide her emotions made me pause. She was good at that. Too good. She knew how to hide her hurt. I didn't know women who could do that. Most wanted the attention.

The door to my right opened, and I stepped out as Branwen leaned over to unbuckle Stevie. I nodded my head to Six, one of the members in the family who Garrett used as security. Stevie had been fascinated with his tattoos and piercings when she saw him waiting by the Escalade when we disembarked from the plane.

Stevie's blonde head peeked out, and I held a hand out for her to take before she jumped down.

"It is weally big," she said, staring up at the Hugheses' mansion while continuing to keep her hand in mine.

Branwen followed her, and the skirt she was wearing had ridden up. Long, tanned legs for fucking miles stepped down, and I tore my gaze off them, only to catch Six's attention being where mine had been. When I cleared my throat, his eyes snapped up, and he stiffened.

"I'll have the luggage brought in and sent to your rooms," he informed me.

I gave him a pointed look. He knew what it meant. Keep his eyes to himself. Or at least off Branwen. I waited for her to move up beside me, but when she stayed a step behind, I almost started up the stairs with Stevie when I remembered Six and decided Branwen would go in front of us. Six didn't need a view of her ass.

"Go ahead," I told her.

She looked unsure, but finally moved in front of Stevie and me to climb the wide steps that led up to the Hugheses' mansion. When we reached the top, she veered over to the side, not wanting to be the one to ring the doorbell apparently.

Stevie was bubbling with energy as she bounced on her feet. With the hand that she wasn't clinging to, I rang the bell.

It had been a few months since I'd been here. Garrett had eased up on his command, and Blaise was in complete control. When we met, it was in Blaise's office at his house or at Huck's motorcycle repair shop.

When the door swung open, Ms. Jimmie—Garrett Hughes's cook and head of house staff—opened the door. Her bright smile went from me to Stevie.

"Oh Mylanta! What a doll!" she said, bending down to look at Stevie, and then she glanced over at Branwen. "Good Lord in heaven, did you grow up to be a raving beauty," she said with a gentleness to her voice.

It seemed Garrett had already informed her of just who was coming with me.

Branwen's smile made her jade eyes shine. "Hello, Ms. Jimmie. You haven't aged a day."

Ms. Jimmie waved a hand. "Oh, I know better. These Hughes men have aged me a thousand years. But thank goodness they're settled and happy now. Just takes the right woman," she said, her eyes swinging back to lock on me.

Then, she looked back to Stevie. "You're the spitting image of your momma as a little girl," she told her. "Well, that is, if Demeter had known how to tame all those curls."

At the mention of her father's name, I tensed, and my eyes flew to her face, but a soft laugh drifted past her full lips.

"Daddy never could get my hair right," she agreed.

"My dad?" Stevie asked with her head tilted back, frowning at her mother.

Branwen shook her head. "No, sweetie. My dad. He worked here, down at those stables with all the horses you saw. I used to play down there all summer, after school, and on weekends while he worked."

Stevie's small mouth opened in surprise. "Weally?"

"Yes."

Stevie's eyes swung over to me. "Did you know my mommy used to play hewah? At youah fwiend's stables?"

"He knew all right. Wasn't a soul on this property that didn't know your momma's favorite was your dad. She was as little as you and would follow him everywhere. It was sweet as could be," Ms. Jimmie informed her.

"He's my favowite too!" she stated with pride and squeezed my hand tighter.

Ms. Jimmie looked back at me. "Seems he's a lucky man."

All right, Ms. Jimmie. Enough of memory lane and making this something it isn't.

It seemed Garrett had left out the part where my daughter had been kept from me and Branwen had tried to make someone else her dad.

"Is Garrett here?" I asked, ready to move this along.

"Yes. He and Fawn are out back. They're expecting you. You know the way. I'll make sure your luggage is taken to your rooms."

"Thank you," I told her, then glanced over at Branwen. "This way."

As we walked through the home, taking the east hallway since it bypassed more—and with Stevie's curiosity, we'd never make it to the patio before nightfall—I worked on putting the memories of that girl back in the corner of my mind, where they belonged. She wasn't a kid anymore. She wasn't sweet and innocent. Me feeling anything other than lust and detachment from her was dangerous. I couldn't trust her.

When we reached the tall glass doors leading onto the back patio, Stevie let go of my hand and rushed outside. This wasn't the side where the pool was, but rather the side where they entertained. I followed her out, not looking back for Branwen. She was a big girl and could manage.

They'd gotten new furniture for out here since I'd seen it last. There was a large U-shaped sofa with plush cream cushions that sat at least a dozen people. In front of it was a table that looked like it was made of stacked slabs of stone. It held a silver pitcher, glasses, several trays of finger foods, and two glasses of whiskey. The flat screen television that he'd had out here had turned into three. One hanging over the white stone fireplace and the other two on the back side of the house. The sofa was placed so that all three were easy to view.

I heard the sounds of a race and knew there wasn't a race happening today—at least that Hughes Farm had a horse in—so that meant he was watching a race that had already happened.

Garrett was in the center of the sofa with Fawn sitting across his lap. They looked to be kissing or talking with their faces very close to each other. Garrett's hand was gripping her ass. I cleared my throat loudly. I doubted he wanted me to get a glimpse of his wife's asscheek, and the way he was pulling her dress up, it looked like I just might.

He stopped and began to smooth the fabric back into place as she straightened. She snapped her head around, looking like a thoroughly kissed woman, and then a smile broke across her face.

"I see them!" Stevie called out, pointing over to the sofa.

Smirking, I raised an eyebrow at Garrett as Fawn stood up, and his gaze found me. An amused look made his mouth quirk, but his attention shifted immediately to Branwen. The pleased expression as he stood annoyed me. Why was it that he seemed to not see what she had done to me?

THIRTY-ONE
BRANWEN

Garrett, like Linc, had aged well. You'd think that men who lived the kind of lives they did would look haggard and old. But nope. It seemed the Hughes and Shephard genes were excellent. There was a touch of gray in his temples, but he still had all his hair, and those bluish-gray eyes of his were still striking.

His wife, like I had already guessed, was stunning and young. The smile on her face was genuine. I didn't know about the wives in between, but I did know that his first wife had not been a nice person. He'd gotten wiser with age when it came to choosing women.

The pink sundress she wore fluttered in the breeze, as did her platinum-blonde hair that hung straight down her back. She was headed directly toward me, then stopped as she reached Stevie and bent her knees as she lowered herself.

"You must be Stevie," she said with a thick Southern drawl that I had not expected. Then, she held out a hand to her. "I'm Fawn, and I am so happy you're here."

Stevie looked at her hand and grinned, then bit her bottom lip as she glanced over at me. I nodded for her to go on, and she giggled as she put her hand in Fawn's and shook it.

"You have a weally big house. It's biggah than my dad's house, and I thought he lived in a mansion," she said matter-of-factly.

Fawn appeared to be fighting back a laugh. "Yes, it is very big. But you want to know a secret?"

Stevie nodded her head vigorously.

"I used to live in a camper. Have you ever seen a camper?"

Stevie's eyes widened, and she nodded again. "I have a Bluey campah, but it's a toy, and I can't live in it."

"I imagine not. But I lived in mine with my daughter, who was once little, like you. We didn't move into this house with Garrett until she was grown up."

Stevie's shoulders rose and fell with a sigh. "She gwowed up alweady?"

I had a feeling she'd been hoping for a friend to play with. I needed to get her to the park or something.

Fawn laughed. "Yes. I feel that way too. I miss having a little girl. But don't you worry. We will have fun. We have a pool, a theater, and you saw the horses when you arrived. And…I don't have a little girl for you to play with, but I do know of a little boy who would like to come swim with you."

She nodded, seemingly happy again. "I like boys! My dad has a pool too!" she said, pointing at Linc.

"Well then, I bet you can swim."

"Mommy says I swim like a fish."

"You are going to have to show me while you're here for sure then," she said, then stood back up and turned to me. "I'd tell you I've heard so much about you, but, well, what I've heard was about your childhood. I look forward to getting to know the grown-up."

She wasn't an elitist because she'd been brought into this world from what sounded like a much different one. I couldn't imagine living in a camper with Stevie. I wanted to hear that story.

"I'm intrigued by the camper. I look forward to getting to know you as well. Thanks for having us. Stevie is well behaved, and she won't be a problem."

Fawn threw back her head and laughed, then looked back at me. "Then, there will be one well-behaved kid around here. Because when Blaise and Maddy bring those boys over, it's wildness."

I grinned, remembering Blaise as a kid. Trev had been little and not around as much. His mother had been Garrett's second wife and a more involved mother, I thought. I wasn't sure really.

"I remember what Blaise was like," I said with a grin.

She blew out a breath. "Whew. I can only imagine."

"You look good, Branwen," Garrett said, coming up behind Fawn. "Glad you came." His voice was deeper, and there was a huskiness to it.

He might have aged well, but the life had changed him. There was a difference in his eyes. As if they'd seen and done things that marked his soul.

"It's good to see you, Garrett," I told him.

He chuckled, and his eyes cut to Linc. "She doesn't look all doe-eyed anymore, ready to follow you to the ends of the earth," he told him.

He had no idea.

"Don't," Linc said, nodding his head slightly toward Stevie, as if that was why he wanted to change the subject.

Fawn turned slightly to him, placing a hand on his chest. I almost choked on my own saliva when the rock on her hand caught the light.

Holy Mother Mary, mother of Jesus! What size was that thing?

"Don't tease," she scolded him. "Let's go sit and visit."

He stared down at her with a possessive adoration, then winked at her while reaching up to take the hand she had on his chest and kissed it. A pang of envy stung my chest. What must that feel like—to be loved by someone you loved so deeply? It sounded like she'd had a Cinderella story, and this was her happily ever after. Maybe, for some, dreams did come true.

"I'm thinking of buying this horse. The last few races he was in were impressive, but he's not done one of the big ones yet. Come give me your opinion," Garrett told Linc. With his hand on Fawn's lower back, he started toward the sofa they'd been sitting on when we arrived.

Stevie rushed ahead and stopped to look over the table of appetizers and treats that were set out in an array of different serving pieces. Sweets were on two-tiered trays that sat in the center while silver trays surrounded them with savory items. The miniature cupcakes with impressive toppings caught her eye immediately, and she looked back at me with pleading eyes.

"They have cupcakes, Mommy," she told me.

"I see that," I replied.

"Ms. Jimmie brought these out for everyone to enjoy," Fawn said.

"All right, you can have one, but only touch the one you are getting," I told Stevie.

She studied them as if it were the most important decision she would ever make.

Linc took a seat to the left of Garrett, leaving several spaces between them, after he picked up a glass of what I assumed was whiskey. He hadn't glanced my way or acknowledged me, so I went over and sat down on the opposite side. Stevie picked up a pink cupcake and came to sit between Fawn and me.

"Would either of you like some mango lemonade?" Fawn asked, reaching for the silver pitcher on the table.

Stevie began to nod her head while chewing her first bite of the cupcake.

"That sounds nice," I told her while I reached over and took a napkin, then placed it on her lap. I had a feeling she was going to need it.

Some kind of cream was inside of the pink cake, and although Stevie was licking it up before it dripped, that was going to be messy.

"Here you are," Fawn said, handing me a glass, then placing one in front of Stevie. "I will have Ms. Jimmie bring out one of the kid cups we keep for the boys when she comes out to check on us. I should have thought of it earlier."

Fawn sat back down, and Garrett's hand immediately went to her thigh, laying his large palm over it, appearing to grip it, but not painfully. It was more of a possessive way. Fawn sank into the plush cushions, close enough that she was touching him, yet her smile stayed on me. They seemed to move together as one.

Could I have had this with Hudson if only I had loved him? No, because Hudson wasn't that type of male—the alpha that other men were intimidated by. He was more the polite, easygoing guy that everyone felt comfortable around.

Linc, on the other hand…

I shoved that thought away. He didn't want me like that. He barely acknowledged me. I had given him what he'd wanted, and now, I was just the mother of his child.

Stevie licked her fingers, then wiped them on the napkin.

"Are you enjoying Madison? Garrett tells me you lived in Nashville. I imagine Madison isn't as fast-paced as you're used to," Fawn said, then took a sip from her glass.

Was I enjoying Madison? That was a loaded question.

"From what I've seen of it, the town is nice, but I've not really gone anywhere," I replied, leaving out that Linc didn't let me have a car to leave when I wanted to.

"There they are."

Garrett's voice caught our attention, and we both shifted our gaze to see a couple walking toward us.

I knew immediately who the man was. He looked so much like Linc. The little boy I remembered was long gone. In his place was a tall man with broad shoulders; light-brown hair, pulled back into a man bun; and a short beard. His features were almost identical to Linc's, except for his hazel eyes.

The auburn-haired beauty, with skin like porcelain, who he held tucked close to his side, was smiling at Stevie. Her green eyes were full of curiosity. She was young, or maybe it was her petite size and smooth, unblemished skin that made her appear so much younger than Levi.

When her eyes lifted from Stevie to mine, her smile deepened. She truly looked like a delicate, fragile doll. Levi, on the other hand, looked like he would make an excellent character on the *Sons of Anarchy*. There was nothing refined about him. He had the dangerous, hard-edged demeanor coming off him in waves.

He nodded in Linc's direction before his eyes briefly shifted to me, then landed on Stevie. I wondered what he thought about this. After all these years, having a sibling. Reading his facial expressions was impossible since they didn't seem to change.

"Levi, Aspen," Linc said, "I'd like you'd to meet Stevie." The trace of pride when he said her name made my chest squeeze. "Stevie, this is Levi. He is your brother. Aspen is his wife." Then, he flickered his gaze to me, as if remembering my existence. "And her mother, Branwen." There was no pride in that introduction. His voice took on a bored tone, as if to say, *Sorry she's here.*

My earlier moment of emotion vanished instantly, replaced by embarrassment. I kept the smile on my face, refusing to react to the way he'd basically dismissed me as an annoyance. My face felt warm, and I couldn't control that.

"I'm assuming she looks like you did at that age," Levi said to me. "Because I have a faint memory of a girl down at the stables with those blonde curls."

"I'd say she's a replica," Garrett informed him.

"It's nice to see you all grown up," I told him, then shifted my gaze to Aspen. "And you look like you found happiness."

He bent his head and kissed the top of hers. "I did," he confirmed.

He was not like his father in all ways, it seemed. The adoration in his face as he looked down at her made my breath catch.

This is going to be fun, I thought pathetically.

I'd get to watch two men who were completely in love with their wives, reminding me of what I still hadn't experienced at thirty-eight years old.

Maybe they didn't have all the flaws I did. They were probably not selfish.

"I've nevah had a bwotha," Stevie piped up.

Laughter came from all directions. Even Levi's lips curled up as his eyes twinkled with amusement.

"You know, I've never had a sister," he told her.

"Weally?!" The excitement in her voice caused another ripple of laughter. Then, she turned back to the cupcakes and looked at them longingly. “Those cupcakes awah yummy,” she told him.

“I bet they are,” he replied.

“I wish I could have anotha one,” she said, sounding so forlorn that I wondered if I should get the kid into acting lessons. She had a natural talent.

“One is e—”

“You can have as many as you want,” Linc told her, cutting me off.

Tensing, I clasped my hands in my lap and glanced over at him.

His eyes went from Stevie, who quickly jumped up off the seat to go over and pick out another cupcake, to me. He had known that I was about to tell her that one was enough. If she ate more sweets, she would be wild, then have a sugar crash, which could get ugly.

He raised his eyebrows at me in a challenge. “What? I missed four years of letting her eat cupcakes. I'm making up for all the lost time.” The taunt and accusation in his tone were clear to everyone.

Going inside and hiding for the rest of this trip wasn't an option, although I was sure he would be thrilled if I disappeared. I dropped my gaze to my hands and said nothing. Making eye contact with anyone right now would likely make the lump in my throat turn into watery eyes.

I took a deep breath in and let it out. I had survived worse things than this. It seemed Linc was going to take jabs at me and humiliate me while we were here. I needed to toughen up and deal with it. I'd made the mistake of letting the man screw me again, which seemed to only make my presence even more distasteful to him than it already had been.

Aspen stepped forward and bent her knees as she lowered herself to Stevie's height. She smiled at Stevie, then peered over the foods on the table. "Hmm," she said, then looked back at Stevie as she picked up some seafood wrapped in bacon. Lobster perhaps. "You know, when I eat too much sugar, it makes my tummy hurt, and I get sad. Sometimes, it even makes me cry," she told her with a serious expression along the lines of a wide-eyed Snow White. She held up the item in her hand. "Also, bacon is my very favorite. I much prefer it. And it doesn't give me a stomachache." She scrunched her nose at the last part.

Stevie studied her closely, then looked at the bacon appetizer as if she was debating the truth in this.

"I like bacon too," Stevie admitted. "And I don't like stomachaches."

Aspen shook her head. "Oh no, those are the worst. I don't like them at all."

Stevie glanced over at the tray where the bacon-wrapped seafood items were. "I think I want one of these," she said firmly, then reached for the stick that it was on and picked it up.

"That's a very good choice," Aspen said with a nod, then took a bite of hers before standing up.

Her gaze swung over to me, and a soft smile touched her lips.

If she wasn't already married to Levi, I might have proposed. She was going to make an excellent mother.

THIRTY-TWO
LINC

“Your daughter-in-law thinks you’re a dick,” Levi said as he closed the door to Garrett’s office and glanced over at me.

“Because he is,” Garrett drawled, then put the cigar back in his mouth.

Shaking his head in disgust, Levi walked over to the bar. “I get you hate Branwen. Damn, we all got that message. You made your disdain for her clear today. If you said another word to or about her at dinner, I thought Aspen was going to throw her drink in your face.”

If they had all stopped acting as if she were important, then I’d not have kept on. But the more the other women drew her into their inner circle, like she was one of them when she sure as hell was not, the worse my annoyance with her grew.

Instead of responding, I shrugged and pulled in the smoke from the cigar to linger in my mouth for a moment before releasing it.

Levi brought his glass of whiskey over to the caramel-colored leather sofa and sat down. "Stevie might be young, but the way you treat her mother isn't going to be missed by her. Sure, this is all new, and you're new. She seems happy with this situation, but the more you humiliate and talk down to her mom, she's going to turn against you."

He took a drink, looking at me the entire time. "I was a boy. It was different. Even when I hated you for the shit you did to Mom, you were my dad. I wanted this life. We had more than just a father-son relationship. We had the family. It gave us a different bond.

"Stevie is a little girl, and that's her momma. You don't get a stronger bond. Hell, look at Fawn and Gypsy. That's what they will grow up to be like. You think she will love you and want you in her life if you hurt her momma?"

Why the fuck was I getting a lecture from my son on relationships and parenting? Did him being married now make him a goddamn expert? Not all women were like Aspen.

"Just so you are clear on something," I began, holding the cigar between my fingers, "the shit with your mom wasn't all me. You're a grown-ass man now, so understand that, although I'm glad you were born, Maggie trapped me with the pregnancy. She found out I had fucked around, and I wouldn't do the exclusive shit with her, so she stopped taking her birth control, knowing if she was knocked up, she'd be able to keep me. Our marriage was doomed from day one.

"As for Branwen, after this year is up, I am moving her into a place in town, and Stevie is going to come stay with me on alternating weeks. She won't see her mother and me together."

There was a smirk on Garrett's face as he listened to me. Why was that fucking funny?

"What?" I asked him.

"You really think that's what's gonna happen? You are going to live with her for a year and then move her out. To live her life. Date men. Fuck other men. Belong to another man."

My nostrils flared as I inhaled sharply. No, she wasn't going to fuck other men. I'd take care of that for her. She'd be addicted to my cock in a year's time. But I wasn't explaining that plan to them. I had a feeling Levi would give me another lecture and Garrett would laugh.

After today, there was going to be some convincing on my part to let me touch her again. There was an uncomfortable tightness in my chest and gut from the pained, dejected look in her eyes when she'd walked upstairs with Stevie tonight. Fuck. Maybe I had taken shit too far. But she hadn't told me about the dentist coming to the house. I was still pissed about it, but not as much as I had been earlier.

"I think we will work it out," I replied.

"You need to give up and admit you just want to fuck her and you don't hate her. You might hate that you want to fuck her," Garrett said. "And don't lie to me about it. I've known you my whole life."

"If he wants to fuck her, then he's shit out of luck. He'll be lucky if she ever speaks to him again," Levi added.

I smirked. He was obviously unaware of my charm.

"Don't underestimate your father," Garrett said. "When he wants something, he usually gets it."

Levi cocked an eyebrow like he wasn't so sure he believed that.

"Just watch," Garrett told him. "When he gets his head out of his ass, it'll look different."

I didn't say anything. Because my head wasn't in my ass. Fawn just had Garrett seeing things in a light that wasn't realistic. His obsession with his wife was unhealthy and had softened him. Thankfully, Blaise hadn't been softened by marriage and kids. The only soft in him was with Madeline and the boys. No one else got that. He was ruthless and ran the family the way the Hughes boss always had. The way Garrett once had. Now, he was making out with his wife on the patio in the middle of the fucking day.

Rolling my eyes, I put the cigar back between my teeth. It was up to me to at least keep my generation of the Shephard name from becoming weak because of a woman. My brother, Stellan, had been married for years, and he'd not been the leader he once had been. Luckily, his oldest son was a crazy fucker, even if he was married. He'd make a good head of the Georgia branch when the time came.

Standing over the bed where Branwen slept with Stevie, I stared down at them. A mess of blonde curls spread out over both pillows. Stevie's arms were wrapped around one of her mother's, and she pressed her face to her mother's shoulder. They were stunning. Both of them.

But then I'd watched Branwen that night at the club, unable to look away. She'd held me transfixed for an hour at least.

Had my subconscious recognized her? I'd been drawn to her, and I couldn't resist walking myself out of the private viewing area to go down to meet her. Hear her talk. She'd not disappointed. Sure, I was high, but she still pulled me in. I hadn't seen the little girl I had once known when I looked at her, but that didn't mean that something deeper inside me hadn't. Now that I knew, I could see it and wondered how I had missed it.

"How did my little Ringlets hurt me the way you did?" I whispered. "What made you hate me so much that you chose to do something I can't ever forgive?" I reached down and flipped one of her curls between my fingers.

But that didn't mean I couldn't fuck her. Own her. Sharing her body with anyone else was out of the question. Her needs would be taken care of, financially and sexually. Levi and Garrett were both wrong. I knew what I was doing, and without relationship shit to get in the way, we'd be better parents.

Stevie would be our only focus.

Love and commitment fucked things up. She didn't need that. She sure as hell didn't need the dentist. The man couldn't take care of her cunt the way I could. I wasn't sure he even had a dick after feeling how tight her pussy was. Tomorrow, I would ease up on her. But I'd get her to tell me about the dentist and make sure she understood keeping things from me was lying. And I fucking hated being lied to.

THIRTY-THREE
BRANWEN

Last night, I had kept it together until Stevie fell asleep. Once she was breathing deep, I let the first tear fall. As I covered my mouth to keep my sobbing from waking her up, the bed shook. But I fell asleep, and rest had seemed to help.

Linc had yet to humiliate me today. I might make it through this day without crying myself to sleep tonight.

Stevie had been slow to warm up to Levi. I thought his appearance made her unsure what to think about him. When he spoke to her, she would get quiet, which was rare for her, and duck her head, as if she were shy. But it seemed they had found a way to bond.

I stood over by the fence post, where I used to sit as a child and watch my dad work with the jockeys who took the horses out to run the practice track. Levi was currently holding Stevie up so she could rub the mane on a large black thoroughbred.

Being here again made the past seemed like another world in one way and like it was just yesterday in another. Helping feed the horses, cleaning up the tack room, even cleaning out the stalls—it had all been a part of my life. There wasn't much that went on here that I didn't know about. These stables had been more my home than the actual house Dad and I lived in. When we were awake, we were here. We only ate dinner, took baths, and slept in our house. The best memories we shared had been on this property.

I glanced over at the buildings that were larger than they had once been. They'd been added on to, and the already-elaborate features had been upgraded. But the land was the same. The smell was the same. I inhaled deeply and wished I could hear my dad's laugh one more time.

"Little Branwen Hester, all grown up," a masculine voice said, bringing me out of my memories.

I turned toward the stables to see the older, more refined version of Kenneth Houston walking up to me. He'd been the worst one to tease me about my crush on Linc.

"You got old, Kenneth," I replied.

He chuckled. "I'm surprised you didn't follow that up by sticking out your tongue at me, then running off."

"There is still time," I warned with a grin.

He leaned up against the fence I was sitting on. "I gotta admit, I came by just to see you here with Linc. When Garrett told me about the two of you, I spit my damn whiskey out."

I sighed. "If I'd only known then what I know now."

"I think we all feel that way about something in our lives," he replied. "She looks like you." He pointed at Stevie with Levi.

"She has my hair and face, but Linc's eyes."

Kenneth smiled. "I have a granddaughter. That little girl is something else. Can't imagine having a daughter. Those sweet smiles can wrap you right around their tiny fingers."

"I know you have a son. Was he your only one, or did you have more kids?"

Kenneth's family had their own stables, and I knew he'd had a little boy back then. I couldn't remember much about him, but he had been young when I left.

"One boy. Saxon. He and his wife, Haisley, live on our land. Their daughter, Winter, is a raven-haired doll. She sure has livened things up for us. Melanie is owned by that child. I swear my wife lives and breathes to make her happy."

The hollow ache in my chest when I thought about Stevie never meeting my dad or knowing him came uninvited. I didn't want to be sad. I'd had enough of that yesterday.

"Well, I need to get up to the house. Garrett is expecting me. I just caught a glimpse of pale blonde curls, and it was like old times. Thought I'd come say hello," he said, pushing off from the fence.

"I'm glad you did. It was good to see you, Kenneth."

He nodded. "You too. And, Branwen, good luck."

I wasn't sure what he meant by that, but I didn't ask as he headed back through the stables. I went back to watching Levi with Stevie. The familiar sound of a cantering horse caught my attention, and I glanced back to see a small blond boy on the back of a dark brown thoroughbred, headed in this direction. The confident way he held himself and the glint of mischief in his eyes left no question on who he belonged to.

He had to be a Hughes.

"CREE!" a deep voice shouted.

The little boy's head snapped around to see who it was, and then he smirked.

"I told you that you could ride Titus! Not Shakespeare!"

"Titus is old and a quarter. I ride thoroughbreds," the little boy called back.

I squinted against the glare of the sun toward the man stalking this way with a black cowboy hat, a pair of jeans hanging low on his hips, and a pair of boots. No shirt and… whew. I felt like I should throw dollar bills at him. Holy crap.

"Get your ass off that horse before your momma comes out here!" He scowled.

"I'm not a pussy! I don't ride pussy horses!"

My eyes widened. He was about Stevie's age. I really hoped she didn't hear him say that. She'd be asking me what a pussy was.

"I swear to God, Cree Elias Hughes, if you don't get down off that goddamn horse!"

And that had to be Blaise Hughes. It seemed the apple hadn't fallen far from the tree with his son. I remembered Blaise being just as wild at the stables when he had been that age. The current boss of the Southern Mafia had the body of a god now that he was all grown up.

"You let me when Momma ain't here!" the boy shouted back.

"If you don't shut up and get down, you'll be riding Hopscotch until you're old enough to drive a car," Blaise threatened him.

"Hopscotch is an old mare. I don't wanna ride her." He sounded so insulted that I almost laughed.

"Then, get down," Blaise said, grabbing ahold of the reins as he reached a hand up for his son to take. "Off. Now."

"Okay." He sulked. "But I don't wanna play with a girl. I wanna ride."

I pressed my lips together to keep from smiling in case he looked my way.

"You will feel differently about that soon enough. Trust me, you don't want to get on the pretty ones' shit list at this young of an age. They remember and will hold it against you."

Cree tilted his head up and looked at his father, scrunching his nose. "Why do they got a shit list?"

"Because guys can be shits. Now, come on over here and act sane for ten minutes, would you?"

Levi walked over to them with Stevie, who was studying Cree with interest. Poor girl thought she was going to have a playmate, but seemed like Cree wasn't on board with that idea.

"You gonna shoot me if I say he looked good up there? Had complete control of Shakespeare," Levi said.

Blaise sighed and took off his hat to reveal blond hair that was long enough to tuck behind his ears. He ran a hand over it to smooth it back and shook his head. "Yeah, well, his momma doesn't like him on the faster ones," Blaise said, then looked down. "You must be Stevie," he said in a softer tone than he'd been using.

She nodded her head, not sure what to think about the overwhelming man in front of her.

"Stevie, this is Cree. Y'all are about the same age."

She nodded and tucked herself back behind Levi's leg some. The fact that she was using him as her security made me smile. I'd almost caused her to miss out on that. Having a big brother. Another fail for me.

"I like your hair," Cree told her.

She smiled bashfully at him.

"It might take her a minute to warm up," Levi told him. "She's met a lot of new people the past two days."

Cree shrugged. "I ain't gonna hurt her. You wanna go get some cookies from Ms. Jimmie? She said she was making my favorite chocolate chip ones."

Levi looked over at me.

I nodded my head that it was fine.

He patted her head. "You can go if you want. Your momma said it was okay."

She smiled then. Chocolate chip cookies could bribe her to do just about anything. "Okay," she agreed.

"Come on then," he told her, acting as if he were older and maturer. It was cute.

When he broke into a run, she took off after him.

"Don't run off and leave her like a little shit!" Blaise called after him.

I was going to have to go over all these curse words with her and what not to say when we left here.

Cree stopped, and she caught up to him.

Blaise swung his gaze over to me, then started in my direction. Levi fell into step beside him. I wondered if they had any idea how much they looked like their fathers back then. It was like watching a replay of my childhood.

Blaise put his hat back on his head and smirked at me. "Well, Ringlets, did you miss us?"

THIRTY-FOUR
BRANWEN

Stevie was asleep minutes after the plane took off. She had played hard all day.

Until our ride to the airstrip, I had seen little of Linc, which led to a much better day. Coming here had been good for me in the end. I wasn't bothered or worried about the fact that these people would be in Stevie's life anymore. Seeing them, being there again, it had given me a sense of peace rather than fear for her attachment to the family. I knew once the year was over, I probably wouldn't see them again, and that thought made me sad, but I wasn't going to dwell on it. Stevie would have them, and I was thankful for it. She deserved a big family. I'd always wanted one, and when Daddy had died, my lack of it had been painful.

Once we were leveled off, I carried Stevie to the small bedroom in the back and laid her on the bed so she wasn't slumped over in a seat. Linc had started to stand, and I shook my head and kept walking with her. I didn't want his help. When I reentered the main cabin, I didn't glance his way even though I felt his eyes watching me. I planned on ignoring him.

Leaning back into the soft leather seat, I sipped the champagne that the flight attendant had brought me. She wasn't the same one who had given Linc a blow job, but she was young and attractive. Her smiles and flirty looks she was giving Linc weren't subtle either. I didn't care. Whatever.

Looking out the window into the night sky, I enjoyed my drink, and we could continue in our silence. I was sure when Linc was done doing whatever he was handling on his phone, he'd take the attendant up on her silent offer. I'd said I didn't care, and yet I kept thinking about it. Real convincing.

"I think she had a good time."

Linc's voice startled me. I hadn't expected to hear it. I turned to look over at him, forgetting that I was going to ignore him.

"She did. She loved it there."

His gaze traveled down my legs, and I wanted to kick him in his handsome face.

"Did you enjoy yourself?"

As if he cared.

"I did," I replied in a clipped tone.

"How long should I expect this pouting to last?" he asked as if I were a child.

My hand gripped the glass I was holding tightly, and I clenched my teeth together. That arrogant ass. I was not pouting. I was hurt. I was angry. I might hate him. But I was not pouting.

"I'm not pouting," I replied.

"You're in a snit."

"A snit?" I asked incredulously.

He nodded. "Yes. I'm the one who should be pissed. But I got over it."

I set the glass down before I broke the damn thing or threw it at his face. "What did you have to be pissed about?"

He took a drink from his glass. His expression seemed to say that I knew exactly what he was talking about. But I was clueless.

"The dentist," he said, his tone harder than before.

I frowned. "What about Hudson?"

His eyes narrowed. "That he came to the house, Branwen."

I nodded, still confused. "Yeah. But I hadn't asked him to, and I got him to leave."

"You didn't tell me."

I shrugged. "Why would I need to tell you? Jayda and Luther knew. You were acknowledging their existence. I assumed they'd tell you. I haven't been spoken to or treated with any respect since the night you came to my room." I hadn't meant to blurt that all out, but I was angry, and it was just bubbling out of me.

He didn't say anything, and I figured we were going back to the silent treatment.

"Did you expect me to treat you differently because we'd fucked?" he asked. As if he wasn't sure what I had expected.

Yeah, maybe I had. But then why wouldn't I? It had felt like we were…different then. Like something had changed.

"I didn't expect to be treated worse. But don't worry. I am not hoping for a repeat. In fact, I'd rather have my teeth pulled out with pliers." Asshole.

I turned to look back out the window and picked up my glass again.

"You sure about that? Because the way you were crying out my name and coming all over my cock and hand, it seemed like you would do anything to have it."

That had been before I knew the outcome.

"You don't have the only dick in the world, Linc," I hissed. "I can find another one to make me come." I didn't look back at him as I said it. The more I looked at him, the more riled up I got.

I could hear him as he set his glass down and stood up. When his shadow came over me, I looked up to see Linc standing there. Too close. He leaned down, caging me in with his hands on either side of my chair. I leaned back as far as I could to get away from him. He had a seat, and he needed to go sit in it.

"Personal space, Linc," I snapped at him.

"No other dick is taking this cunt," he growled and grabbed my leg to uncross it, shoving his hand beneath my skirt.

I tried to push him away, but he was hard to budge.

"Stop it," I hissed.

"No one else can take care of this pussy like I can, and you know it. Has anyone ever fucked you and gotten you off that many times in a night?" he asked. Then, he leaned down, his beard brushing my skin, as his mouth was close to my ear. "Has anyone else called you their slut? Spread your legs and gotten you off while finger-fucking you as his cum leaked out?" He slid a finger inside my panties. "You like being called names. It made you so fucking wet."

I whimpered, hating myself for it. I was torn between wanting him to stop and wanting to open my legs wider. I tried to mentally fight this. My body's craving for this man.

"Don't you have a flight attendant you can have suck you off?" I asked him, but my voice sounded breathless rather than snide.

A deep chuckle tickled my ear. "Careful. You sound jealous."

I was, and I wasn't. Because just like the flight attendant he'd used, he'd also used me.

His finger rubbed my clit, and the wetness pooling down there was unfortunate. I had no control over it. If I had, I'd have made sure to stay bone dry.

"That's it." His voice was husky as he ran his finger down to my aching core. "You might not like that you want me, but you do. Your body wants me. It wants to be my pretty little slut. Spreading your thighs for only me."

Oh God, please don't let me have an orgasm.

I fought against lifting my hips. I would not enjoy this.

"I wasn't lying. This pussy is the sweetest, tightest one I've ever had." He pressed a kiss on my neck, and I shivered. "I'm not gonna share it. And you're gonna give it to me when I want it."

I shook my head. "No, I won't," I said, wishing I'd sounded firmer.

His tongue flicked against the pulse in my neck. "Ringlets, your pussy is dripping wet." He thrust his finger in and out of me to prove his point.

The door to the front of the plane opened, and I watched over his shoulder as the flight attendant stepped out. I tried to push him away and press my thighs together, but a sadistic laugh rumbled in his chest as he replaced his one finger with two.

"Stop," I told him. "The attendant is in here."

The trail of his hot breath and lips moved up my neck. "She can't see your pussy. My hand is covering it up."

"She can tell what you are doing."

"Mmhmm," he murmured against my skin.

She looked unsure of what to do and glanced at his empty glass.

"Ah fuck, Ringlets. You keep that up, and there will be a puddle in this seat," he said as another gush came from my traitorous body.

I gripped his arms, not sure if I was trying to stop him anymore.

"She can hear you," I panted.

His thumb began to rub my clit, and I dropped my face to his shoulder, closing my eyes tightly as I tried to fight off the climax building.

"Please, stop," I begged.

I jerked as his teeth sank into the curve of my neck.

"Your cunt is squeezing my fingers, and your clit is swollen and pulsing under my thumb. Do you really want me to stop?"

No. Yes. Oh God.

"Linc." His name sounded like a moan.

"That's a good girl. Show her how sweet you come for me, Ringlets. Coat my fingers so I can lick them clean."

"I can't. She's gonna hear me," I said in a strangled whisper.

"She offered me her cunt to fuck, but whose cunt are my fingers buried in? Show her whose cunt I want. Whose cunt I take care of." His dark, tempting words were right against my ear.

My legs opened more.

"Ah, there we go. Open wide for me. Show her that I already have my own naughty slut."

I gasped, trying to hold it back, but it slipped away from me. He could have fucked her, but he was finger-fucking me. My body began to shudder, and I muffled my cry as the orgasm hit me.

"That's my good girl," he praised. "Ride my hand. Get the taste of that sweet pussy all over it."

I didn't know if she was still in here or not, but I hoped she had gone. I couldn't believe I had given in to him again.

He removed his hand from between my legs and grabbed my wrists, then tugged me up from the seat. My knees were wobbly as he turned us so that he could sink down onto it instead. His hooded eyes slid up my body while he unzipped his jeans. What was he doing?

I glanced over to see the attendant eyeing him hungrily.

What the hell?

"Get the panties off and come straddle my cock," he said as he pulled it out and began to stroke it.

I looked at him, then back to the attendant. Was she just going to stand there and continue to watch? I...I wasn't about to orgasm this time, and there was no way I was doing this.

"Leave," he barked at her, then reached for my thigh. "Take them off, or I'll rip them off."

The door closed as she exited the cabin.

I looked back down at his erection and swallowed. "What if Stevie wakes up?"

"We will see her come out. I'll tell her Mommy was just sitting on Daddy's lap."

"You can't tell her that," I hissed.

"Get off the panties, or I will shred them."

His large hand continued to stroke while he stared at me with lust. I was weak. I wanted this. Not only the pleasure, but also the connection. When we were like this, I felt like he was mine. That he cared for me. I knew he didn't, but for that blissful moment, it felt like he did.

Sliding them off, I stepped out of my heels and then pulled up my skirt and placed one knee on each side of his hips. His free hand slid around to my bottom and pulled me closer.

"That's it. Now, sit on my lap and ride," he said thickly.

He held his cock while I moved over the swollen tip and eased down until the head was inside my entrance. Hissing as he stretched me, I grabbed his biceps.

"Come on, Ringlets," he said coaxingly as he held my butt with both hands now.

I let more in, then held my breath and went down fast. "OH!" I cried out as he instantly filled me.

"Fuck yes," he groaned, laying his head back on the seat. "Pull your shirt up so I can watch your tits bounce."

I reached for the hem and pulled it up and over my chest. He tugged the cups of my bra down and freed them. His fingertips brushed over one, and he made a pleased rumble as he felt my nipple.

"Fuck me," he said, lifting his hips enough to push even farther into me.

I'd only done this position once; it had been with him, and it had been on a bed. I placed my hands on his shoulders and lifted my hips up, then dropped back down. That was amazing. I moaned with each movement.

"Fucking hell, Ringlets, you're killing me." He slapped my bottom hard. "Faster."

I started to speed up, and his fingers dug into my butt cheeks.

"That's it. Make those titties bounce for me. Ah God, fuck, Ringlets. FUCK."

My breathing was coming in a hard, fast pant as I looked down at him. His eyes were glazed over in pleasure, watching my boobs. Having this control was heady. Knowing that I was making him look that way. I loved it. The tingling ache was so tight now that I felt ready to burst.

"Oh, Linc, oh," I gasped as I grew closer.

"Yeah," he groaned. "You gonna come on my cock like the perfect little slut?"

At the degrading word he kept calling me, my body ignited like a firework, and I threw my head back while slamming down hard onto him until my climax hit so deep that it was almost painful. I began to rock as pulse after pulse of bliss pumped through me.

Linc worked me up and down with his grip on my butt. Then, his hips lifted up, and his body shuddered beneath me. I felt the heat of his release as it unloaded deep inside me. The connection. The moment when he was mine. I held on to it. Soaked it in. Wishing I could keep it.

"Goddamn, that pussy is sucking me dry," he grunted. His body twitched again, and a low, deep growl came from his lips.

We sat there as our heart rates slowed. The euphoria faded. This was the part I hated. The end. When reality came back and I was no longer important to him. Just the slut he'd called me.

"Lift up onto your knees and let me slide out, but stay here." His voice was hoarse.

I did as he'd said and waited to see what I was supposed to do next. I had become his puppet.

He slid his hand over my tender folds, and I jerked.

"Easy. You know I like to feel my cum inside your pussy."

Oh. We weren't done. My eyes went to the door leading to the bedroom. We should stop. I couldn't be sure she wouldn't wake up.

"Here it comes." His deep hum that followed made me shiver. He slid his two fingers over my folds, running his semen around. "I want this plump pink pussy to have my seed all over it. It needs to know who it belongs to."

The door behind us opened, and I stilled, looking down at him, wide-eyed.

"I'm sorry, sir, but we are getting ready to land, and everyone needs to be in their seats and buckled." The attendant's voice was nervous as she stammered over her words.

"All right," he drawled as he continued touching me.

"Linc," I hissed.

"Hmm?" He didn't look up.

"She can see you."

"She can't see your pussy, Ringlets. She just knows I'm playing with it."

I covered my face with my hands. I couldn't believe we were doing this. That I was letting him do this.

He finally stopped and held a finger up to my mouth. "Suck it."

I opened my mouth, and I sucked it the way I would his cock, tasting the saltiness of his cum, mixed with mine. His eyes flared.

He wasn't immune to me. I had some power here. If only I knew how to use it.

THIRTY-FIVE
LINC

Luther came walking out of the patio door, holding a six-pack in one hand and Maui in the other. I'd left Maui in Jayda's care while we were gone, but it seemed he had stayed with Luther most of the time.

"Jayda made a grocery run. There will be more stocked in the fridge out here soon," he said.

"Are they cold?" Mal Bowen asked.

"Did I bring them out here? Of course they're fucking cold," Luther replied.

"Then, I want one," Mal told him, leaning back on the sofa and looking at the television, where ESPN was discussing predicted outcomes for the first game of the NFL preseason.

"Oz has more riding on this game than any previous first season game," Hale Carver said as he stood up with a cigarette in his mouth to go get a beer instead of asking Luther to give him one.

"Are all the boys watching it over at Locke and Gathe's place or the Cash hacienda?" Luther asked Mal.

Mal's two sons, Locke and Gathe, shared a home that had belonged to Their grandfather. The rest of the younger generation lived in a house the Cashes owned. Bane Cash had shared it with his brother, Crosby, who had been shot and killed two years ago. Bane was married now with a baby, and I knew he was looking to get them a place alone. I doubted he'd kick the others out even if he did own it. I had a feeling he was going to build something.

"The hacienda. It's bigger, and with Oz having to deal with all the betting going on, it's easier for him to be there," Mal replied.

"Than's fucking attached to that kid, man. If Bane up and moves them out, he's gonna have withdrawals. I sure as hell don't want him getting locked down with marriage at his age and having babies," Hale said, opening his beer.

Hale had two sons and a daughter. Ransom was his oldest, and Than was his youngest. The middle child was a girl, Opal, who had gone political in college and was a direct in for us at the White House. She lived in DC and wasn't around a lot.

Luther laughed as he set Maui down to explore, then lit up a cigarette. "Than's ass ain't getting married. You're safe. The boy is a slut."

"If it keeps him from doing something stupid, then fine," Hale replied.

"Speaking of babies," Mal drawled, looking at me pointedly, "where is yours? All I've seen is her dog that Luther seems to have stolen."

"Taking a nap. I had a new swing set put in while we were in Ocala, and she played on it all morning," I replied, still not sure if I was ready to navigate Branwen around these two.

They were the only single men over thirty in this branch of the family. Hale's wife had been dead for fifteen years, and he had no desire to get remarried. He hadn't wanted to get married the first time, but that was a guilt he lived with now that she was gone. Mal's marriage had ended much like mine. He was never meant for one woman, but Celeste had walked out on his cheating ass way sooner than Maggie had left me.

Luther took the cigarette from his lips and let out a laugh. "That ain't a fucking swing set. It's a damn playground. Fifty kids could play on the motherfucker at one time. Y'all go look at it," he said, pointing in its direction. "It's even got a two-story house on it with a kitchen and bedroom."

Mal grinned and shook his head. "You having a daughter is funny as fuck, and you know it. First dick who breaks her heart for doing the same shit you've done to women, you'll put a bullet in his head."

I hadn't thought that far, but, yeah, if someone broke her heart, I couldn't say he was going to see the next day.

"Just wait until his baby momma struts her hot ass down here. You'll understand why that accident happened," Luther told them as he sat down in one of the seats and Maui came hurrying over to him.

Getting pissed off about him talking about her hot ass was not going to help anything. They wouldn't understand, and then they'd all think this was something that it was not. I had to make sure she didn't get it in her head that we had some kind of relationship. If she came out here and the men started talking like we did have something, it would give her the wrong idea.

Last night, when we had gotten home, I'd carried Stevie to bed and walked away with a simple, "Good night."

That had been hard but required. I'd wanted to follow Branwen into her room and fuck her again, but I hadn't. Because the urge to kiss her on the fucking plane had been like a wake-up call. One I'd needed before I did something stupid. I did not need to kiss her. I knew that was a road that

I would not be going down. I didn't trust myself if I tasted her mouth. Felt her lips move under mine. Fucking was one thing. Kissing was intimate. I'd only kissed one woman since Maggie, and it was Branwen. The night in Vegas. I had vivid memories of it that loved to come back to me in my dreams at night.

"I gotta ask," Mal said, and I didn't much care for the grin on his face. "Are you fucking her while you have her under your roof? I mean, I'm assuming you aren't bringing women here to fuck with the kid here, and you haven't gone to Glow with us in two weeks. So..."

Gow was the strip club we visited. It was members only with a price on it that made the place elite. I grabbed a beer and stuck a new cigarette in my mouth, then lit up. "We got a kid. That's it," I snapped, annoyed.

"She'd so open those sweet legs for him too," Luther said. "I'm waiting until she gives up on his ass, and then I'm sweet-talking my way between them."

My hand gripped the bottle as rage rolled through my body. "I'll put a gun to your goddamn head," I snarled without thinking about the words.

His eyebrows shot up, and he took a drink from his bottle as he looked at me. "Huh," he said. "Thought so. Just wanted to hear you say it."

"Pass me the nachos. I need a snack for this," Mal said with a smirk.

"What the fuck does that mean?" I scowled at Luther.

He leaned forward, resting his elbows on his legs while Maui placed his paws on his knee, trying to get his attention. "It means you want to fuck her. That she was more than a high, drunken fuck in Vegas. Maybe she's got a voodoo pussy. I don't know. But there is more to this shit than you put on. Why?" He pointed his beer at me. "Because you have never ignored a gorgeous female in your goddamn life. You are charming. You work your shit. But this one? You will go out of your way to ignore her. Poor thing stood in the doorway of the kitchen, watching you and Jayda decorating those pancakes for Stevie, looking so dejected. Then, when you realized she was there, you didn't even acknowledge her. I was ready to fucking cry for her. It was painful to witness."

He was so full of shit. Half the time, I wondered why the hell I'd agreed to share a house with him.

"What does Jayda have to do with it?" I asked. "And Branwen wasn't dejected," I added. I'd seen her. I always saw her, even when I was trying like hell not to see her.

"You and Jayda were all close and touching while you made the face on the pancakes. It looked very intimate."

"Jayda has a fucking girlfriend! You know she doesn't want my dick or yours. She likes pussy as much as we do," I was almost shouting.

He was pissing me off.

"Great. Now, I have a boner," Mal drawled, taking another drink.

Luther nodded, then put his cigarette back in his mouth. "Yeah, I know that feeling. I worked up the image in my head the other day of Jayda going down on Branwen and had to jerk one off. Jayda walked in on me, and I shot off like a goddamn water hose."

Mal started coughing as he choked on his beer. "Where were you?" he asked in a strangled voice.

"Great room. Branwen had just been in there, wearing a bikini, and I got carried away with the fantasy."

Hale cut his eyes to me as my temples started pounding.

When the fuck did this happen?

"Don't worry," Luther said, holding out a hand to me, as if to stop me. "Branwen saw that I was gonna pull out my cock and ran out the door like it was a damn anaconda."

The smack of my beer bottle hitting the table as I climbed over the chair to grab Luther by the collar was followed by an animalistic roar that tore from my chest.

"Shit, Luther," Hale said as I shoved him against the wall.

"Easy," Luther said as his eyes fucking danced with amusement. "I didn't think you wanted her. You gotta tell a brother."

"I said not to touch her," I sneered.

"And I didn't touch her. I touched my cock that she'd made hard."

I slammed his back against the wall again. "DON'T FUCKING LOOK AT HER!"

He nodded. "Okay. Noted. We will both ignore her, and she can be sad and cry."

"Jesus, Luther, shut up," Mal groaned.

The door opened, and I let go of him, turning, afraid it was Stevie or Branwen. Jayda looked at the two of us as she held two cases of beer.

Her eyes narrowed, and then she nodded. "Ah. You told him about jacking off to me going down on Branwen." She rolled her eyes and muttered, "Dumbass," then brought the cases over and set them on the bar.

Luther straightened his collar. "I was unaware he'd react so strongly."

Jayda let out a bark of laughter. "Yeah, right. She's the mother of his daughter. Don't share with him when you masturbate to her. But for the record, if I were single and Linc wouldn't kill me, I would try my hardest to convince her to let me down there. She's fucking gorgeous. A complete sexpot," Jayda said, then pointed a sharp nail at me. "Don't slam me against a wall. I'm just stating something everyone else is thinking."

"This is so not helping my boner," Mal said.

Jayda looked over at him and grinned wickedly. "What? The idea of me licking Branwen's clit until she screams has you hot and bothered?"

"Fuck."

"Jesus Christ."

"Jayda!" I snapped as the other men groaned. "Don't."

She held up both hands. "Sorry, boss."

"God, I love having a hot lesbian working here," Luther said, then took a deep pull from his cigarette.

I was tempted to lock Branwen in her room until they all left, but that would be late tonight, and Stevie would need her. I was going to have to drink more before she showed up out here. The fact that all of them were going to get off to Jayda's head between her legs the next time they jerked one off made me livid.

THIRTY-SIX
BRANWEN

One would think that a four-year-old who had played nonstop on their own personal playground for four straight hours would sleep longer. But the excitement of waking up this morning to find she had a child's fantasyland in the backyard had been too much. After a nap that had lasted only one hour and thirty minutes, she was up again, ready to return to the outdoors.

Jayda was coming out of the kitchen, carrying a tray of what looked like hot wings, some chips and dips, and meatball sliders.

"Do you need help?" I asked her, as it seemed she had her hands full.

"Well, there is another tray in the kitchen. It's not this full," she said, sounding reluctant.

I wasn't her employer. There was no reason for her to make two trips when I was right here with perfectly good hands that worked.

"I'll get it," I replied.

"If you're sure," she called out, but I was already headed inside the kitchen.

She'd been busy in here. There were several things happening. Cookies looked like they were in the works. What was going on? Why all this food?

Taking the tray back out to the hallway, she stood there, holding hers as she talked to Stevie about her playset and assured her that Maui was outside, waiting on her.

When she saw me, she nodded her head for me to follow. "These are going outside. I have some sunflower butter and jelly roll-ups for Stevie when she's ready to eat. I wasn't sure what she would eat from all this."

"What is this for?" I asked her.

"Pregame day. Football is back. The guys have some friends over to watch it."

I wondered if Stevie going out to play would be okay. The playset was far enough away and out of sight from the patio with the way it was placed, but if Linc and Luther had friends over, I wasn't sure if we should be coming and going.

It had been different today.

Linc hadn't come in my room last night when we returned, but simply said, "Good night," and left after laying a sleeping Stevie in her bed.

This morning, I had been prepared for him to ignore me again, but he'd spoken to me. Granted, it was formal and polite. Nothing more. He acknowledged my existence, but he didn't try and interact with me as more than Stevie's mom. When he told her about his surprise outside, he asked me to come with them. While she played on it, he asked me if there was anything that could be dangerous on it or that I was uncomfortable with. It had been weird. I didn't know what to think about it. When he was acting like I didn't exist, then I at least felt like there was something there under the surface. This had seemed…detached.

We reached the patio door, and Stevie rushed to open it and hold it. Jayda thanked her for being such a good helper, which made her beam. Following her out the door, I winked at Stevie, and she giggled like we had a secret.

A loud male curse and something about calling Oz was the first thing we were greeted with. I focused on Jayda for directions instead of the men gathered out here.

"Just put it over on the counter. I'll handle the rest," she told me.

Stevie rushed over to pick up Maui, who was at Luther's feet. She bent down to pet him, then turned to look at Linc. Leaving Maui where he was, she walked over to Linc, glancing at the other men with uncertainty. Linc picked her up and placed her on his right knee. Nervously, I watched while Linc talked to her, and she nodded her head, causing the blonde curls to bounce.

"This is Stevie," he told them.

There were three new faces that I hadn't met. Luther I obviously knew.

Linc glanced back over his shoulder. "And this is her mother, Branwen."

It seemed I was getting introduced this time.

"Ladies, this is Mal, Jonas, and Hale," he informed us, pointing the bottle of beer in his hand in the direction of each one as he said their name.

All three men were attractive. They had the *Southern wealth* vibe about them that reminded me of the men on *Yellowstone*. I would guess they were all between forty-five and fifty-five maybe.

"You copied and pasted, didn't you, darlin'?" One of them grinned at me, leaning back on the sofa with one booted foot resting on his knee.

"Lucky for her, she didn't get her daddy's ugly mug," the one with the most salt-and-pepper hair and pale gray eyes said.

I believe that one was Mal. I wasn't sure exactly if that was right. Linc had introduced them so fast and pointed from one to the other, and I didn't want to say their names in case I got it wrong. Hopefully, I wouldn't need to address them.

"My dad is not ugly," Stevie said defiantly, sitting up straight, as if to challenge the man.

Linc smirked. "Seems the prettiest girl in the state of Mississippi believes otherwise, Mal."

"You put damn Disney World in the backyard for her," the one that I thought was Hale said. "You are a king in her eyes. Don't let it get to your head."

"We all know I'm the best-looking one," Luther drawled, and then his eyes swung to me. "Ain't that right, Branwen?"

My eyes widened. I was not getting in this conversation. I especially wasn't going to give Luther any wrong ideas. I'd already seen some of his penis.

"Fuck, Luth, Jesus," Mal said, reaching over and shoving him on the arm while chuckling and shaking his head.

I felt like I had missed something they all seemed to find amusing, except Linc. His jaw was clenched, and the veins in his neck were standing out.

"Mommy, my dad is the most handsome, isn't he?" Stevie said, turning to look at me.

Why, Vivi Lu, are you bringing me into this?

"Stevie, sweetheart, don't do that to your momma," Luther drawled. "God knows he's barely spoken to her today..." He trailed off. "She doesn't want to defend him."

An embarrassed flush rushed up my neck.

"For Christ's sake, Luth, when he has you by the neck again, I'm not stepping in to stop him," the one I thought was Hale said.

Luther only flashed me a wicked grin, then turned his eyes back to the television.

"I don't know how he lives with your ass," the third one, speaking for the first time, told him. He'd be Jonas, if I was right about Hale.

"I own half the house," Luther drawled. "He ain't got a choice."

Linc whispered something to Stevie, and she smiled, then hopped down from his lap to hurry over to me. "Let's go play on my new swing set," she told me, then bent to scoop up Maui, who had followed her.

He was ready to get rid of us, and I didn't blame him. I wanted to get out of this situation too.

"It was nice to meet all of you," I told them before letting Stevie start to lead me away.

"You too, darlin'," Mal called out.

We were almost around the corner of the tree line when I heard one of them say. "Holy fuck, Luther wasn't exaggerating. Jesus, Linc. If you're gonna knock one up, that's sure one I don't blame you for."

A pleased smile tugged on my lips, and I hoped Stevie hadn't been listening. Her vocabulary was getting larger—and not in a good way.

"Shut up, Hale." Linc's voice sounded like an angry growl.

"She's young too. I didn't know she was that young. Damn, man. Whew. Beauty and youth. What did Levi think about her being so young? Is he older than her?" I thought that might be Mal.

"She is older than Levi." Linc sounded pissed. "She looks younger than she is."

"Eh, let's not forget that she was a little girl when you were already married and had a kid," Luther piped up. "I might have only been a teenager back then, but I remember her. She followed you around, worshipping the ground you walked on."

I hadn't realized Luther had been in Ocala back then. He'd never mentioned it. I tried to think back, but I didn't remember him.

Whatever else was said after that, I could no longer hear them as I kept going. Stevie was basically pulling me in her attempt to run to her new playset. Linc had wanted to outdo the one that I had wanted to get for Hudson's backyard. He'd succeeded far beyond any expectation. My jaw had dropped when we walked out here this morning.

There was a round teak sofa with cream cushions and a canopy that came over the top for shade, along with the playground that he called a swing set. Two tall, skinny teak tables stood on either side to hold drinks. I walked over to it and slipped off my sandals before climbing onto it and stretching my feet out in front of me. The furniture came apart into four pieces, making a curved sofa; two small, padded benches; and a round one in the middle to use as a seat or perhaps a table. But when pushed all together, it was large enough to stretch out on like a bed. I preferred it this way.

Maui began running toward someone about the time I heard footsteps, and I turned to see Jayda carrying a glass of lemonade and a child's cup, which I assumed was filled with the same thing.

"I thought you might need drinks," she said, placing them on the table to my left.

"Thank you," I told her. "I meant to grab something from the refrigerator out here, but—" I stopped.

"But the guys were talking shit, and you wanted to escape," she finished and gave me a knowing look. "I don't blame you. Unfortunately, they will be here until late. More could also stop by. The younger guys most likely. The other two older men in the fam—uh, circle of friends won't show up. Fender is more uptight, and he rarely comes here for game nights. He spends more time with Gannon, who has Parkinson's, and it's progressed to the end stages from what Linc says. They are close, and it's been harder on Fender; plus, he lost his youngest son two years ago in a shooting. He's not been the same since." She said all this as if I knew who in the heck she was talking about.

But I listened. This was Linc's world, and I wanted to know about it. These would be people in Stevie's life.

"Anyway, it'll probably be Hale's oldest, Ransom, and Mal's oldest, Locke, who stop by, if any of them do. Jonas's oldest is the bookie among them, and he will be working all night. The younger crowd…well, from what I've heard, there are topless women—mostly strippers from Glow—and light drug use involved. But I guess they won't be doing that at Cash's house anymore. Not with Bane married and the baby." She shrugged. "I'm rambling. I'd better get back to the kitchen. I have cookies to put in the oven and Rice Krispies treats to make."

"Thank you for the drinks. I'd help you if I didn't have Stevie wanting to live on this, well, whatever it is," I said, waving a hand at the massive structure.

She grinned. "It is something else. She's loving it though."

That she was.

Determined to go back outside and tell Linc good night before going up to bed, Stevie went out onto the patio, and I had to follow. When I had brought her inside for dinner and a bath, they had all been wrapped up in the game, and Linc hadn't done anything but nod and wink at her. Facing them again seemed exhausting because I never knew how Linc was going to treat me.

Stevie opened the door and went running out to him, wearing her Bluey pajamas and slippers. Her blonde curls were still damp and hung longer in the back because of it. Linc had moved from beer to whiskey, and there was a cigar in his mouth. When he saw Stevie, he put his glass down and immediately put the cigar in an ashtray, then shoved it toward Mal to move it away from her.

She scrambled up into his lap. I stayed silent as I waited by the door.

"There is plenty of room here if you want to sit," Luther told me, patting the space between him and Mal.

Mal repressed a grin and shook his head, as if Luther was crazy.

"I'm good, thanks," I replied. "She just wanted to tell him good night."

Luther waved at the table full of food. "Get something to eat. No rush."

Linc appeared tense, as if he was afraid I'd take him up on it and invade the party.

Not something I want to do, bud. Chill.

"We ate in the kitchen with Jayda," I replied.

Mal let out a small groan and closed his eyes for a minute.

Hale chuckled, and Luther grinned wickedly. I was missing something here.

"What the fuck is wrong with y'all?" Jonas asked, frowning at them.

"I'll explain later when the little ears have left," Luther told him, then glanced back at me with a glint in his eyes that made me nervous.

The door opened behind me, and I turned, expecting to see Jayda, but instead, two younger men walked outside.

One had dark brown hair, cut short, but there was a hint of a curl to the flipped-up edges that could be seen from under his cowboy hat. His face was chiseled with a firm jawline and a cleft in his chin. The stubble on his face looked like he hadn't shaved in a week.

The guy behind him was taller, maybe even six-five, with a slightly lighter shade of brown hair and a beard. He didn't wear a hat, but he looked like he'd just walked off a ranch or maybe a calendar shoot for sexy cowboys. When his eyes met mine, he did a complete up and down of me, and then the corner of his lips quirked.

He reminded me of the one I believed was Mal. That would make this one his oldest, Locke. Which, if Jayda was correct, the other would be Ransom.

"How much did you lose on the Patriots game?" Mal asked them.

"Not a fu—" The one I was almost positive was Locke stopped before finishing the word as his eyes landed on Stevie sitting in Linc's lap, looking up at him. "Not anything. Didn't bet on them."

"I'm down three grand. Oz's ass has already called to taunt me about it," the other said as he picked up one of the sliders from the table. "Y'all always have the better food."

Locke held out his hand to Stevie. "Hello, Stevie," he said formally.

She looked at his hand, then back at Linc, who smirked, then nodded. Slowly, as if not sure she was okay with this, she reached out and placed her much smaller one in his, and he gave it a shake.

"I'm Locke. It's nice to meet you. Gathe has told us all about you."

Her eyes lit up at the familiar name, and then she swung her eyes to me. "He knows Gathe, Mommy!"

I nodded, smiling at her enthusiasm.

"And I'm Ransom, Goldilocks," the other one told her, then stuck a chip into his mouth.

"And that is Branwen," Luther said. "These are Hale's and Mal's boys. Ransom belongs to Hale and Locke to Mal."

Both of the younger men turned to look at me.

"It's nice to meet you," I said, feeling awkward and on display.

"Than did not exaggerate," Ransom said. "Shocker."

Linc cleared his throat and stood up, holding Stevie in his crooked arm as if she weighed nothing. "I'll go tuck this one in," he said to the men, then started toward me.

I couldn't tell if his expression was angry or not. But he didn't look happy.

"Where's the puppy?" Luther asked.

Grinning at his concern over Maui, I looked back at him. "We just took him to his bed for the night."

He looked disappointed, and I wanted to laugh. I wasn't sure if Maui was Stevie's or Luther's anymore.

"Night!" several of them called.

I gave a small wave, then followed Linc inside, not sure what to expect from him and wishing he didn't tie me up in knots so easily.

THIRTY-SEVEN

LINC

As I closed the door after waving back at Stevie one more time, tucked into her large bed, my chest was tight with the reminder that I'd missed so many of these nights already. Nights I couldn't get back. Moments that would never be mine to cherish one day when she was grown and living her life.

"She's easy to put to bed," I said as I turned to look at Branwen, standing over by her door with her arms crossed. "From what I can remember, Levi was hell to get to sleep. Refusing to stay in bed."

"We had times when she was more difficult, but it seems we've moved past it," she replied.

The way she stood was pushing her tits up, making her cleavage all the more visible. A champagne-colored lock of hair curled just over the right side, and the tip would be touching her nipple if she were naked. There wasn't a blemish on her skin. It was as if she'd been airbrushed. All smooth, golden perfection.

Listening to the others talk about her and even with the ones who hadn't said anything, I knew they'd looked at her for too fucking long. I'd seen their gazes. She was intoxicating with or without that tight velvet cunt that sheathed my cock like a vise.

My fingertips were digging into my palms. I hadn't realized I was clenching my hands until I felt them. Forcing myself to relax, I took a deep breath. How was it that I wanted to shake her for stealing memories I could have had with our daughter, but also wanted to throw her against the wall and fuck her until I was completely sated at the same time?

There was also an unwelcome and uncomfortable ache in my chest every time those jade pools looked at me with longing. As if she'd give anything to have more of me. She didn't have to say it. I could read her expressive face easy enough. She was letting us fucking make her want something we would never have. I wasn't built for that shit—and especially not with a woman I couldn't trust. She would be a weakness. I would be worrying about the lies she could be keeping from me every day.

"Good night, Branwen," I said before heading back toward the stairs, needing distance before the sexual ache for her became too much and I followed her into her bedroom.

"Good night, Linc." Her voice was soft, and there was a touch of sadness to it.

I winced, thankful she couldn't see my face as I walked away.

I'd treated her with respect today. I hadn't ignored her, yet I had kept a firm distance with her otherwise. If I could get into this habit and guide her into this type of relationship, we'd survive this year.

I'd fuck her every damn night if I could, but I didn't just worry about her getting attached anymore. I was starting to be concerned about me. I still intended to own her. I wasn't going to give up on taking that pussy and losing myself in it, but I had to limit it. Fuck other women in between. Otherwise, I might get obsessed with it and make a massive mistake.

The guys were still outside when I returned.

Luther glanced over at me first and raised his eyebrow. "I thought you'd be a while, tucking Branwen in."

Why he thought pushing me was fun I didn't know, but when I broke his nose, he'd fucking stop.

"Didn't tuck her in. Just my daughter."

"She wants you to," Mal said, then shrugged a shoulder. "Don't scowl at me. I'm just pointing it out. She looks at you like she'd do anything for you to notice her." He stuck his cigarette back into his mouth. "I always knew you were a hard motherfucker, but, damn, man. You are stronger than I am. I'd have had her naked and on the bed with—"

"DON'T finish that sentence," I warned him through clenched teeth.

My gaze scanned all of them. I hated knowing that they would all fantasize about her. If I could scrub her from their brains, I would.

Mal held up both hands. "Sorry."

No, he wasn't.

"Branwen and I aren't a couple, but understand this: Her cunt is mine. No one else touches it or fucking thinks about it. She belongs to me."

Luther cleared his throat. "So, just to be clear, you're touching it then?"

"Luther." I seethed, my eyes locked on him as rage pounded in my temples.

"I'm just making sure. Because someone needs to. It's a fucking abomination for a face and body like hers to go untouched. It is meant to be fucked."

"Luther, if you don't shut the fuck up, not one of us will get up and save your ass when he puts a gun to your forehead," Jonas warned him.

Luther sighed. "I'm the advocate for hot pieces of ass across the world. Okay? They should all be taken care of properly."

Ransom spit out his drink, trying not to laugh, then choked.

Mal chuckled and shook his head.

I should have stayed upstairs. I'd be buried balls deep in Branwen, listening to the sexy sounds she made. Instead, I was down here, listening to Luther say shit to piss me off.

THIRTY-EIGHT
BRANWEN

Linc: Issue came up in Georgia that my brother needs backup on. Had to leave too early to tell Stevie goodbye. Let her know I am sorry and I'll bring her back a surprise. This will take a few days. Locke will be at the house every day by ten to take you both wherever you want to go. He'll stay with you for security purposes.

I read the text, then put my phone back down and stared at the ceiling. He was gone again. I should be happy about that, but I wasn't. I'd held on to the hope he'd come back to my room last night. That was pathetic, and I knew it, but I couldn't seem to control my head and heart. After living the days with him when he was withdrawn and aloof, I craved that connection with him. It was getting worse, and I didn't know how to stop it.

Tossing back the covers, I stretched, then got up. Stevie and I had a way to get out and do something today. At least Linc had thought about it before running off and leaving. He'd listened to me. My head started going in the direction of maybe he was softening toward me and perhaps he felt something too. Or some emotion could be growing.

"You have got to snap out of it, Branwen. Jesus, you aren't that little girl anymore. Grow up," I muttered as I made my way to the bathroom to take a shower.

I needed to plan our day. Decide what we would do and where we would go. Stevie would probably be happy to stay here with her new playset and Maui, but there would be time for that later today.

Once I checked my bank account and knew what money I had left after bills were paid, I'd know just what we could afford to do. If I could find somewhere for her to play with other kids, that would be good. She needed that.

The Mississippi Children's Museum in Jackson had been phenomenal. We'd stayed there for four hours, and Stevie still hadn't gotten to see and do everything.

She asked if we could go feed the ducks on our drive back to Madison. Locke stopped at a grocery store for me, and I got a loaf of discounted bread for the ducks and a pint of strawberry oat milk ice cream and a small pack of plastic spoons.

While we sat down by the water and ate from the container, Stevie talked about the things we had done today, asked when her dad would be back, if she could play outside on her swing set when we got home, if Jayda would roll Maui his ball so he wouldn't get lonely, and what my favorite color was. Her little brain never seemed to take a break.

When she jumped up with a slice of bread she had taken from the loaf, I glanced back at Locke. He stood maybe a yard away, leaning against a tree. I felt bad that he'd had to spend his day at the Children's Museum, following us around while Stevie ran from one thing to the next.

"I'd offer you some, but since we ate out of the container, I doubt you want to share our germs. I should have asked if you wanted any. I'm sorry."

"I'm good," he said. "But thanks."

I turned back to watch Stevie as she tore off pieces and giggled happily as the ducks hurried to eat it. Some of the fish would pop up and snatch a bite as well from time to time. After twenty or so minutes, she tired of it and decided it was time for her to go home.

She'd started calling Linc's house "home" the past few days, and it had been odd for me at first. It definitely did not feel like home for me, but I guessed it would always be her other home, so it was good she felt that way. Even if a part of me was jealous of having to share her. Knowing there would be a home for her that I wasn't at stung, even when I knew it shouldn't. I had time to work on that. Myself. How sharing her would affect me.

Her eyes closed on the short drive back to Linc's, and she slumped over on me as she slept. When we arrived, Locke offered to carry her, and I let him because it was a long walk from the front of the house to her bed. Once she was in bed, I thanked him, and he left.

We repeated basically the same routine the next day, except instead of the Children's Museum, we went to the zoo.

Stevie spotted a stuffed monkey, whose hands Velcroed around your neck, hanging on several other kids and begged for one. I was having to budget these outings, so I bribed her with a picnic and more duck feeding if we didn't get the monkey. I could tell she was disappointed, and I felt a twinge of guilt over it, but she couldn't have everything she wanted. The thought that, one day, she might prefer living with Linc instead of me because he gave her elaborate gifts began to dig in and taunt me. I knew she loved me, and I didn't have to buy that love, but when she was a teenager…no. Not going there. This was now. I'd cross that bridge when I came to it.

On our way out of the zoo, she needed to make a bathroom stop, and when we walked out, Locke was waiting on us with a damn stuffed monkey in his hands. She saw it immediately.

"You bought a monkey! I wanted one too." Her voice didn't even mask her envy.

He held it out to her. "Your dad said to tell you he misses you."

She squealed and squeezed it to her chest. My throat clogged, my eyes stung, and all those fears came rushing to the forefront. I could not compete with Linc's gifts.

The rest of the day was easier. While eating, we discussed facts about monkeys that she'd learned at the zoo. I offered to let Locke sit beside us, and this time, I remembered to feed him too. I offered him a sunflower butter and jelly sandwich, and he took it.

On day three, I felt bad for Locke. He had to be tired of this. I almost texted Linc several times to ask if he could give Locke a break and send someone else, but then worried it would sound as if I were unhappy with Locke. There was also the fact that other than that one text, he'd not contacted me again. Not even to ask about Stevie, but I figured he was asking Locke and Jayda instead. Luther hadn't been around, and either he'd gone with Linc or we had just not crossed paths in the house, which was possible.

The Museum of Natural Science ended up being my favorite out of the three. Stevie loved the preschool discovery room and watching the scuba divers feed the fish in the large aquarium. It was another long four-hour visit, and my funds were getting low. Thinking ahead, I'd asked Jayda if I could pack us lunch in a cooler to take to the park with us instead of me going to get groceries. She had done it for me before I got down to the kitchen today. She'd also mentioned that the pond we had gone to had a playground on the other side.

This time, we had a picnic table to eat on, and it was much easier to set out the food. Jayda had added several things and sent enough for Locke too. My sandwiches paled in comparison to our spread today. Stevie ate her strawberries while talking about the fish in the aquarium.

I had already decided to tell Locke he had the day off tomorrow. I didn't want to deplete my bank account, and three days in a row of fun things to do was enough for the week. The pool and playground at Linc's would be just fine for a couple of days.

As I picked up my turkey club roll, out of the corner of my eye, I saw Locke move and glanced over at him to see he was focused on something behind me. Confused, I turned around and then froze. The sandwich I was holding slipped from my hands to the grass at my feet.

Hudson stalked toward me; his face was red, and a furious scowl was on contorting it. It was a look I'd never seen him make before.

What was he doing here?

"IS HE WHY?!" he shouted.

Oh my God. I glanced around, and there weren't any other families close by to hear him.

"YOU'RE FUCKING SOME GODDAMN TWENTY-YEAR-OLD!"

What? My eyes swung back to him. What was he talking about?

"Hudson," I said, standing up, "what—what is wrong with you? What are you talking about?"

Locke moved to stand in front of me. Blocking my view of Hudson.

"Oh, is that it? You're gonna be tough?" Hudson let out a demented-sounding laugh. "You think I'm scared of some Gen Z. Jesus." His tone sounded disgusted. "I can't believe this is why you broke things off with me, Branwen. Telling me that her father wanted to spend time with her. Wanted to get to know her. But you're out every day with this guy. Where is the so-called father? I thought you were staying locked up on that property with him, but now, you're out with this one? Can't make up your mind?"

"Stop this," I told him sternly, stepping over to see him around Locke. "This isn't your business, and what are you, stalking me?"

He pointed a finger at me. "Don't turn this around on me. I was worried about you. Then, I see you out with him. You used me. You took my money. You're a gold-digging WHORE!" He shouted the last word as his face morphed into a crazed look that made me take a step back.

Stevie let out a sob. "Don't yell at my mommy," she wailed, then ran around the table to cling to my legs. Her little body trembled as she pressed against me.

"It's okay," I told her, bending down to cup her face and wipe away the wetness from her cheeks.

She sobbed again. "But he is scweamin' at you," she said, her face crumpling. "It scaywas me."

"Yeah, go ahead and make me the bad guy. That's just great. I loved you. I love you now! But you tossed that away for this—this?! Does he have Daddy's money? Is that it? I didn't have enough money for you? What happened to Stevie getting to know her dad? Huh? Did you lie about that? You're cheap white trash, just like my mother warned me, but I let your face and body blind me!"

Stevie sobbed and buried her face in my chest as I winced at his words, closing my eyes, as if I could make him go away. I covered Stevie's ears with my hands, waiting for more awful words to be hurled at me.

But there was only silence.

"Take her to the car." Locke's tone had me snapping my eyes back open and looking at him.

He'd moved over to stand in front of Hudson. I heard Hudson's heavy breathing. He wasn't moving away from Locke or shouting at him. What had changed?

Then, I saw it. The reason why Hudson had stopped talking. Locke had a gun shoved inside his mouth.

Oh dear God. I sucked in a breath and kept Stevie's face buried in my chest.

"Locke," I said very slowly so as not to startle him, "don't do it."

I didn't want Stevie to hear what he was doing. She was too young for this.

"I won't. Linc will want to handle him. Now, you two go to the car. I'll be there in a moment." The twinge of satisfaction in his voice was almost evil.

I shivered. It sounded nothing like the polite guy who had followed us around the past three days.

Standing while keeping Stevie's face against me so she couldn't see anything, I picked her up, holding the back of her head so she didn't lift it, and hurried to the car. She was shaking in my arms, and her hands held fistfuls of my top.

"I'm scaywud, Mommy," her muffled voice said.

"It's okay. We are almost to the car, and Locke is making sure that Hudson goes away and leaves us alone."

"I want my dad," she said on another sob.

I'd like to blame him for this, but the behavior that Hudson had just displayed wasn't sane. The realization that I'd almost moved my baby into a house with a man who could turn into that sent a wave of horror through me. Oh God, what if I hadn't come here? What if Linc hadn't seen her? I felt sick.

I heard the doors click and knew Locke must be close behind. Jerking the back door open, I put her inside her car seat, then hurried around to the other side. There was no view of Hudson. Just Locke as he headed our way, carrying the cooler we'd brought our lunch in. When I had Stevie buckled, I held her small hand in mine, and she squeezed me before peeking out at Locke, afraid of what she might see.

Locke opened the driver's door and climbed inside. He looked up at the rearview mirror at me. "Are y'all okay?" he asked with a concerned expression.

I nodded.

"Will you tell my dad that I want him to come home?" Stevie asked as her voice wobbled.

There was a pause, then, "Yeah, I will."

She sniffled, then looked up at me. "I want my dad."

I sighed and ran a hand over her hair. She trusted him to protect her already. How easy it had been for him to walk into her life and become so important.

"I know, but he has work, and I'm here," I replied, pressing a kiss to her head.

"But he will keep us safe," she said with a hiccup.

He had kept us safe today. She just didn't realize it. I'd thought that the security was silly. That he was going overboard. How wrong I had been.

THIRTY-NINE
BRANWEN

Long after Stevie fell asleep and her death grip on me eased, I lay there, holding her. The what-ifs torturing me.

How had I not seen that side of Hudson? I replayed every instance where he could have gotten angry, and not one time had he ever exhibited that unstable, dangerous behavior.

Living here might be hard for me. Linc might break my soul. But it was right for Stevie. She had her father. He would always protect her. If she was safe and happy, then I could survive the effect it had on me.

When I finally got up and tucked her in tightly, then pressed a kiss to her head, I stepped into the hallway and stared at my bedroom door. I'd left my phone in there, but I had no one to tell. No one to talk to about this. The ladies from work I'd gotten close to all believed whatever Hudson was saying about me because not one of them had checked in with me. My world had been built around him.

It seemed I was meant to be alone. I had no lasting friendships. That should tell me something. The common denominator was me. I was the problem. When they had to choose, they didn't choose me. Not Idris, not the women from work. I must be a bad friend. I tried to think about what it could be that made me the one no one wanted to keep.

I headed for the stairs. It was later than I normally stayed up, but I wanted to get something to drink. Maybe some wine. With my heart heavy and in a complete pity-party state, I stepped into the kitchen to find Luther, shirtless, in a pair of jeans that were unbuttoned, as if he had been about to remove them and stopped or had just put them on and not taken the time to fasten them. He was pouring a glass of milk, and there were cookies in a container beside his glass.

He glanced up at me. "Coming for a snack?" he asked as he put the top back on the gallon of milk.

I shrugged. "I was thinking more along the lines of a drink."

His lips twitched. "You want wine or something stronger?"

"Wine."

"Red or white?"

"Red."

He put the milk back into the refrigerator, then walked over to the other side of it and pulled out a hidden rack that held at least three dozen bottles of wine. He stood in front of it, looking at different ones, then slid one out and pushed the rack back into the wall.

"Figure you're not gonna drink it all, so I chose one I'll finish off," he said, then placed it on the counter and began to uncork it. "Sounds like you had some excitement today." He cut his eyes up at me.

I scrunched my nose and pulled out a barstool across from him, then sat down. "Not what I'd call excitement."

"At least you didn't marry the crazy fucker." He pointed out what I had already been dwelling on.

"Yep. That's going to mess with my head for a while."

He walked over and got down a wineglass, then filled it almost to the top. I looked at it, wide-eyed.

"Just drink it. You need it. You're pale and wounded-looking," he said, then reached for a cookie. "You know, I wasn't so sure about this sunflower butter stuff, but, damn, these cookies are just as good as my peanut butter ones. I can't even be mad about it."

I picked up the glass as he took a bite and began to chew.

After taking a sip, I nodded my head toward his unbuttoned fly. "You often forget to button your jeans?"

He took a drink of milk, then shook his head. "Just sent my fuck home and didn't have the energy."

I choked on my wine and covered my mouth as I coughed.

Luther leaned over and patted my back. "Easy there."

It took me a moment to get my voice back.

"I wasn't, uh, expecting that answer, I guess," I replied. "Although I should have. You were probably the one who told me about the threesome the first time I came here."

He had a cookie halfway to his mouth and stopped. "What first time?"

I took another drink, then swallowed. "When I came to tell Linc I was pregnant."

Luther lowered the cookie back to the table. His eyebrows drew together. "You came here to tell him you were pregnant?"

"Yep, and when I pressed the intercom button on the gate, a man answered and informed me that Linc was involved in a threesome, and when he was ready for another cunt, then he'd give me a call." I picked up my glass and tilted it toward him. "My bet is, that was you."

Luther rubbed his face and blew out a breath. "Fuck," he muttered, like this was bad news. "Linc doesn't know about this."

It didn't sound like a question, but more of a statement, but I answered anyway. "No. He never asked me or gave me the chance to explain. He assumed I'd never come here, and honestly, admitting that I knew he had threesomes was… uncomfortable and awkward.

"And after that night, I'd decided he had given me the morning-after pill. He said in his note that he didn't want a kid. I couldn't stand the thought of my baby ever feeling like it had a father who didn't want it." I sighed. "So, I told her he was dead instead. That way, she'd never feel like he didn't want her. He wasn't around because he wasn't alive. At the time, I thought I was doing the right thing. I see now that I was wrong, and I will live with the guilt of it for the rest of my life."

I gave him a tight smile. "Sorry, I am lost in my own pity party tonight, wallowing in my bad decisions and loneliness."

Luther turned and took down another wineglass, then poured some in it before taking a long swig. When he set it down, he groaned. "Jesus H. Christ."

I drank mine, saying nothing, while I watched him almost scowl as he stared down at the glass.

He finally blew out a breath and looked back up at me. "Here, eat a cookie," he said, pushing the container near me.

"I'm not—"

"They're delicious. Eat a fucking cookie," he cut me off.

"O-kay," I replied and reached into the container.

He looked to be in deep thought as he took another drink of his wine.

"I thought I heard voices in here," Jayda said.

I turned to see her enter the kitchen, wearing a pair of cut-off sweatpants and a tank top. She had on no bra, and I was almost positive her nipples were pierced.

God, I wanted to dislike her. I knew Linc had slept with her. They were too familiar. He was nice to her, and they got along. With me, he fucked me, then treated me like I was a random stranger or dirt on the floor. It was me. Something was wrong with me. I had to face it.

I took a much bigger drink this time, hoping the wine would numb the pain and regret.

"Come eat some of my cookies so you have to make me some more," Luther told her, then held up the bottle of wine. "Get you some of this too."

She sauntered in, and he watched her like she was about to perform for him onstage. The lust in his gaze blatantly on his face. Not even attempting to hide it.

When she reached him, she picked up a cookie and grinned. "Told you you'd like them."

He put his arm around her shoulders and pulled her against his side. "Almost as much as I like your pierced nipples and you walking around without a bra on."

She slapped his chest and rolled her eyes while taking a bite of her cookie.

I watched them, wishing that I could be like her. Have sex with a man and live with him and be friends. Not let emotions get in the way. Not want or ache for more. Maybe that was my problem. I had delusions of romance and being loved the way that I'd witnessed in Florida with the wives of Garrett, Levi, and Blaise. The way they looked at them as if they were all they could see. All they wanted to see. I wasn't one of those women. I didn't inspire that in a man like them. Like Linc.

But if I could be a Jayda…maybe then I'd have Linc in a way. Where he didn't treat me like a fling that wouldn't go away.

Which is kinda what I am, I thought sourly.

Hudson had given me a false sense of comfort. I clearly sucked at picking out men.

Luther filled my glass back up, and I watched him, not having realized I'd drunk all of it.

"I have a raspberry cheesecake in the fridge," Jayda said, walking over to get it out.

"Grab another bottle," Luther told her and held up the one he had. "This one is almost gone."

I should probably go to bed. Picking up my wine, I decided against it. Why start doing the smart thing when I was so good at doing the stupid one?

FORTY
LINC

My veins burned, as if they were pumping violence instead of blood throughout my body. Stalking from the plane that had taken me from Georgia to Nashville toward the black Escalade that waited for me, I felt like I was going to snap at any second, leaving a path of destruction in my wake.

I hadn't been completely sane since Locke had called me.

I'd been in the underground my grandfather had built that sat on the back side of my brother's land for over five hours when I finally stepped out of it to check with Locke on how the day had gone with the girls. Once I was aboveground, seeing five missed calls and ten text messages hit my phone made my blood run cold. I'd never been gripped by terror like I had in that moment. If he was calling, something was wrong. I didn't take the time to read the texts. I called him and started for the closest vehicle. I hadn't told my brother or the other men with him that I was leaving. I'd just left.

Hale, Ransom, Than, Locke, and Bane were all inside the vehicle when I climbed inside the passenger seat.

"Where the fuck is Luther?" I demanded, looking at Bane, who was in the driver's seat.

"He's been drinking. Apparently with Jayda and, uh, Branwen. I mean, it's just wine, but he's tipsy," Bane replied. "I thought Hale would be a better choice. He's not drunk."

Narrowing my eyes, I listened to him. "Why the fuck is Branwen drinking?" I seethed.

"Probably because she's traumatized," Locke said. "The dude was yelling shit at her, and Stevie was sobbing and clinging to her mom. When I left them at your house, Branwen was barely holding herself together."

I was shaking. Every muscle in my body was clenched so tight that I started vibrating with rage.

Bane hadn't started driving yet, and I was seconds away from slamming my hands down on the dashboard and roaring at him to fucking move.

"I know you're the one who makes the call. But this time, it's personal, and I know from experience that when it is personal, we don't think clearly. We act and get sloppy. Take a breath. They are both safe. Locke put a gun in the bastard's mouth, and when he took it out, he used the butt of it to knock him out cold before dragging him over behind the bushes and leaving him. He never got close enough to touch either of them," Bane said.

I already knew all this. He needed to drive.

"What call do you think you're gonna be making, Bane?" I challenged.

He didn't lead the branch yet. I did. And if he thought he was going to step in before it was time, he was gonna find out how wrong he was.

"Linc, listen," he said. "We are going in and making sure he never comes near her again. Break his nose, beat the shit out of him, but don't kill him. That's a bigger mess to clean up. If he'd have touched her, then yeah. But do you want to explain to Blaise why we slaughtered a man in his house who hadn't taken, hurt, or even touched something of ours?"

"If he had, he would already be dead," Locke said matter-of-factly.

Bane nodded. "Right. But he didn't. This is a revenge visit. One that will keep him in line, quiet, and far away from Branwen and Stevie."

She could have married that bastard. She and Stevie would have been in his house. For the first time in my life, I didn't give a fuck what the boss told me to do or would want me to do. The compulsion to beat the dentist until he was unrecognizable, then cut his dick off and shove it up his ass was dominating all other thoughts.

"Just drive," I demanded, pulling my gun from its holster to make sure it was fully loaded.

"He's right, Linc," Hale said from the seat behind me. "You know he is. I understand he attempted to get near your girls, but he didn't. Because you had protection on them. You kept them safe. All that is needed is to make sure he never tries it again."

My girls. He'd called them my girls. I glared out the window as my chest rose and fell. Those words hammering in my head. Stevie was my daughter. But Branwen…she was… she was mine. I wasn't letting anyone else touch her and live. I wasn't even sure Luther would be safe from me when I got back.

"He lives in a suburban neighborhood," Bane said. "I went online and pulled up a video from the real estate company that had sold the house to him. I have the layout. We know the points of easiest entry."

I unclenched my hands and laid them flat on the tops of my thighs. I had to restrain the savage fury that felt like claws sinking into my back, wanting to consume me.

They were okay. He hadn't gotten close enough to touch them. I kept repeating that over and over in my head while we drove out of the city lights and onto the dark streets, lit only with streetlamps.

When we turned onto a dirt path, I didn't question it. I knew we weren't going to pull into the driveway and park. Bane had done his research while they tried to get me on the phone. We moved off the road, and the dirt path ended as we drove slowly over limbs and debris.

"I called Brock," Bane said. "He sent me this location. It's family-owned by their branch. Belongs to a sister-in-law of one of the wives. He's sending two guys to stay with the vehicle for backup."

Brock Keller was the head of the Tennessee branch. It was smart. Bane had used his head.

I just nodded. I'd thank him later. Right now, I had one focus. Not snapping the dentist's neck the moment I saw him.

The Escalade came to a stop, and two figures stepped out of the dark woods. I recognized Brock's oldest son, Arrow, but I wasn't sure who the other one was. All four doors opened at once as we joined them.

Arrow looked from Bane to me. "Higgens and I will stay here. Call if you need us."

"Thanks," I told him.

"No problem," he replied.

Bane moved to the front. "All right, boys, this way," he said.

We moved in behind him almost silently, except for the crackle of limbs and leaves beneath our feet. But even then, it was quieter than any other footsteps would be.

We stepped out of the tree line into a backyard. I thought about the fact that they'd almost lived here. My girls had almost been his. I wanted to burn the place to the ground and watch it until all that was left were the embers. This backyard wasn't big enough to hold the playset I'd bought Stevie. She wouldn't have had a pool here. My eyes cut to the driveway, where that fucking ugly blue car he had given Branwen was parked beside his luxury sedan.

They were never his. He'd almost stolen them. Taken what belonged to me.

"You look like you're about to torch the place. Don't," Bane said under his breath.

He nodded his head, and the others moved out, going to their entry point. I followed Bane as we headed for the downstairs door.

"It has an alarm system, but I used the code Wilder gave me to hack into the system and disarm it." His voice was almost too quiet to hear.

Taking out his tool, he slid it into the dead bolt and turned it. After the metal bar slid out, he moved on to the keyhole in the doorknob and eased it slowly around. His gloved hand wrapped around the handle and turned, and then we moved inside.

It was dark, but I could make out the game room. It had a mediocre pool table, a couple of arcade machines, and a well-worn leather sofa. The stairs weren't anything impressive, and the railing needed tightening. The dentist didn't take care of his shit properly. Much like he hadn't taken care of Branwen's cunt properly.

The main floor had some light coming from the left, but it went out quickly, meaning whoever had come in that way was inside without issue. I didn't ask who had cut any phone lines he might have, knowing it had been handled.

Ransom stepped into the hallway, followed by Hale. Which meant Locke and Than would be coming in on the opposite side of the house.

The others took their places, and Bane led me down another hallway and then to a room with two double doors that stood open. The king-size bed with the dentist forming a lump under the covers made my stomach turn. Knowing Branwen had been in that bed, that he'd had her in this room, ignited a roar in my ears that drowned out everything else as I took long strides to the bed. Needing to see him suffer. Hating every inch of this fucking house and what it represented.

I stood over him. Loathing that he breathed. He had called her names. Screamed at her in public. In front of Stevie.

Hearing the words he'd said had sent a bolt of remorse through me. I'd wanted to make her the word he'd lashed out at her. I'd planned to make her my whore. Use her when I wanted her. Problem with that was, my cock only wanted her cunt now.

I had requested the flight attendant who had sucked my cock like a professional for the trip to Georgia. But her hands had felt wrong. She smelled wrong. Her voice was wrong. I had to tell her I'd changed my mind. I'd not gotten as far as unzipping my pants, and I knew it wasn't happening. She even sat down on the sofa and opened her thighs to play with her cunt for me. The fact that it didn't look like Branwen's had annoyed me.

The dentist's eyelids started to move. Then, his eyes opened, and he was looking up at me. There was a moment of confusion, then panic. I stood there as he scrambled to sit up, reaching for his cell phone that he'd left charging by his bed. But it was gone. Bane had pocketed it while I waited. When he realized there was no phone, he swung his gaze back to me.

"What the fuck do you want?" he shouted.

Bane moved up, grabbing his hair to jerk his head forward, and then Than tied on his gag to muffle the screams he was trying to make.

"Touch the gag and I'll put a bullet between your eyes," Bane warned him. When they both stepped back, his eyes looked frantically around the room. When he recognized Locke, I knew it because he began to try and move backward, as if he could push through the headboard behind him.

"Remember me?" Locke drawled.

The dentist tried talking, but his words were hard to make out. I was almost positive he'd said something about the police.

"You made the grave mistake of getting close to what is mine. You yelled at Branwen, called her names that no one gets to call her but me." An evil smirk curled my lips. "She likes it when I slam my cock into her tight cunt. When I call her my pretty little whore, she gets off on it. Screams my name while her orgasm milks my load right out of me."

His eyes flared with hate and jealousy, overtaking the fear.

"You made my little girl cry." I shook my head and made a tsking sound. "No one does that," I told him, taking another step closer.

He reached out a hand to hold me back, and I grabbed his forearm and twisted until the sound of the bone cracking sent a smile to my face. His muted wails only had me forcing the abnormal bend further while the continued snapping sent a balm over me.

He began to go limp, as if he might pass out from the pain, and I dropped his arm. He fell back, and his head bounced off the headboard, but his eyes remained opened.

"You didn't touch her, so you get to live. This is your only warning. If you are caught within a thirty-mile radius of Branwen or Stevie, I will hang you up by your wrists and slice you into pieces while you bleed out."

I closed in on him, wrapping my hand around his neck and squeezing. "And if you tell the police, I'll know within minutes, and you won't see another sunrise."

Tears ran down until the cloth, jammed in his mouth and wrapped around his head, soaked them up. He was trembling from not only fear, but also the injury to his arm, which, I was sure, was breathtakingly painful. He wouldn't be able to fix any teeth for a while.

I grabbed the cloth tied around his head and tore it off.

He let out a gasp.

"Go ahead and scream. See how long I let you live," I taunted him, wanting him to make that mistake.

"Ah, Linc, now, you're just trying to get him to give you a reason to kill him," Hale said from the other side of the room.

"Sh-she was my fiancée," he stammered.

"That was a lapse in judgment," I replied. "One she corrected."

"Wh-why ar-are you do-doing this? You barely know he-her."

I grinned. "That's where you're wrong. She was mine long before she was with you."

FORTY-ONE

LINC

Luther was sitting at the table, drinking from his cup of coffee, while holding Maui. My gaze swung from him to Jayda, who looked surprised to see me. She must not have gotten the memo that I was back.

"Good morning," she said. "Wasn't expecting you. I'll get your breakfast going. Let me finish these up real quick before Stevie comes down."

"Oh yeah, Linc is back," Luther drawled over his cup.

She rolled her eyes and continued what she had been doing.

"What are you making for Stevie?" I asked.

"Chocolate chip waffles."

"I'll just have those too," I told her.

She paused and looked at me as if I had grown two heads. "You will?"

I nodded. "Yeah. Sounds good."

I went over to make my coffee and could feel her eyes following me. So I was going to eat something different for breakfast. What was the big deal?

"He cracked the bones in the ex-fiancé's arm last night and broke his nose. Then left him in a puddle of his own blood, knocked out cold on his bed," Luther told her. Sounded like he had talked to Hale.

"Ohhh," Jayda replied, as if that made sense.

"Whose got blood on theyuh bed?"

I turned around at the sound of Stevie's voice to see her standing in her favorite Bluey pajamas and slippers. Her blonde curls wild from the bed and a wide-eyed look on her face. When she saw me, she beamed and came running. I set my cup down before she wrapped her arms around my legs.

"You came back!"

"Of course I came back. This is where you are, isn't it?" I ruffled her hair.

She tilted her head back to stare up at me. "We had a scaywee thing happen." Her expression turned serious.

Maui had been set free from Luther's arms and came straight to Stevie, wagging his entire backside.

She glanced down at him. "Wait a minute, Maui. I have to tell my dad something." Then, she turned back to me. "Hudson came to the pawak, and he yelled at Mommy. I cwied. And Locke made him leave Mommy alone. I told Locke to tell you I wanted you to come home. I was scaywud. Did he tell you?"

I should have killed the dentist. She'd been scared and wanted me. I hadn't been here. Damn, the lump in my throat felt as if it might choke me.

"He did. And I will make sure Hudson never gets near you or your mommy again. I promise."

She sighed loudly and smiled.

Maui was still demanding her attention, and she bent down to play with him.

"I made chocolate chip waffles," Jayda said in a singsong voice.

"You did?!" Stevie asked, then squealed. "I love chocolate for bweakfast."

I watched her as she and Maui tumbled around on the floor. This house had never been so lively. She made the dark shit go away.

"You two are a bad influence," I heard Branwen groan.

My gaze shot up to see her standing in the doorway, looking fucking perfect. Her hair appeared as if she'd only run her fingers through it. The baggy pink-and-white striped pajama pants she wore hung on her hips, and her white tank top didn't meet her belly button, leaving her flat, tanned stomach bare.

Her eyes met mine, and they widened. "Oh," she said. "I, uh, I didn't know you were back."

"For the record, I'm not the bad influence. Luther is," Jayda piped up, taking a waffle and putting it onto a plate.

Branwen blinked, as if she had been slightly dazed and was coming out of it. I continued to watch her, wondering how I thought I could live under this roof with her for a year and not be affected by her. I couldn't trust her, but it wasn't like I was going to propose. There were other options.

"Just to get it out there and over with," Luther drawled. "The three of us shared three or so bottles of wine last night."

"Six, Luther. We went through six bottles," Jayda corrected him.

He shrugged. "Whatever. We drank, ate some cheesecake and cookies, threw darts." He pointed at Branwen. "She's good. If you ever play her, do not place any bets. I owe her a hundred dollars."

"Five hundred, Luther. I was there. You kept going double or nothing," Jayda said.

He rolled his eyes.

Branwen looked so nervous that she was slightly pale. I studied her. She shifted her eyes to me, her throat bobbed as she swallowed, and then the tip of her pink tongue darted out and licked her lips.

"I-I…uh…" She smiled, but it was a nervous one. "I don't want your money."

"You are taking his money," Jayda said.

"No. Really. It was fun." She reached up and touched her forehead. "*Was* being the operative word. My head isn't feeling great this morning."

Jayda chuckled. "I'll fix that. Sit down and let me give you my hangover cure."

Stevie stood up from tussling with Maui. "Mommy! My dad came home."

Branwen nodded. "I see." She went to sit down at the bar, still looking uneasy.

"She could also sing every word of every Fleetwood Mac song I could think of," Luther said.

Her eyes darted to me, as if she feared my reaction to that. I'd made her wary of me. My plan to use her for sex and otherwise treat her as unimportant had created this. It wasn't what was best for Stevie. Branwen had done something that I couldn't forgive her for, but I could move past it. Friends with benefits would be a better fit than whatever I'd worked up in my head. That plan had too many flaws. The worst one was that hurting Branwen would hurt Stevie. That hadn't occurred to me when I set out to get my revenge. But the more I was with them, the more I realized that being in my daughter's life meant being in her mother's life.

"I can take the credit for that," I told him, walking over to pull out the stool beside her and sit down.

Jayda placed a glass of water with some powder she'd mixed in it and two pills in front of Branwen.

"Really?" Jayda asked, sounding surprised.

I nodded. "Yep. I was a big Fleetwood Mac fan in the '90s, and since Branwen worshipped me, she liked whatever I liked. Except beer. She tried mine once and spit it all over me."

Branwen's gaze snapped up to me. "I did not worship you, and you should have never let me taste that beer. I was ten years old."

"Yeah, you did," Luther chimed in, and I smirked.

She narrowed her eyes at him. "Stay out of this. I don't even remember you. You couldn't have been around much."

I threw my head back and laughed.

"And I thought we were friends," he said.

She shrugged, and her eyes seemed to sparkle with the morning sunshine filtering in through the windows as she looked at me.

Yeah, we could do this. Be friends. I could let it go. Learn to move on from it. I had Stevie now. I wouldn't miss any more of her life.

"I let you taste the beer because you were very hard to tell no."

"I was ten."

"You were adorable, all puppy-dog-eyed and begging for one taste. I figured you'd either like it and become a teenage alcoholic, or hate it and you wouldn't touch it again. I was so damn relieved when it spewed out of your mouth."

I watched her face soften, and a smile spread across it as the tension faded. It was that easy with her. If only I had this gift with all females.

Jayda was silently watching us when I reached to pick up my cup. She smirked at me, getting the wrong idea.

"Waffles are ready, Stevie," Jayda called out while looking at me.

Stevie left Maui behind and jumped up onto the stool to my left. "You know what we did?" she asked me.

"What?"

"We went to the museum, and the zoo, and the othah museum with the scuba divahs." She listed them off as she held up a finger for each one.

"Sounds like you were busy."

She nodded her head at me, then reached for her fork and stabbed a piece of waffle with it. "We was vewy busy," she agreed, then shoved the waffle into her mouth. Her cheeks looked like a chipmunk as she caught me watching her and grinned at me.

Breakfast had never been something I looked forward to or thought much about. Rarely did Luther and I eat at the same time. But with these two here, the kitchen was an entirely different experience. The room even seemed brighter. Laughter, puppy growls, dimpled smiles, and ringlets had managed to turn it into one of my favorite parts of the day.

FORTY-TWO
BRANWEN

After breakfast, Linc told us he had a surprise, something to show us.

I was trying to process his treatment of me and gauge what he'd meant when he said it.

He had to repeat himself for me, saying, "for y'all," not just Stevie.

He had a surprise for *us*.

Stammering, I told him we would go get dressed. He then told us to wait a minute and left the room for only a minute or two, then returned, carrying a large shopping bag that said *Ariat* on the front.

When he walked over to me, he held it out for me to take. "You will both need these."

The "these" were cowboy boots. Mine were a Western style with pretty aqua-blue thread woven into the brown leather. The soles were the same blue as the thread. I was smiling so hard as I studied them that my cheeks actually hurt. I'd not had a pair of actual riding boots since I had been a kid. Since…my dad.

Stevie pulled out her box and opened them up before I could help her. She held up a brown-and-teal-blue leather boot and grinned. "I got boots too, Mommy!"

I knew he hadn't gotten them because of me. There was no way that he'd ever remember it, but I'd once begged my dad for a pair of teal cowboy boots, like the ones Kimberly Brown had worn to school. He'd told me no. That work boots weren't meant to be pretty and cowgirls didn't care about silly things such as that.

Stevie stopped to show off her boots to both Jayda and Luther on our way out the front door with Linc. Once we reached his truck, he paused with his hand on the door handle.

"We aren't leaving this property," he told me. "It's a dirt road, and I will be the only vehicle on it. Is it okay if she goes without her car seat?"

I had no idea how much property he and Luther had behind the tall privacy fence that enclosed the backyard. From the balcony in my bedroom, I could see the fields and trees beyond what I thought was the end of their property, but a row of what looked like pecan trees cut off my view from seeing any farther.

"Sure, that'll be fine," I told him.

The crooked smile he gave me sent off the wild beating of butterflies in my stomach who honestly had no shame. They had no pride. They were pathetic, and I couldn't seem to control them.

He helped Stevie into the truck, and she bounced in the seat, excited about sitting in the front without a car seat.

"You like the boots?" he asked, turning back to me.

I nodded. "Yes, thank you. They're beautiful."

"And comfortable? Jayda told me the size you needed."

"Yes."

He looked down at them. "Unfortunately, I couldn't find any in a teal blue that would work well for what you needed them for. This was as close as I could get. But I did get Stevie some, so I hoped that would make up for it."

I stared at him. What did he mean by that? Because what I thought he meant would be...sweet. Possibly the most thoughtful thing anyone had ever done for me. It would also mean he...had thought about me. Made an effort to please me. None of those things seemed possible.

"Uh, these are great. And Stevie loves hers. She's never had real boots."

The corner of his lips quirked, and he tilted his head. The dark blue of his eyes seemed lighter in the sunshine, more like the sky than the deep ocean. "But are they what your eleven-year-old heart wanted, Ringlets?"

I blanched. My breathing hitched, and my mouth fell slightly open. He'd remembered? The reckless butterflies flapped their wings, as if to mock me and my doubt.

"You—you remember that?" The question was almost a whisper.

He smirked at me. The crinkles fanning the corners of his eyes were even sexy. "Of course I do. I had to spend twenty minutes just trying to get you to smile again. Not even the fact that I brought you two daisies helped."

This was a memory. He didn't mean anything by it.

I sucked in a breath, then let it out. "Dad wasn't one for flashy things, and I was dramatic back then," I said, trying to play it off.

If he thought I was reading anything into it, then he'd stop being nice. I'd already figured out he didn't want me to think it was okay to cross any and all lines he had firmly set in place. Not that I would try.

When he held out a hand for me, my gaze dropped down to it as if I didn't know what it was or what to do with it. Touching him when it wasn't sexual felt foreign and forbidden.

"I'm just trying to help you up into the truck, Ringlets." His deep drawl made warmth rush through my body.

I placed my hand over his, and that single touch of his skin on mine sent a shiver over me that I hoped I masked as I stepped up into the truck. Then, I quickly pulled my hand free and placed it in my lap. It was if he'd branded me.

We drove slowly back through his property as Stevie chatted about her new boots and being a big girl in the front seat while I worked on pulling myself together. The tingle that still covered my palm from his touch wasn't much help.

With my gaze out the side window and my thoughts on everything that had happened since I had woken up, Stevie's, "I SEE A HAWSE!" caused me to jump.

I snapped my gaze from the fenced-off fields on my right to look directly ahead. Several yards away sat a red barn, and just outside of it was a buckskin quarter horse.

"I want to pet it!" Stevie exclaimed, her hands clasped together at her chest as she peered over the dashboard.

Linc slowed the truck and came to a stop outside the barn.

"Then, let's go," Linc said as he swung open his door.

"Is that…do you have stables?" I asked him.

He reached to take Stevie as she crawled over to him, and his eyes lifted to meet mine. "They're part of the reason we bought this property. Cash Stables is where the family raises their thoroughbreds in Mississippi, but I wanted something smaller. Mine. But I just never got around to getting horses moved into it. These two had been at Cash Stables for about a year now. I'd bought them on a trip to Alabama with Bane to look at a thoroughbred he wanted to buy."

He had stables. This was not the surprise I had expected. I'd not really thought too much about the surprise, honestly. I'd been too wrapped up in my boots and Linc buying them because of a memory I hadn't realized he had.

Stevie slapped his back as he held her. "Let's go!" she urged him.

He nodded, smiling at her before looking back at me. "Get out, Ringlets."

I reached for the door handle and pushed it open, then hurried to get down out of the truck. My gaze took in every detail of the scene around me. There had to be over thirty acres out here that was fenced in. That wasn't bad for only two horses. The barn looked freshly painted, although the rustic older-style feel to it remained intact. I loved that. It wasn't flashy, like the rest of his life seemed to be. This was simply functional.

Linc put Stevie down, and she took off running over to the fence where the pale golden horse watched us. Its black mane and tail fluttered gently in the breeze.

"I'm ashamed to say that she'd never been around horses until we were in Ocala," I told him.

"She mentioned that. But she's young. We've got plenty of time to turn that around."

I smiled and watched her as she held on to the wooden fence with her head tilted back so that she could stare up at it.

Linc walked up behind her and picked her up under the arms, then sat her on the post while keeping his arm wrapped around her waist. "Stevie, meet Diane," he said as he reached out and ran a hand down the horse's head.

"Diane?" I asked, scrunching my nose. "Odd name for a horse."

He cut his gaze to me. "Shh, you'll hurt her feelings."

I suppressed a grin.

Linc let out a whistle. "Jack!" he called out, then pointed toward the barn as a blue roan quarter horse emerged.

I'd only ever seen photos of a quarter horse this color. They weren't easy to breed for, and they weren't cheap.

The names clicked then, and I swung my gaze back to Linc.

"Jack and Diane," I said aloud.

He nodded. "Yep. Life goes on."

A laugh bubbled out of me.

"Don't laugh at theyah names, Mommy," Stevie scolded me. "It's not nice."

I nodded, looking at him one more time before shifting my attention back to Jack. "You're right, Vivi Lu," I replied. "I'm sorry."

"Can I wide them?" Stevie asked, turning her head to look up at Linc.

He nodded. "Want to go inside and check out your tack?"

She had no idea what tack was, but she nodded her head as if she did. I watched as he put her booted feet back on the ground. She immediately reached for his hand, and seeing him wrap his much larger one around hers never got old for me.

They started in that direction, but I didn't follow. He hadn't mentioned it, and I didn't want to intrude on a bonding moment they might have.

Just before I went back to admiring Jack and Diane, Linc glanced back over his shoulder at me. "You coming?"

Oh. He wanted me to go too.

"I wasn't sure if this was a, um…bonding kinda thing."

He raised his eyebrows slightly. "It is, but she has two parents."

Seven words couldn't have held more security in them if they tried. She did have two parents, but I often feared that he wished she hadn't.

I licked my lips. "Okay."

They continued to the wide double doors, and Linc pulled one open. Stevie let go of his hand and darted inside. He held it for me, and every hair on my body came alive as I passed by him. His eyes following me didn't help.

The inside momentarily distracted me. The ceilings weren't vaulted with extravagant fixtures. Instead, they were mass timber beams that had a rustic feel I loved. The ground was paved with black brick, and the far wall had been built from stacked stone. On the left were six stalls. On the right was an open door that I could see held the tack. A barrel had been built into the wall, made with the same stacked stone as the wall down at the end. On the other side were two more doors, but both were closed.

There were no connecting buildings or flat screens hanging on the walls. It was simply a functional, well-kept stable. Stevie ran ahead, peering into each stall, and then peeked out the far-right exit that led into the fenced-in fields, where Jack and Diane were currently.

"What do you think?" Linc asked, and I couldn't help but smile.

"I think it is perfect. I love it," I finished and turned to him.

The pleased glint in his eyes continued to add to my confusion about his sudden change in personalities. At least where I was concerned. He'd always been this way with Stevie. But me? Not even in the same ballpark.

He nodded his head toward the tack room. "Come check out your saddle, Stevie," he called out, keeping his eyes on me.

Stevie's little legs ran back toward us. "I got a saddle? To wide a hawse?" she asked, wide-eyed.

Linc turned his attention to her. "You're a cowgirl, aren't you? And you've got your own horse."

She frowned. "I don't have a hawse."

He rubbed his bearded chin with his thumb and forefinger. "I could have sworn that Jack's registration papers said that he belonged to a Stevie Hester."

Her mouth opened wide, but this time, I wasn't surprised. I'd assumed he had chosen to give her one of the horses. His elaborate gifts were getting to be the norm.

"It does?" she asked in awe.

He nodded and adjusted his hat on his head. "Sure does. Now, let's go see if we can find a saddle in this tack room that will fit you just right."

Stevie rushed past us and into the open door. Her eyes scanned all the items until she found a tan child-sized barrel racing saddle with a turquoise padded seat, matching crystals on the trim, and other splashes of bling that were worthy of a show saddle rather than an everyday one.

"I like this one!" she called out, going directly to it. Her eyes swung back to me, and she grinned. "See it, Mommy?"

I nodded. It was fit for a princess. I didn't want to dampen the moment, but one day soon, we were going to need to discuss that if he continued with the gifts, she was going to turn into a spoiled diva. Mix that with her teen years, and whew. Neither of us wanted that. He just didn't know it yet.

"It's beautiful," I replied.

She pointed at her chest. "It's mine." Then, she reached to pick it up. "I want to wide now."

Linc chuckled. "Looks like it is time for the first lesson."

I stood back and watched as he squatted down and began to talk to her about the saddle and what every part on it was for. I couldn't remember my dad ever giving me that lesson. Sometimes, it felt as if I had been born riding.

Dad would have loved this. He'd have wanted his granddaughter to ride horses. For them to be a part of her. Something else that Linc could give her that I couldn't.

FORTY-THREE
BRANWEN

The exhilaration of today had not only made combing through Stevie's hair with the detangler after her bath easy, but she had fallen asleep almost as soon as her head hit the pillow.

We had spent several hours at the stables while Linc worked with Stevie on basics and then put her on the back of Jack with him to go for a longer ride. It had been so many years since I'd ridden that I hadn't even asked if I could ride Diane. I felt as if I needed lessons too.

I hadn't realized just how bad I'd missed it until today. Even being at Hughes Farm hadn't brought back the desire to feel myself on the back of a horse with the wind in my face like it had today. There had been a few other saddles in the tack room, and if Linc continued being so…friendly, I might get brave enough to ask.

Glancing down at my phone, I saw it was after twelve, but I was thirsty, and sleep wasn't coming for me. My brain refused to shut off. Getting up, I headed out the door and toward the staircase.

Linc had left with Luther shortly after we got back from riding, and they still hadn't returned by the time I brought Stevie up to bed. Jayda had taken Maui and put him in Linc's room for me.

It wasn't until I reached the entrance to the kitchen that I heard voices coming from the great room. Considering the time, I was curious as to who was up this late. Jayda had said she was going up after she finished cleaning the kitchen, and that had been three hours ago. I hesitated and then decided to just go peek. As I got closer, it sounded as if the television was on, but I heard something else too. Loud, feminine laughter caused me to pause.

That wasn't Jayda.

It could be someone with Luther…and Linc. I winced at the stab of jealousy.

I should turn around and go back to the kitchen to get a drink and head back upstairs, where I belonged. Today had been a good day. Linc had treated me as if I was human, and I'd like not to mess that up. If he had woman here, he had waited until well after he knew Stevie was asleep. Yes, it was painful to think about, but that was something I'd have to learn to live with.

Before I could do something stupid, like go see who was here, I went back to the kitchen, not stopping until I had my glass and was filling it with the pitcher of cold water from the refrigerator.

"Linc," a female's voice said with a purr in the hallway just outside the kitchen.

I stopped pouring, sat the pitcher back up, and stood there, staring down at my glass, trying to decide what to do.

"Where's your room?"

"Not going to my room." His deep voice was slightly husky.

"Oh," she breathed.

Then, I heard her gasp, and something hit the floor.

"You want my cock, then you're gonna get it on your knees." His tone turned hard.

I was going to have to stand here and listen to this. My eyes darted around the room for any escape that I hadn't noticed before.

"God, I forgot how big it was," she moaned.

Apparently, she wasn't new.

"When you fucked me at the club, I was sore for days," she told him with a reverent tone.

I didn't know what club, but I'd bet it was one where she had on no clothing and there was a pole involved. Pressing a hand to my stomach, I put the glass on the counter, no longer wanting it. Reality was a mean bitch, and I was getting a strong dose.

"Shh," he said. "Don't talk. Just suck. Ah, that's it. All the way down that throat. Fuck yeah."

The sounds of his pleasure were difficult to hear. The jealous pang in my chest was mixed with the fact that it turned me on. I just hated knowing it wasn't me making him sound that way.

"Open that throat up," he growled. "I'll shove it down if you don't. AH fuck. That's the way."

"Such a good girl, Barbie," Luther drawled with a dark chuckle.

My eyes widened. Why was Luther out there too? Was this about to become a threesome?

Shit. Crap. I didn't want to have to listen to more of this.

"You suck him off real good, and then I'll fuck you while you eat Arabella's pussy," Luther said.

Make that an orgy. There were two girls. Jesus, how many of them did they need? I already felt inadequate at sex, but this…I would never do this for Linc. In fact, the next time he did attempt to get my panties off, it was not happening. I needed to go get tested. God, I could have some STD and not know it.

"That's right. Play with my balls." Linc's tone was thicker.

I was staring at the door, wondering if I could hide in the pantry and muffle the sound of this, when Luther walked into the kitchen, completely naked. My breath hitched in my throat, and I felt my face instantly heat up from the embarrassment of this entire situation. He stopped, and his head tilted to the side. The edge that always seemed to be there in his expression, even when he was joking around and appeared relaxed, was sharpened. Of their own will, my eyes dropped to his penis, and seeing his semi begin to thicken and the metal at the head sent my gaze shooting right back up to his face.

"I'm sorry," I stammered. "I came to get wa-water…" I stopped trying to explain this and ran for the door.

Luther's hand shot out and grabbed my arm, almost too tightly. I let out a yelp, and my eyes swung back to his face. The threat that hung in the air as his eyes traveled down my body made me tremble. His nostrils flared, and he moved his gaze back to mine.

"Mmm," he said, then shook his head slightly before releasing my arm.

I didn't wait for him to say anything more before I broke into a run, thinking I could get past Linc without seeing what was happening even if he saw me. It was a mental image I didn't want.

His demanding words as he told her she was gonna swallow his load meant he was about to come. Maybe his eyes would be closed.

When I reached the door, his back was against the wall, and he was facing toward the kitchen, only a few feet away from me. My hope that his eyes were closed was my only good luck. The actual act, however, I wished I had never had to see.

The veins bulging in his neck; his fingers threaded through blonde hair, holding it tightly as he moved her head back and forth in rhythm with the pumping of his hips; teeth clenched; the muscles in his arms and chest flexing—he looked like a depraved god. The sight of her hand, with long hot-pink nails that had rhinestones on them, lying flat against his abs sent a stab of vicious jealousy through me.

I hated her. Everything about her. And it wasn't her fault. She was just a reminder of what I had been to him. While I had felt a connection, he'd gotten his pleasure and used my body to do it. I was just another willing place for him to bury his cock.

Shame took any other emotion I might have been feeling and moved them to the side. It needed all the space in which to fit. My eyes stung, and I forced myself to move. But in that second, Linc's eyes opened and locked on me. The surprised flare in them was followed by his gaze running down my body.

When his eyes snapped back up to mine, I saw the crest begin to take him as he reached his climax.

"Ringlets," he groaned.

Helpless to move away from this, I watched his body jerk as he thrust into her. He went lax while he held her head still and released into her. His eyes never leaving mine.

I had stopped breathing when he said, "Ringlets."

Sometimes, pain made it too hard to inhale. Calling me that name while he had his dick down another woman's throat...I wasn't sure I would ever recover from it. Before I could break down crying and humiliate myself any further, I ran.

When I reached my door, I slipped inside and closed it quietly so as not to wake Stevie, then locked it. If she needed me, she would knock. Stepping back from the door, I blew out a breath, then let the first tear fall. The fact that I was even crying was ridiculous. I was ridiculous.

How long would I want that man? Was I doomed to this… this need for him…my entire life? I hadn't been enough in Vegas to get him to even leave me a number or tell me his name.

The fear that this obsession I had for him, this longing for him, would one day completely break me was a real threat. He made me weak. He made me think that if I tried harder, I might be the one for him. That he might see me and feel the same way I did. That…that he could love me.

I was a fool, and I continued to be one. Time and time again.

FORTY-FOUR
LINC

"Fuck!" I snarled, letting go of Barbie's hair and reaching for my boxer briefs and jeans to tug back up.

How long had Branwen been there? She was supposed to be in bed. Dammit!

"You done? Because I need to fuck," Luther's voice was tense.

I nodded as I walked past her to the kitchen. Stopping inside, I stared at the glass of water sitting on the counter, and I ran a hand through my hair, groaning. She'd come down for water. Didn't look like she'd drunk it.

"Get pissed at me if you want, but whatever shit is happening with Branwen needs to end," Luther said angrily.

I turned around to glare at him. He was naked. His damn cock was fully erect, and he'd been in here with Branwen. She'd seen him like that.

"No. You don't get to be mad," he said, shaking his head. "You were the one with your cock down a woman's throat while she watched it. Then, you called her the nickname that you had given her as a kid," he said with disgust. "You wanted to hurt her because she'd hurt you. She stole fucking years of Stevie's life from you, yada yada. Well, being the one who had to watch her listen to that out there, I can assure you that you've hurt her. Mission fucking accomplished.

"Now, you can either stop this bullshit or I am going to stop it. I'm done watching this. She doesn't deserve it. Let her go. You don't want her, then release her to have a life. Get joint custody. Share Stevie. But this, making her stay here a year, is horseshit. You hear me? It is HORSE. SHIT."

He pointed his finger at me. "You can't admit to yourself that she's here because you don't want anyone else to have her. In your head, she's yours. But she ain't a goddamn possession. She's a woman. A mother. A real fucking incredible one. Treat her with the respect she deserves and let her go."

My chest was rising and falling as I seethed. Listening to every word he said, hating him for the fact that he was right about some of it.

I felt like shit over the fact that she'd just seen that and that I'd said, "Ringlets," as I shot my load.

But the sight of her face and those tiny satin shorts and matching camisole had been why I exploded. Not the woman on her knees.

"This isn't your business," I warned him.

He let out a mocking laugh. "It's about to be. Because if you aren't gonna treat her right and you're gonna keep her locked up under this roof without her own life, then I'll make sure she's treated right."

My eyes narrowed as fury rolled over my back. "Are you threatening me?"

"Just making it clear. I like her. She deserves better."

I let out a hard laugh. "And you're better? You? You think you can be a relationship man? That she would want you?"

He shrugged. "You saw her in that outfit. I think I'd do some crazy shit to call that mine."

I lunged as a roar ripped through my chest. All I saw was red. The threads of my sanity had been snipped, and the possessive rage consumed me. I was going to kill him.

FORTY-FIVE

BRANWEN

If I stayed in my room any longer this morning, Stevie was going to come looking for me. I'd waited until the normal time breakfast was over and the guys left. The thought of seeing either of them this morning made me want to curl into a ball and die.

I'd been in bed last night and heard the female screams. Linc hadn't even cared that his daughter might hear him. That she might wake up and be scared that someone was dying. It was way over the top. Yes, he had a big dick, but, Jesus, it wasn't a weapon of mass destruction, and I doubted she had been a virgin.

Giving myself one more pep talk, I headed out the bedroom door and down to the kitchen. It seemed quiet. I didn't hear anything until I was almost at the door. Stevie asked Jayda if she liked the color purple or pink better. There was no sound of masculine voices. A small twinge of relief came with that, and I peered in the door, just to be sure.

Stevie was on her knees, sitting on a stool, with a plate in front of her while Jayda leaned against the bar with a cup of coffee. No one else. Thank God. Maybe I could time it this way every day. Even better, I could dodge them altogether. Never lay eyes on them again.

Jayda looked over at me. "Morning," she said. "Latte first?"

I nodded. "Yeah, thanks," I replied, wondering if they'd said anything to her about last night.

I moved over to take the stool beside Stevie and put my arm around her shoulders to pull her close so I could kiss the top of her head.

"You slept late," Stevie said.

"Yep."

Jayda glanced back at me while she worked on my latte. "You okay?" she asked.

The flicker of concern in her eyes made me want to crawl under the table and stay there all day. Or the rest of the year. Probably the latter would be best.

"Yeah, I'm fine," I lied.

She didn't call me out on it or push. I wondered how I'd feel about her if I had found her with Linc's cock down her throat. It was hard to imagine hating her, but I wasn't so sure. I hoped that day never came. I wanted to continue liking her. She would be in Stevie's life, even when I wasn't. It would help, knowing there was a woman here who I knew cared about her.

Stevie wiggled down off her stool when I let her go and ran over to where Maui lay, resting on one of the beds that had been bought and placed around the house for him. He saw her coming his way, and his head perked up as his entire body seemed to wag.

Jayda brought my drink over to me and set it down. "You didn't have to wait up there so long," she told me. "They weren't here."

Oh. They'd left. When? After Linc had apparently ripped the woman's vagina open with his cock? The bitter thought settled over me. I needed to schedule an STD test today. I could ask someone to take me.

I didn't respond as I took a sip from the cup.

She stood there, watching me as she chewed on her bottom lip. After a minute or so, she sighed. "Are you not going to ask where Linc went?"

I shook my head. Absolutely not.

The exasperated look on her face would be funny if I wasn't a bitter, broken soul.

"Okay, fine. Don't ask. I'm telling you anyway. They are both in the hospital rooms in the basement with Doc Burl."

I set my cup down slowly. There were many questions that statement brought up.

"There are hospital rooms in the basement?" I asked.

She rolled her eyes. "Yes. Seriously, is that your first question?"

No. "Yeah, because that's intense."

Jayda tilted her head. "Look, I know you know who they are. When things happen, most of the time, they don't want to go to a hospital. It involves too many questions. Police would be called, et cetera. They even have an operating room down there. Doc Burl works for them privately."

Well, now that she'd explained it, that made sense.

She glanced over at Stevie, who was on the floor, playing with Maui, then back at me. "They got into a fight in here last night," she whispered. "Linc lost it and attacked Luther. The women they had with them were screaming like banshees, and I came running in here to find them beating the hell out of each other. I had to mop the floor to get the blood up before I went to bed."

Was she joking?

"What?" I whispered, my eyes bugging out of my head.

She smirked. "I dumped the pitcher of cold water over them while on the phone, calling Bane. They'd stopped by the time he arrived with Locke and Oz, but they were still seething and glaring at each other. They each have a cracked rib, which is what probably kept them from going at it again."

I shook my head. "What in the world happened?"

They had cracked ribs? Jesus.

She waggled her eyebrows. "You."

Me? I frowned. "What?"

She bit back a laugh and leaned closer. "All I know or got from their angry hissing and snarling was that Luther threatened to take care of you sexually if Linc didn't stop leading you on and using you."

That stung—no, it was more along the lines of a knife right in the chest.

"Seems you saw Luther naked and Linc getting a blow job. It escalated from there."

I dropped my head into my hands and rubbed my temples. I shouldn't have come out of my room. This was worse than I'd imagined. Luther had gotten into a fight because I was pathetic. That was basically what she was telling me.

I looked up. "Why did Linc lose it?"

She gave me an amused look. "Please tell me you're joking."

"No," I said slowly, trying to figure out what I had missed in this entire thing.

Placing her hands on the counter, she leveled her gaze on me. "Because he is possessive of you. He gets jealous. Doesn't like the other men to mention that you're hot."

Not for the reasons she was clearly thinking.

I sighed heavily. "That all has to do with Stevie. Not me."

Jayda pursed her lips. "I don't think so."

It was. I started to explain that I was an easy lay for Linc and he used it to his advantage, but seeing as she was, too, but managed to not be clingy or territorial with him, she wouldn't understand.

"Mommy, I want to go play outside," Stevie called out.

Taking my cup, I stood up. "Okay," I replied.

"Thanks for the latte," I told Jayda. "And sorry about last night."

She grinned at me. "I'd say it wasn't your fault, but, well, it was."

"What was youah fault, Mommy?" Stevie asked.

I heard Jayda cover up a giggle.

"Nothing. Get Maui, and let's go outside to play."

FORTY-SIX
LINC

Cursing, I sat up after opening my eyes and staring at the ceiling for a few minutes. My hand went to my rib, and I winced.

"Fucker had better be dead," I snarled.

"Afraid not," Luther drawled.

My head snapped up, and I glared at the bastard standing in the doorway of the room Burl had left me in after giving me enough pain meds to knock me out for hours.

"Then, I will finish the job," I threatened.

He'd cracked a damn rib. I'd had too much to drink and actually let the motherfucker crack a rib.

Luther smirked at me. "You'll try."

"I'll be sober next time. But you're gonna pay for my rib."

He pulled up his shirt to show me his wrap, which was identical to mine. "You already did. It was an even fight. Except you cracked one of my molars. Thanks for that. I fucking hate going to the dentist."

A hiss came from between my teeth as I stood up. He sure as hell didn't look like he was in the same shape I was, but Luther rarely showed any signs of pain. It was part of his sadistic DNA. His father had been the same way.

"What do you want?" I snapped.

I didn't want to have to look at his face first thing after waking up from a drunk brawl with him.

"Eh, cure hunger, to be fifteen years younger, Margot Robbie and Megan Fox in a threesome—you know, the basics."

I held in my groan as pain shot through my ribs when I straightened.

"Doc left pain meds." He nodded his head toward the counter to the left of him.

My eyes swung to see a cup of water and two large pills. Thank fuck. I went over to them and swallowed both, then finished off the water before tossing the paper cup into the trash can. Luther was still standing there.

"Would you get out of my face?"

Jesus, he could annoy the fuck out of a person.

"I could, yeah. But I think there is something you need to know," he said, then leaned his shoulder against the doorframe.

"Then, tell me and get the fuck away from me."

"First, answer me truthfully," he replied, as if this were a goddamn game. "You attacked me last night because?"

I narrowed my eyes at him. Was he serious? Yes, I had been drinking. But he pushed me. Said shit he knew would set me off. I'd felt exposed and raw from the look on Branwen's face when she fled. Fuck, I reached up and rubbed my chest with my fist. That was even harder to think about sober.

"You know why," I replied. The anger in my tone was directed more at me this morning though. I'd fucked up.

As much as I had planned on hurting her in the beginning, that idea no longer appealed to me. In fact, it was making my chest hurt far worse than my rib.

"Is it because you want her, or that you have feelings for her that go deeper than your cock, or that she's your baby momma and that makes you feel possessive?"

I said nothing. It was all three, but I'd be damned if I admitted that to him.

He nodded. "Yeah, that's what I thought."

He winced as he shifted his stance. I was glad to finally see some pain on his face.

"Seems, five years ago, you were having a threesome here, and someone buzzed at the gate. It was a woman. She was here to see you. I figured it was one of your usuals who was hard to shake once you fucked them a couple of times. I gave her details on what you were currently involved in at the moment and told her when you needed another cunt, you'd give her a call. I vaguely remember it."

I stared at him, waiting for him to get to the point.

"Anyway, it wasn't one of your flings. Well, I guess, technically, it was, but she hadn't come here to fuck. She'd come here…" He paused, and a flash of regret crossed his expression. It was so out of place on him that I almost questioned it. "To tell you that she was pregnant."

That last sentence replayed in my head over and over again. Then, what he had told me all began to click together and sink in. For a moment, I didn't think my heart was beating. I didn't inhale a breath. I stood, unable to speak or move.

She'd come here. She had found me and come to tell me. Even though I'd left her the note and the pill. She would have planned on admitting her identity. Knowing that I'd question how she had known my name. How she had found me.

I sucked in a breath when my lungs began to burn, and my eyes bored into Luther's. "How do you know?"

If he'd known all this time, I was going to go get my Glock and end his life. Blaise could string me up if he wanted to, but I wouldn't be able to forgive that.

"Recently. The night we drank wine and played darts. She'd said it as if it wasn't important. As if you wouldn't care either way. I realized she had no idea that was the only thing holding you back from going caveman and laying claim on her ass. More than just sexually, of course."

Remorse, regret, guilt. Fuck, I didn't know what this was slamming into me with such brutal force that I would be bent over with my hands on my knees, gasping, if my broken rib wasn't in the way. Turning, I gripped the counter and held on tightly. Rage pounded through me, and if I could pick up the goddamn table and hurl it at the wall, I would.

"Yeah," Luther drawled. "That's the reaction I expected. So, I'm gonna go on upstairs now." His words were muffled by the thudding in my head—or was that my heartbeat? I wasn't sure.

She had come to me.

Those five words repeated over and over in my head until they chiseled their way into the wall I kept around me. Then, I felt it. The first crack. The one that would lead to the crumble. The wall that protected me from feeling anything that made me weak. Anything that had the power to hurt me. The wall I had constructed years ago. The one that had eventually sent my ex-wife away.

It was in danger of being brought down for the first time since I'd firmly put it in place.

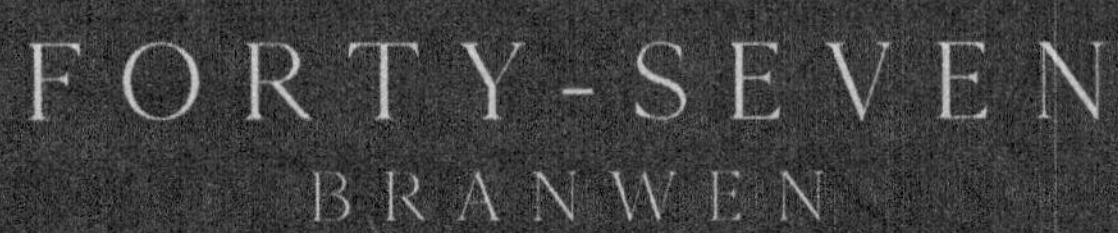

FORTY-SEVEN
BRANWEN

Stepping out of Stevie's room after she finally fell asleep for her nap, I froze at the sight of Linc standing outside in the hallway. His face didn't look as bad as Luther's had when I saw him in the kitchen at lunch, but there was swelling in his left eye, a cut on his cheekbone, and bruising.

I'd had most of the night and all morning to think about what I would say to Linc. I had even gone as far as rehearsing it in the mirror while using concealer to cover the dark circles under my eyes.

None of that came out though.

Instead, I blurted, "I'd like someone to take me to get tested for STDs."

His flinch was as if I had slapped him hard across the face. The look in his eyes as they stayed locked on me were different. As if I had hurt him instead of the other way around.

Nope, just because I called you out on your whore lifestyle does not mean you get to be hurt. I have every right to get tested.

I crossed my arms over my chest and stared back at him.

He blew out a breath slowly. "Okay. I, uh…I deserve that."

A hard laugh fell from my lips as my heart, which he'd shattered internally, lay in shards around me.

Whatever he came here to say, I didn't want to hear it. If it was an apology for last night, why? There was no point. It had served a purpose.

"Last night—" he began, actually looking remorseful.

I held up a hand and shook my head. "No. I don't care, Linc. I get it, okay? I also get that I am just a fuck for you. One of many. I don't want to talk about it."

I started to walk around him, wanting to be as far away from him as possible. Seeing him only made the damage I'd allowed him to cause me roar back to life.

His hand shot out and grabbed my arm to stop me. Closing my eyes, I took a deep, calming breath. I could not yell at him and call him names outside our daughter's door.

"What?" I snapped, not looking at him again, but keeping my gaze straight ahead.

With one hard tug, he pulled me against him, causing me to lose my balance and fall onto his chest. He inhaled sharply, and I realized I'd probably just hit his cracked rib. Well, good. He deserved it. He was the one who had pulled me over here.

Angrily, I glared up into his eyes, only to momentarily forget to breathe. His hands cupped my face, and I had no time to process the look in his eyes before warm lips pressed against mine. The tip of his tongue flicked out to trace my bottom lip, and I opened. The need to have this kiss, know what it felt like, was far greater than my common sense and self-worth.

A low growl vibrated through him as he began to plunder and explore with hungry strokes, as if I tasted like a treat he couldn't get enough of. My hands went to his biceps, and I held on, needing something to steady me. The pads of his thumb brushed over my cheekbones. I could no longer tell if the quickening beat I felt was my heart or his. This went beyond any connection I had experienced before. It was far deeper.

This could destroy me.

That thought was a cold splash of reality, and I pulled back, breaking the kiss, but Linc didn't release me. He continued to hold my face, and the darkened gleam in his blue eyes held me transfixed.

Why was he doing this to me?

The gentle touch of his thumb ran underneath my eye, as if he saw the shadows I had tried to hide.

"Even when you were a kid, you tugged at my soul." The corners of his mouth quirked beneath his beard.

"Drunk and high in Vegas, I was drawn to you, but when I looked at you the next morning, the threat that you could own my soul sent me running."

He leaned down and pressed another soft peck against my lips. "And even when I wanted to hate you, when I wanted to hurt you, I couldn't. Because it was you." He lifted his head, and his eyes met mine. "It was always you."

We stood there for several moments, and the things I saw in his eyes confused me. I wanted so much from him, but I had been fooled too many times before, and I knew my wishful thinking misread him every time. His hands fell away, and his eyes felt like a caress as they drifted over my face.

"I'll have Doc come here for the STD testing," he told me, his voice raspy and deep.

Then, he turned and walked away.

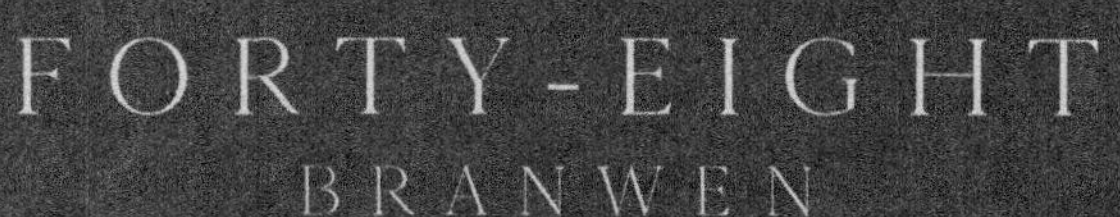

FORTY-EIGHT
BRANWEN

I was sure I looked completely engrossed in the episode of *Bluey* playing on the patio television to anyone else, but that was so far from the case. My head was spinning with so many different thoughts that I didn't know what to focus on first.

Stevie was curled up beside me with her hair still damp from her bath, wearing her pajamas. I'd gone ahead and bathed her early because we'd spent the afternoon at the pool after she woke up from her nap.

During that time, Jayda had come to get me, and she stayed with Stevie while I went inside to meet Dr. Burl.

He was pleasant and took my blood quickly, telling me he was sure there was nothing to worry about, but that I was smart to be safe. Feeling the need to defend my request, although he hadn't been negative at all, I mentioned Linc's variety of women.

Burl smiled and nodded, as if he understood. He then said that Linc was tested monthly and that he'd never known him to not use protection with a female. That this was unlike him, but my wanting to be tested was smart. That one could never be too careful.

The knowledge that Linc was tested regularly had eased my concern. The thing about Linc always using protection though? Nope. Didn't believe that. He might lie to the doctor, but I knew that when Linc was worked up, it was easy to get him to go without one. I'd pleaded once, and he'd sunk into me.

His kiss this afternoon had messed me up for a few hours. My lips warmed at the memory. Dammit. That had been… well, I'd never felt that before with just a kiss. As with everything when it came to Linc, my body only responded to him that way. I had actually made a grocery list in my head once while kissing Hudson. With Linc, I was sure there had been a moment when I forgot my own name.

The sound of the door opening and closing behind us snapped me out of my deep thoughts, and I turned my head to see Linc walking toward us.

I'd not seen him since the kiss. Since he'd said things that still confused me, as I wasn't sure what to make of them. Had that been him trying to apologize for last night? If so, as mind-blowing as that kiss had been, it didn't make the night before go away. His words, well, he'd said many things to me before that made me feel special—granted, he had been inside of me at the time, but still. He was good with words.

I turned my attention back to *Bluey*.

Linc came around the sofa and sank down carefully on the other side of Stevie. I saw the slight tightness around his mouth. It was the only indication that he was in physical pain.

Stevie looked over at him and grinned, sitting up from lying on me.

I held her shoulder to keep her back. "Your dad is hurt. One of his ribs is cracked, so you can't climb on him or lie over on him."

Her smile fell, and she frowned, looking every bit concerned. "Did you go to the doctow?" she asked him.

He nodded, then held his arm open. "I did, and I'm okay. If you want to come over here, you can."

Stevie tilted her head up to look back at me. "He is okay, Mommy. The doctow fixed him," she told me reassuringly, then shifted her body over to lie on his cracked rib.

A flicker of a wince crossed his face as she settled into him, and his arm lowered to rest on her shoulders, holding her to him.

The softness in his eyes as he dropped his gaze to her made my heart do all kinds of crazy crap. It needed to chill. But that scene would make any woman hard-pressed to look away from it. He was hurt and in pain, but letting her lie on him anyway. She had no idea how hard that had to be for him.

"How was your day?" he asked, and my eyes swung from Stevie and his hand resting on her arm to his face.

"Uh, good," I replied awkwardly.

He smirked. "I was hoping for spectacular."

I waited for him to say more, and when he didn't, I turned back to the television. The new episode that had come on was one where Bluey was grown up and gave a glimpse of what she wanted in her future.

I'd seen it at least five times. Stevie loved this one.

"So, why a dental assistant?" Linc asked me after a few minutes into the show.

I turned to look at him again. God, I wished there weren't a flutter every time I saw the man.

I shrugged. "I was able to get a loan and a grant. It was only two years of college, and I needed a job more substantial since I had a child to raise."

"You always talked about becoming an equine veterinarian," he replied. "The only other person who came to the stables that you gave as much attention to as me was the vet. You followed her every move and asked a million questions. What happened to that? Just grow out of it?"

I wanted to laugh. Oh, how it must be to never worry about money. To have it there at your fingertips whenever you needed it.

I turned back to the television. "Life happened. I realized that my good grades weren't enough to pay for my undergraduate degree, much less veterinarian school. That took money that I did not have, and they wouldn't give loans to those without credit."

He didn't speak for a moment, and I wondered if he was struggling to comprehend being broke.

"What happened to the money that Garrett had sent your aunt? That was supposed to cover your needs and college."

I scrunched my nose. What? I looked back at him and shook my head. "I have no idea what you're talking about, but Garrett didn't give my aunt any money. I worked full-time hours while in high school, and I still wasn't able to buy a car until the June after I graduated. My aunt made me pay her three hundred dollars a month for bills to cover what my living there cost her. Trust me, there was no money. She reminded me daily how thankful I should be that she had taken me in and what a burden I was on her financially."

Life with Aunt Catherine had been the worst years of my life. I rarely spoke to her, and if I did, it was because she called me. The calls normally consisted of her needing money because her Social Security check wasn't enough to handle the bills. She always blamed me for her not having retirement savings. Yet the summer I'd moved out, she had gone on a cruise, taken a trip to Hawaii, bought a new Mercedes sedan, and sold her house and moved into a more expensive neighborhood. I always wanted to point out that was where her savings had likely gone, but I never did. I'd just send her a couple hundred dollars and hope I didn't hear from her for a year—or ever again.

I noticed Linc's jaw was jutted and his neck veins were standing out. What was wrong with him?

"Where is your aunt now?" he asked, his voice sounding tight.

"In the uppity neighborhood she moved to after I graduated and got the hell out of there."

"Does she contact you still?" His question sounded almost like a demand.

Frowning at him, I nodded. "Yeah. When she wants money."

His eyes flared with…anger? Was he mad? About my aunt? I was confused.

"Do you send her money?" The words were clipped, as if he already knew the answer and wasn't going to like it.

I nodded, watching him warily.

"How much?"

"Uh, normally about two to three hundred dollars."

His throat bobbed as he swallowed, and his nostrils flared. "How many times have you done that since you moved out?"

I shook my head. "I don't know. Why are you asking me all this?"

"Branwen, how old were you when she started asking you for money?"

I glanced at Stevie, wondering if I should pull her back over to me. Linc was looking more severe by the second.

"I guess the year after I moved out. I don't know exactly."

When he remained looking like he was about to go put his fist through a wall, I asked him, "What is wrong with you?"

He took a deep breath, his chest rising and falling while he studied me, as if he wasn't sure he was going to tell me or not.

"Garrett gave your aunt money. Money to take care of you, make sure you had all you needed. A car. To pay for your college. I don't know the exact amount, but I know it was significant."

I sank back onto the sofa as a rush of air left me. "He…he did what?" My question was just above a whisper.

"Demeter was part of the family. Garrett made sure you were taken care of for your father. He thought letting you go live with your aunt would be a better life for you, but he still provided for you."

I shook my head. "My dad was the lead trainer. He was an employee of the family." Did they do that for all their employees? I didn't ask that though.

"No, Branwen. Your dad was family. So was his father. Your dad was our bookie, just like his father had been, but then he took over as head trainer after proving how successful he was, working with thoroughbreds."

Everything I'd thought I knew about me, my life…had just been sent spinning like a wheel while I waited for it to stop on something that made sense.

FORTY-NINE

LINC

The silence on the other end of the line I understood. I waited while Garrett processed what I'd learned this evening. Nothing had prepared me for the sheer hate that had come over me. It surpassed that of the dentist who had thought he was going to take what was mine. This was another level of loathing that I'd never experienced.

"I'll have her location and all her financial records pulled," he said, his voice the hard, unyielding one I'd not heard in a while. This was the sound of the boss. "Once it's all together, I'll call you with details."

"Okay."

"I failed Demeter," he said. "I should have watched her closer. Trusting some bitch I didn't know was a mistake that she'll pay for. But, Linc, I won't fail him again. If you don't love her, then you'd better set her free."

The underlying threat took me by surprise. I stared at the bookshelf in my office, letting it sink in.

"The family takes care of our own. She's ours."

My body went rigid, and I gripped the phone tightly. Like hell she was ours. She wasn't fucking *ours*.

"She's mine." The words came out like an animalistic snarl.

Silence.

He wasn't the boss anymore, but that didn't mean he wasn't a Hughes. Right now, I didn't care. He'd said something I wouldn't allow. No one got to claim her. She was already claimed.

"Good," he finally said with a sigh. "Fawn assured me as much when you left here. I had my doubts, seeing as how you treated her, but my wife reminded me of my treatment of her in the beginning, so I was giving it time. Having Luther update me on how things were going with the two of you."

I narrowed my eyes as I let that process. Luther had been telling him shit? That motherfucker!

"And what has he said?" I asked between clenched teeth, ready to go break another bone in his goddamn body.

Garrett sighed and then laughed. "That you're so fucking messed up in the head over her that you're showing signs of insanity."

I sank back into my chair, feeling most of my rage fade. I opened my mouth to argue, but closed it. What the fuck was I going to say? That it wasn't true? Because the fact was, Luther's words had described the way I was feeling so damn accurately that I was tempted to laugh.

But I didn't.

Because he was an asshole.

FIFTY
BRANWEN

This would be the third night I didn't get enough sleep, it seemed. I kept tossing and turning, my brain refusing to shut off. If I wasn't thinking about how Linc had sat beside me at breakfast, engaged in conversation with me, made me laugh, then I was thinking about him reaching down to hold my hand today when he'd taken Stevie and me to go see a colt he was looking at buying to keep at his stables here. I was struck speechless and let him hold it while in shock. By the time I'd snapped out of it, yanking my hand away would have caused a scene, so I'd…endured it.

"God," I muttered. "You're so full of shit."

Nothing would have made me take my hand out of his.

It had been all too good to be true, which meant that it was going to crash down around me in the light of day. I'd wake up, and—poof—the other personality that Linc had would be back, and he'd ignore me. Or worse, he'd be cordial to me and treat me like someone he had to speak to, but didn't want to.

Rubbing my face with both hands, I groaned, then dropped them to my sides and stared at the ceiling. Linc Shephard would be the death of me.

It should say on my tombstone, *Died because she loved a man who shouldn't be loved.*

The click of my lock caught my attention, and my eyes dropped to the door as it opened. The tall, dark shadow that entered didn't frighten me, but it should have. Because I knew he was more dangerous than anything else when it came to my well-being.

My eyes followed him as he walked silently over to the other side of the bed. The moonlight coming through the window illuminated him. He had something in his hand that he laid on the nightstand. It was papers.

I then watched as he pulled the shirt over his head and dropped it. His ribs wrapped up didn't even take away from his perfection. When he began to take off his jeans, I started scolding myself for letting him get this far, but said nothing. I tensed up, as if preparing for a battle, while he slid beneath the covers, then moved his body over to mine until the heat of it sent shivers through me. I tried to put up walls. Forge a backbone or willpower. Something to protect myself from him.

"What are you doing?" I hissed between my teeth as his arm wrapped around me, tucking me against his chest.

"Holding you."

I…that…was not what I'd expected.

"Linc, what are you doing? And I don't mean just right now."

He reached up to brush hair away from my face and pressed a kiss near my ear. "Holding you. Enjoying you. Letting myself have what I've wanted since you came storming back into my life, waving divorce papers in my face," he whispered huskily, then ran his nose along the curve of my earlobe.

I closed my eyes and tried to calm my racing heart. "I don't understand," I breathed. "And stop doing that. I watched you shoving your cock down another woman's throat."

"Mmm," he hummed. "I was drunk. Trying to get some relief from the constant ache to be inside you. I was imagining you in my head. Pretending that it was your mouth taking me deep. Then, I opened my eyes to see you standing there." His voice dropped. "Your hair mussed, messy blonde curls draped over your bare shoulders, with only small scraps of satin touching your skin. I could see your hard nipples. Then, I looked at your face and unloaded."

His hand slid over my stomach, and a pleased rumble came from his chest. "I shouldn't have brought her here. It was one of my many mistakes." He nuzzled my neck. "Forgive me."

There wasn't a nerve in my body that wasn't buzzing.

Grasping at any ounce of sanity I could muster, I blurted, "The STD test results. I can't..." I couldn't what? Let him touch me because I would spread my legs and let him take me without a condom again?

His arm left me, and his body rolled away. I almost cried out and reached for him to come back. But he didn't sit up. He reached for the papers he'd brought in and handed them to me.

Taking them, I moved to sit up and leaned toward the light from the window.

It was the STD results, but they weren't mine. They were his.

I glanced up at him. "These are yours."

He nodded and took it away to show the sheet below it. My name was at the top. I let my eyes scan over it, knowing it must all be fine or he wouldn't have brought them to my bed.

He put his in front of me again. "I'm clean."

"I see. I didn't ask for yours."

His fingers moved a lock of hair off my shoulder, and then he took it and began to twirl it around his finger. "Yours is the only cunt I've ever considered sinking into bare, Ringlets," he told me. "And I want you to feel safe when I do it again."

I sucked in a breath. "Again?" I asked, shifting back from him. "I didn't agree to that. Or sex at all."

A slow smirk touched his lips, but his eyes darkened as he held my gaze. "Are you going to punish me? What about if I just kiss it? You spread your legs for me, and I'll make you feel so good." The tips of his fingers ran over my collarbone, then down to my chest before circling one of my nipples poking against the camisole I was wearing. "I can suck on these too," he added.

I fought back the urge to pant and beg him. Wanting all of that.

"So I can be treated like I don't exist tomorrow?" I asked. "No thanks. I-I can't do that again. It hurts, Linc. I don't deserve it. You don't treat Jayda that way." Saying this to him helped remind me why I had to get him out of my bed.

He paused, and I looked at him, my chin held high. I would not be embarrassed by admitting this to him. It was true. He was hurting me, and I was no longer going to just take it.

"I know I hurt you, and I'm sorry. That's over. I can't push you away anymore. I need you, Ringlets. In my life. In my bed. Just you."

Just me? I fought off the wave of joy because that wasn't possible. This was Linc.

"Don't promise things you can't do," I said.

His words were already painful, and he hadn't broken them yet.

He tilted his head and cupped the side of my face. His thumb ran over my lower lip, and his hooded eyes went from my mouth to meet my gaze. "No one else compares, and trust me, I've tried. The woman was sucking my cock because I couldn't bring myself to fuck anyone else. I'd been trying, and it wouldn't work. With her on her knees and her scent away from my nose, I could imagine it was you. Think about you. It was the only way I could get there. Just you. It's just you."

I let out a ragged breath. Wanting this to be real. Terrified it wasn't.

"You'll change your mind. The other women won't disappear. You'll get bored with me. Jayda is here every day, and I like her, which just causes me more pain."

He grinned as he moved in close, and his lips touched mine. "Are you jealous of Jayda?" he asked, his husky voice sounding amused.

If his hand wasn't currently between my thighs and his breath wasn't mingling with mine, I might be able to slap him.

"Yes," I whispered, hating it.

"Ringlets"—he trailed kisses along my jawline as his fingers slid over the crotch of my panties—"I've never fucked, Jayda."

The laugh of disbelief was mixed with a moan as his finger ran along the slickness he'd caused. "I've seen you with her," I panted as my fingers fisted the sheets.

"Mmhmm. She's my employee, my friend even. But that's it," he replied as he sank a finger inside me.

"AH!" I cried, rocking against it.

"If anyone needs to be jealous, it's me. Because while I've never touched Jayda, I know she's thought about how sweet this pussy is and imagined tasting what is mine."

I stilled, and a deep chuckle came from him as his mouth moved back to hover over mine.

"Good thing Jayda is faithful to her girlfriend," he murmured, then took my mouth and thrust his tongue inside as his finger worked in and out of me.

I moaned into his mouth as I sank against him. I gave up. I had no way to keep myself from allowing him to take what he wanted. I'd handed him my childish heart, and he'd broken my adult one. Now, here I was, letting him consume what was left of my soul.

"Fuck, get this off," he swore, reaching for my top and pulling it over my head.

Then, he moved to my bottoms, and I saw him wince when he put pressure on his side. I'd forgotten about his ribs.

"You're hurt," I reminded him.

"My rib will be forgotten the moment my cock is deep inside your tight cunt," he said, throwing my shorts and panties to the floor. "Lie back and spread your legs for me."

I shook my head. As much as I wanted his mouth on me, I didn't want him in that position. It would hurt him more than he was already hurting.

"You lie on your back," I told him, moving back and onto my knees.

His eyes followed me as if he was mesmerized. If only he would stay that way. Truly mean what he was saying.

"Okay," he finally agreed and eased down onto his back slowly.

I crawled over between his legs and smiled at him.

"What is it you wa—uh—oh fuuuck." He groaned as my mouth slid down over his tip, and I let it go as far back as it could, which wasn't that far. His hands fisted in my hair. "Fucking hell, Ringlets, that sweet mouth feels amazing."

I wasn't sucking him nearly as deep as the other woman had been, and I hated to think that his imagination of me was better than reality. Swallowing, I focused on relaxing my throat and letting it open so I could slide him farther in.

"Shit," he hissed as his hands tightened on my hair. "That's it…take more of it."

My eyes watered as I forced another inch down. Knowing that was about as deep as I could go, I began to suck and move my lips up and down. His hips bucked.

"God, baby," he panted. "Seeing your head down there is going to make me come. Let me see your eyes."

Keeping him deep, I lifted them to look up at him.

"My beautiful girl with my cock down her throat. You gonna swallow it?"

I nodded, running my tongue along the shaft as I worked my way up, then down, pushing to try and go deeper.

"Fuuuck." His hands pulled at my hair.

I watched as his mouth opened and his eyes glazed over.

"I'm—GAH!"

His body jerked as his salty, thick release began to pump into my mouth. I swallowed quickly, wanting to take it all.

"Holy fuck." The tight grip he had on my hair eased. "Come here."

I let him pop free of my mouth and looked up at him.

He cupped my face. "Here. Now."

Smiling, I sat back on my knees and climbed back over his leg to move up beside him, not wanting to touch his wrapped ribs. He pulled me to him anyway and buried his face in my hair.

"That was by far the best blow job of my life."

I laughed and rolled my eyes. "No, it wasn't. I couldn't take all if it."

He slipped a finger under my chin and tilted my head back so I had no choice but to look at him.

"Having your eyes looking up at me, seeing your mouth wrapped around my dick, and burying my fingers in your hair, not having to close my eyes and just imagine it…yeah, Ringlets. You could have just sucked the head, and it would have been the best."

His eyes said things that my heart was too afraid to believe. But, God, how I wanted it. I wanted him.

Being Linc Shephard's, loving him, having his heart—it was all I'd ever wanted.

FIFTY-ONE

BRANWEN

The summer heat beat down fiercely, and I was thankful for the little shade I had. I glanced out at Stevie as she splashed in the water, and I was tempted to join her. Getting wet would cool me down. If I took off my cover-up, she might see the hickey on the top of my right boob and the small outline of where Linc had spanked my bottom so hard that he'd left a handprint. My bikini bottoms didn't cover it well.

I loved having him leave marks on me, but hiding them from our curious four-year-old was difficult.

For the past two weeks, I'd lived in my own fairy tale. Well, almost. It was as close as I was likely to ever get, but thinking about that would take away my current bliss. Linc was in my bed at nights, and I woke up in his arms every morning. He kissed me whenever we had a moment with no eyes on us during the day. He had taken Stevie and me to the movies. We'd gone back to the zoo, with him this time, and gone on picnics. It felt like a real family.

Today, he'd had to go handle family stuff early and said he wouldn't be back until late. I'd wanted to sulk at the idea of him being gone, but that wasn't fair. He couldn't always be by our side.

Giving in to the temptation of the cold water, I stood up and slid my cover-up off. I'd keep my bottom turned away from Stevie's view. She'd be so busy; she wouldn't be paying attention anyway. I bent over to grab the towel on the other side of the lounger bed when I heard footsteps and stood back up to turn around.

Linc was closing the distance with long strides as he came toward me.

He was back early, and happiness rippled through me. When he reached me, he grabbed the towel I was holding and wrapped it around my body.

"Fuck, I'm gonna be hard now that I saw my handprint on your ass," he said in a hushed whisper as he looked down at me.

"I was going to cool off in the pool," I told him.

He held me in the towel. "Not yet. We have company," he said, then let go of me to turn around just as one of his lawyers turned the corner from stepping down off the patio and headed this way.

"Wh-why is your lawyer here?" I asked nervously.

Was this about the divorce papers? I hadn't thought about those in weeks.

He patted my towel-covered bottom, but didn't reply.

"Stanz, you remember Branwen," Linc said.

Stanz was holding papers and a pen. I felt sick. Was he signing the papers? Why now?

"Yes, of course. It's good to see you again," he replied.

I gave him a shaky smile. "You too," I lied. It was not at all good.

Linc's gaze moved back to me. I turned to look up at him for answers that just might break my heart yet again.

"Stanz has all the legal work handled to have Stevie's last name change to Shephard. He just needs your signature, and then he can file it."

I blinked. Stevie's last name. We'd never talked about it. He had never brought it up. I wasn't sure what to think. He was her father, and the only reason his name wasn't on her birth certificate was because he hadn't known about her. But shouldn't he have asked me or just mentioned it? Why bombard me like this?

Was that what this had all been about? The past two weeks. The family time. Being together. Sleeping in bed with me. Had he been prepping me to just do whatever he told me to? Panic, disillusionment, and—as always with him—pain. Eventually, it came.

Stevie called out for him and told him to watch as she did a trick. I stepped past him, no longer able to make eye contact. Taking the papers from Stanz, I looked down at them.

He held out a pen and showed me where to sign. Once I was done, he took them, and I turned to look back at Linc, who was watching me.

"All you had to do was ask me. When have I not given you what you wanted? I'm an easy yes for you, aren't I, Linc?"

Tears clogged my throat as I thought about all the nights I'd thought I saw something in his eyes when he looked at me. But it was always me and my wishful thinking. Emotion boiling over inside me, I let out a sob I hadn't wanted to.

"Heck, Linc, you've owned my heart for most of my life. I've loved you for so long that I can't remember a time when I didn't. With that kind of power, why not use me like your puppet? Because I clearly allow it."

Spinning around, I started for the house. Stevie had heard me. I was too loud. I'd let myself break down in front of her.

I heard his heavy footsteps just before his fingers wrapped around my arm and he stopped me. I used my free hand to wipe at the tears.

"Just let me go," I pleaded.

Using both of his hands, he pulled me back until I was pressed against his chest. His warmth made me shiver. Mocking me and all that I represented.

"Say it again, Ringlets." His voice was hoarse as his breath tickled my skin.

"What?"

"Tell me you love me."

I closed my eyes as another whimper escaped me. "Why?"

He reached up and pulled my hair over to one side, then pressed a kiss on my bare shoulder. "Because I need to hear it again. Hear the woman who owns me—and will own me until I take my very last breath—tell me she loves me. That she can love me after all the darkness and shit I've put her through." He pressed his lips to my temple. "I think I fell in love with you in Vegas and ran to save you rather than me. But fate brought you back to me, and I almost fucked that up. Please, tell me again."

Sniffling, I wiped at my face. I turned to look up at him, not sure I trusted this. But when my eyes met his, my heart stuttered, and I sucked in a breath. "I love you," I said, letting it back out.

He grinned, then lowered his head. His lips brushed over mine.

"Dad! What awah you doing?" Stevie called out, sounding alarmed.

Linc's arms held me firmly, not letting me move away as he lifted his head to look at our daughter. "I'm kissing your pretty momma," he replied.

Stevie's giggles brought a smile to my face as Linc's gaze dropped back down to me.

"Thank you," he said simply.

"For what?" I asked.

"For loving an outlaw," he replied with a sexy smirk.

"Linc Shephard, my heart never gave me a choice."

ABOUT ABBI

Abbi Glines is a #1 New York Times, USA Today, Wall Street Journal, and International bestselling author of the Rosemary Beach, Sea Breeze, Smoke Series, Vincent Boys, Boys South of the Mason Dixon, and The Field Party Series. She is also author to the Sweet Trilogy and the Black Souls Trilogy. She believes in ghosts and has a habit of asking people if their house is haunted before she goes in it. Her house was built in 1820 and she finally has her own haunted house but they're friendly spirits. She drinks afternoon tea because she wants to be British but alas she was born in Alabama although she now lives in New England (which makes her feel a little closer to the British). When asked how many books she has written she has to stop and count on her fingers and even then she still forgets a few. When she's not locked away writing, she is entertaining her first grade daughter, she is reading (if everyone in her house including the ghosts will leave her alone long enough), shopping online (major Amazon Prime addiction), and planning her next Disney World vacation (and now that her oldest daughter Annabelle works at Disney she has an excuse to frequent it often).

You can connect with Abbi online in several different ways. She uses social media to procrastinate.

Facebook: AbbiGlinesAuthor
Twitter: abbiglines
Instagram: abbiglines
Snapchat: abbiglines
TikTok: abbiglines

Printed in Dunstable, United Kingdom